Emperor's Sh~~a~~

Published by Ink And Quill Press, 2023

For more excellent works of fiction, visit Inkandquillpress.com

Cover artwork by Dustin Stech
Edited by Hannah Brickey

Dedicated to my wife, Letisha, my daughter, Charlie, and of course to the noble adventurers themselves - Charlie, Dusty, and Dan. Your journey through Scera was the fuel behind this story, and it was my incredible pleasure to be your Dungeon Master. I hope that this story - our story - can inspire future adventurers, and bring back fond memories for the seasoned ones like ourselves.

Prologue

Rarely does one recognize one's own place in history. Often it is the duty of those who follow us to determine our impact - and to judge us accordingly. Thus it is, and thus it has always been across the vast breadth of this world, Scera. But every rule has its exceptions, and there is perhaps no greater exception than the Emperor, founder of the Sunset Empire and god-ruler to all of her citizens. He formed the Empire centuries ago, and has watched over her ever since.

The Empire in its current form extends some 5,200 miles East to West, and fully 1,500 North to South. Her geography is varied, as are her people. From the nomadic wanderers of the frozen tundras in the far east of the Empire to the temperate forests, sprawling farms, and rolling plains of the West; from the ever-warm summerlands in the South to the craggy steppes in the North.

The full history of the Empire is shrouded in mystery, known only to a few within her borders, but legend says she was born of a hero who broke free from a tyrannical neighbor to the North, beyond the mountains that ring the vast land.

Even without her history, however, one thing has remained certain throughout the past centuries since the Emperor first began his long slumber - the course of the Empire is kept steady in the ironclad grip of the Sisterhood, the divine mouthpieces of the Emperor.

This is accomplished in a variety of ways, but the most effective of those must surely be the Black Hand. This ancient order has its beginnings in the early days of the Emperor, and they form the martial backbone of the Church. They arbitrate justice throughout the Empire, as well as serving as the most trusted and capable of military assets. They are, for all intents and purposes, a monolith of unwavering faith and unflinching lethality.

The Empire's laws protect her from discord within, even in a world of powerful eldritch forces and across such a breadth of land and a patchwork quilt of peoples.

Another tool in the Imperial toolkit is the central Academy that trains all sanctioned Imperial Wizards - in fact all those with the potential for higher magics are identified as children and sent there to learn. These students enter as uncontrolled youths and emerge as masters of terrifying power, beholden to the Empire for their gifts.

A word regarding magic. Magic is ubiquitous across Scera, those who can actually use it are considerably less common. The lowest form of magic is known by simple names like "spirit" or "ki" and is accessible to nearly anyone if they have enough time, discipline, and access to a master. It allows those who master it to perform feats that seem at times superhuman.

Then come the higher orders of magic - those of Nature and Divinity. Legends tell of druids who can move mountains, change the course of rivers, and assume the forms of wild animals through a deep, supernatural connection with Life itself. Druids coax nature with kind and gentle patience, bending to Her will as much as she bends to theirs.

Clerics, priests, and other champions of the Gods can heal grievous wounds, call fire from the heavens, even turn back the hands of Death if their divine patrons will it. Like the powers of Nature, Divinity is accessible only to a select few, chosen by the Gods, the Universe, or some other force. Those chosen to wield these powers do so as humble servants, forever indebted to their cosmic masters.

And then come the masters of the Arcane. Only those with the drive, the strength of will, and perhaps the hubris to defy the very nature of reality can wield arcane forces. Practitioners are born with natural conduits within their blood that allows the channeling of immense energies, and they use their will and the energy that flows through all living things to bend reality itself. These individuals, once grown to the full potential of their blood and attuned to the chaotic energies of the planes, are capable of warping flesh, stone, and steel to their whims, able to travel vast distances in an instant, and to function as the ultimate weapon of war, a one person army.

Amidst these mighty forces the Empire runs on. Noble houses form the aristocracy of the Empire, intermingled with business magnates, and other socialites. The common citizenry underpin this grand tapestry, grateful they weren't born into danger that lurks outside the Empire…

Chapter One

Arcus took a deep breath, soaking in the night sky, the cool spring breeze, and the sounds of the world around him. From his vantage point atop a low hill, he could see the glittering sprawl of Sunset Isle, the goal towards which he had strived the past few months. The Sunset Imperium was the bastion of humanity and reason, a shining beacon in a dark and cruel world, and here was the beating heart of it. The ranger couldn't help but compare it to the serene tundras of his own home, in the distant east of the Empire. Out there in the snow-covered plains, he and his people, the D'Ari, lived at one with nature. Those wind-swept plains were a far cry from the jungle of stone that stretched before him.

A soft whine interrupted his thoughts, bringing his attention to the snow-white wolf sitting beside him.

"We'll be alright, little brother," he reassured the creature with a soft pat, adjusting the leather satchel on his back and setting off down the slope towards the nearest city gate.

"Come on, Kodja," he added, looking back at the animal and smiling at the nonplussed look in the creature's eye. "Just stay close to me. I don't know how city dwellers will react to you, and I don't want any harm to come to you here."

The wolf huffed before obediently padding along after him.

"Hold there, stranger," one of the guardsmen called to him, causing Arcus to stumble to a halt.

He'd expected the same type of friendly greeting he might receive upon returning to his homestead back on the plains, not the suspicious glare he was currently enduring.

"Hello, friend. I'm Arc--" he began, but was cut off abruptly as the surly guard shouted over him.

"Speak only when spoken to!"

The man, a bit shorter and considerably stockier than Arcus, brandished a half-spear and wore a shining breastplate over his deep blue uniform. He called to his companions, three other similarly dressed guardsmen, who slowly encircled Arcus.

"What is your business here, outlander?" The leader growled.

"I . . . er, I don't *have* any business really," Arcus explained haltingly. "I'm a simple traveler, seeking to experience more of the land I call home."

The guard didn't seem to find this answer satisfactory at all.

"You have the look of the barbarians of the eastern wastes," he frowned. "Your kind don't like cities. And besides, you certainly can't bring that wild animal into the city."

"I assure you, sir, my companion is very well behaved," Arcus gestured to Kodja, who tried to appear as non-threatening as possible. "He'll be no trouble at all, sir."

"Must be one of those druids the stories tell about," another of the guards chimed in. "Shamans that speak with animals and all that."

"Don't be stupid, he's a filthy barbarian with a pet dog," the leader snapped before turning back to Arcus with a menacing grin. "They use money where you're from?"

"Er, yes," Arcus replied. "When necessary we use coin, but generally--"

"There is a fee for entering the city with an unregistered animal."

The leader lifted his chin and narrowed his eyes, and the hairs on the back of Arcus' neck prickled. This was a situation that could very easily turn ugly. Somehow he had found trouble before he even made it into town.

Fantastic.

"Of course . . . a fee. How much is it?" he asked as neutrally as possible.

"Five silver rellis."

Arcus' heart dropped. That was enough money for room and board for a week. Unfortunately, he didn't see another way out of the situation. He couldn't abandon Kodja and he didn't think that the 'fee' would change regardless.

"That's all I have, sir," he lied, hoping the guards would believe him.

The leader's grin turned into a scowl.

"But I am, of course, willing to comply."

He handed the money over as the guards sneered at him.

"Well then welcome, barbarian," the leader said, not even bothering to hide his laughter. "Feast your eyes on the crowning jewel of the Imperium, home to the Emperor himself."

"May the sun never set upon His rule," Arcus mumbled, automatically speaking the traditional response to any mention of the Emperor.

He kept his head down and felt a tension grow between his shoulder blades as he continued - albeit a little less confidently - into the city, working his way into the maze of cobblestone streets and the crush of people before him.

Elbaf's breaths were labored as he jogged down the dark, winding alley that was Bolin street. He reminded himself that he was almost home, almost back to Brine street. He'd long ago lost the Cair Street Boys - somewhere about a mile back he guessed - but he wouldn't really be comfortable until he was back in the Brine, where he was a respected force.

There, the Brawler of Brine Street could rest easy under the watchful gaze of friends and allies. He slowed his pace to a walk as he rounded one final corner, allowing himself to relax and take in the seedy sights of his neighborhood. The looks he got from passersby were generally friendly, if a bit frightened. Of course he was impossible to mistake for anyone else, his towering 6 foot 9 inch frame filled the narrow, crooked street and his green-hued skin shone a brackish color in the dull light of the oil lamps placed sporadically along the road.

Those lights also revealed the blood on his lips and across his knuckles.

Tonight the Brawler had won. Cair street would respect their boundaries a while longer and his own people were that much safer for it. Though he claimed to

5

fight only for the joy of it, Elbaf did feel a certain sense of responsibility for the Brine, a certain *protectiveness*. He shook the feeling as best he could though, no one looked to half-orcs for altruism.

Elbaf was young, by human standards, but at sixteen years of age he was nearly a third as old as he could expect to reach, and he'd matured early thanks to a hard life of struggle and loss. Often he claimed a higher number - early twenties usually - because the people here didn't really understand his shorter life span and were quick to pounce on anything that could be perceived as weakness.

He followed Brine street almost to where it intersected with Corning Road, the main thoroughfare from the Eastern Gate. He exchanged meaningful looks with several of his fellow Briners, members of his gang, as he traveled. They would keep watch over the neighborhood tonight, and he would be able to relax.

The lights of the Tilted Table shone brightly ahead of him, welcoming him to a well-deserved rest. A raucous tavern on rest days, it was fairly subdued tonight in the middle of the work week. Perfect for a quiet pint before shuffling upstairs to find his bedroll.

"Elbaf, yer' all blooded up, mate," the barkeep, Dorm, called out from behind an old worn counter top as Elbaf entered. "Good night for the Brawler?"

A few of the patrons looked up from their stews and ales and then promptly back down again. Elbaf was not such a source of excitement that he drew attention from tired laborers, after all.

"It was, old friend," he sighed, as the last bit of tension left his neck and shoulders.

"I'll send Theresa 'round," the friendly, older half-orc winked. "You'll have your usual table, I imagine?"

Elbaf nodded and turned towards the far corner of the establishment, looking for his table. It was his favorite for a good reason. He could lean back against the walls and still have a commanding view of the room. To his irritation he saw that his table already had an occupant - a frail, elderly man who seemed utterly consumed with his stew.

"Dorm," he grumbled. "Who is . . ."

But his friend had already moved off to tend to another customer.

Elbaf took to his usual tactic and tried to look as imposing as possible as he approached, moving closer until his shadow towered over the old man.

The old man, however, didn't seem to notice. In fact, as Elbaf neared the table he realized that somehow the ancient fellow had fallen asleep while sitting up, his head nodding gently as he slumbered.

Elbaf was at a loss. He couldn't afford looking weak, but he truly had no desire to pester this old man. Rather, he had hoped the fellow would simply catch sight of him and shuffle off. Not knowing what else to do, he sat himself down and waited for Theresa to come by with his supper. Perhaps she would take care of the pesky old-timer for him.

Darko stumbled, nearly falling to the ground as he meandered along the uneven street. He looked up, pulling his nose from the book he was reading and glaring at the offending stone that had nearly done him in, as though the object had deliberately attempted his downfall.

He took the opportunity to review his surroundings and realized he was near the Eastern Gate. His wandering ways often led him into unfamiliar territory - not that he ever really worried for his safety - but this part of town was particularly unknown to him. Even in this rougher area his fears were minimal, though. After all, he wore the robes of an imperial wizard, a sanctioned mage. He was unmistakable in the deep red robes of his station, complete with the golden-runed trim that marked him a Master of his art.

Respected or not, magi were distrusted and feared by most common folk. Darko tended to forgive their ignorance, recognizing how easy it was to fear things beyond their comprehension.

Darko Branislav was a very serious student and had been for nearly all of his 101 years of life. He was still a young man in the reckoning of his race, though his age was indeterminate to the humans he lived among. Having been born into a fairly well-off elven family - a rarity on Sunset Isle - and identified at an early age as a potential candidate for magical learning, the path of his life had been set for many decades now, and he was admittedly quite comfortable in it.

In truth, all candidates on the island and, theoretically, in the Empire at large, were identified in this way and brought up through the Imperial College here on the island.

The wizard had a restlessness of mind that his body struggled to keep up with, and so he had taken to going for long wandering walks whilst reading. Unfortunately he was not as gifted of body as of mind, and his left leg was club-footed, a defect with him since birth that left him slower than most and caused him constant aching pain. He chose not to think of himself as a cripple, per se, but rather as having traded a whole and healthy body for an unusually sharp mind and an exceedingly powerful gift.

While not unheard of, magic users were fairly rare. Less than one in ten thousand souls had the gift of manipulating arcane energies, and far fewer could ever hope to attain the mastery that Darko had.

His attention lifted from his reading, Darko realized just how sore he was. He'd wandered much farther than usual and he felt rather inclined to rest a while. The area he was in seemed fairly residential but there was a promising looking tavern just down the street that he could see.

"The Tilted Table," Darko chuckled as he made his way through the door. "Well, I certainly hope not."

A broad common room - and a fairly quiet one at that - met his gaze as he entered the establishment. The smell of a robust stew graced Darko's nostrils as he entered, and he made a mental note to eat something while he rested.

Darko rarely frequented taverns but, on the occasions he did, he preferred a quiet corner when one was available. Ignoring the more crowded central tables, he looked into the darker recesses of the room. The tables were all fairly packed with patrons who seemed to have the same inclinations. All except for one corner, the sole occupants of which were an old man and a large, grim half-orc.

Curious.

The wizard was surprised they shared a table, but reasoned that perhaps if the half orc didn't mind the company of an old man he wouldn't mind Darko reading quietly as well.

Darko hobbled to the same corner and approached the table.

"Unbelievable," Elbaf mumbled under his breath as the wizard approached his table. "Am I to share my space with every forsaken outcast in the damn city tonight?"

"Pardon me, good sir," the spindly mage asked. "But as seating is rather limited, I wonder whether or not I might share your table?"

He tried to look foreboding, but the elf seemed determined to make a nuisance of himself.

"I'm sorry, I do tend to speak rather softly," the man cleared his throat and spoke up. "Sir? Might I sit at your tab--"

Elbaf glared at the elf, doing his best to look intimidating.

The wizard switched to Orcish, which grated Elbaf's nerves and lit a fire in his belly. Surely this delicate fool was unaware of the gravity of his insult. When Elbaf still said nothing, the man began to pantomime his desire, his actions drawing confused looks from several of the patrons nearby.

Seeing that the mage couldn't take the hint, Elbaf finally responded.

"Fine!" Elbaf roared. "But be silent!"

The common room fell quiet, pausing to see if the Brawler was about to demonstrate how he'd received his moniker. When it became clear that no violence would grace the bar, the crowd reluctantly returned to their own conversations.

Darko was appalled at the man's rudeness, but his leg ached and he needed rest. He took up a chair with the old man in between himself and the orc, stretching out his leg and positioning himself so that the light from the center of the room would shine over his shoulders enough to read. He pulled a book from within his robe, took one last look around the table, and cracked it open, promptly losing himself once again.

His course of study tonight was the Sisterhood, the so-called Holy Handmaidens of the Emperor.

It was said that divine magic was a gift from the God Emperor himself, and it was far more prevalent than the more chaotic arcane variety that Darko wielded. This divine power was granted to the Sisterhood to accomplish the great works of the Empire, and practitioners of great power filled the ranks of the Sisters of the Imperium. They were a strong and mysterious order of Warrior Clerics who upheld the Emperor's will and maintained his health in the Imperial Palace.

Their order was structured in three levels, those of Inferius, Mediatus, and Superia, and they all had their place in the great machine of the Church.

They acted as his mouthpiece throughout the lands, as defenders of the faith and of the realm, as healers for the sick and injured, as arbiters of Imperial Justice, and as caretakers of the ideals of the Empire. Through the divine works of the Sisters, and the military mastery of their martial arm, The Black Hand, the Empire held steady as a mountain against the dark forces of the world. From demi-humans like orcs and goblins to the cruelty and tyranny of the savage lands that lay beyond the borders of His Holy Domain.

Talia walked boldly down the dimly lit avenue, her carriage proud and her head up high. To onlookers she was incredibly out of place in the seedy darkness of Brine Street, but if she was aware of it, it didn't show.

Her slender frame and youthful look was the envy of many a passing woman and the stuff of dreams for many of the men. She walked with careless ease - oblivious to the stares she received - her long blonde hair bouncing in luxurious curls and her sandals softly clicking away. She wore the robes of a priestess, and her face beamed a radiant smile as she walked. She wore more wealth on her small body than many of the people around her would ever know. A full coin purse and a shining, silver reliquary adorned her belt, and a slender golden necklace with a seven-star lily pendant - crafted from expensive pearl - hung delicately around her throat. Only her clothing was simple: a cream colored cloth robe, cut to mid thigh and featuring a crimson crown on its front, and a pair of simple leggings of the same crimson.

Her clothes marked her as a fledgling priestess of the Emperor. All who saw her knew she was the embodiment of His will. It was partly due to this, and partly due to her youthful naivety, that she strode so casually through one of the roughest neighborhoods on Sunset Isle. She'd been selected at an early age - only 11 - and had been training with the Sisters here in the Capitol for the past eight years.

As the youngest daughter of House Lorraine, her parents had been delighted to learn of her selection. The majority of her learning was yet to come, of course, but so far she had learned scriptures, histories, and a smattering of magic. She'd begun the journeyman phase of her learning just six months ago, and she was still getting used to the liberty provided by not spending every waking moment in the Cathedral. She was tasked now with going out into the Empire and doing good works. When she was deemed ready, the Sisterhood would recall her and formally induct her as a Sister Inferius, a full fledged member of the Order.

She'd spent the last half year doing charitable work throughout the Isle and the surrounding communities. Tonight she'd attended a charity ball hosted by her parents, and it was her goal to distribute the coins she had in her purse to the poor.

Thinking of her mission, she couldn't help but smile. How wonderful it would be to provide much needed relief to the less fortunate. The only question that remained now was where she ought to start. She knew there was a shrine to Dostor, patron of the charitable and kind-hearted, near the Eastern Gate, and she was headed there to see if the caretaker had any ideas.

Shadows moved in an alleyway beside her as she walked past, but she didn't notice. A figure stepped out after she had gone a dozen feet or so and began to trail quietly behind her. Any sound of footsteps was masked by the jingling of coins and her softly humming hymns.

Arcus wandered yet another nearly empty street, indiscernible from the rest of the city and no help whatsoever in helping him determine where the hell he was. Night had long since fallen and his patience with it. Every building in this garbage heap of a city looked the same, and every passing citizen was either terrified of his companion or rude beyond measure. He'd stopped to ask several people for assistance, and the kindest response he'd gotten so far was a hearty 'piss off' from a child who couldn't have been more than six.

"Damn this city, Kodja," he said as he ran a hand through his hair and looked around for some kind of bearing. "Perhaps we shouldn't have come here after all."

His companion was characteristically silent, but he'd swear he saw a glint of amusement in the canine's eyes. That gleam quickly faded as Kodja's ears perked up. The wolf cocked its head to the side and then flattened his ears, a warning if Arcus had ever seen one.

The ranger's hand drifted to the sheathed scimitar on his hip and he slowed his pace, ready for anything. Much to his surprise, a young woman stepped brightly around the corner. The girl was clothed in the garb of an imperial priestess, but she still looked like a child to his eyes. Surely she couldn't have been more than a journeyman, or perhaps she was on her mission already?

She smiled widely at him and gave him a slight nod as she strode past, humming softly. Arcus let out a breath and cast a judgemental glance at Kodja, only to find him growling softly.

He didn't have long to wonder why.

A cloaked and hooded man slipped softly around the corner a dozen steps behind the girl. The man stood straighter as soon as he caught sight of Arcus, but his intent was clear.

Arcus recognized a hunter's gait, a predator's gaze. Alarm bells rang in his head, immediately amplified when another two men in similar clothing followed just after.

He made a split decision, bending at the waist and pretending to retrieve something from the ground.

"Priestess!"

He lifted his closed fist from the ground, turned around, and jogged past the men to catch up with the girl, who turned at his call.

"I believe you dropped this, ma'am," he said as he approached her, holding his hand out.

"I'm afraid I don't understand. Dropped what?"

He laughed loudly, throwing an arm around her shoulder, then dropped his voice down low.

"I think it would be wise for you not to be on the street for a little while, ma'am," he said as he flicked his eyes back towards the men, hoping to draw the girl's gaze and understanding. "May I escort you home?"

She caught sight of them and he could see a vein in her neck throb as her pulse quickened.

"O-of course," she answered, a tremble in her voice. "I would be delighted to walk with you, sir."

He gave a curt nod and stepped around to her right, leaving his sword arm on the outside of them.

The hairs on his neck rose as the men closed in on them slowly over the course of the next few blocks until he could swear he could feel them breathing down his neck. Worse, he could now see three *more* men ahead of them, waiting just outside the illumination of a nearby street lamp. They pushed off from the stone wall where they were leaning and headed his direction as the distance between them closed.

Trapped, the ranger cast around for a place to make their stand. An alley ahead looked promising, but in order to make it there first they'd have to run, doubtlessly escalating their problems.

He flinched as he stepped unexpectedly into the light of a newly opened door to his right, barely avoiding a man who stumbled drunkenly out and into the street. He caught a glimpse of a crowded bar room as the door swung shut behind an exiting patron, and inspiration hit him like lightning.

That'll do.

Arcus gripped the girl's arm and pulled her inside the establishment. He stepped immediately to the side, moving the young woman out of the way of the entrance and scanning for a next move. Kodja slipped in and stood behind them, his fur brushing the backs of their legs and his watchful eyes at the door.

A full but subdued common room and a worn wooden bar stretched out before them, both packed to the gills with tired laborers and other blue-collar types.

A quick scan of the room revealed that seating was incredibly limited. In fact, the only table with open seats already housed an unusual hodge-podge of characters - an old man, an elf in wizard's robes, and a gruff looking half-orc.

The half-orc gave Arcus pause, he'd met precious few of them in his time abroad and they'd all been . . . surly to say the least. But the six men outside were a far more certain threat, so he ushered the young woman ahead of him and they moved toward the table.

"May we join you for a short while, friends?"

The orc was about to answer, and from his face, none too kindly, but the old man beat him to it.

"Of course you may, tundra-dweller!"

Arcus was surprised but grateful, while the half-orc seemed equal parts furious and perplexed. Nonetheless, he nodded his gratitude to the old man, taking his invitation at face value. The orc seemed ready to burst, and a deep scowl had set itself across his features as first the young woman and then Arcus himself took their seats.

The ranger glanced back at the door just in time to see that three of the men from outside had come in and pushed their way to a crowded table nearer to the door.

"I'm Arcus," he introduced himself, turning back to his new companions. "And let me thank you again for allowing us to share your table, I--"

The orc growled his displeasure, but the red-robed wizard seemed excited enough for two.

"You are a wastelander," he interrupted. "Truly?"

He peered at Arcus inquisitively, and the ranger took a moment to further evaluate the elf. He seemed harmless enough, but his welcome in the city so far had been anything but warm. Further, the imperial magi were well known - and rightly feared - even in his distant homeland. Their eldritch powers were not to be trifled with, and Arcus had no choice but to equate the elf's age with power until he knew better.

"I am what the folks here seem to mean when they say wastelander," he replied cagily. "Though we call ourselves by our true name; the D'Ari."

The wizard practically quivered with excitement as he retrieved a small leatherbound notebook and a curious looking pen from one of his many pockets.

"Go on, go on," he pressed. "The *D'Ari* you say, did I pronounce that correctly?"

"You did, mage," he shrugged. "But I'm not sure what there is to tell. We are druid-folk. We live at the whims of nature, enduring her most extreme temperaments in tune with the unforgiving wilds."

He spoke, and in his mind's eye he was standing again on endless plains of ice and snow. Glaciers that stretched for leagues and mountains that rose jagged as broken glass from the hostile land.

"We live a nomadic life, for the most part," he continued, "following the snow-elk on their great migrations."

The mage was scribbling furiously.

"And you, ah, worship nature then? As a concept?"

Arcus furrowed his brow, unclear exactly what the magician was trying to determine.

"Worship?" he asked. "I would not choose that word, no. Rather, I would say that we revere the majesty and power of nature. It does not require our belief, nor our faith. It is beyond us, and yet also around us. We are part of it, but completely at its mercy. There is a divinity in the natural world, to be certain--"

"I-I'm sorry to interject," the young priestess beside him said as she shifted uncomfortably. "But that's not quite right, is it?"

The mage stopped scribbling and glanced back and forth between the two.

"How do you mean?"

The girl straightened her back and spoke with more authority.

"I mean that of course nature is divine," she explained, her posture rigid but determined, "but in a way no different from any other of the *lesser* Gods. Nature is represented by The Huntress, Alia'anara. She serves beside the Emperor himself, below and to His left at the Grand Table," Talia nodded, snipping off the end of her last syllable as she snapped her mouth shut into a thin, aggressive line of determination.

"I beg your pardon, priestess," Arcus began in a placating tone, "but your ways are not our ways. We do not worship as you do - we do not hold one god above another in our--"

"Blasphemy," Talia banged her fist on the table, cheeks flushed red. "And I'll not stand for it. Your people live - as do we all - within the cradle of our glorious Empire, and by the grace of the Emperor, may the sun never set upon His rule."

Tensions mounted in the growing silence until the old man, all but forgotten, spoke again at last.

"Tis' indeed a dangerous statement to make, tundra-dweller," he pointed out. "But sure as man still draws breath, the freedom to worship as you choose is still your own."

Elbaf growled low, rumbling his dissent.

"So long as you're silent about it, I suppose."

Talia shot the massive half-orc a dagger glare.

"And what do *goblinkin* believe?"

Elbaf bristled at the insult. He leaned in close to the woman. Half-standing from his seat, the table groaned under his grip.

"I believe in strength, girl," he snarled, revealing inch-long canines. "And I suggest you watch your tongue. You are far from the clean-swept halls of your convent."

"Youth is often a bitter drink," the old man cut in again. "She knows nothing but the kindness of the Empire, Elbaf, son of Elbain."

Elbaf stood abruptly, the table scraping a few inches across the rough wooden floor as he did so.

He eyed the man with newfound suspicion. There were no more than a handful in the city - in the whole of the world perhaps - that knew his lineage. *This* man was a stranger to him and a stranger to Brine Street. He certainly had no right to his father's name.

"You overstep as well, old-timer," he threatened. "And I do not suffer strangers who pry too deeply."

"I know, Brawler, your reputation far precedes you," the old man raised his hands, palms out, in an obvious attempt to placate the warrior. "I have no quarrel with you. My only desires are a stiff drink and a warm fire, and here I have both."

"The Empire *is* kindness," Talia huffed, but the man's words deflated her considerably.

"For some, perhaps," Elbaf growled again, still staring unbroken at the old man.

"Let me apologize," the old-timer soothed him. "And perhaps soothe the injuries of the night with a round for the table at my expense. May I impose upon you all?"

The group nodded their agreement, and the old man gestured with a surprising surety across the room.

Elbaf, keenly aware of how busy the two-person staff was tonight, was stunned to see Theresa turn and catch the man's wave immediately. She made a beeline for his table and smiled brightly as she approached.

"Apologies for the fullness of the bar tonight, gents and lady," she smiled winningly. "But tight quarters can breed fast friends, no?"

"My dear, I would like to buy a round," the old man smiled back. "Whatever these fine folks would have to drink and a glass of chilled mead for me, if you have it?"

"Best in the city, sir," she winked. "And for the rest of you?"

Elbaf tapped his glass, indicating another of the strong, smoked beers he loved so well. The rest of the group ordered an assortment of wines, brandies, and a glass of water for Talia.

Theresa nodded along with each order, then bounced away toward the bar with another dazzling grin.

"You still have much to explain, old-timer," Elbaf started again.

It was clear that Elbaf would not let the conversation drop. His heavy brow was furrowed with a focus that would not be distracted.

"Please, be at peace, Brawler. I meant no disrespect. I know only what I have heard," he answered earnestly. "As your legend grows, you must expect others to hear of your deeds."

Elbaf snorted doubtfully at the man, but he could not help enjoying the idea that he had a legend, or that it might be growing. The ugliness in the air was not quite gone, though. It lingered heavily between them as silence grew. They received their drinks in short order, but none yet dared breach the ever-widening maw of discomfort.

"Let us break the tension," the old man said at last, sitting up straighter in his seat with renewed energy. "How about a game of riddles with a prize to the winner?"

Elbaf rolled his eyes as the others were pulled from their shells, each agreeing with varying degrees of enthusiasm. Finally, only he had yet to voice his agreement, and the gazes of the table fell upon him. He sighed heavily before uttering a gruff affirmative and re-took his seat.

"Very well," the old man rubbed his hands together. "A weightless cover, a blanket that brings only chill, it covers all eventually, and few can pierce its veil."

The group exchanged questioning looks while the old man took a happy sip of honey wine.

"Do we . . . do we simply answer?" Talia asked uncertainly.

"Yes, yes, you're not schoolchildren," the old man chuckled. "You need not raise your hands."

They again fell silent, each working through the problem in their own way.

Elbaf looked around the table, analyzing each of his competitors. The answer seemed glaringly obvious to him, but he feared the simplicity of his guess. Finally, he could wait no longer.

"Darkness," he mumbled.

"Come again?" the old man asked. "I am afraid my ears are no longer young."

"Darkness," Elbaf said again, louder this time.

The eyes of his companions shifted to the old man, who smiled and clapped his hands softly.

"First point to the Brawler," he announced. "Darkness, indeed!"

The group nodded, acknowledging his success - all save the wizard that is. Darko put his notebook away and leaned forward, his pride injured and his focus redoubled.

"Another, another," the man muttered. "Let's see now, let's see . . ."

He scratched his chin absentmindedly before settling on a new puzzle with a snap of his fingers.

"A war," he began, "of wholeness and void, never-ending til' the death of both - and then only to fulfill another."

Elbaf quirked up an eyebrow. This was considerably trickier. He stole glances around the table - the rest of his companions seemed similarly stumped, until at last the wastelander spoke.

"Hunger," Arcus thumped the table with his hand, smiling broadly as he proclaimed his guess.

"Excellent work, druid! Yes, hunger, the war that ceases only when we feed another. Much can be learned of humility in the understanding that one is but a small piece of an endless wheel."

Arcus nodded at the man, finding a greater appreciation of the old-timer.

"In D'Ari lands, we learn the value of hunger alongside the value of life," the druid pointed out. "Living so close to starvation lends itself to solemn introspection."

"Another!"

The assembly looked in surprise at the fervent proclamation of the frail-looking wizard, who straightened his robes and repeated himself more calmly.

"Another, please."

"Yes, alright, let me think, let me think . . ."

Already the air was clearing above the table, the group exchanged smiles at the wizard's outburst and shared smalltalk as the old man thought of another riddle. Introductions were made at last, and the group finally knew each other's names. All fell silent though when the old man began to speak once more.

"Mortal men and gods alike fear this, the all-consuming night."

The wizard stood up, his abrupt movement jostling the oaken table and upsetting the drinks upon it.

"Death," he shouted triumphantly. "It's death!"

The bar fell instantly silent, and a score of curious faces turned to their table as Darko's face swiftly reddened until it matched his robes for depth of scarlet. He took his seat again swiftly, mumbling under his breath and sinking lower into his chair.

Dorm, the barkeep, seemed just as taken aback as his patrons. He stood with a clay mug in one hand and a rag in the other. Reading the hesitation in the room and sensing a dip in sales, he cleared his throat loudly.

"Next round is half-price!"

The crowd roared in approval, and Theresa was busy taking dozens of new orders immediately. The wizard's outburst was quickly drowned by cheap ale and the camaraderie of the night, but Dorm sent an irritated glance to the table anyway. Elbaf caught the glare, and waved him off with an apologetic shrug.

"Perhaps, wizard," Elbaf sighed, "you can refrain from embarrassing us further?"

Talia giggled at the Orc's admonishment, and Arcus cracked a smile as well.

"Yes, well . . . I *apologize*. Perhaps I did get a tad excited . . ."

"You don't say, wizard," Elbaf muttered under his breath.

"So?" Talia asked expectantly, her eyes glued to the old man with whom they shared their table.

"Oh, I suppose I have a few more . . ."

The table grew quiet once more, all eyes trained on the man's sparkling blue eyes.

"Right, yes, here we go," he began, taking a deep breath. "The wind beneath a poem's wings, it can bring tears to the eyes of kings. No mortal can resist its call, it begs us each to cherish all. It lifts us up, it brings us low, at times 'tis fast and others slow."

Several minutes passed without a word as the party chewed on the riddle. Several times a member started to speak, only to be stopped by self doubt.

"Well, I suppose a shot in the dark is no sin, is it?"

The old man smiled at Darko's question.

"No, mage, no sin at all."

"Then I guess language. Am I even close?"

His guess was met with a slow shake of the head, and the old man smiled broader.

"No, Elf, but you're on the right track."

Elbaf chuckled at the wizard's flush of embarrassment, and the old man turned to him instead. Upon being caught, Elbaf's wry smile disappeared immediately.

"And you, warrior? Have you a guess, then?"

Elbaf balked while the table waited, until at last he finally gave a gruff reply.

"Love, probably," he said. "Something stupid like that."

The old man shook his head, a twinkle in his eye, and opened his mouth to speak, but halted when Talia's small, lyrical voice answered instead.

"It's music, isn't it?"

"Very good, priestess," he clapped excitedly. "Yes, *music*, the language that transcends all others, the language that loves."

Elbaf rolled his eyes, but kicked himself internally. Of course it was music. The rest of the table nodded appreciatively too as focus returned to the old man.

"It seems we have a tie," he announced. "Perhaps just one last riddle then, no?"

All four of them leaned forward intently as the spirit of competition took hold - the old man was right. They were tied at one all and that simply would not do.

Even the rumble of the common room seemed to quiet as he spoke at last.

"That which warms and brings the light, shadow's lament and life's delight. The death of darkness."

Darko was first to answer, though he did so tentatively.

"The Emperor, I suppose?"

Elbaf noted a slight scowl as the old man shook his head. He expected another gentle answer but none came.

"No," the man said curtly.

"What about fire?"

Arcus' answer received the same shake, but the man was not as cold about it.

"The sun."

Talia's answer was so soft, her voice so low, that the assembled members barely heard it over the background noise. Contrary to the old man's earlier assertion, he seized on her quiet answer instantly.

"But of course, my dear," he beamed. "Of course it should be you."

"I'm not sure I understand what you mean, sir?"

He smiled broadly and reached into a pocket at his belt. Gently, he retrieved a small, intricately carved wooden box.

"It's nothing, child," he said with a hint of melancholy. "But I believe you are owed a prize."

Talia raised her hands slightly and seemed embarrassed to actually take anything from the man.

"Your company was our prize, sir. Please, I need no material gifts."

"Nonetheless," he insisted. "I gave my word, and I'll keep it. May this keep the darkness in the world at bay a while longer."

He pushed the box to her and waited for her to open it. The group stared at the box, its dark wood and glimmering golden trim entranced them. Even Elbaf, who generally held a strong poker face, found himself staring in rapt attention as the young woman snaked a small hand out and lifted the tiny bauble.

The top slid open beneath her thin fingers and Talia gasped in awe. She gently pulled a silver chain up from the box and then, as the last links were lifted clear, an exquisite golden medallion followed. The disk was carved to resemble the burning sun, with radiant rays of glowing metal extending in a circle around its core.

"Sir, there's simply no way I can accept this," she insisted. "This must have cost a fortune!"

The old man laughed, a genuine heartfelt laugh that brought warmth to the table.

"It was a gift to me as well. Besides, you wouldn't begrudge the doting of an old man, would you? Truly it is my honor to pass it on."

Elbaf decided at last that he liked the old man, suspicious or not. He raised a hand, gesturing to Theresa and catching her attention after a moment.

"I did not think that I would share my table with strangers tonight. In fact, I never do," Elbaf began, lifting his nearly empty drink, "but . . . you have my thanks for sharing these past few candle marks with me."

The table raised their glasses in unison and downed their dwindling drinks just as Theresa arrived to take the orders for their next round.

"On me, Theresa. I insist."

The group was placing orders when the sound of bells started ringing in the distance. The Imperial Cathedral, a towering structure nestled in the Emperor's palace in the heart of the city, could be heard for miles, even beyond the city's outer walls.

"Can it truly be midnight?" Talia stood up swiftly, no small amount of fear in her eyes. "Mother Superior will have my hide! I apologize, friends. I must take my leave of you. I've missed curfew and I'm likely going to spend the next fortnight scrubbing latrines for it."

"Sir, thank you again for this necklace," she gave a short bow to the old man. "I will wear it with pride for all of my days."

The group began to protest, but Talia wouldn't hear it. She quickly gathered her things and headed for the door.

Chapter Two

Elbaf's gaze followed the young woman as she made her way through the crowd to the door. She was so full of youth - and so naive. She didn't belong here in the Brine, he decided. No, it was best she left for safer neighborhoods where the lamp-men kept the streets well lit and the guard had regular patrols.

He silently wished her well, then returned to his drink. He took a hefty swig and turned to the ranger from the wilds. He had more questions and the drinks were loosening his tongue. On turning, however, he saw the ranger already moving to stand, one hand on the hilt of a saber at his side.

"What is it?" he asked, rising and following the smaller man's gaze. "What's wrong?"

Elbaf saw his target immediately: three men, their eyes locked on Talia's slight form, who were all rushing to the door after her.

Elbaf rolled his neck, letting out a satisfying crack and pulled a dagger from his side. He raised his blade and with a sharp flick of his wrist he whipped the palm sized weapon across the barroom where it buried itself deep in the oaken door just as the lead man reached for the handle.

"Who are you," Elbaf growled, "and what're you doing on my turf?"

The bar fell silent, and many of the more seasoned regulars pushed back from their tables, hands drifting to their own weapons if they had any, while Arcus and Elbaf made their way across the room.

"What's it to you, half-breed?" The leader retorted, disdain dripping from his words.

"This is the Brine," Elbaf chuckled darkly. "And you must be a long way from home."

Where he walked the patrons swiftly cleared space, for they knew well of the Brawler's wrath. He came to a stop a few feet from the men with Arcus and his wolf at his side.

"I said, what's it to you, *greenskin*?"

Elbaf smiled. He could smell fear on the men, but they looked willing enough to fight if it came down to it. He didn't recognize them, and with steel on their hips a bar fight could swiftly turn deadly.

"Last chance," Elbaf took another step, a large one, putting himself inside an easy arm's length of the man who'd spoken. "Sit down, finish your drinks."

Elbaf flexed his fingers then balled his fists. The gloves he wore held pockets of lead filings on every knuckle, and they packed a mighty punch when driven by his well-muscled arms. He could feel his blood pressure spiking, the prickle of sweat on the back of his neck as his heart pounded a wardrum's beat.

"We're done here," the man scoffed as he reached out for the door handle.

His hand never made it.

One-hundred and sixty pounds of muscle and teeth erupted from behind Arcus as Kodja's jaws locked around the man's wrist with a sickening crunch. He cried out in pain, trying desperately to pry the wolf's jaws open with his free hand. Elbaf silenced him with a leaden haymaker, dropping him to the floor where he spit blood and teeth, then promptly passed out.

With that, the bar erupted.

The two men still facing them drew short daggers and took a few steps back, shoving several onlookers out of the way and clearing a small space between them. The one on the left - whether from courage or stupidity - chose to make the first move.

"You'll pay for that," he growled, murder in his eyes.

The man lunged forward, slashing wildly with his dagger before unceremoniously slipping and falling to the ground as, with a loud crack and a bang, a pool of slick, shimmering oil appeared beneath him on the worn hardwood of the barroom floor. The slippery liquid left him sprawling on the floor, flailing about as he struggled to stand and his companion backed further away.

Elbaf resisted the urge to turn around. He felt the hairs on the back of his neck rise and his skin crawled at the unfamiliar tingle of arcane energies behind him.

"Rest assured, my next incantation will be substantially more lethal," Darko called from across the room, his voice threateningly magnified. "Lay down your arms."

The brawling crowd scrambled to clear a path between the wizard and his target, and Elbaf spared a glance back at his dinner companion. Darko's eyes were jet black pools with neither whites nor pupils and his hands glowed a deep purple with halos of sparking, crackling energy cascading off of them.

The man on the floor froze. He raised his hands and dropped his daggers to the ground, where Arcus kicked them away. The lone troublemaker that was still standing followed suit, falling to his knees and dropping his weapons with a clatter.

Elbaf strode over to the man on his knees and gripped his woolen tunic with both fists. He lifted the man with both hands and bared his teeth.

"This is the Brine," he growled. "Here there is only one authority. *Mine.*"

Whatever reply the man had went unheard as a loud, piercing scream tore through the room from the street outside.

"Talia," Arcus bolted for the door, yanking it open and disappearing into the night.

Elbaf threw the man into the wall, then followed the wastelander, yanking his dagger from the door as he passed. He burst from the bar just in time to see Talia, kicking and struggling, being dragged into an alley by three hooded men. She was putting up a fight, but one of her assailants had her mouth covered with a gloved hand and he was clearly stronger than the slender woman.

Arcus was already halfway across the street, Kodja at his side.

Elbaf roared a challenge and charged as well. Hot on Arcus' heels, he rounded the corner into the alley and skidded to a halt to evaluate the scene.

The alley was effectively a dead end, with a tall fence blocking the men's escape some twenty feet in. The man holding Talia pressed a long dagger to her throat, and the other two had short swords drawn and ready.

"Let her go," Arcus said, drawing a long, lightly curved scimitar from his waist. "This doesn't need to end in your deaths."

The one holding Talia seemed to consider, and judging from the looks the other two gave him, he was the leader of the trio. He had the desperate look of a cornered rat, glancing at his men and then back at Elbaf and Arcus before lifting his hand and striking Talia in the back of the head with the butt of his dagger. She crumpled to the ground in a heap in front of him. The man stepped over her unconscious body as he pulled a second blade with his free hand.

"You don't look so big to me, mate," he sneered. "Let's dance."

Elbaf sized the trio up. He had his dagger, but bringing a knife to a sword fight was hardly his idea of a good time. Each of these men seemed well used to the blades they brandished, and their confidence was . . . unexpected. They wore no emblems that he recognized and their faces were unfamiliar to him, so he reasoned they must be wandering predators poaching in his area, rather than members of a rival gang.

"You have one final opportunity to leave this fight unharmed," Arcus threatened, his words punctuated by a deep growl from Kodja.

"No," Elbaf interjected. "That time has passed."

He strode past the druid, watching the men for any sign of weakness.

There.

The man on the left casting small, furtive glances at his companions. *There* was his weak point.

Elbaf feigned a lunge to his right, only to plant his foot and redirect to the left at the last second.

While the leader and his henchman on the right bristled and made ready for contact, the one on the left hesitated. Elbaf closed the gap in an instant, simultaneously grabbing the man's sword arm by the wrist and jamming his dagger into the poor bastard's thigh.

His prey dropped the shortsword he was holding, which Elbaf caught deftly mid-air before spinning around to bring the hilt crashing into the man's temple, felling him immediately.

The leader sprang back, throwing one dagger then the next, both targeting the half-orc. Elbaf managed to dodge one, but the other caught him a glancing blow in the forearm. It was a deep cut, a half inch at least, but he couldn't afford to let the searing pain slow him down - the man already had two more knives in hand.

The other henchman was locked in a duel with Arcus, who's superior swordsmanship and longer blade was proving too much for the thug to bear.

Running out of options and growing visibly more desperate, the leader threw another pair of daggers - one each for Elbaf and Arcus - and backed up further, putting his back to the fence. Arcus neatly sidestepped his throw, and the blade left nothing more than a streak on his sturdy leather armor. Elbaf was less fortunate, and the second dagger bit deeply into his side.

Elbaf gritted his teeth against the pain and charged, his blade bared. The leader faced off with the half-orc and, in doing so, exposed himself to Kodja's surprise attack. He cried out and fell backwards as the animal erupted from Arcus' side. Kodja tackled the man, bearing him to the ground where his jaws locked around the squirming man's throat. A gurgling scream was cut off by a sickening crunch, and the man was left twitching on the ground as Kodja tore out his throat in a spray of blood.

"P-please, I yield," the final man begged, throwing his blade to the other side of the alley and backing away until he hit the stone of the wall.

Arcus kept his blade out, holding the man at bay.

"Dammit, ranger," Elbaf breathed heavily, his mind racing. "It's murder charges for us now."

"It was *self defense*," Arcus retorted incredulously at the half-orc. "Have you gone mad? We were rescuing Talia!"

"Good luck convincing the guards of that," Elbaf groaned. "We need to get out of here."

He turned to the man whose fate had yet to be decided, still cowering against the wall.

Heavy footsteps drew all three men's gazes to the entrance of the alley, but it was only Darko. The wizard hobbled into view, painfully favoring his good leg.

"By the nine, what happened here?"

"We've no time, wizard," Elbaf snapped tersely as he lifted Talia onto his shoulders. "You can dwell on it at length when you return to your gilded tower. Right now--"

His words were punctuated by a loud, unmistakable whistle from down the street.

"Someone at the bar must have called them," Elbaf cursed. "Move!"

Elbaf headed for the main street, only to be stopped by Arcus calling out behind him.

"What about this one?"

The ranger jerked his thumb at the trembling thug.

Elbaf clenched his jaw and turned on his heel, glancing down at the shortsword still in his hand.

"Actually," Darko interjected, "I may have a--"

"Then do it. We have no time!"

Darko began to softly chant, his hands adopting a dim silver glow.

"N-no, wait," the man begged. "I swear, I won't say any--"

The thugs's words were cut off as his eyes rolled back in their sockets and he collapsed in a heap.

"What did you do to him?" Arcus asked, returning his blade to its scabbard.

"He's asleep," the wizard explained. "His memory of the last few hours should be a blur when he wakes up."

Arcus nodded, visibly relieved that the man was still alive.

The group left the alley with Talia in tow and Kodja trailing a few feet behind, only to find a cluster of activity at the entrance of the Tilted Table across the street. Four guards in uniform - each brandishing a lantern in one hand and a polished steel longsword in the other - were questioning Dorm, who looked to be less than cooperative. The men they'd fought in the bar were all seated on the edge of the street in irons, looking rather worse for wear.

"There they are!" one of them shouted, pointing with both his chained hands. "Them's the men who attacked us, officers!"

The leader of the guard troop turned and, upon seeing them, pointed his blade.

"You, there," he shouted. "Stand fast in the name of the law!"

The man marched into the street, making a beeline for the party, and Elbaf bolted.

"I said halt!"

The man's cries fell on deaf ears as Darko and Arcus took their cues from the half-orc, following him into the darkness of the night.

Elbaf had scarcely gone a block when he realized that only Arcus and the wolf had kept up with him. Looking back, he could see Darko had already fallen considerably behind. The guards had taken a moment to organize themselves, but two of them had pursued and were now nipping at Darko's heels.

"We can't leave him," Arcus said through labored breaths.

Elbaf adjusted the woman on his shoulders and hissed as his wounds captured his attention again.

"Says you, ranger."

But despite his gruff reply, leaving the wizard did not sit well with him, either.

"Ugh, *fine*. Take the girl," he sighed, handing her over. "Go down this road, take a left there at the lamp, then three more streets, and then a right. I'll see you in the park, just . . . just stay there until I get there. Do not leave the park."

Arcus nodded, taking Talia from Elbaf and putting her over his own shoulders.

"Kodja," he glanced down at the animal. "Go with Elbaf, he'll need you more than I."

"No, I won't," Elbaf shook his head, waving the wolf off. "Stay with your master, keep that girl safe."

Elbaf didn't wait for a response. He took one last look at Talia's unconscious form and, with a bellowing roar, sprinted back down the street. He saw the guardsmen balk at the sound, allowing Darko to widen his narrow lead.

"Follow the ranger," he shouted as he passed the elf. "I'll join you when I can."

The lead guard stopped, clearly leery of the charging warrior.

"S-stop there," he called out, holding his lantern high.

A mere sixty feet separated them. Then forty. Then twenty.

The men put their hands on the hilts of their now sheathed swords, sharing a look of concerned disbelief.

"I said sto--"

Elbaf cut the man off as he hit him like an avalanche, spearing the man in his mid-rift and lifting him from his feet in the process. They collided with such force that they both traveled several feet before they hit the ground with a heavy thud. Elbaf rolled to the side, narrowly evading the reaching hands of the second guard, and sprang to his feet. A strong left hook to the jaw sent him sprawling into his companion, who was only now standing up. Elbaf spared a glance back at Darko, relieved to see he'd nearly caught up to the ranger by now.

Unfortunately, his lapse in attention earned him a blow in the stomach and another square on the nose. He could feel his nose break under the impact and blood poured from it immediately.

"You're under arrest," the leader growled at him as his companion grabbed hold of his wrists.

Elbaf said nothing, choosing instead to headbutt the man holding him, sending him backwards with a cry of pain. He successfully yanked his left arm free, but the guard had a surer grip on his right. Elbaf spat a mouthful of blood into his stunned face. The guard let go in shock, wiping his face feverishly as he backed away retching.

Elbaf took the opportunity to tear off down a side street.

As he'd hoped, the guards pursued him - his companions all but forgotten. It took all of five minutes for the guards to call off their pursuit, then another ten for him to make his way to the park.

Every breath brought fresh, sharp pain to his side and his head was growing foggier by the second. He looked down at his side and was unsurprised to see blood steadily leaking from between his fingers. His head and heart were pounding in sync and he felt a bone-numbing tiredness spreading throughout his entire body. He looked back, cursing when he saw the winding trail of blood on the stones behind him. He'd lost no one, he realized, but simply delayed his own capture.

He shook the fog out of his mind and moved with renewed haste into the lush darkness of the park. It was only an acre or so, but filled with all manner of barely maintained shrubbery and trees. Once a well-used picnic spot, the grounds had fallen into horrible disrepair decades ago and were now largely avoided.

These days, they made an excellent place for clandestine meetings and shady dealings, but most other folk gave them a wide berth.

Elbaf looked around, but even after searching quietly for several minutes he found no sign that his companions had made it.

"Damn it," he groaned. "Will this night not simply end?"

The half-orc contemplated leaving. By rights he'd done far more than was required of him. It was the thought of Talia that pushed him to keep searching - she was too young, too innocent to face the streets at night. Rather than turn back, he picked up the pace again, working out in his mind the most likely path the ranger had taken by mistake.

This part of the city was old, dating back almost to the Founding, and was laid out in a relatively organized grid of major streets connected by smaller, narrower alleys and paths.

Elbaf headed west, and three blocks later he heard the shouting.

He cocked his head, trying to pick out the direction of the sound amid the warren of stone walls around him. His heart sank and his blood ran colder when he realized where the noise was coming from: Coral Street to the south, the very edge of the Brine that butted up against the Cair Street Boys' territory.

Fresh from a loss, they'd be out in force tonight and hungry for revenge on any unfortunate soul to pass their way. Elbaf took off, following the sounds of the commotion to their source.

He could hear jeers and raucous laughter from up ahead, punctuated with whistles and cat-calls. The noise grew louder and he slowed his pace, approaching each new intersection with care.

He shouldn't have bothered.

The scene was well-lit by one of the few functional street lamps in the area. Arcus, supporting a conscious but injured Talia, was brandishing his blade at a dozen men, all with saps and clubs in hand. Darko stood behind them, bright green light emanating from his hands. They were backed against a wall and surrounded by a semi-circle of men who were, for the time being, keeping their distance. Several of them sported injuries - nicks and cuts from Arcus' blade, no doubt.

Elbaf watched the men taunt the small group, feigning attacks and bursting out in derisive laughter every time Arcus flinched. Even from here he could see Arcus was exhausted, his blade wavering.

Another feint elicited a wild swing from Arcus, then another, even less coordinated.

Elbaf cast around for a weapon. His small blade would be a poor choice, and he'd already gotten lucky once tonight. A pile of rubbish nearby offered a promising option: a four-foot wooden board that was a few inches square and studded with nails on one end.

He retrieved it as quietly as he could before turning back to the group. They'd closed in by several feet already, barely out of blade range and Arcus' seemed barely able to hold his sword anymore. Elbaf swore and threw caution to the wind. He hefted the board and stepped into the dim light of a flickering oil lamp, gauging the group and trying to determine a point of entry while running out of time.

One of the men grew bold, stepping inside Arcus' range and leaning in to taunt him up close. Elbaf was as stunned as the gang when Arcus ducked and dragged his sword across the man's belly, laying it open like a side of beef. He followed with a powerful kick that sent the man backwards, trying and failing to hold his guts inside his body.

His blade returned to its unwavering position and his deception was revealed - he had plenty of energy left to fight. The mockery and taunting stopped immediately and the men's faces hardened with newfound anger.

Elbaf chose this as his moment to enter, striding into the light with his chest puffed up and his stance wide and menacing.

"Seems your prey has a bite," Elbaf yelled with authority. "Perhaps you'd like to try your luck with me again, instead."

He stopped some fifteen feet away, tapping the club in his hands on the stone street before pointing it at the leading man.

To his surprise, the men backed warily away, not only from him, but from Arcus as well.

"C'mon, boys. We're done here," the leader hissed as they collected their fallen companion and headed for the nearest street.

Elbaf shuffled over to the others, looking them over quickly for injuries. He scarcely had time to close the distance before loud whistles rang out down the road the Cair Street Boys had taken.

The gang came pouring back into the intersection, scattering in each of the other three directions. Identical whistles rang out from each street, this time coupled with the shouted commands of the town guard.

They'd come out in force it seemed - at least six to a street and closing in fast.

The gangsters made ready to stand and fight, and Arcus did as well.

"No, friend." Elbaf held a hand out to the wildman. "There's no fight to win here. Make peace with what gods you have."

Arcus had a look like cornered prey and seemed at first unwilling to disarm himself, but as the guards waded into melee with the Cair Street boys he was faced with the reality that their situation was indeed hopeless.

The ranger said something to his wolf that Elbaf couldn't understand - a sort of lyrical language that slipped from his mind as soon as he heard it. The animal hesitated, then bolted down one of the streets, dodging guards and disappearing into the night.

Elbaf hit his knees, tossing aside his makeshift club and placing his hands on the back of his head while the brawl in front of him tilted more and more heavily in the favor of the guardsmen, and he indicated with a nod that Arcus and the others should do the same.

Several guards were injured - at least one fatally by the looks of it - in the time it took for the squad of men to subdue the Cair Street Boys and close in on Elbaf and his company.

"Do as you're instructed, druid," Elbaf hissed. "Trust me when I say it's easier that way."

The last few members of the gang were still being loaded into the back of a wagon as the guards shackled Elbaf and his companions and threw them roughly to the ground. Elbaf grunted as his fresh injuries met the pavement, but kept his composure as best he could with his face pressed against the cobblestones.

"Wha' about this lot, sarge?" A gruff voice called from above him. "Ain't wearing Cair Street colors, but this 'un is the Brawler, I think."

A pair of black leather boots approached Elbaf's face, stopping a few inches away.

"Take 'em back to the station and we'll sort 'em out," another voice answered as the boot raised up.

The last thing Elbaf saw was the heel of it coming down.

Then nothing.

When he woke at last to a pounding headache, Elbaf could feel that he was laying on smooth, cold stone. One of his eyes was swollen so badly he could barely open it and his whole body felt sluggish, but he forced himself to move. He could feel his side stick to the floor as he rolled over. He hissed as dried blood crackled and his clothes peeled free from the ground.

"Elbaf," Talia's voice was laced with fear, but it brought Elbaf to his senses immediately. "Are you alright?"

He tried to speak, but couldn't - his mouth was bone dry and his throat was hoarse. He licked his lips and tried again, managing to croak out a weak reply.

"I'm alright," he coughed. "You?"

He sat up painfully and found himself in a small cell. He was surrounded by bars on each side save one, which was a stone wall. His cell was joined with Talia's on one side, and an empty cell on the other. He could see an identical row of cells on the other side of a narrow hallway that seemed to run down the center of the rows. Though the area was dark, Elbaf's orcish heritage lent him clear sight of the area - albeit in black and white.

"Come closer," Talia was pressed against the bars of her own cell, her human eyes wide as she peered through the darkness at him. "You need medical attention."

Elbaf was prepared to protest, but his vision was blacking out around the edges and he could scarcely feel his extremities. Instead, he simply nodded and dragged himself over to their shared wall.

Talia waited until he got close, then reached out a hand to him. She found his shoulder in the darkness, gripped it firmly, and to Elbaf's surprise she began to sing. He gasped, unable to contain his shock as moments later the young woman started to glow with a soft white light.

Elbaf felt *instantly* revitalized.

He'd never seen true clerical magic before - no one in the Brine ever had, to his knowledge. Within seconds the swelling in his eye deflated, his vision was restored, and his pain levels were reduced to that of a modest bruising.

He reached up to find his face uninjured, then quickly inspected his other wounds. The cuts were half-healed - the sort of scabbed over but not-quite-scarred look that should have taken weeks to occur.

"I-I'm sorry, that's the best I can do," Talia sighed, breathing as heavily as if she'd just done wind sprints.

"Priestess," he responded in a reverent whisper. "You . . . honor me with your gift."

Restored, he took another look at their surroundings. He was no stranger to the jails of the city, and this was certainly not one of them. No clapboard siding or loose shackles here. No, these bars were straight and tightly set, the stone cleanly cut and level.

They must be somewhere else.

"Any idea where we are, Talia?"

"They took us to the heart of the city," she said, her voice quaking. "We're below the Cathedral."

Elbaf's heart rate spiked, but he would not let it show.

"And Arcus? The wizard? They live?"

"I d-don't know," she stammered. "The guards came and took Arcus at least a candlemark ago, and Darko was taken not too long after."

Elbaf shook his head. He'd never heard of anyone being taken here before, but he had enough sense to know it was not good.

"Don't worry, priestess," he tried his best to comfort her. "You're innocent here, not to mention a servant of the Emperor's will. You're going to be ok."

Whatever reply she might have had was cut short by the approaching sound of heavy boots.

Three guards marched down the hall, preceded by the even light of the lantern that one held. He seemed to be in charge, as he walked a few feet ahead of his companions. In his other hand he held a clipboard with several sheets of parchment on it.

"Talia Lorraine, of House Lorraine," he read from the clipboard. "You are hereby called forth to stand trial for murder, evading arrest, assaulting the city guard, inciting violence, and fraternizing with known criminals. Will you come peacefully?"

Tears poured from her eyes as he read the list aloud, but she nodded silently.

"She did no such thing," Elbaf protested. "I--"

"Quiet," the leader barked, as the two guards flanking him drew batons. "Your time will come soon enough!"

But Elbaf wouldn't be silenced so easily. He stood shakily and approached the bars.

"It's ok, Elbaf," Talia's voice broke. "It's ok. I'll come peacefully."

She stood and walked to the door of her cell, holding her arms out for shackles as the two escorts entered. She didn't look back as they led her away down the hall.

Elbaf was alone.

The silence of the prison was deafening.

He started to pace, tension mounting in his clenched jaw and across his tightly drawn shoulders.

"Dammit, ranger," he cursed under his breath. "How hard could it have been to simply turn left?"

But inside, he blamed himself as much as them. They were strangers to the ways of the city, and he should have kept them under closer watch.

"You carry it well, Elbaf."

He jumped, looking around for the source of the familiar voice.

"Here," the voice rang out from the distant corner of a cell on the other side of the hallway.

Elbaf looked again and, sure enough, there sat the old man from the tavern.

"How is it *you've* come to be here, old man?"

His query was met with a soft laugh.

"Oh, the same as you, I suppose, warrior."

He stood and walked to the edge of the cell and peered down the hallway where Talia had been taken.

"They'll be back for *you* soon."

"I suppose they will," Elbaf straightened up, doing his best to look resolute.

They shared a silent, solemn moment before the man spoke again.

"Can I beg a favor of you, Elbaf?"

"Sure," Elbaf shrugged after a moment's consideration. "Though I don't know what I could possibly do for you, given our current situation."

"Even so," the old man said, drawing a small object from his pocket. "Talia dropped this in the alley. I would very much appreciate it if you could return it to her for me."

He tossed the object - a tiny cloth-covered bundle - across the intervening space. Elbaf caught it easily and knew straight away what it must be. He unwrapped it and marveled at the beauty of the sun pendant that Talia had won during their contest earlier in the night.

Elbaf wrapped the bundle back up and stuffed it into his pocket, eyeing the old man with an equal measure of suspicion and wonder.

"I think you are more than you seem."

It wasn't a question, but the old man answered anyway.

"As are you, warrior."

The sound of the guards returning brought a close to their conversation, and Elbaf moved away from his cell door, putting the wall to his back where he could better fight without being surrounded.

The man bearing the torch was the same guard who had escorted his friend away, but instead of two escorts he now had four.

"State your name, orc."

"Elbaf," Elbaf puffed his chest. "Son of Elbain, Brawler of the--"

"That's plenty," the guard interrupted, holding a hand up to cut Elbaf off.

The man scribbled something on his clipboard with a quill pen.

"You are hereby called forth to stand trial for murder, evading arrest, assaulting the city guard, inciting violence, and fraternizing with known criminals. Will you come peacefully?"

He thought about resisting, but simply nodded and walked to the door.

"On your knees," the guard instructed. "Face away from the door."

He complied stiffly.

He felt the guards pull his arms back, shackling them together at his wrists and above his elbows before yanking him to his feet. The men started marching him away and down the hall - two on each side and the lantern-bearer at the front - when a final thought occurred to Elbaf.

"You said I carry it well," he called out behind himself. "What did you mean?"

"All the weight on your shoulders," came the reply. "All the weight."

He didn't have time to respond, nor do much else. The hallway extended forty feet or so, terminating in a stairwell heading up. The broad spiral stairs allowed the men escorting him to stay at his sides, not that there was anywhere for him to run should he break free successfully. Still, he thought to himself, he was alive.

He still had a chance.

The stairs brought them to a vaulted, well-lit hallway that was tiled in midnight black. The floor was so dark it seemed to almost swallow the clear, steady light of the lanterns that were spaced evenly along it. No, not lanterns he realized, something else entirely. Elbaf studied the next pair of the objects as he passed them. They looked like lamps, but the light emanating from the soft white globes was far too steady to be a flame. He knew the Sisterhood was rumored to practice powerful magic, and given what he'd seen from Talia he had no reason to disbelieve those rumors now.

He reasoned that this hallway must have been at ground level, since he could see a clearing ahead. Sure enough, a courtyard came into view as they neared the end of the hall. The courtyard was tiled in the same dark stone, and ringed with an overhanging ceiling. The center of the broad square was open to the sky above, but the walls of the cathedral towered up on every side.

One feature captured his attention, however. A broad stone platform dominated the center of the square and on it stood a guillotine.

The thick dark blade hung from an onyx cord, glinting in the light of the lamps that ringed the courtyard with a menacing gleam. Two men in polished black platemail stood on the platform, and another pair stood at every exit. They all held greatswords in their hands, the tips resting gently on the ground between their feet. The guards he was with hesitated. They stopped at the entrance to the courtyard, unable or unwilling to pass the two towering men standing there.

"Elbaf, son of Elbain," the leader said with a faint quake in his voice. "You will proceed to your sentencing."

With no further ado, the guards shoved him into the courtyard and then promptly left, making haste back down the hallway.

Elbaf stumbled a few feet into the courtyard, but kept his footing.

At first, no one in the clearing moved.

The world felt unnaturally still. Not a single sound pierced the thick veil that hung over the courtyard like the heavy shadow of a passing stormcloud.

At last, several long heartbeats later, the warriors beside him stepped in closer - not touching him, but nonetheless threatening his noncompliance.

Elbaf weighed his options.

It took only a moment for him to realize that he had none. None save to die with dignity. He straightened his back and took steady, measured steps towards the platform. As he drew closer, he could see a set of stairs built into the side of it. His heart thudded in his chest as he climbed the stairs, but he would not give them the satisfaction of seeing his fear. When he got to the top, he could see an inlaid silver pattern, a sort of path that led to the center of the platform, just in front of the guillotine itself.

His feet carried him - a semi-willing victim - along the path until he stood at the end of it. He felt heavy, like his legs were made of lead, and he was entranced, staring at the razor edge of the blade hanging above him.

"Elbaf, son of Elbain. A violent criminal. A *murderer*."

The voice belonged to a woman.

It rang out strong and clear from across the courtyard, drawing Elbaf's gaze with it. At some point while he was walking she must have entered, though he hadn't noticed. She was wearing a form-fitting ebony breastplate, a skirt of black chainmail, and a flowing, fur-lined onyx cloak. Her arms and legs were adorned with cleric's cloth, not much different than that which Talia had worn except that it was of finer quality.

The woman's eyes and hair were midnight black, her lips a vibrant crimson, and her skin as fair as fresh-fallen snow. For all of her cold, piercing beauty, it was her voice that enchanted him. It was thick with passion, but held a core of barbed iron.

He wanted to speak - to deny her words - but he felt himself unable to even open his mouth to try.

She approached the stand, her opalescent armor making no sound as she mounted the stairs and strode over to him, one hand on a sheathed longsword at her side. As she drew closer, an emblem embedded in her armor caught his eye. It was a hand, palm outward, carved in incredible detail over her left breast above her heart. The hand, about four inches tall, captured his gaze and held it trapped. It *called* to him in his very soul, filling his heart with fire and his veins with ice.

No citizen of the Empire was ignorant of this symbol, that of the Black Hands of the Emperor. They were the living instruments of his will. Unquestionable, unassailable and, to the common folk, utterly foreign. They were rumored to harbor eldritch power, and their word was absolute law.

"You have committed grievous crimes against the Empire," the woman began softly, bringing his attention back to her face. "Blackened her very heart with violence and disorder. You have corrupted a priestess of the order, murdered citizens and guardsmen alike, and besmirched the reputations of the Sisterhood and of the Imperial Academy. For these crimes, and by the Hand of the Emperor, you are sentenced to die."

At her words, the two men on the platform, who had been standing still as statues until now, marched over and gripped Elbaf's arms. They helped him to his knees, not so roughly as the guardsmen before, and placed his head upon the cradle of the guillotine.

His heartbeat was roaring in his ears, but still he couldn't move. Partly from stubborn pride and partly because the weight of the woman's gaze held him as surely as any chain could have. Still, he managed not to break eye contact. Though it took a monumental force of will, he stared her down as he prepared to die.

As he continued to hold her gaze, she walked closer to his head and knelt next to him. She cocked her head to the side, her eyes catching the light such that it looked like fires blazed in her pupils.

"Are you ready?"

He chose to answer, suddenly finding his voice once again.

"Get it over with, then. I've no wish to linger."

He turned his gaze forward, staring off into space and bracing himself. He saw her crack a wide, genuine smile at his words as she stood and walked to where the rope waited, ready to be cut. She was still within his field of vision and so he saw as she slowly and smoothly drew forth her sword - an enamel-handled masterpiece of black steel. She held it in front of herself and bowed her head. He could see her whispering to the blade, her eyes screwed shut in concentration.

Then, in one sweeping motion, she sliced the rope.

The jet-black blade was whisper-quiet as it descended, slowly at first then with startling speed. Elbaf took one last mighty breath and locked eyes once again with the woman.

The guillotine hurtled downward, but instead of the impact of the blade Elbaf felt a sudden, penetrating chill. His neck was banded with ice and he felt a strong, cold wave wash across his throat as the blade passed through his body harmlessly, burying itself in the wood below his neck.

He was startled to silence, his eyes wide in disbelief and his mind dumbfounded. The icy cold faded, and was replaced by a ring of fire around his neck that brought tears to his eyes and made him cry out in pain.

Just as quickly, it too was gone.

"Elbaf, son of Elbain," the woman announced in a clear, even tone. "Your sentence has been delayed by the will of the Emperor. You are not forgiven. Death is too small a price to pay for your crimes. By his will, you will serve the Empire until you perish or dishonor yourself or the Emperor. Should you be found derelict in your duties, your sentence will be carried out immediately. You have been granted a path not to redemption, but to an honorable death."

Chapter Three

Day 36.

"Keep. Moving!"

The instructor wasn't screaming at him - not this time at least - but Elbaf looked back nonetheless.

From his position at the head of the pack, he could see Talia on her hands and knees retching. She was surrounded by instructors, all screaming at the tops of their lungs in her ear while the rest of their class ran on.

The girl was red-faced, with tears streaming down her cheeks, and it looked as though she might pass out at any moment.

With a snarl, he slowed and broke from the formation, Arcus hot on his heels, and together they sprinted back to Talia's position.

"Get back with the group, you two."

"With respect, sir," Arcus frowned, "no."

The instructors in the course were in good shape and more than capable of violence. Elbaf had received a great deal of reminders of that in the few weeks they'd been there already. They were not, however, the merciless monsters they portrayed. At least, Elbaf suspected as much. They seemed intent to prove him wrong, however, but even so he muscled his way between them and helped Talia to her feet.

"This doesn't concern you, cadets."

"Sir," Arcus answered. "Anything that concerns our classmate concerns us, sir."

Elbaf was grateful for Arcus' silver tongue - his own reply would have been less respectful.

"You three will be missing dinner chow tonight," the lead instructor looked them up and down derisively. "Report to the Master Sergeant at the company area upon your return."

"Acknowledged, sir," Arcus snapped a crisp salute as Elbaf ignored their cadre.

The instructors jogged off, chuckling darkly at the group as they left them behind.

"Come on, Talia, get up."

She looked up at Elbaf, then wiped her mouth on the shoulder of her slate-gray training uniform before reaching out a hand.

Elbaf yanked her to her feet, slapped her on the back, and then gave her a reassuring smile.

"Move it."

Talia rolled her eyes, still breathing hard.

"I don't know if I can go on like this."

"You can," Arcus encouraged her. "And I'd rather not find out what happens if we are much later than we're already bound to be."

Talia nodded in agreement and set off at a jog with the two men flanking her a few paces behind.

The trio finished out the last three miles of their run, pushing Talia as hard as they dared.

By the time they made it back to their company building, a drab three-story stone building that had come to represent both pain and sanctuary to them over the past month, it was well past chow, anyway.

"Time to pay the tab," Arcus sighed. He rolled his neck and shoulders, easing the tension there.

Each of them had taken to the course in different ways. Their strengths were honed, and their weaknesses beaten out of them by force. Where one fell short, the others often excelled, and so far they had been successful at helping each other through.

Arcus, for instance, was barely winded from the punishing run. Elbaf also held up well to the physical training, but neither had taken to their other coursework as easily as Talia.

They walked the last fifty paces, crossing the bare dirt of the sparring field to climb the three steps into their building.

Upstairs, in the living quarters, they could hear the tired laughter of their comrades and classmates. But that warmth would have to wait.

They made their way instead to the long narrow hallway where the living quarters and administrative offices of their instructors were, a place normally forbidden to cadets.

"Cadets D'Ari, Elbainsen, and Lorraine reporting as instructed," Arcus called out.

His clear voice echoed down the stone corridor before fading into silence. A moment passed before they were answered.

"Proceed, cadets."

The voice was softer than they expected, and they exchanged confused looks as they made their way ahead. They passed the empty offices of most of their instructors, ending up at the last door. It was cracked, and firelight poured from it and out onto the cold stone floor. A worn but polished brass nameplate was centered on the heavy wooden door, and above that a door knocker.

Master Sergeant Roland E. Parrek.

The Master Sergeant was rarely heard from directly, though he was in charge of their formations in the mornings. His authority was absolute, and he was rightly feared by the cadets and even - so it seemed, at least - the instructors.

Arcus looked to Elbaf, who shrugged and knocked firmly on the door.

"Enter."

They filed in, Talia ensuring the door closed behind them, and stood in a row at attention. Their eyes were fixed forward, but Elbaf took in the details of the room as best he could. The office held a large wooden desk, an iron-grate fireplace where a small fire blazed, and a variety of worn, utilitarian cabinets, chairs, and accents. A short flag hung from a pole at the back corner of the room. It was brilliant blue and gold, but Elbaf couldn't make out the crest on it, only that it hosted a variety of campaign streamers and decorations as well.

The man behind the desk was by far the most eye-capturing feature of the room.

Master Sergeant Parrek was not an overly large man - Elbaf had him beat by more than a head - but at just under six foot and about two-hundred pounds, he was far from scrawny. His deep brown skin showed the scars of many battles and close calls - including a long horizontal scar across his throat. He wore his hair trimmed close to his head, and the flecks of gray among the tight black curls were the only sign of his age.

At present, he was scribbling neat, compact lines of notes on a piece of parchment, one of many that were precisely and purposefully arranged on his desk. Every quill, every stack of letters and official documents, they all had a place.

They stood silently as he finished his note, then pushed back in his high-backed leather chair and examined them through a set of silver-framed glasses.

His uniform, a black kidskin version of their own training grays, was adorned by only two medals. One, his Black Hand Insignia, and the other a golden horseshoe with crossed spears behind it and a large golden sun on the inside. Elbaf wasn't sure what it meant.

"So."

They waited, silent.

"Why did you go back for Cadet Lorraine?"

Arcus looked over at Elbaf and they met eyes.

"Ah, sir, we . . . *I* went back because she's my friend. She needed help and I provided it as best I could."

"Was she in danger?"

"No, sir, but--"

He held a hand for silence.

"You went back because she is your friend?"

"Yes, sir," Elbaf answered for both of them.

He mulled over the half-orc's words.

"We couldn't leave her behind, sir. It . . . it wouldn't have been right."

He quirked up an eyebrow and leaned forward.

"Would you have done the same for any of your classmates, or just Talia?"

"Any of them," Arcus replied without hesitation. "We're a team."

"And you agree, Cadet Elbainsen?"

"Yes, sir."

The corner of the man's mouth turned up ever so slightly.

"Very well."

He pulled open a small drawer on the left side of his desk and selected a pair of small objects before shutting it again and standing. He walked around the desk, speaking as he approached the three of them.

"Cadet D'Ari, you will assume the responsibilities of platoon leader. You will take responsibility for their actions, and their performance will be a reflection of your own. You will own their failures and share in their victories. Above all else, you will accomplish the mission."

He fixed a brass badge, a smaller version of the rose insignia worn by junior lieutenants, to Arcus' lapel.

"Each morning, one hour before formation, you will report to me for your daily assignments and guidance. You are then to provide guidance and direction for your men. Do you understand your duties as explained to you?"

"I do, sir!"

He turned to Elbaf.

"Cadet Elbainsen, you will assume the responsibilities of Platoon Sergeant. You are to care for your men, enforce discipline, and provide for their needs. Your responsibility is to execute the direction of your platoon leader, and by extension myself and your instructors. You will guide and counsel your men and craft them into a more perfect and cohesive unit. Above all else, you will care for your men. Do you understand?"

He placed a similar insignia on Elbaf's lapel, this one reflecting the upturned silver chevrons of a Master Sergeant. Elbaf hoped his surprise and confusion weren't as clear on his face as he suspected.

"Yes, sir. I understand."

"Excellent."

He turned at last to Talia.

"Cadet Lorraine."

"Sir!"

"Are you injured?"

"N-no, sir."

"You are to consume not less than three canteens of water tonight and," he looked her over, taking note of her sunken cheeks and loose uniform, "you've lost weight?"

"Sir, a-about twelve pounds since we arrived, sir."

Elbaf looked at her in alarm. How had he not noticed how thin she'd gotten?

"You're on double rations, then, effective tomorrow. Cadet Elbainsen, I will be checking in with you regarding her progress. You are all three dismissed."

They snapped a salute in unison, then quickly and quietly filed out of his office. No one spoke as they hurried from the hall and made their way upstairs to their straw bunks. They could scarcely believe what had happened.

Day 90.

"You will *fight* as a unit, or you will *die* as a unit!"

Elbaf's arms ached, his muscles felt like minced meat, and his brain had turned to mush hours ago.

"Again!"

Captain Odum strode up and down the field, his gleaming armor almost too bright to look at. He spoke with surety and projected his voice so as to fill the large practice field without shouting.

"The score stands at three to two in favor of the Favored Few."

The captain looked young, but spoke with a maturity and confidence that belied his true age. Though for all the world he looked a lad of twenty, he'd spent that and more in the service already. He was a veteran of a dozen border conflicts, though he wore his scars beneath his youthful face.

Elbaf took from his lack of insignia that he was not a Hand, but over the past few weeks he'd learned the man was an unparallelled fighter.

"First to five gets dessert and the morning off."

Both sides of the field mustered a rousing cheer as the stakes shot high.

"Swordsmen, *up*! Spears, at the ready! Archers, *hold*!"

This time it was Arcus who called out, drowning out his counterpart's instructions from across the battlefield.

Elbaf could see he was tired, too - dark circles ringed his eyes and sweat poured from his friend's brow.

Dutifully, Elbaf rose from where he'd been sitting and drinking water.

He couldn't afford to look weak. Not here. Their men counted on them and he would not let them down. He took his place beside Arcus once more while the men of their company formed around them.

Across the field their enemy mirrored their actions - Charlie company, the Ragged Foxes.

"The morning off," Arcus sighed, rolling his shoulder. "Can you imagine it, Elbaf?"

"I can't," Elbaf shook his head. "And I won't - not until it's real, brother."

"Too true," Arcus managed a wry smile.

Their men had formed a sloppy line. One row of swordsmen, a second of spears, and a dozen archers in the back. Elbaf frowned at the wobbly formation, the drooping spear tips, and the half-raised shields.

"Come on, you dogs," he roared. "Hold those blades like you've some idea what to do with them!"

The men snapped-to, his powerful bass shaking them from their exhausted stupor. With a deep breath he roared again, puffing his chest and muscling his way up to the front of the formation. He held his blade aloft, a fire-hardened wooden replica of the imperial longswords they'd all been issued.

"I've no stomach for losing, men."

A rumbling of agreement rose.

"So, I'll give you the option," he paused for effect, though the men knew his ritual well. "Any man or woman here can challenge me for the right to first blood, and if I lose I'll follow them into battle. Otherwise, the honor is mine and you lot can clean up. Any takers?"

The group chuckled. Not since Norrick had lost teeth during his challenge five weeks ago had anyone dared. But Elbaf could see the gleam in their eyes, the grit in their teeth, and the strength in their backs returning as he boasted. It was no idle threat. Elbaf had been the first to meet the enemy in every fight they'd had so far, and with four broken bones in the past three months, he'd paid for it dearly.

The company was assigned a medical team, a mixture of clerical healers and more traditional, non-magical folks, but the pain was still a strong motivator to do better in each successive fight.

"Let's hope they can manage a good fight before we grind them to a pulp," Elbaf called out, reciting the ages-old poem from which they drew their names. "I've no stomach for easy victories, and nor, my friends, should you."

More and more voices joined him as the group spoke aloud the words that had long-since been drilled into their memories.

"I would fight beside no others, for no others stand as true," he continued. "There's blood to be drawn--"

"*By us, the Favored Few,*" the entire company yelled together, their battlecry echoing over the field.

Captain Odum, now at the edge of the playing field, raised his hand high. Arcus waved in return, as did the student-commander of the company across from them. Seeing both sides were prepared, Odum dropped his hand swiftly to his side.

Elbaf roared again, this time a guttural, animal cry of rage and strength. He raised his blade again and turned to face the enemy, shield and sword in hand.

"Stand ready," Arcus called from behind the archers, unslinging his longbow and pulling a blunt, lead-tipped arrow from his quiver.

The Foxes charged, the distance rapidly closing between their lines. At sixty feet, Arcus loosed his arrow, triggering a volley of heavy, leaden hate that arched up over the shielded fronts of the men, and rained down onto them with staggering blows.

Forty feet melted into ten, then five, then a clap like thunder rolled out across the yard as weapons and shields clashed together. The Foxes broke upon them like a wave crashing against a rocky shore. They held, but even so there was bloodshed on both sides. The weapons were blunted to prevent a killing blow, but bones broke and shouts and cries of pain competed with fervent orders, all promising that the healers would be working late into the night to make the men ready for the next day.

Captain Odum watched closely - a leatherbound notebook in one hand and a charcoal pencil in the other - silently taking notes from the sidelines as the battle raged a few dozen feet away.

Day 157

"Take your seats, please," Matron Artemia's voice carried easily in the stone amphitheater - more easily than her frail appearance would suggest - and her words were heeded instantly.

The entire company sat as one, each cadet sitting straight-backed and attentive as their instructors prowled the outside of the aisles. The black-clad forms of their instructors were as familiar to them now as their own shadows, and as omnipresent. They maintained a distance now, allowing the student leadership to learn - but they were never far away. It was no longer fear that kept the cadets rooted in place, kept their eyes trained carefully and thoughtfully on their teachers. No, that had long ago been replaced by understanding, respect, and, above all else, discipline.

"Thank you." She smiled at the assembled students. "Tell me, what is your purpose?"

Her question was carried on the soft, steel-hearted melody of her voice and it floated out amongst her charges unanswered for several minutes before a cadet stood at last.

"Cadet De'Clinton, go ahead."

Even after weeks of tutelage, Elbaf still found himself impressed by the power of the old woman's mind and memory.

"Ma'am, the Hands of the Emperor serve as warriors, dedicated to the defense of the realm and unwavering in their commitment to His will."

"A good answer." She indicated he should retake his seat and smiled softly. "But an incomplete one."

Talia stood.

As a squad leader, she was at the outside of her row, but the Matron noticed her at once.

"Sister Talia."

Matron was the only one of their cadre that ever referred to them by anything other than cadet, and she did this only for a rare few of them.

"Matron, ma'am, they serve not only as warriors, but also as the voice of law and justice. They are the sword arm of the Sisterhood. They enforce the law, serving as judge, jury, and, if need be, executioner in the pursuit of the Emperor's divine justice. They are impartial arbiters, trusted and revered throughout all the lands of the Empire. Their commitment to fairness is unequaled, they cannot be bought nor can they be swayed from absolute truth."

"Excellent answer, as always, Sister."

Talia glowed at her praise, and Elbaf saw the hint of a smile as she sat back down.

"Today will mark the beginning of your education in the legal framework of the Empire."

Long used to note-taking, the students began to quietly rummage for charcoal and paper in their belt pouches.

"No."

Everyone froze, the sudden coldness in the woman's voice taking them by surprise.

"In this course you will take no notes," Matron Artemia announced. "You will memorize the laws of our land by heart. You will learn them word for word from the first line of the first book to the last of the last."

She looked out over the crowd of students, meeting each gaze in turn with a look of deadly calm.

"In this you cannot fail. In this you *must not fail*. You will be the blood that carries justice to the furthest corners of our lands, places you cannot possibly hope to bring a stack of law books and references with you. Do you understand?"

The class nodded and Elbaf felt sweat pooling at his back. He was no simpleton, but he'd never considered memorizing such a monumental amount of information.

Was it even possible?

The warrior forced himself to breathe evenly, pushing his self-doubt to the back of his mind and focusing instead on the task at hand.

"There are eleven volumes of Imperial Law. Your company library has enough copies for you to share them during your allotted study time, and you will be responsible for studying them when you are not in class."

A solemn, sobered hush fell over the class.

"Make no mistake, the far reaches of our peaceful land are not as ordered as our blessed Capitol. There are lawless lands where you and you alone will be the light of the Emperor."

She stood, suddenly much more menacing, and slowly scanned the crowd. She seemed to be reaching deep into each cadet's heart and gripping it with her gaze.

"You will repeat after me."

Silence.

Elbaf noted that the matron had no notes or books in hand for reference, either.

"Imperial Law, volume one, chapter one."

She paused, and the entire company echoed her words back in clear, even voices.

"These shall be the laws of the Sunset Imperium, as laid down by my hand. By my grace they shall govern the peoples of our lands and ensure harmony and justice for all of the citizens of the Empire who dwell therein. They shall exact righteous vengeance upon those who would break them . . ."

Day 235.

"Where's my damned curist?"

Elbaf was shouting, the fear of an avalanche or rockslide now a moot point, his only concern was the safety of his men. Through the swirling snow he could make out the struggling shapes of the others who'd been caught when a section of the narrow mountain path had broken away. Fifty feet up the mountain they could see the vague blurs of the rest of their company still on the path above.

"Hold on, Reichart. Keep pressure here."

The man did as he was told, wincing a little as he wrapped his hands around the broken pine bough buried in his guts, but keeping his composure. Elbaf could see that most of the tree, which had broken the man's fall, was buried under the same rockslide that had claimed a dozen riders and their mounts. He glanced at Reichart's legs, or what was left of them. A mangled mess of fabric, leather, flesh and pulverized bones lay crushed beneath jagged chunks of ice and rock.

"Arcus, how far out are we?" Elbaf called out through the swirling snow. "We passed the last marker at least a candlemark ago."

Arcus picked his way nimbly amongst the fallen stones, dancing from one to the next with an uncanny grace that never ceased to amaze Elbaf.

"We've another two leagues yet."

Elbaf swore.

"I've sent outriders to the front, but they'll have a hell of a time in this."

Arcus gestured around them and Elbaf looked to the skies. They'd been steadily darkening since midmorning and they looked ready to unleash hell at any moment. They *needed* to move, but Reichart wasn't going anywhere in his current condition.

"Is Talia above?" Elbaf wiped blood out of his eyes with the back of his hand. "I didn't see much after the fall."

"She's on her way."

Elbaf nodded his understanding, and Arcus took off to search for other survivors.

The groans and shouts of the injured competed with the whistling winds of the pre-storm air. Already more ropes were being cast down from the path, and a second wave of rescuers were on their way to tend the wounded.

And recover the dead.

Elbaf turned his attention again to Reichart. The young man was barely nineteen. His once olive skin was paler than it ought to be, all save his windburned cheeks and nose. He was far from his home in the Southlands, somewhere north of Jala on the border in a land of endless summers and warmth.

"Am I gonna be ok?" Reichart coughed and flecks of blood dotted his lips.

Elbaf could smell fear on him - the deep and visceral fear of a dying man - so he lied.

"You'll be fine," he smiled shakily. "Sister Talia is on her way."

By the time she arrived with a pair of the company's medics in tow, Talia's hands and forearms were already soaked with the blood of previous patients.

She wasted no time with pleasantries, kneeling beside Elbaf and reaching for the wounded man.

"Damn it, we don't have the supplies for this," she muttered to herself just barely loud enough for Elbaf to hear. "I *told* curist Elaria we needed surgical gear."

Reichart was still conscious, but he was white as a sheet now. His eyes brightened at her arrival, but he did not have the strength to speak.

"Reichart, right?"

He nodded almost imperceptibly.

"You're going to be ok, Reichart. I'm here now. I need to move your hands, ok? No, no, don't move anything else. Just blink once if you understand, ok?"

He blinked slowly.

"Ok, this is going to hurt," she admitted.

She pried his hands away from his stomach, dried and frozen blood crackling in the air. He winced, and tears streamed from his eyes, but he didn't cry out.

Elbaf could read Talia, but he didn't think Reichart noticed the way her eyes looked. Talia assessed his wound swiftly and thoroughly, but he could tell that she had already come to her conclusion.

"Ok, Reichart," she flashed him a warm, heartfelt smile. "It's ok. I'm gonna help you sleep now, alright?"

Talia reached a hand up to Reichart's forehead and began to pray quietly. Within seconds the young man was fast asleep, his breathing softer and the lines on his face eased.

"He's dying, then?"

Talia didn't answer. She only nodded curtly, then stood and headed off to her next patient.

Elbaf sat back down, his hand resting on Reichart's shoulder.

They were fewer now by half already, the course having taken its deadly toll. Less than fifty cadets remained of their entire class, and they'd all been folded into the ranks of the Favored Few several months ago.

Elbaf would not abandon his brother, so he sat there - heedless of his own cuts and bruises, heedless of the biting cold - until, at long last, with a soft wheeze Reichart's chest stopped rising.

Graduation.

"Company, present . . . arms!"

The Favored Few snapped one unified salute with flawless precision as the soft morning light glinted on the mirrored blackness of their polished steel armor. Thirty-five arms held perfectly still in the absolute silence of the drill yard. Elbaf executed a crisp turn to face Arcus, whose purple helmet crest distinguished itself from the white crests of the rest of the student company. He performed a slow, exaggerated salute, which Arcus returned before conducting his own turn. They stood at the front of their formation alongside their bannerman, Cadet Tobrin, who stood silently holding the waving black and gold flag of their company.

Across the yard was a short wooden platform, and Elbaf couldn't help but be reminded of the guillotine he'd stood at before, almost a year ago.

It felt like a lifetime.

A clump of observers sat in a small section of risers, just off to the side of the platform. Among them were the scarlet robes of imperial wizards, the opalescent black armor and midnight capes of other members of the Hands, and a handful of clerics and priestesses of the Sisterhood. Their instructors were also present, not sitting in the stands but in one of three smaller formations beside their own.

Along with their instructors, there were two more small arrangements, one of freshly inducted wizards, and one of newly appointed clerics. Elbaf dared not turn his head, but tried desperately to see if Talia and Darko were among them. He hadn't seen Darko since they'd started training, and Talia had been taken from them - along with anyone else with the divine gifts - some three moons past.

A woman walked in from behind the stands and made her way to the stage, silencing Elbaf's internal monologue and capturing his focus. She wore the now familiar combination of black armor and cleric's robes that marked her as a member of both the Black Hand and the Sisterhood. It was the same uniform that Elbaf had seen the day he was dragged from his life and inducted into this mess. This, however, was a very different woman than the one he had spoken with at the guillotine - of that he was sure. Still, she had the same steel in her gray eyes. Her warm brown skin and ebony hair perfectly complemented her soft, round face and gentle features.

"Order . . . arms!"

The command rang clear as a bell in the cold morning air, and the company returned their arms to their sides in one smooth motion.

"I am Mater Superia Colonel Caramina Westmoore, the commandant of this, the finest military training school the world has ever known. I am here today on the auspicious occasion of your graduation into the ranks of the Hands of the Emperor. When you leave this field today it will be as newly commissioned lieutenants, and you will receive the insignia of the Hand, marking you as initiates of our hallowed order."

The woman spoke with passion and clarity, and Elbaf could feel the fire in her heart.

"Eleven months ago you entered this academy as the walking dead, the condemned, the wretched dregs of our society. By the divine grace of the Emperor, you are reborn into glorious servitude of the highest purpose."

Elbaf kept his emotions carefully in check.

He felt a sort of perverse gratitude, it was true. In part because he was in the finest shape of his life. He'd built friendships that were stronger than the hardest steel. He'd learned, grown, and pushed himself beyond every limit he thought he had. But he'd never accepted the narrative that he had, by circumstance or choice, ever been the *wretched dregs*. His pride would not allow it. He had done right by himself and his people in the Brine, and it was that protective streak that had carried many of the men and women around him through their training.

A few feet away he heard the tiniest scoff from Arcus, disguised as a cough. At least he wasn't alone in his dismissal of the Colonel's speech.

Arcus stood perfectly still, his eyes dutifully forward, as the Colonel spoke - but his mind was elsewhere. The heavy metal armor he wore was stifling, and he felt cut off from the majesty of nature while he was in it. He could feel his connection to the living world around him dulled and he was internally counting the seconds until he could be rid of it.

Something in the Colonel's tone shook him from his reverie and he focused on her words once again.

" . . . and you will be there. *You* will be the hammer of the Emperor himself, bringing the force and power of our sacred way of life to even the most stubborn provinces."

She paused for effect as Arcus held back a frown.

"Therefore, I hereby grant you the commission of an imperial officer. Welcome, lieutenants, to the most elite fighting force the world over. Welcome to the Hands of the Emperor."

The small crowd in the bleachers broke out into mild, scattered applause.

"Fall out!"

Arcus saluted firmly before turning around and addressing his men.

"Favored Few, it has been a distinct honor and a privilege to serve as your student commander. In the tradition of my people, I would say just a few words. May the skies above you be clear and, should they rain, let them cool you from the heat of your labors. Let the paths before you stretch straight and true and carry you ever back to your loved ones. Should they turn difficult, let them fill you with accomplishment as you conquer them. Let the land around you share its bounty and, should it prove scarce, let it hone you into a finer hunter. But most of all, let not the distance of this world diminish the friendships forged here. You are dismissed."

A hearty cheer rose up as the men and women of the Favored Few broke ranks. Their celebration was short lived, as a loud, piercing whistle rang out from the cadre.

Master Sergeant Parrek waved his hand in a tight circle, indicating that they should reform around him.

"Come here, sirs. You're not done quite yet."

For once, smiles dotted the faces of the cadets as they formed a tight horseshoe formation around the man. He looked a little older to Arcus, who wondered how he hadn't noticed how tired the man appeared, nor how kind his eyes were.

"You know your duties. You are prepared to use the blades at your sides and the space between your ears," he began, tapping his temple to a chuckle from his audience. "With a bit of favor, you'll be doing the latter more often."

Arcus smiled, finding himself next to Elbaf. He gave him a nudge and got one in return.

"Hear that, Elbaf? You can't simply stab every problem to death."

The Master Sergeant sobered a bit, and his eyes took on a distant, melancholy quality.

"In all seriousness, you've been thrust into a dangerous job. This . . . *calling* will more than likely claim your lives. I am one of the few who remains from my own class, less than a dozen when last I checked, and it may surprise you to know that only a scant twenty years separates us."

The smiles faded and the laughter died.

"Look after each other. No one else will," he paused, and they saw his face harden once again. "Trust yourselves, trust your judgment, trust your training."

The man paused again, this time overcome for a moment by emotion - a fact which every single cadet promptly overlooked - before continuing.

"You will report back to your barracks, where you will find your individual orders and assignments on your bunks. Clear out your footlockers and move out, Favored Few, and never forget where you came from."

With that, he snapped to attention and rendered a slow, textbook perfect salute to the assembled soldiers, who returned it as one.

They headed for the barracks, which they could just see poking above the trees behind the parade field, breaking into small clumps and joking together as they went.

"Elbaf, Arcus!"

Arcus barely had time to turn before he was engulfed in a hug.

Talia slammed into him, wrapped her arms around his neck and planted a kiss unceremoniously on his cheek before turning and giving Elbaf the same treatment. She looked different, a little more tired. She had a thick white streak in her hair that extended from her left temple to the tight, no-nonsense bun she had her hair in. Her armor matched that of the Colonel, her cleric's vestments below shining ebony scalemail.

"Talia, we haven't seen you what, three months? How've you been?"

Her smile faltered, but swiftly returned.

"I've been . . . good," she replied shortly as she punched him playfully in the shoulder. "I missed you both terribly. I felt awful that I left you, but our training was very . . . comprehensive."

Arcus thought about pressing, but something told him not to.

"But that can wait. What about you? I'm much more interested in the rest of your training, there's so . . . few of us left."

Elbaf and Arcus exchanged dark looks, and it was their turn to shift topics.

"We're off to find out our assignments, *ma'am*," the half-orc nodded towards the barracks.

Arcus glanced at Elbaf, surprised by his choice of words, then returned his gaze to Talia. Sure enough, she wore three roses to his one.

"You're a *captain*," he gasped in surprise. "How the hell does that work?"

Talia's laugh was the same innocent joy that Arcus remembered, and her mirth brought a smile to his face.

"Well, *Lieutenant*, if you must know it is because I successfully completed the Rites and I'm now, officially, *Soror Mediatus* Talia Lorraine!"

"Congratulations, Talia! You must be so proud." Arcus clapped her on the back with a smile. "Care to join us as we discover our fates?"

Talia opened her eyes wide and stiffened.

"I . . . I see a vision!"

Arcus let go of her, stepping back.

"Talia? Talia are you alright?"

She began to shake, her eyes darting back and forth.

"You two will be assigned to the . . . Brazen Hawks! Alongside the mage Darko Branislav and the most *talented* young cleric you shall ever hope to meet . . ."

She trailed off into a laugh, pointing a finger at the look of concern on Arcus' face.

Elbaf swiftly joined her laughter, but Arcus was too nonplussed to share in their humor.

"That wasn't funny, Talia."

"Oh, I disagree. That was hilarious," Elbaf was laughing so hard he could barely speak.

It had been a long time since they'd laughed that hard together.

"I'll tell you what isn't a joke," Talia wiped a tear of laughter from her eye. "We'll be together, the four of us. I requested Madrie Van Cleigh's unit, and she allowed me to choose my team."

"*Your* team?"

"Well, *our* team, I suppose." She rolled her eyes at Arcus. "Now come on. She's an inspiration, but she's far from patient."

A half-hour later, they were standing at attention in their new commander's office, separated from the woman by a heavy desk laden with scattered maps, notes, and tally sheets.

"I am Mater Mediatus, Major Madrie Van Cleigh. I've no time for idle talk, and you'll find I run a tight ship."

The woman in front of them had the look they'd grown to expect when it came to the sisters of the order, but none of the coldness. She was a passion-filled firebrand at five-foot-six, and she had the build of a farm girl with plenty of upper body strength and a healthy glow.

"The Brazen Hawks is my company, and mine alone. Each of you four has a role to play in it, and I expect you to fulfill that role."

Her gaze fell to each of them, but it lingered longest on Talia.

"Lieutenant Elbainsen, you'll take first platoon. Lieutenant D'Ari will have second. Sister Talia, you will be studying under my executive officer, Soror Superia Captain Annabelle Montagne."

They each nodded in turn.

"And me, ma'am?"

Darko was still something of an enigma to his friends. He had returned from his studies more sober, but also more sure-footed. He still limped, but his gait was undeniably stronger. As was the menacing aura he projected. It was easy for the three of them to fall back into their friendship, but he had remained somewhat to the outside, though not for want of the others trying.

"I've not been assigned a wizard before," Madrid frowned. "Though I have seen some of what your kind can do. You'll advise me on matters of mystical nature, you'll keep your infernal powers to yourself unless I direct you to use them, and you'll not corrupt my men, understood?"

"Ma'am, I am hardly a threat to you or your men. I am an asset that can--"

"A simple 'yes, ma'am' will do."

He paused, and an uncomfortable silence filled the confines of Madrie's quarters.

"*Yes, ma'am,*" he finally responded.

He did his best not to allow his frustration to show in his voice, but didn't succeed very well. If Madrid noticed, she ignored it.

"Excellent. Pack your things. We ride for Galmead the morning after next. Until then, your time is your own."

Chapter Four

Elbaf looked at the old, worn door of the Tilted Table.

He'd not yet dared to enter it, but his appearance in the Brine had already caused quite a stir. It had been years since one of the Hand had entered the dingy streets and alleys of the neighborhood, and everywhere he walked he could feel the stares and hear the whispers of the passerby.

He kept his visor down, hiding his identity from the people he once considered his own.

He was still standing there when the door swung open and he was greeted by the sight of a very irritated Dorm.

"Beggin' yer' pardon," Dorm spoke with respect, but no small amount of frustration. He held his arms crossed around his chest and wore a surly scowl. "But yer' scarin' all my customers away."

Elbaf didn't know what to say, so he simply nodded curtly and stepped towards the door. The surprised barkeep stepped aside and let him pass into the building. Elbaf headed at first for his normal spot, but stopped himself midway through the common room.

"Somethin' wrong with the seatin?" Dorm asked stonily.

He shook his head silently and resumed his walk, pulling up his old, familiar chair and sitting down gingerly. It was sturdy, but he was wary of putting an extra fifty-five pounds of metal against the worn wood.

His fears proved unfounded.

Elbaf looked around the bar, noting that none of the handful of patrons were eating or drinking. Instead, all of them were staring openly at him.

Moments after he took his seat, Theresa cautiously approached.

"A drink for you, m'lord? We've stew and bread, as well."

Seeing the fear in Theresa's young eyes pushed Ebaf to speak at last.

"Kranell's smoked."

The girl did a double take. Scarcely anyone knew of their small collection of smoked beers - and certainly no one who wasn't a local.

" . . . *Elbaf*," she whispered incredulously.

He looked at her for a moment, then reached his hands up to his chin strap. He undid the buckle and slowly removed his helmet.

"Aye, it's me, Theresa," he grinned sheepishly.

She stared, slack-jawed, then burst out into laughter and wrapped him in a bear hug.

"Elbaf! I can't believe it!"

He stood, lifting the girl off her feet as she clung to him.

"Alright, alright," he chided, chuckling. "You'll ruin what's left of my reputation."

She let go at last, taking in the sight of his armor as if for the first time.

"Oh, I doubt that, *m'lord*."

Elbaf thanked his orcish heritage - and the ruddiness it brought to his skin tone - that she couldn't see him flush with embarrassment.

"Elbaf," Dorm called out from the kitchen before poking his head out into the common room. "Elbaf! You old bastard, what the hell are you doing running around in that tin suit and scaring half the damn Brine into hiding?"

His roaring voice was accompanied by a wide, genuine smile and outspread arms.

"Drinks on the house. The Brawler returns!"

The folks eating and drinking all visibly relaxed, their eyes alight with wonder at this unprecedented development.

"To think," Dorm said as he approached, "one of our own, a Briner, becoming a *Black Hand*. In all my years I've never heard of such a thing."

"I can't stay," Elbaf returned the man's embrace. "Not for long."

Dorm's face fell.

"But--"

"I'm sorry, old friend. Were it up to me, I'd never have left at all," Elbaf admitted sadly. "I've come for the sword and to say goodbye."

The last of Dorm's smile faded, and he nodded solemnly. He turned and headed to the back of the bar, where he lifted a cellar door and descended. A moment later he'd returned, an oilcloth-wrapped object nearly five feet long in his hands. He held it out gingerly, moisture in the corners of his eyes.

"Been nearly ten years I've held this blade for you," the barkeep raised the weapon up and held it out for Elbaf. "If yer' takin' it now . . . well, I suppose we won't be seeing you again."

"That I wish I knew," Elbaf lifted the object gently from his friend's hands. "But I cannot see the future. I know only that my fate will demand bloodshed, and I would have my father's blade in the battles to come."

"Then Kullum be with you," Dorm nodded, putting a hand on Elbaf's shoulder. "May the strength of the warrior flow in your veins and lead you ever to victory."

Arcus sat quietly on a hill overlooking the city. From his position, cross-legged in the grass, he pondered just how much had transpired during the past year. The view had scarcely changed from when he and Kodja had first laid eyes upon the Capitol, but he was not at all the same man.

He stopped his thoughts before they could tumble into turmoil, consciously clearing his mind and detaching from himself, instead.

He focused outward, feeling the cool breath of the land as it swept the smell of far-off rain into his nostrils. He felt the warm brush of sunlight on his hair and on the branches and the leaves of the forests in the distance. The cool trickle of an underground spring hummed past the silent work of diligent insects.

Each sound and smell, each living thing was met, regarded fondly, and then let adrift back into the great sea of life around him. He floated in the midst of that energy, patiently waiting, hoping.

Then at last, he felt him. Kodja.

They couldn't speak to each other. Arcus' mastery of nature had not yet deepened to that point, but they could *feel* each other after a fashion. They could catch hints of each other's surroundings, share feelings of joy or fear or excitement. Arcus caught the smell of crushed pine needles and last night's dinner. A rabbit, unused to prowling wolves this close to the city.

Kodja noticed Arcus, too; their minds touching briefly from miles away. A warmth was shared as their bond, which had been strained by time and distance, proved itself as strong as ever.

Arcus opened his eyes, a wide smile on his face, and turned to the west. Though he could not yet see him, he could feel Kodja's excitement as he closed the distance between them.

Darko was breathing hard, but as he climbed the last few steps of the Academy's looming Northwest Tower, he was impressed with himself. Eleven flights of stairs would have taken him over an hour a year ago. Now, he'd done it in less than a quarter of that. His body was physically stronger than it had ever been. Moreover, the *peculiar* methods of instruction he had endured the past few months had greatly expanded his knowledge of the arcane as well.

He mulled over the past year as he headed for his dormitory. The door was still locked, still marked by the arcane seals he had placed there all those months ago when he left for a simple evening stroll.

A wry smile crossed his lips - what havoc time must have played in his absence.

With a wave, the seals flashed brilliant white, then faded like mist on summer morning as Darko reached for the iron handle of the door and pushed it gently inward.

The room was dark, but Darko fixed that with a flick of his wrist. His gesture sent an orb of soft yellow light orbiting around his head.

The small sphere provided plenty of illumination for him to make his way past quiet stacks of textbooks and discarded clothing over to his tightly shuttered windows. He breathed the dust of familiarity as he undid the latch and pushed open the stubborn hinges. Disuse and the elements had gotten to them, and they squeaked in resistance but eventually gave ground, allowing daylight to stream into the room.

The room was exactly as he'd left it. His desk was covered in what had been his most pressing research. An inkwell sat dried up and dust covered, a quill still sitting within it, and his bed remained in disarray from his unexpected departure. A plate of what had been dinner held the mummified remains of cheese and grapes.

Behold, the prodigal son's return!

The voice in his mind dripped with a haughty irritation.

"Don't be so dramatic, Reia."

You masquerade as a series of harmless woodland creatures for almost a year and try to maintain your cheer, Master.

"Quit fooling around. Get down here," he called out the open window.

Yes, Master.

A sparrow landed on the window sill and executed a funny little bow.

Darko rolled his eyes.

The sparrow shuddered, then began to twist and contort itself into impossible shapes, disappearing into a small but growing cloud of deep purple smoke. Electricity arced inside the cloud, casting flickering light around the room.

Darko wrinkled his nose, waving his hand to clear the smoke. He quirked an eyebrow and then, his impatience growing, muttered a soft incantation.

A strong gust of wind shot out of his palm, blowing the smoke cloud into wisps and sending them out the window. With the cloud gone, Reia was at last revealed.

"Gather your things, Reia."

Reia bristled, her seven-inch height doing nothing to diminish her irritation. She stretched her jet-black bat-like wings and stomped indignantly, her hoofed foot producing a tiny, frustrated thump.

"You know, Master. Where I'm from that would be considered *very* rude."

Darko stole a glance at his familiar. Her deep purple skin was, as ever, wreathed in a tiny coat of pink fire. Her arms were crossed over her chest, and the miniscule ring of horns around her brow crackled with electricity.

"Yes, yes, I suppose in the plane of eternal flames that would be quite off-putting," Darko mumbled as he packed clothing into a canvas duffle bag. "But we are not on the Q'Jralli homeplane. We are here, on Scera."

"We're a *noble race*, Master," she pouted. "You know, I didn't have to answer when you called."

"And yet you did."

She sighed.

"And yet I did."

She caught his eye and they both smiled. For all their nitpicking, they'd been together most of a century now. As with all imperial wizards, he'd been charged with binding a familiar spirit. The binding usually took the form of confining an unwilling spirit into an otherwise normal animal, but sometimes young acolytes would impart a fragment of their own magical power into their chosen vessel, rather than binding an innocent creature to their will.

Darko's experience had been, at least at first, quite different.

Even now he maintained that he had performed the ritual perfectly, but rather than a captive spirit he had been met instead by this hellion, Reia.

To say she was independent would have been an understatement.

Somehow, after a series of small fires and other mayhem, they had indeed come to terms. Rather than bind herself solely to him, they had bound themselves to each other. A unique relationship in the Imperial Academy as far as Darko knew.

"Now who is wasting time, Master?"

He glared at her, his cheeks red from being caught daydreaming.

"Perhaps in your dotage you've simply taken to staring off mindlessly," she put on a look of sarcastic concern. "Worry not, Master. I shall care for you in your twilight years."

Darko smiled despite himself.

With a heavy sigh, he shoved the last few items he needed into his duffel, then cast one more wistful look around the room.

"Ready?"

Reia sighed as well, a subconscious homage to the bond between them.

"Will we be back, Master?"

Darko snapped his fingers and his duffel bag shrank to the size of his palm. He tied it to his belt and wondered at Reia's question.

"I don't know, Reia," he admitted, turning back to the door just as she resumed the form of a bird and flitted up to perch on his shoulder. "But I suppose if we do we shall be very different."

"Captain Lorraine!"

"Yes, ma'am," Talia jogged the last few steps towards her commander's office.

She rounded the corner to find her superior officer hunched over her desk, a quill in one hand and the other holding down a detailed map of the region. She was jotting down notes in a small leather-bound book in eloquent, flowing script.

Another woman, one Talia didn't recognize, was standing at the Major's left and just behind her. She wore the black garb of a Soror Superia and had a captain's insignia.

The woman didn't acknowledge Talia's entrance.

Major Van Cleigh looked up to see Talia stiffly saluting her.

"As you were, Captain," she turned her attention back to her notes. "Are the men assembled?"

Talia dropped her salute when it became clear it wouldn't be returned.

She was still trying to sort out how to read her commander. On some things, she stood very soundly on protocol, and in other ways she was uncomfortably relaxed when compared to the training environment Talia had just left.

"Yes, ma'am. They are assembling outside now and making final preparations to depart."

"Excellent. I'd like you to meet my executive officer, Soror Superia Captain Annabelle Montagne."

The woman looked up at last, meeting Talia's gaze with an icy stare. Her pupils were a shade of green so dark they almost looked black, and her skin was as pale and flawless as freshly fallen snow.

"It's good to meet you, Sister," Talia said, approaching and holding a hand out. "I'm Talia Lorraine. I understand I'll be studying under you and I'm looking forward to the . . ." She trailed off as Annabelle pointedly ignored her offer of a handshake.

An awkward beat later she dropped her hand and stood, unsure of what to do. She was rescued by the brusque words of their commander.

"Excellent, you've met. Sister Captain Montagne, you are to take Sister Captain Talia under your tutelage. I want her at your side as frequently as possible, observing."

Annabelle nodded curtly, snapping a salute.

"Yes, ma'am, I'll ensure she's ready."

"See that she is." Madrie gestured towards a long, meandering dotted line on the map at her fingertips. "Our rotation will take us out of the interior of the Empire in just four short months, and I want her battle-ready by then." With that, the Major closed her notebook with a snap and walked out of the room.

"Ma'am, I--"

But Annabelle had already turned on her heel to follow the commander.

Talia gritted her teeth and rolled her head side-to-side, cracking her neck in frustration before following the pair.

By the time they made it outside, Talia had caught up and fallen into step just behind Annabelle.

Together, they walked out into the large grassy assembly area in front of the barracks building.

Rows of men in standard issue scale-mail emblazoned with the imperial sigil, a white tower in front of a setting sun, stood in loose formation on the grounds. The men all had heavy canvas packs at their feet. Their weapons were slung loosely at their belts or, in the case of the platoon of spearmen, resting against their shoulders as they chatted idly.

Off to the side, the company's small contingent of officers stood next to their horses. Talia caught the gazes of her friends and wondered if they could read her frustration from this distance.

"Comp'ny! Atenn-*SHUN!*"

The booming voice of the Sergeant in charge of the men echoed off the stone facade of the company building, and all of the assembled soldiers straightened immediately.

Arcus, who held not only his own reins but those of Madrie's horse as well, jogged over and passed them to the commander as she approached.

Madrie took the reins and pulled herself effortlessly into the saddle. The armor she wore seemed no obstacle as she adjusted in her saddle and pointed her horse's nose at her men. When she spoke, she did so in a clear, loud voice - she didn't shout, yet her voice carried like a trumpet in the air.

"Brazen Hawks!"

Her horse huffed and pawed the ground.

"The majority of you are new to our company." She looked through the crowd. "Hell, most of you are new to the ranks. Children of summer. Look around you, and understand this; the last time the Brazen Hawks were here in the Capitol was six years ago - a full rotation. For every one of you that stands in my formation in unsullied boots, I lost a man of worth. A man of caliber. They did not fade idly into retirement, they faced the cold realities of steel and worse outside these sheltered lands in the bosom of the Empire."

A deathly silence was punctuated only by the distant call of crows on the wing.

Some of the men shifted uncomfortably, stealing brief glances to their left and right. It was true, perhaps one in eight of those assembled were veterans.

Those men stood rock steady, their gazes forward and their grizzled faces set. Here were men who had once held the carefree smiles and bright eyes of the recruits they now shared ranks with, but who had long since been worn down by the truth of the world.

"The safety you thought you had is gone," she continued. "A blanket reserved for others. A shelter for the ungrateful who know only the warmth of their hearths and remain blissfully ignorant of our duties."

As she spoke, she seemed to meet the eye of each of the soldiers, her passion mirrored in the redness of her cheeks and her voice as strong as steel.

"Look to the men who have traveled this road before. Learn from them. Heed their advice and better yourselves so that when at last we ride into the darkness - and make no mistake, we *will* ride into darkness - you may yet survive it."

She nodded to the Sergeant in charge and gave her horse a gentle kick in the flanks, trotting off towards the main road.

"I want this column on the road ten minutes ago," Captain Montagne yelled.

Where Madrie's voice was a clear trumpet, Annabelle's was a roaring wave.

Her shout galvanized the men instantly.

The Sergeants shouted orders, and the men slung their rucksacks and began to file out towards the road in an ordered double column.

Annabelle gave a short, sharp whistle and her horse trotted over, pulling its reins from a surprised Darko as it went. She climbed into the saddle of the enormous black stallion almost as gracefully as the commander had and rode out after her, leaving the others to scramble onto their own horses and try to catch up.

"Cheery," Arcus muttered to the others as they cantered after their leaders. "Isn't she?"

Talia mulled over the situation, trying her best to see both sides of the encounter.

Elbaf, however, was not silent.

"I disagree, ranger. I think her bluntness is more . . . honest," he replied as he waved towards the column of men beside them. "Half these men - or more - may well be dead by the time we return."

For nearly a fortnight they'd been on the move and they'd long since left behind the congested, wagon-filled roads of the Capitol region. Darko remarked how the urban sprawl of the Capitol had given way to broader streets and larger houses. For a while they'd passed through wide expanses of well-kept green dotted with manors and estates belonging to minor lords, but even these gave way at last to small villages and hamlets barely worthy of their own names.

Now they scarcely saw other traffic at all, and even then it was usually a lone traveler content to keep their own company, or else the occasional merchant caravan. Even these were no longer the unguarded trains they'd grown used to, but often accompanied by armed men, mercenaries, and private guards.

The men's spirits were still high, and the column still broke out in spontaneous laughter or even song, but Darko mostly kept his own company. The elf didn't see what common ground he would find in the soldiery. Darko and his fellow officers were condemned men forced into servitude - and for all their trappings of mystery and power, Darko at least knew the truth.

They were slaves.

Darko, for his part, could *feel* the animosity and fear that often accompanied the stares he received from their men. Even if he'd wanted to build the types of friendships he saw his companions forging, he doubted he'd be given the chance.

So be it.

The year of training he'd endured had hardened his body, but spending day after day in a saddle still left him sore and battered. He was grateful that they'd been stopped all morning, finally giving him a chance to leave the saddle and sit on solid ground for a moment.

When they'd stopped at this crossroad last night, he'd expected they would follow their pattern of moving out at daybreak. Sure enough, the men were roused with the rising of the sun and their gear packed and stowed.

They did not, however, depart.

After three or four candlemarks of waiting in place, the order had been given for the men to drop their rucks and stand ready to leave. He knew not what they'd been waiting on, but he could see the growing irritation of both Madrie and of Annabelle. The women kept no other counsel - save Talia's, on rare occasions - and frankly, he didn't mind the limited interaction. Darko felt certain that his gifts would demonstrate his worth with time, and he was content to have them come to him.

As if summoned by his musing, he watched as Annabelle broke from her quiet conversation with the commander and headed his way. He made no move to stand, nor did he acknowledge her approach until she was a few feet away.

"Sorcerer, we have need of you."

Talia, Elbaf, and Arcus all saw the interaction and took the leave of their men, heading over to Darko's fire as well. Darko stood, his bad leg slowing him only a little, and brushed the dust from his robes.

"And what service might I provide for the Empire?"

Annabelle's lips were drawn into a faint, disapproving line.

"Our rendezvous with Lord Altimeer is behind schedule, considerably." She glanced up at the late summer sun, which was nearing the middle of the sky. "He and his entourage were to meet us here hours ago."

The meeting was news to the four of them, but they took it in stride.

"What would you have us do?" Talia asked.

"You four will take a few men and horses and travel up this path. It's a half day's ride to the Altimeer Estate, but hopefully you will meet their party on the road. Lord Mortimer Altimeer's son, Roren Altimeer, was to journey with us on our way east. Unfortunately, we cannot wait any longer. We have to push forward towards Bethlir if we are to meet the courier there on time. You are to collect Roren and his men, and then catch up with us as swiftly as you can. Do you understand?"

They nodded in unison.

"Excellent."

She looked pointedly at Darko.

"You have the capacity to send messages with your . . . witchcraft, yes?"

"I am so trained, yes."

"Then you will apprise me of your progress. That will be all."

Darko recognized a dismissal when he heard one, so he turned to gather the few things he'd laid out and began packing them back into the bags around his saddle.

Annabelle turned on her heel and headed back to Madrie, who was busy consulting maps on a small folding field desk.

"Elbaf, Arcus, select six men each," Talia instructed. "Experienced riders only, and ensure they have rations for a week, just in case."

For her part, Talia selected Sergeant Cormorant - one of the more experienced veterans in the company - to serve as their squad leader.

Meanwhile, the whole column made ready to move, leaving only their small contingent of mounted men at the campsite.

Darko analyzed the men that had been selected to accompany them. He was surprised to note that most of them were fresh recruits. Were it his decision, he'd have selected veterans. Admittedly though, he was no warrior, and this was not his area of expertise. The men brought their horses into a rough semi-circle around the cluster of officers and awaited more detailed instructions.

"Alright, men," Talia announced from the saddle of her warhorse. "We're to find Lord Altimeer's son and escort him safely to the rest of the column. I don't have to tell you that there are dangers to be had. However, this should be a fairly simple task, and I expect no trouble." She looked at Arcus. "The detachment is yours, Arcus."

He nodded before speaking.

"Alright. Tomlin, Elric, and Felder, you're with me in the front."

The three men named were all skirmishers, and they nodded their understanding. They carried shortswords and longbows, as well as broad-tipped half-spears slung across their backs, and their armor was much lighter than the rest of the groups'.

"Elbaf will take the rest of the column, followed by . . ." He surveyed Elbaf's choices of troops. "Derrin, Merryl, Jennings, and Garland. Then Darko and Captain Lorraine."

Darko was pleased to hear he'd be riding in the middle, and even more so to find he might get a chance to speak more closely with Talia. He'd been trying to catch her for a private word since they'd departed.

Their guards were strangers to him, but they wore the metal-scaled armor of infantrymen. Their longswords and steel-rimmed shields glinted in the sun, and they looked considerably less comfortable in their saddles than the scouts had. Nonetheless, they must've been competent for Elbaf to choose them.

"That leaves Julias, Gideon, Kardon, Rennault, and Thellik to bring up the rear guard. Any questions?" Seeing none, Arcus continued. "Excellent. We leave immediately."

He spurred his horse down the road, his fellow rangers in tow.

Elbaf gave a quick nod to Talia and followed suit, setting the group upon their path.

Darko fought his way into his saddle while the horses of the rear guard stamped impatiently. The riders kept their criticisms to themselves, but he could not help theorizing their disdain for him.

Talia waited as well, her face drawn tight and her stare distant. She seemed almost to start awake when Darko finally steered his horse towards her.

They rode for several hours in relative quiet, each content to mull over their thoughts internally.

Darko dwelt on his frustration and his newfound doubts regarding his companions. He glanced over at Talia - something was definitely on her mind. She fidgeted with her reins absentmindedly and paid no heed at all to the woods around them or the path at her horse's feet. As the sun began to dip in the sky above, his curiosity at last got the better of him.

"Something troubling you, Talia?"

She glanced back at their men who rode some fifteen feet behind them. When she spoke it was nearly a whisper. Not that Darko's keen ears had any trouble with her words.

"The Altimeers are one of the oldest families in the Empire. Their lineage dates back to the Founding. Father often spoke very highly of Lord Altimeer, and I remember his son Roren from my youth."

"You are concerned for them?"

"Roren Altimeer was . . . odd." Talia chewed her bottom lip. "*Dark* in a way, I suppose, but altogether charming. No . . . that's not the right word, either. He was captivating. Handsome, strong, and dedicated to the Emperor with a passion that would shame many of my order. I cannot see the man I knew being late for our meeting."

Darko nodded, adding her words to the notes and calculations in his mind.

"Then you suspect foul play."

She nodded grimly.

They rode in silence a while longer and Darko's discomfort grew. It took him a moment to put his finger on why he was so ill at ease, but finally it clicked.

"Where have all the birds gone?"

"What?" Talia looked over at him quizzically. "What do you mean, where have all the--"

Darko held up a finger for silence and strained his ears. His senses were far keener than any human's - he could pick out the sound of a whispered word at fifty paces. He identified and dismissed each sound around him. The rumbling thud of hoofbeats, the creak of leather and the clink of armor. Even the restless breathing of the riders.

Beyond that, nothing.

"Darko," Talia insisted. "What is it?"

"Tell the men to halt."

Talia's eyes narrowed and she set a hand on her hilt. The other she raised in a closed fist.

The men behind her reined in their mounts instantly while a short, sharp whistle sent the message forward. Silence fell as the entire group shuffled to a stop.

"Something isn't right, Talia. *Listen.*"

She cocked her head to the side.

"I don't hear anything, Darko."

He sighed in exasperation.

"*That's the problem.*"

He mulled over his options. He was reluctant to reveal more than he had to, even to Talia.

"Wait here."

"Darko," Talia shook her head. "I don't think you should be going off on your own."

"Talia, I just need a moment." He rolled his eyes. "I'll be a few paces off the road, that's all."

"Let me rephrase." She straightened in her saddle and glared at him. "You're not leaving this column alone."

Her rebuke caused Darko to bristle.

He narrowed his eyes at her and his tongue fairly dripped acid when he spoke.

"Or what, *ma'am?*"

Months of pent up frustration simmered to the surface as this woman - no, this *girl* - dared to treat him like an errant toddler.

"Am I so untrustworthy? Am I a trained *animal* to be held by a leash until, and unless, you need my gifts?" He did not wait for her reply, but kicked his horse into a swift trot off the path and into the woodline.

"Darko! Lieutenant!"

He ignored her call.

Reia, I have need of you.

He could feel her in the back of his mind, already well aware of his pending request.

A raven flew down from the sky and landed on a nearby branch. When it opened its beak, it spoke with the soft seductive tones of his companion.

"Yes, Master. I sense it, too." The bird peered out into the forest. "Something is off here."

"Go. Look ahead and return to me with what you see."

The bird leapt skyward and made a large, lazy circle above the road.

Be careful, Reia.

She sent him a feeling of reassurance, then headed off down the road.

Darko was still watching the sky when Talia crashed through the underbrush, a heavy flanged mace in one hand and her reins in the other.

"Damn you, Darko," her cheeks blazed as she spoke. "I gave you an order!"

He was about to reply when the rest of their rear guard rode into sight. He cast a look over Talia's shoulder at them. They had their hands on their weapons as well and were eyeing him warily.

"We are on the same side, Darko." Talia said to him as she leaned in from her saddle. "I am not your enemy."

"You're right," he replied. He dropped his gaze to the ground in a show of obedience, but in his mind he was following his familiar closely. "I'm . . . sorry."

"What in the Infinite Hells has gotten into you?" Talia hissed. "You're spooking our men. Hell, you're making *me* nervous."

"Not here, Talia," he mumbled in a distant, distracted tone that only served to stoke the fires of her irritation.

He felt her heated stare and focused on the woman, pulled from his connection with Reia. Talia was nonplussed, her head cocked to the side and her cheeks bright red.

"Yes, here," she snapped indignantly.

Darko, attempting to turn inward once more, muttered something noncommittal.

"That's not good enough, and this isn't over," she warned him with a pointed finger before raising her voice. "Now get back to the damn road!"

Talia was still fuming an hour later.

How dare he?

She'd insisted he ride ahead of her since his little jaunt into the woodline, so she'd spent the time glaring daggers at the elf's back. Whether he was equally frustrated with her, she didn't know, but he'd barely spoken a word since their altercation.

His foul mood had infected the group as well, and even the younger men were surly and quiet - a fact made worse when Talia had the men eat and drink in their saddles, rather than halt the column for a midday meal.

The crushing quiet of the area around them seemed more oppressive with every mile they traveled, and the group was on a razor's edge; the atmosphere had an ugly, electric charge. The clear sunny skies of the morning had given way to steely thunderheads, muting the colors of the landscape until even the grass seemed dull.

And still they'd seen no sign of Lord Altimeer's party.

No one voiced it aloud, but they all knew that the further they made it without a trace the more likely it was that something had befallen Altimeer and his men, and might well befall them, too.

She stewed a while longer, but at last could not keep her silence. She spurred her horse and rode up beside Darko, who seemed to hardly notice her presence.

"What's gotten into you?" she chastised him. "You've been broody and sullen since we left from the Capitol--"

"We are *slaves*, Talia," he interrupted her. "And something rotten here dwells, mark my words."

"We are being punished for our crimes, Darko," she frowned. "And we have been given a chance to right our wrongs."

Reflexively, she reached a hand up to her neck. Her gloved fingers traced the inch-wide black mark around her throat. She, like the others, had been branded by the blade of the guillotine that fateful night a year ago. She remembered it all too well - the terror and the certainty that she was going to die.

Even now the blade sometimes came to her in dreams, and usually when it did she woke drenched in sweat with a racing heart.

She knew not what sorcery had made the mark, only that ever since she'd worn a band of dark black on her skin that neither faded nor washed away. In the quiet hours of the night she had often prayed to the Emperor that he might let her heal the wound - or at the very least conceal it - but she never felt his presence when she asked this.

Eventually she'd stopped asking.

Darko laughed dryly, humorlessly.

"We are bound by *enchantment*, or weren't you told the same?"

She nodded.

They had indeed received the same instruction. The band upon their necks was as much a badge of their station as the emblems of the Hand upon their chests. She could well recall the words of their instructors telling them that should they act against the interests of the Empire or exhibit disobedience, the magic that kept them alive could just as surely kill them where they stood.

"Talia, can you truly tell me this doesn't strike you as *wrong*?"

"It is His will, Darko," she steeled her resolve. "And my faith is strong."

She heard him sigh and saw him start to withdraw into himself again.

"Darko, there is more you're not telling me."

It was no question. For his poker face was sorely lacking.

"Yes, Talia, there is. But these men already mistrust me. I would not abuse myself further by revealing more of my arcane arts."

There it was - the core of the issue at hand was finally revealed to her.

"Darko," she reached out a hand to grip his shoulder. "I am not these men. I am not Annabelle or Madrie. I am your friend."

He shrank from her grip, but finally met her eyes.

"These men fear you, as do our superiors, I believe. But I do not call you witch, I do not mock your gifts. Your powers are a boon to all of us. I *know* your worth, not just as a tool to be used, but as a companion."

He visibly relaxed.

"Have I changed so much, Darko, that you would count me as an enemy?"

She tried not to show how deeply she was cut by his mistrust, yet could not help feeling like she'd somehow betrayed him.

"I'm sorry, Talia," he said, this time genuinely. "I should have given you the merit you deserve. This cloud of suspicion and hatred frustrates and offends, but my quarrel is not with you."

He turned his gaze back to the road.

"I only want to make the best of this situation."

She sensed he had more to say, so she remained silent.

"We are young, Talia. If the fates smile upon you, you may yet live another six, even seven more decades. I pray that you are so blessed."

He locked eyes with her again.

"But I am staring at *centuries* of servitude. The timeline of my race is played out over hundreds of years, and I am barely at the end of my first century. Would you be so willing, I wonder, if you looked at a millennia of slavery?"

Now it was Talia's turn to break away. She felt doubt flutter in her heart and no longer wondered at her friend's anger.

Would my faith be strong enough?

Her internal dialogue was interrupted by a large black raven cawing above them. She looked up at the creature, wondering at its behavior.

"We need to hurry, something is indeed amiss."

Darko spurred his steed as he gave his warning, breaking into a gallop. Talia and the rest followed suit, pounding down the trail with the sounds of thunder.

Within minutes they were met by the scouting party. Arcus was nowhere to be found, but the other three scouts were all standing beside their mounts, each pale-faced and looking around nervously.

"Where is Lieutenant D'Ari?"

Tomlin, a tall, gaunt man with sunken features, saluted and then pointed up the road. The path bent out of sight some fifty yards distant.

"Ma'am, he said to wait 'ere for ye, and to send you 'round when ye' arrived."

His voice was steady, but she could see the sweat on his brow and feel his nerves on edge.

Elbaf looked meaningfully at her and unshouldered his massive blade.

"Darko, Elbaf, with me. The rest of you, form a perimeter here. Water your horses."

She gave her mount a small kick and continued down the road. Darko and Elbaf both fell in line beside her, neither speaking.

They rounded the corner and saw that the path was blocked by a large wrought iron gate set into a tall, well-crafted stone wall. The wall itself was massive, easily twelve feet tall and made of smooth gray stones cut with such precision that they were nearly seamless. Either side of the gate was flanked by a tower that rose another six feet above the top of the wall and featured tall, narrow arrow slits. Both towers had long, elaborate banners depicting the briar rose and stag of House Altimeer, each hanging limply in the still air.

But it was the gate that captured their attention.

It dwarfed Arcus as he stood before it. The gate looked as though it had been designed to open from both sides, like a wide double door, but it was hard to tell in its current state. Bars as thick as a closed fist and topped with wicked barbs a foot long were twisted and tangled like ill-used yarn. To say it was inoperable would have been to shame the word. The once proud entrance was ruined, the lock broken and the two sides entwined inseparably.

Talia was so stunned by the sheer force that must have been required to cause such damage, that she was entirely unphased when the raven circling above came to rest on Darko's shoulder with a dry rustle.

Chapter Five

"Darko?"

Her eyes hadn't left the gate, and neither had his.

"I see it, Talia."

His tone held neither contempt nor disrespect. He simply didn't know what else to say.

Movement at his side caused him to turn in time to watch as Elbaf rode up to the gate and cleanly dismounted. Darko watched him hand his reins off to Arcus and share a whispered word with him.

"Hello, the tower," Elbaf called out through cupped hands.

Darko was unsurprised when the half-orc's call went unanswered.

He treated Talia to a mystified shrug and rode closer as well. As they approached, she seemed to finally notice his passenger.

"Darko," she began slowly, reaching for her mace as she spoke. "There's a . . . *bird* on your shoulder."

"Yes, there is," he waved her off before raising his voice so the other two could hear as well. "I'd like to introduce you all to Reia."

Are you sure about this, Master?

"She is very dear to me. We are *bound* to one another."

Elbaf and Arcus both shared a confused look, and Talia had her brow furrowed suspiciously.

"Darko, that is no natural bird," Arcus warned, pointing at Reia's glossy feather coat.

Darko chuckled at the druid's concern.

"No, no she isn't. She's more of an, uh . . ." He looked up at Reia, unsure how to explain her properly without alarming his companions further. "A familiar spirit. A creature of magic, if you will."

Elbaf had already lost interest, and was wandering closer to the gate, but Talia and Arcus seemed inclined to listen further.

"She and I are connected, and she enhances my magical-- Elbaf, don't!"

He cut himself off and his heart skipped a beat as he watched Elbaf reaching out to touch the ruined bars of the gate. The man froze, his hand still several inches away from the metal.

Darko hurried down off his horse and approached.

"What is it, wizard?"

"We don't know *what* did this," Darko began carefully inspecting the gate, the lock, even the ground below the entrance. "But I suspect strongly that magical forces are at play. There may yet be harmful energies lingering here."

He held his hands to his temples and began to murmur softly. As he spoke, white fire flickered into life along his fingers and spread out over his eyes. The flames licked harmlessly at his skin and then faded into his pupils until they turned a soft, silvery-white.

Darko blinked a few times to clear his vision as the enchantment set in, then examined the gate more closely. A faint haze covered everything in his sight, the residual magic that lay over the world. He could see wisps and motes of energy as they danced through the air, unbound by spell or purpose. Some were bright, like sparks from a fire, and others so faint as to nearly blend in with the background.

He looked over at Talia, unsurprised to see that she radiated a fair amount of power. Her energy was bright, golden like the sun. Arcus too was alight, though his aura was more neutral, browns and greens of the natural world. Darko noted with interest that the ground the ranger stood on seemed also to glow with concentrated energy, as did the grasses and the trees nearest to him. Not much, but enough to stand out. Both also shared the distinctive black ring around their throats that they all wore. He tried his best to ignore the deep, swirling purplish-black of that energy.

Elbaf was a surprise, though.

Darko expected no other evidence of magic upon him, but Elbaf's heart pulsed red and black with traces of gold. With every beat, tendrils of energy whisked through his veins, only to return to the core in his chest.

"Cast your gaze elsewhere, wizard."

Darko realized he must have been staring. He quickly looked aside, making a note to explore the phenomenon more fully later.

Next he set his eyes upon the gate.

"As I expected," he announced to his patiently waiting companions. "No mundane force wrought this destruction."

The bars were coated with the fading light of a powerful spell. It felt heavy and dark in his mind. He looked closer, noting that the spell had all but disappeared and that no part of it seemed still active. Drawing near, he reached a hand out to the bars. The transmutation magic that had bent the steel was slippery to his arcane touch, and he could feel in it a power that outmatched his own by a wide margin.

"Can you undo it?"

Darko turned back to Talia.

"I couldn't have done it in the first place, Talia. This would require magic beyond my current skill."

He returned to his inspection.

"Perhaps with more study I could accomplish such a task, but it would take a very learned wizard to do this."

"Then we go over the wall," Elbaf said, pulling ropes and a grappling hook from his saddle bags.

"A little faith please, Elbaf," Darko huffed.

He pulled a leather-bound grimoire from within his voluminous robes while the party looked on. He opened the tome, the pages flipping themselves to reveal the incantation he sought.

"Here we are."

He began to speak eldritch words of power, one hand holding the book and the other outstretched and pointing at the ground. He drew his hand in a slow circle as he spoke, and to the surprise of the group a small blue fire began to burn upon the ground some ten feet in front of him. The flame followed the path of his hand, tracing a blazing circle five feet wide. As he completed his incantation, so too did he complete the circle. When the ring of fire was finished it rushed inward, filling the whole circle with a disc of flickering, whorling blue light.

Darko slumped a little, then regained his posture. His brow was dotted with a few beads of sweat, which he hoped his companions hadn't noticed.

"Alright, who will go first?"

No one moved, but instead all eyed him incredulously.

"First . . ." Arcus voiced the confusion of the group. "Meaning?"

"It's to lift us over the wall," Darko explained, nonplussed.

Still no volunteers.

"Oh, very well," Darko sighed, stepping into the circle.

He raised a hand and the party gasped as the disc lifted into the air. It carried him softly, slowly, up and over the wall, only to set him gently on the other side where he stepped lightly off.

"I'll get the others," Arcus said, hopping back into his saddle.

He rode off while the group, now reassured, followed Darko.

Elbaf was just touching down when Arcus returned with the rest of their party. Some of the men made warding signs against witchcraft and many of them looked nervous, but they followed their orders admirably. Each man was lifted gently over - one at a time - and released safely.

They had to leave the horses, which were too skittish and too heavy for Darko's peculiar mode of transportation. They left them tied on loose leads with their contingent of scouts. Kodja, too, could not be persuaded to enter the blazing circle, no matter how Arcus coaxed him, and so rather than reveal his presence, Arcus had him keep watch in the surrounding trees.

"If we aren't back by sunrise," Talia warned through the bars of the gate, "send Private Tomlin back to the Capital garrison and Private Elric forward to link up with the company."

"Aye, ma'am," Corporal Felder said with a salute.

Darko fought the urge to shiver as they turned their backs on the men and headed up the path. The sense of foreboding that had blanketed them on the path was stifling here, as though the walls around the estate held it a captive cloud.

Arcus still led the party, but only by a dozen paces. He made sure never to fall out of the eyesight of Elbaf and the infantrymen at his side. Sergeant Cormorant, Sergeant Merryl, and Corporal Garland were all veterans of the previous rotation - taciturn and gruff. Private Derrin on the other hand was young and fresh-faced, but seemingly capable enough. He had the muscled build of a laborer, but all the discipline of a professional soldier.

They walked with their hands firmly on the hilts of their blades, as did the men who followed behind Darko and Talia. With his vision still augmented by sorcery,

Darko cast around for the source of his discomfort. The background levels of magic were not abnormal here, nor did any ley-lines run through the ground close enough for him to detect. Nonetheless, he felt a great weight bearing down on him. Finally, his arms covered in goosebumps, he could hold his silence no longer.

"Talia, something is *wrong* here."

The way she jumped when he spoke made him realize that no one had uttered a word since they'd left the gate more than a candlemark ago.

"I'm not overfond of the atmosphere either, Darko," she laughed nervously. "But we are charged with finding Lord Altimeer, and that is what we will do."

He chewed on the inside of his cheek a moment, pondering his words carefully.

"We should send a message to the captain."

Talia set her mouth into a thin line.

"No. We can handle this."

Her tone left no room for argument, and further discussion was cut off as they rounded a final wooded corner and came at last to an open field. The manor itself sat at the center of several acres of lush grasslands. Clumps of heather and native grasses covered the softly rolling grounds of the estate, flanking the path that they walked upon. The path, which turned from dirt to flagstone at the edge of the clearing, led directly to a massive set of iron-bound wooden doors.

On a sunny day the grounds must have been beautiful, but under the overcast afternoon skies above them, the broad two-story structure seemed menacing. No lights burned in the windows of the vast manor, and across the whole of the grounds not a soul was in sight.

Talia felt the hairs on her neck prickle, but she refused to display her doubts outwardly.

"Talia, *think*," Darko pleaded quietly beside her. "Where are the guards? Why do lights not shine from within? Lord Altimeer has dozens of men-at-arms and servants--"

"What would you have me do, Darko?" she hissed back at him. "Call our superiors at the first sign of trouble? Prove ourselves incompetent before we have even reached our first assignment?"

She glanced at their soldiers.

"Would you have us be cowards in the eyes of our men? Would you have us cast away any respect they might have for us so quickly?"

He matched her gaze steadily.

"I would have us live, Talia. Something isn't right here, and I know you feel it, too."

She wouldn't deny it.

"Yes, something here is deeply amiss, and we shall reveal it in the Emperor's name."

She ignored the huff of indignation she received and turned her gaze forward once again.

"Men, gather 'round."

The small group huddled around her in a loose circle. Elbaf, Darko, and Arcus stayed a few steps behind the rest of the men, but their attention was squarely on her as well. She waited until they were still before clearing her throat to speak.

"Men, you too have likely felt the presence of something . . . *foul* here. I don't know what danger awaits us, but something troubling lingers in the air. You are men of caliber, of strength, and together we will face whatever is within. Kneel that you might receive the Emperor's blessings."

Her voice radiated authority, and they knelt as one around her.

Talia bowed her head, her helmet in her hands.

"Holy Emperor, Lord of Light and Bane of Darkness, we, your humble servants, ask for your blessings as we execute your will. Though we sense great evil, we will not falter. For your light shines upon us."

As she spoke she began to emanate a soft white light. It began in the center of her chest, then spread to cover her entire body. The light bathed the men and put them at ease. Each man breathed easier and felt renewed.

"No evil that walks the earth nor fills the skies nor slithers beneath the ground can stand before you, and we will drive the taint of wickedness from these lands with hearts free from fear - for we know the strength of our faith will be our shield."

Talia felt herself filled with energy, as though she could run a marathon in full plate. Her doubts were eased - *here* was the power of her faith. Her muscles rippled with divine energy and her lungs filled as if with their first breath.

"In the name of the Emperor, His will be done."

"His will be done," the men echoed solemnly, each enchanted by the undeniable power of her magic.

Talia set her polished helm upon her head as the glow began to fade. It softened and dulled until only her armor still shone, and then only just. Nonetheless, the soft purity of the light gave heart to those who saw it.

She removed the scale-shaped metal shield from her back, strapping it to her right arm, then hefted her mace in her left. She held the weapon in front of herself for a moment, eyes closed in concentration.

Suddenly, the mace burst into radiant golden light, shining twice as strong as any torch the men had seen. They gasped in admiration as she led the way, glimmering like a beacon, toward the front door of the manor.

Elbaf kept pace with her, staying at her side as the rest followed them to the door. They climbed the broad stone steps and Elbaf shot a quick glance at Talia before raising his fist and pounding three times on the door.

"Lord Altimeer!" Talia called. "Are you here, m'lord?"

An eerie silence was their only answer.

"The hard way, then," Elbaf growled.

"Don't just--"

But Talia's words were unheeded. Elbaf stepped back a pace and then slammed into the wood door with all his might, buckling it inward with a mighty crack. The door hadn't been barred, and in fact may not even have been locked, so both sides of it banged loudly off the stone walls within.

The dull booms echoed in the empty halls of the manor.

Talia stepped into the foyer, taking in the sight of a broad double staircase, polished stone floors, and hanging tapestries. Everything seemed in order. No signs of struggle within - nor any signs of life.

The men filed into the room, all armed and expecting trouble.

"Talia . . ."

"Yes," she looked at the wizard with narrowed eyes. "Yes, I agree, we should split up."

"Talia," Arcus cautioned quietly. "That seems a bit hasty."

She glared at him.

"Team up, no less than three. Rennault and Thellik, you're with me. Light your torches, and tread lightly. If you run into trouble, make some noise. This is a big place, but not so large that we shouldn't hear each other."

"Elbaf," Arcus said, nudging the half-orc. "*Say* something."

The warrior locked eyes with Talia and shrugged.

"Yes, ma'am."

With that he pulled the gleaming greatsword he wore on his back from its cradle.

Nodding, Talia took stock of the layout of the room and made a quick assessment based on the outside of the building and her memory.

"I'll take the west wing upstairs," she gestured. "Elbaf, you'll take the ground floor to the west. Arcus the ground floor to the east, and Darko you're upstairs to the east."

Her fellow officers divided up the rest of the men, while Thellik and Rennault walked over to her side, their blades drawn and uneasy frowns on their faces.

"Ma'am, I'll be firs' ta' say I'm glad I'll be with you." Rennault gave a small nod toward her glowing weapon, his messy orange hair poking out from underneath his helmet.

"The Emperor protects, Corporal."

"Aye, he sure does, ma'am," the fellow nodded. "And by your grace, I don' mind being a little nearer ta' his favor."

Thellik didn't speak, but Talia knew he was grateful as well. She could see it in the shifting glances of his pale blue eyes behind his ruddy complexion.

She'd picked them precisely *because* they were both young and unsure - better she keep them close to watch out for them herself.

"Come on, we're headed upstairs. If memory serves, the Master suite is this way."

She hefted her mace and headed up the stairs while the rest of her troops headed off to their respective areas. The stairs were covered in thick red carpeting and their footfalls were nearly silent despite their armor. At the top of the stairs they found a long wide hallway running east to west. She cast a look over her shoulder at Darko and his team. She watched as Darko raised a hand and spoke a sharp word, his hand erupting in a blazing arcane fire that cast a light down the hallway in front of his group. He seemed to sense her staring and looked back to meet her gaze - frustration clear in his eyes.

Talia fortified her resolve and turned away.

Her weapon still emanating enough light to guide their path, she led her men down the hallway, past staggered doors on the left and right. It had been a decade since she last wandered these halls, but she remembered more with every step. Here was a library, there a parlor where Lord Altimeer and her father had enjoyed repugnant cigars. She left those doors unopened, focusing instead on the end of the hallway. To the left was a broad, ornately decorated wooden door. On it was carved and painted a bold scene of a hunter drawing down upon a mighty stag.

They'd nearly reached it when Talia heard a sound, a whisper like cloth being run across a blade. She froze in her tracks, her men following suit, and looked to her right for the source of the sound.

A door, ever so slightly ajar.

"Now where does this go?" she murmured softly aloud.

She searched her memory, but was nearly certain she'd never entered the room as a child. *Why,* though? Why, when they'd traipsed through every other room with the careless abandon of children, would she have neglected this one?

She inspected the door more closely. It was quite ordinary - smooth, dark-stained wood with a wrought iron handle. She gave a curt nod to her men, who gripped their weapons tighter, before she softly pushed the door open with the face of her shield.

It opened smoothly and silently, revealing a sitting room with large cushioned couches and a small fireplace. The room had only one other entrance, an opening at the other end - a sort of archway covered with curtains of fine silk. Talia's mace shed plenty of light to fill the space, and she took her time examining the room as she took a few tentative steps inside.

She heard a clink of glass as her foot caught some small object, sending it rolling softly across the hardwood floor. She looked down at the spinning object and remembered.

It was a baby's bottle.

"The nursery," she muttered.

As she watched, the curtain across the room fluttered softly in an unseen breeze.

A window must be open.

With growing dread she walked toward the curtain, her pace increasing as she drew near. She held out her mace and parted the thin fabric, metal rings singing softly as the cloth slid to the side.

The first thing she noticed was the woman on the floor - she was facedown, laying just inside the room. Judging from the puddle of sticky, dried blood around her, there was nothing Talia could do.

Talia glanced around the attached room, it was small - only fifteen feet to a side - and there were no other exits save a large window that sat open on one wall. The only features of the room were a few low dressers and four bassinets, all horribly, horribly silent and still.

"Secure the window," Talia ordered with a shaky breath. "And see to the woman."

She would not leave the darkest duty to her men.

Talia walked to the first of the cribs and let out a sigh of relief when she saw that it was empty.

The second wasn't.

As she drew near, the deep red staining the blankets within and the still, unmoving bundle of cloth brought tears to her eyes. She blinked rapidly, trying and failing to keep hot tears of rage from spilling down her cheeks. The third and fourth were the same, and each time Talia forced herself to reach a hand in to check for a heartbeat or a breath - but she found none.

"Ma'am . . . 'er throats been slit."

Rennault's words galvanized her. Talia whipped around, no longer particularly interested in stealth, and stormed out past her men. She turned crisply on her heel out into the hallway and strode up to the door of the Master suite.

She didn't knock.

Instead, she raised a booted foot and kicked the door in. The heavy, well-balanced entrance slammed open revealing a massive, luxurious bedroom. There, at the foot of the bed, knelt a man with his back to Talia. He was holding a woman in his arms as she lay upon the ground. From where she stood she could see his shoulders shaking as if he were weeping.

The man wore rich red sleeping clothes, and his long gray hair hung to his shoulders in the well-recognized ponytail that Lord Altimeer often sported at court. He didn't turn at her entrance, despite the light and the noise of the door.

"Lord Altimeer!"

Silence, or rather near-silence.

Talia cocked her head, trying to identify the soft, wet smacking noise that she heard from across the room.

Righteous anger fueled her, and the glow from her armor intensified. It spread to her skin until her eyes shone bright ivory.

"Lord Altimeer!"

Overcome at last by the light, the man spun on all fours, hissing like a wild animal.

Talia heard her men swear and step backwards at the sight of what was once surely a man.

Lord Altimeer hunched like some feral beast, his teeth bared and bloodsoaked. Blood and viscera coated his mouth, his chin, and all the way down his throat and chest. She could see now that the woman he'd knelt over was Lady Belinda Altimeer. He had been . . . *eating* her.

The monster's cold, cloudy eyes focused on her and it growled, crawling on all fours as it prowled at the edge of her radiance.

"Is that . . . Is that the Lord Altimeer?"

"Stay behind me, Thellik."

Talia raised her shield, holding it out in front of her with her mace back and ready to strike.

"Lord Altimeer, in the name of the Holy Emperor, I sentence you to death for the crimes of blasphemy of the highest order, murder, and of defiling the sacred dead."

The creature hissed, spraying bits of slobber and blood, and charged. It moved with a lilting and unnatural gait, transitioning from four limbs to two and stretching out bloodsoaked hands to grab her.

Emperor, guide my hand, that thy justice be served.

She timed her swing, and with a satisfying crunch she intercepted the wide jaws of the man with a crushing blow from her mace, caving in his skull and shattering his jaw at the same time. The fury of the blow knocked him off to the side, where he lay still.

Talia smelled a faint stench of smoke and stared in wonder at her mace head. Thick, clumpy blood and brains coated the heavy, bladed flanges of the weapon. The gore sizzled and popped, boiling on the bare metal of her holy weapon.

She turned back to her quarry, still laying silently on the floor.

Talia approached cautiously, then rolled the man over with her foot. She could see now quite clearly that his throat had been slit wide open long before she arrived, but the *thing* before her had been far from dead.

Or perhaps far beyond it.

Darko was right.

Only powerful dark magic could bring a man back from the dead. She'd heard legend of evil sorcerers who could accomplish such tasks, but centuries had passed since a necromancer had prowled within the Empire. Even so, she could not deny what she saw before her own eyes.

"We need to leave," Talia turned with sudden fervor to her men.

"Ma'am?"

"I . . . I've made a terrible mistake. We need to leave, *now!*"

She turned back toward the door of the bedroom suite and headed for the opening. She stepped briskly out into the hallway only to be greeted by the hunched figures of a half-dozen servants just a few feet away. Their jerky, stumbling walk told her everything she needed to know.

She tried to step backwards, tried to warn her men, but they reached for her instantly.

She managed to fend off one with her shield and land a glancing blow to another, but a third creature grasped her by the shoulders and pushed her backwards hard enough to lose her footing.

She landed hard on her back, covered in an instant by the ravenous ghouls.

"Get . . . get back!"

She tried her best to blockade the door, to keep the threat bottlenecked, but the creatures crawled over her and into the room. She lost sight of Thellik and Rennault, but heard them shouting and the ring of steel.

The creature on top of her reeked of death - it had clearly perished several days ago. An open slit across the man's throat dripped blood onto her chest as snapping jaws and bleeding fingernails scrabbled for purchase across the plates of her armor.

She could see and hear the sizzle of dead flesh as the monster's skin burned and stuck to her armor and shield.

The Emperor protects.

She had to get to her men, but her mace was useless while she was being grappled. She dropped the heavy weapon and instead reached out with a gloved hand, wrapping her fingers firmly around the neck of the once living man on top of her.

She chanted the rights of battle and, in a fit of inspiration, channeled the energy within herself that she normally drew upon to heal others. Brilliant white light engulfed her hand, and where it touched the creature she could feel flesh and bone turn to ash and dust.

The monster recoiled, hissing, as white fire spread from its throat and consumed it entirely, leaving behind only black dust.

Talia rolled to her feet, scooping up her mace as she did. She regained her footing in time to see Thellik fall beneath the onslaught, a bloodcurdling scream leaving his lips - and being cut short - as the creatures bore him to the ground.

Rennault looked soon to follow. Talia waded in with her mace, laying into the creatures with unmatched fury. Whether stupid or utterly mindless, the creatures noticed her assault too late and could not stand before her. She laid low the two attacking Rennault, then turned her baleful gaze upon the three atop Thellik. She raised her mace to rescue him, but she could see he'd already been fairly dismembered - there was no hope of saving him.

"Go, Rennault," she pushed the shell-shocked soldier toward the door. "We have to get out of here!"

He cleared the entrance with her a half-step behind him. She pulled the heavy door shut behind them, and then took the lead. They could hear shouts from across the house - it seemed their friends had met similar resistance.

"Elbaf, Darko, Arcus!"

Her shouts didn't go unanswered.

As they neared the top of the stairs, she could see Darko was already there. He was bleeding badly from his shoulder and his men, Gideon and Jennings, were nowhere in sight.

"Talia," he cried. "Get downstairs!"

She headed down the steps as he turned to face the hallway he'd come from. She saw his hands swirl in arcane circles as a red glow began to coalesce at his fingertips. The light intensified, leaving swirling trails of light as he moved faster and faster.

Talia could see a pack of the monsters nearing him, shambling down the hallway toward the unarmed mage.

"Darko!"

But she needn't have called out - no sooner did the word leave her lips than a cyclone of flames burst forth from Darko's hands, roaring down the tunnel and consuming everything in its path.

Darko held on to the torrent of fire until the last of the creatures crumbled to ashes, then dismissed the flames just as swiftly as he'd summoned them.

He looked down at the broad waiting room, taking stock.

Elbaf was holding one of the hallways, his massive greatsword singing death as it cleaved arms, legs, and torsos. Arcus was helping what remained of their small force out the door, and Talia was making her way downward as well. He took a deep breath to steady himself from his expenditure and worked his way down the stairs as quickly as he could.

He saw Arcus turn toward him, his bow drawn and an arrow nocked.

Darko instinctively turned as well, just in time to see the pale, staggering corpse of Lady Altimeer catch an arrow through the eye socket. Her body crumpled in place and Darko made a mental note to thank the druid - if they made it out of here.

"Darko, come on!"

Talia waved at him, pointing to the door, then turned to smash an undead servant boy in the face, leaving him alongside the steadily growing pile of bodies that was filling the foyer. Darko cursed - not for the last time - his leg and the frailty of his body. Fighting through the pain, he made it to the wide double-door. As soon as he ducked out into the night, the rest of the officers followed him.

Elbaf came last, pulling the broad doors shut and doubtless regretting the fervor with which he had kicked them open earlier.

"Darko, send a message to Annabelle," Talia ordered him grimly. "But make it quick. We're going to need you."

But she needn't have bothered - he was already kneeling on the dewy grass, his eyes closed in concentration. The elf whispered quietly into cupped hands, oblivious to the world around him. As he spoke, a tiny pinprick of blue light appeared on his forehead. It grew steadily into a spark, getting brighter and brighter until it was difficult to look at directly.

"How much longer, wizard?"

Elbaf's call fell on deaf ears. Darko couldn't allow himself to be distracted. He did his best to ignore the pounding of flesh against wood as the monsters within the manor tried to escape, did his best to ignore the grunts of his allies as they struggled to hold the door shut in the face of the tide.

Finally, he muttered the last words of the spell, and the spark drifted down into his cupped, waiting hands.

"Come at once. Lord Altimeer is dead. The corpses of the fallen walk the living world. We are in danger of being overrun."

With that, he snapped his hands shut and the spark winked out of existence with a sharp snap.

"Darko!"

"It is done," he said as he turned and stood with some difficulty, his cheeks red with frustration. "Now we must simply hope she receives it in time."

He caught Talia's eye and could see remorse there. Remorse and crushing sadness, both cloaked in a fiery rage. He shook his head softly, trying to convey some measure of reassurance, but she looked away.

He readied himself, taking a wide stance and digging deep within his magical reserves, considering carefully how to spend the last of his energies.

His gaze landed on the cluster of warriors fighting to hold the massive doors of the manor shut, and a thought occurred - a relatively simple spell, but one that might make all the difference.

He pulled the incantation from memory and struggled to recite it as he made his way up the stairs towards the door.

"Mage, what are you *doing*?" Elbaf grunted as he approached. "I cannot defend you here, get back down the stairs!"

Darko couldn't break the spell, but he shook his head no and kept up his approach. The door shuddered again, and Elbaf and the other men were pushed back a few inches across the stone. A crack appeared between the two halves of the door and clawing, grasping fingers pushed through as the men began to tire.

Darko's hands turned a deep, earthen brown as he spoke and swelled to more than twice their usual size. He was not yet finished with the spell when he reached Elbaf, but he placed his hands on the half-orcs' back.

"What . . . what are you doing, wizard?"

Darko uttered the last syllable of the spell, and his hands began to shrink back to their normal size and color.

Elbaf's eyes widened as his muscles bulged and his skin darkened. The veins in the half-orc's arms, already prominent, stuck out like corded steel and he grew a full three inches in a matter of moments. His muscles rippled and flexed and he roared as his body filled with magical strength.

He gave a mighty shove and slammed the doors back shut with such force that the fingers and hands poking through were crushed like twigs.

Darko all but collapsed as the last of his energy was consumed by the spell.

Seconds later, a hot dark gust blew over the group from the south - a rush of wind that smelled of ash and chlorine. Darko's skin prickled as latent magical energy flowed through the air, and he looked up in time to see a swirling pillar of black smoke roar down from the heavens.

"What fresh hell is this?" Elbaf growled. "You four, take up arms. I can hold the door."

Sure enough, he edged closer to the middle of the doorway and placed a hand on each door. Though the rest of the men holding it broke away and drew blades, his empowered body easily held the portal shut.

Talia, too, raised her mace and shield, turning her efforts towards the pillar of darkness.

Arcus drew a bead on the column just as it disappeared into a swirling cloud of black smoke.

Annabelle strode out of the cloud with the grace of a panther, a mace not unlike Talia's in her hand.

"Get behind me, now!"

Everyone but Elbaf moved quickly, rushing to stand behind the woman.

"Annabelle," the young cleric gestured. "The *dead* walk within, they will--"

Talia's words were cut off by Annabelle's raised hand.

"They are like dry wheat before the scythe of the Emperor."

Darko could see as he passed the woman that her dark hair floated as though in a breeze, even though the winds had stopped. Her eyes, too, were different. Where the white should have been, there was nothing but inky blackness. Even her voice had a dull, hollow tone to it.

"Stand aside, orc!" she yelled to Elbaf.

Darko studied her, his keen eyes following her off hand, which reached into a pouch at her belt. Though observers often assumed his senses were as frail as his health, they were in fact far keener than any man alive. His vision in particular was flawless and his elven heritage made picking out her movements child's play.

She drew something from within the pouch: a small, cylindrical piece of chalk, black as charcoal. Darko didn't need half the knowledge he had to know it was an item of magical nature - the tiny object fairly radiated power - but it was unlike anything he'd ever seen before.

"Move," Annabelle roared again at Elbaf, who still barred the door.

With a frustrated growl, the warrior leapt from the doorway, landing at the bottom of the stairs almost ten feet away and whirling to face the flood of undead that poured forth through the now unmanned door.

Darko caught sight of Annabelle's hand tightening and time seemed to slow. The monsters at the top of the stairs surged forward just as his ears picked up the sharp *snap* of the stick of chalk.

A sudden and complete stillness swallowed them.

It lasted only a fraction of a second, less time than it took to blink, and was followed by an all-consuming roar. Thick black smoke poured from Annabelle's closed fist, swirling around her and then bursting forth in a thick wave toward the manor. It engulfed the oncoming enemies, and Darko saw it shred them down to dust as it rolled over them.

But it didn't stop there - it swept out to engulf the whole of the manor, roaring over the structure like a tidal wave. The smoke coiled around the building like a great black serpent, wrapping it in thick banks of smoke, each spinning and rolling until the whole of the structure was buried beneath the boiling clouds. For several minutes the group looked on as the magic silently wrought its devastation. Stone was torn from stone, wood from wood, and all turned to dust in total, incomprehensible silence.

Darko gaped in awe as the cloud finally settled, revealing only a raw pit in the ground where the wine cellar had once sat. No trace of the manor remained, save the bare earth where it had been. Even the stones of the cellar were gone, replaced with wind-blasted dirt and ash.

Silence fell. What could there be to say in the face of such power?

After a moment, Annabelle turned to face the group.

"Any man who breathes even a single word of this will be executed on the spot. Am I understood?"

The group nodded in unison.

"You four, over here."

She strode away, coming to a halt some ten paces distant from the rest of the group, and turned to the officers.

"I need not tell you that this is highly . . . irregular."

They said nothing.

"I must speak with the commander and with the order back in the Capitol." She paused, hesitating a moment. "You are to take your men back to the main road and follow the signs towards Bethlir. In light of the . . . *gravity* of this discovery, the Brazen Hawks will be proceeding at half pace until you rejoin us. I will report the happenings here to Commander Madrie, and *you* will ensure the silence of these men - and yourselves."

Chapter Six

Silence hung like a heavy cloak over the hours following Annabelle's departure. They'd rejoined their scouts outside the gate to a flurry of questions - but none among them dared answer. Talia alone spoke to them, and then only to instruct them solemnly that they were to forget anything they *thought* they knew - anything they might have heard or seen. But the empty saddles of the last four horses of their train were a sharp reminder that no matter how hard they might pretend, the events at the manor had indeed taken place.

They departed immediately afterward.

There were no graves, no prayers aloud for the dead to carry with them on their path to the Undying Battlefield. It sat poorly with the group, but especially so with Elbaf.

"Talia."

She looked up at his gruff voice, her eyes bloodshot and nervous.

"Will we not honor our fallen?"

She turned back to the road, her face stony.

"You know as well as I the price of disobedience," she said as she reached a hand up to her throat, rubbing it self consciously.

Elbaf's thoughts turned to the first time they'd seen the power of their mark exercised, and he tried to suppress a shudder. They'd been fresh into their training cycle, four, maybe five days at the time. In the wake of the horrors of the day, his tired mind wandered freely into the past.

"Recruit, you will obey my orders," the instructor screamed, pulling a short black baton from his belt.

Colton ignored him, his broad back to the instructor and his focus entirely upon the man he was straddling. He raised a fist and brought it crashing down on Errol's already brutalized face. Bones cracked and blood sprayed from the unconscious man's mouth and nose, but still Colton pummelled him.

The instructor wrapped the baton around Colton's throat, locking it in place with an elbow and trying to pry him off of the much smaller man.

But Colton was a monster of a human, bigger than Elbaf by a head - and at least sixty pounds. He pulled the instructor's grip loose as though he were wrestling a child, and tossed him like a plaything to land several feet away.

"Enough," the instructor cried out, struggling to his feet. *"Stand down!"*

Colton continued his onslaught, ignoring the instructor's command outright. Another blow landed, then another. Elbaf saw that they had drawn the attention of one of the senior instructors, a priestess who was looking down on them from the hill at the western edge of the training yard some sixty yards away. She turned to face them and he watched as she raised a hand, pointing it menacingly at Colton.

Colton froze.

He clawed at his throat, a gurgling, high-pitched scream escaping his lips as smoke started to curl from the black band around his neck.

Aside from his agony-filled screams, the training yard fell silent as instructors and trainees alike all fixed their gaze upon the dying man. The skin of his neck, then his face, and then finally his whole scalp started to blacken from within. He clawed at his own flesh until it bled, screaming as the meat and skin slagged off in chunks beneath his fingers. In short order he fell silent and keeled over, but the smell of burning meat lingered, sizzling and popping until all that remained of the man's head was a charred skull.

"Such is the price of disobedience," the instructor growled, eyeing the trainees. "Now back to work!"

"Road's clear ahead."

Arcus' words pulled Elbaf from his daydream with a start, and he had a hand on his sword before he knew it.

"Steady, friend," Arcus raised his empty hands in the shadowy darkness.

Elbaf let his breath out slowly. He was still on edge, still struggling internally to work his way through what he had seen. He looked over at Talia, who was staring off into the blackness as they rode side by side.

"Even so," he grumbled aloud, returning to the matter at hand. "It is cowardice."

Arcus quirked up an eyebrow, while Talia reacted more strongly, her face turning red as she turned to face him.

"I will not be accused of cowardice, not after--" she cut herself short and glared at him before snapping her reins and trotting ahead of them, closer to the front of their small band.

"Dare I ask?" Arcus said softly, matching his horse's pace to Elbaf's.

"Do you need to?"

Arcus didn't respond, other than to tilt his head knowingly to the side.

"We spilled blood with those men," Elbaf growled, mostly to himself. "And we are to ignore their sacrifice? For what? For our own safety?"

"Elbaf . . ." Arcus tried in vain to placate the warrior as his voice started to rise.

"To the hells with our safety, to the hells with the convenience of the Empire." He gestured to the men following them before continuing. "These men know what happened, so what harm is done if we acknowledge our dead?"

His question hung in the air, and though none answered it, Arcus could see the steel in the mens' eyes glinting in the torchlight as they rode.

They shared his rage.

A sharp whistle from Talia at the fore put a halt to any further discussion. Elbaf glowered at her hand signal, an indication that she wanted to pick up the pace, but spurred his horse forward nonetheless.

They rode for hours in relative silence. Midnight came and went, the stars and the twin moons wheeled slowly across the skies above them until, at long last, Talia signaled from the front that they should slow. The horses' sides heaved, their breath thick and foggy in the chill of the morning.

Talia allowed herself to fall back towards the middle of the column, eyeing her fellow officers.

"We'll camp here, three hours and *no* fires."

Elbaf looked over their exhausted men. They'd been awake for almost an entire day and had fought for their lives in that time.

"Talia, these men need more than twelve candlemarks' rest."

She looked ready to argue, but Elbaf's conviction matched her own. She backed down, her sturdy facade crumbling a little in the shadows. He saw at last the pain behind the anger, the guilt. Elbaf wondered if Talia knew he could see clearly in the darkness, or if she thought her silent tears were hidden from him.

"Men," he announced with loud, clear authority. "Circle up. We've five hours to rest. Make the most of it."

The men breathed heavy sighs of relief as they dismounted and began to unpack rations, bedrolls, and other amenities.

"No fires," he announced to scattered groans. "Derrin, Tomlin, you've the first watch with me."

"Elbaf," Talia began, her voice soft and cracking.

"Rest, Talia."

She nodded, then rode off for the far edge of the camp to see to her own sleeping arrangements.

"She's in a good deal of pain," Arcus sighed, just barely above a whisper.

Elbaf shared a look with him, no words needing to be spoken.

"You should rest as well, ranger."

Arcus' rueful smile did not go unnoticed, but Elbaf chose to ignore it as he dismounted and set out his bedroll. He pulled a waterskin and some jerked meat from his saddlebags and made his way to the perimeter, his eyes scanning the dark forest surrounding them.

Hours later, Arcus was awoken by a gentle nudge at his booted foot. He snapped his eyes open and, aided by the moonlight, made out Elbaf's shadowy outline.

"Your shift, friend," the orc said simply before turning and walking off towards his bedding.

"Good morn' to you as well," Arcus grumbled in response.

With a groan, he rolled to his feet and stretched out the kinks in his back. He'd slept in his armor, but the supple leather didn't bother him much. He'd spent many a tundra night sleeping in leather during a hunt; sometimes to keep warm, other times to better defend himself from the nocturnal threats of the frozen wastes.

He could see that Tomlin and Derrin were already asleep and that Elbaf was now waking Garland and Merryl. Arcus scooped up his saber and buckled it around his waist, then grabbed his longbow and quiver. With the weapon slung comfortably, he went to meet his men.

"Good morning," Arcus greeted them softly.

The two men saluted but he waved them off.

"Take your ease, men. There's no need to stand on ceremony at this hour."

He looked around the camp, listening to the soft snores of the soldiers. He could feel Kodja's presence just inside the trees. His was a strong, warm heartbeat amid the sea of life that teemed around them.

"You two can stay within the confines of the camp. I'll take the perimeter."

They nodded, and he slipped out into the trees.

Kodja was there in an instant, settling into a slow walk beside him, rubbing his shoulder against Arcus' thigh. Arcus reached down and gave the wolf some well-deserved attention, rubbing through his coarse, thick fur and scratching his neck, ears, and back.

"I know, friend. I missed you, too."

It was true. For months traveling west the wolf had been his only companion, and now he tended to linger about in the shadows, unwilling to trust the company of so many strangers. He cursed, not for the first time, the insular and intolerant nature of the Empire. He'd learned many hard lessons in his years, but perhaps the hardest had been finding out that his entire way of life was condemned as savage, uncivilized, and barbaric. More and more he was coming to realize that the Empire was not the kind and gentle light he'd always heard, at least not for everyone.

Kodja could sense his unease and whined softly in agreement.

He looked down, lamenting that they'd ever left the snow and ice of their homeland. But now they had a new tribe, a pack beyond themselves, and more than the cursed mark upon his neck to hold Arcus here.

The pair settled into an easy silence as they prowled the woods. It was unlikely that anything would surprise them - Arcus could feel the lives of the creatures they passed, and the forest knew him as a friend. He allowed his mind to unfocus and turned outward into the great web of life that surrounded them. He traced the veins of the leaves in the trees, felt the breath of the grass, breathed deeply the smell of moss and dew. A nearby stag, alerted to his presence, raised its head in alarm. The majestic creature eyed him cautiously, instincts at war as it studied him.

Arcus reached out with his mind, using the subtle magic of his craft to calm the animal. The energy that normally flowed so freely between his heart, his mind, and the natural world was sluggish and clumsy. It took more effort than it should have, considerably so. Nonetheless, he pushed harder and felt the stag's heartbeat slow as it finally relaxed.

He wondered if Talia or Darko experienced similar difficulty with their magic. If they had, they'd made no mention of it. He needn't wonder the cause, that much at least was as clear as a midsummer sky to him. He could feel the presence of the mark on himself and the others. It clung to them like the smell of some long-dead fire. But not the clean ash of a wildfire, no. It was an acrid, *unnatural*, haze that clouded everything around him.

He resolved to ask with the coming of the dawn. Certainly it was not worth disturbing their slumber, but in light of the recent events, it did perhaps bear mentioning.

Their watch passed swiftly, the two hunters sharing the comfortable quiet of fast friends. Before long, dawn kissed the sky with the first hints of daybreak and Arcus made his way back to the camp. Restless minds lead to restless feet, at least in Arcus' case, and he found that they'd ranged far and wide, covering several miles during the two hours of watch that they shared.

They parted ways at the edge of camp, Kodja returning to the greenery while Arcus strolled into camp just as Merryl and Garland were starting to wake the rest of the group.

He gave the soldiers a silent wave, which they returned. Arcus left them to continue their duties as he headed to his sleeping area and packed up the few items he'd pulled loose the night before.

"How was your shift, ranger?"

Arcus was surprised at Elbaf's approach. In the time they'd known each other it was rare that the towering half-orc began a conversation freely.

"It was quiet. Yours?"

Elbaf grunted, a much more expected response. After an awkward pause, he turned to leave.

Arcus sensed hesitation in the warrior and chose to extend an olive branch.

"Elbaf?"

He turned his head to look back at Arcus.

"The events of yesterday . . ." Arcus shook his head softly. "They sit poorly with me."

Elbaf looked him over silently, and Arcus wondered at his thoughts.

"With me as well, Arcus," he finally agreed. "But the cleric is correct - what recourse do we have?"

"Perhaps none, but let it be said that I dislike it. I would have my dissidence known."

Elbaf agreed, but he was not so willing to wear his discontent on his sleeve.

"We have a duty, Arcus," he said simply.

"A duty to *whom*, Elbaf?" Arcus pressed. "To these men perhaps, to ourselves. But to the Empire? I disagree."

"Then let it be a duty to ourselves and our men," Elbaf snapped. "I see no one else who would care for their lives, do you?"

Arcus let out a frustrated sigh.

"Perhaps not, but you must agree that there are foul forces at play here."

Elbaf's lips drew a hard line.

"I saw the dead walk as well as you did, ranger. I need no lecture on foul forces."

"No," Arcus continued. "Not just those abominations. These marks upon our throats, they reek of the same fell magics at work at the manor."

"Neither Talia nor the elf have made mention of this. Perhaps you are mistaken?"

"Perhaps I'm not," Arcus mumbled, allowing doubt to creep into his mind. "Perhaps *they* simply have yet to speak of it."

"And why shouldn't they have said anything?"

Arcus had no answer for that either, and he chewed his lip in frustrated silence.

"I know only what I feel, Elbaf, and this I feel more strongly than any warning my heart has ever given."

"Do not mistake my obedience for contentedness, friend," Elbaf surprised him with a slow nod. "I have my own doubts, as well."

Arcus felt his hope renewed.

"But we are bound, not simply by the honor of our words, but by the lives of these men and, as you have rightly mentioned, the enchantment we wear."

Arcus pondered the warrior's words and was forced to agree.

Elbaf shrugged, expressing their mutual frustration with the simple gesture, then turned and walked away.

"Morning, Talia," Elbaf greeted the cleric as pleasantly as he could muster.

"Good morning," she replied with a yawn.

He was pleased to see that she'd gotten some rest. Her eyes were less tired, less anxious, and though he could see the evidence that she'd been crying throughout the night, he sensed she'd regained some of her strength and composure.

"The men will be ready inside a candlemark," he said simply. "I believe at the pace we maintained overnight we should be able to catch up with the rest of the company by nightfall."

He contemplated saying something further - perhaps something to put her guilt at ease - but he struggled to find the words. Instead, with his report concluded, he turned to make his way back to his horse.

"Elbaf, wait," Talia called softly after him.

Twice in one morning. You've gone soft.

"Yes, ma'am?"

Talia, now on her feet, rolled her eyes and stepped in close, wrapping him in a bear hug.

"I'm sorry, Elbaf," her voice cracked, and Elbaf could tell she was in danger of breaking again. "I'm sorry. I . . . I just don't--"

He wrapped her in his arms and squeezed, perhaps not as gently as he'd intended because he cut her sentence short. The hug lengthened and his discomfort deepened. With a firm pat on her back he turned her loose.

"I have faith in you, ma'am." He looked deep into her eyes. "Truly. As do we all."

He could tell she didn't know what else to say, yet she straightened her back with newfound strength and nodded firmly.

"Men!" he roared, turning to the troops. "You'll be out of this clearing before the sun clears the woodline or there'll be hell to pay."

The sleepy grumbling in the clearing quieted, and the men set their hands and minds to the task of packing their gear. Whether from their own military discipline or Elbaf's not-so-idle threat, they were indeed ready to depart in short order.

Elbaf, the last to mount his horse, took one last look at the assembled troops then smoothly lifted himself into the saddle. He gave Talia a salute and a reassuring nod.

"Move out!"

They rode in silence as dawn broke over the quiet forest. It was not the uneasy void of the day before, but rather the comfortable silence that follows a thunderstorm. Their bond was tested, but unbroken.

"Talia," Elbaf broke the rhythm of hoofbeats finally. "There's nothing you could have done at the manor. What we faced was a power far beyond us."

She shook her head sadly.

"You're wrong. I could have waited, I could have trusted the mage," Talia sighed heavily. "I could have *listened* to my doubts, trusted them instead of dismissing them as weakness."

Elbaf nodded sagely, all too familiar with the burden of doubt.

"Did you do as well as you could with what information you had?"

She raised an eyebrow at him.

"Did you believe you were making the right decision at the time?" he rephrased.

"I suppose, yes. Why?"

Elbaf searched her eyes, finding only truth there.

"Then you could have done no more. Our duty now is to honor the fallen and to see to the living."

She opened her mouth to argue with him but reconsidered, allowing them to fall back into mutual introspection once again.

The easy creaking of leather and hoofbeats were their only company as the troop logged mile after mile. Elbaf kept a weather eye on the men, watching them for signs of stress and disorder. He'd been in many fights, some of them lethal, but he had to admit he was still rattled by what had taken place at the estate the night before.

Even now his skin crawled and his heartbeat quickened as he recounted the events internally. The smell of rot and decay, the pallid, crumbling flesh of the monstrosities that had assaulted them, and the coppery tang of blood and death.

The devastation of Annabelle's sorcery.

He willed himself to relax - he could not allow his men to see his weakness.

He pushed down the memories of the battle, locking them away far from the light. Elbaf cast around for a distraction instead, finding one in Arcus and Darko. They made an unlikely pair, but they rode together at the head of the column engaged in what appeared to be a spirited debate.

"No," Darko sighed condescendingly. "You misunderstand. The nature of magic is *finite*, it follows strict rules and adheres to basic, fundamental principles."

Arcus rubbed his temple.

"That's not what I'm asking," he retorted for the umpteenth time. "I'm asking you if this damned mark is interfering with *your* magic."

Darko stared blankly back at him.

"I'm not explaining this well," he searched for the words to describe his feelings. "It's as if . . . as if all the magic and the majesty of the world is somehow *muted*. As though where once I felt the vastness of the seas, I stand now before a lake."

"Majesty of nature? Lakes and seas? Muted?" Darko sputtered. "Well it's no wonder you're struggling with your magic - you've got the whole thing . . . *wrong*! This mark is just another *form* of magic, and a simple one at that. See, this is just more evidence that careful study and practice will always outperform ritual and superstition."

Arcus bristled.

"There are no *forms* of magic," Arcus replied acidly. "There is only *magic*. It exists independently of either of us. It simply is."

"Nonsense," Darko scoffed.

"You believe yourself a Master of the arcane," Arcus scolded the much older mage. "But though you command some small measure of power, you wield it clumsily. You try to *force* your will upon every situation, believing any problem can be overcome by sheer stubbornness when the truth is so much deeper."

"A bold hypothesis, ranger," Darko laughed. "But where is your evidence?"

Arcus allowed himself a token of vengeance as he extended his mind to that of Darko's horse. The creature's thoughts were beautiful, but simple. His own spirit greeted that of the horse, and for a moment their lives linked.

Darko was left cursing as his mount suddenly froze, refusing to take even a single step further.

"Perhaps your magic will assist you, mage," Arcus taunted as the distance between them grew.

"Very well," Darko replied tersely, his face a deepening red.

The wizard rubbed his hands together and with a muttered word a thin tendril of smoke rolled from his fingers to the nostrils of his steed.

The horse's eyes opened wide with fear and it bucked and kicked immediately. The elf was thrown unceremoniously from the animal's back as it bolted down the path.

Arcus intercepted it, calming the creature enough to bring it back under control before grabbing ahold of the reins and heading back to his friend.

"Are you alright, wizard?" he called out with genuine concern.

"*I'm fine*," Darko yelled back at the top of his lungs. "And as you can see, the damned creature *did* move."

Arcus roared with laughter until a sharp, piercing whistle brought him to heel. He looked sheepishly at Talia, who was glaring at both of them.

"Ranger," she called. "A word?"

Embarrassment reddened his cheeks, but he made no pains to hide his smile as he rode back past Darko, handing off the reins of his wayward mount as he did so.

"Careful, mage," he winked. "These animals can be difficult to handle."

"Arcus!"

"Yes, ma'am. I'm coming," he relented.

"*Why* are you torturing that old man?"

Arcus' smile faded a little as he was brought back to the seriousness of the conversation they'd been having.

"Actually, Talia, we were discussing a matter of some urgency," Arcus replied. "Something I'd like to speak with you about as well."

She looked unconvinced, but gave no argument.

"And if he wasn't so damn stubborn, I would have--"

"Arcus," Talia warned.

"Alright, Talia. Alright." Arcus raised a hand to ward off her angry glare. "I need to ask you a rather personal question . . ."

She scowled at him.

"It's just . . . have you had any, er, *difficulty* concerning your magic since we were branded?"

"What do you mean, difficulty?"

"I've tried to explain it to Darko as well," Arcus began. "But that elf--"

"Arcus, your point, please?"

"Right," the ranger sighed. "Essentially, my connection to the natural world feels . . . suppressed. It's distant and faint where it should be strong and vibrant."

She seemed to mull over his words carefully.

"And for this you blame the mark," she shook her head softly. "I'm sorry, Arcus, but I feel no such interference. It feels to me much the same as any other work of the clergy."

"Well, then perhaps the clergy is the problem," Arcus grumbled irritably.

"That's a poor way to solicit my assistance," Talia rebuked him.

"I'm sorry, Talia. I'm uneasy with this state of affairs." He gauged her reaction to his words before continuing. "We did nothing wrong, so why have we been pressed into servitude for a cause that is not our own? Where is the merciful Emperor of legend and lore? Why are we held on pain of death to . . . to *slavery*?"

"We are simple mortals, Arcus," Talia said in a conciliatory tone. "It is not our place to question the will of a god."

Arcus could tell he was getting nowhere, but couldn't resist the urge to try once more.

"Talia, please. I know in my heart that the magic that binds us is not what it seems. I can *feel* how . . . how unnatural it is. May I be frank?"

She nodded.

"It reminds me in no small way of the forces we encountered at the manor."

"You stray too far, Arcus," she glared at him. "Your accusation is as bold as it is unfounded. Or do you truly think so little of my own power that I would not recognize the work of the Emperor were it directly in front of me?"

Arcus sighed, defeated.

"Very well, Talia. Have it your way."

Any further discussion was cut off as the group rounded a curve in the path and found themselves suddenly and unexpectedly in the midst of the rest of the Brazen Hawks.

Talia shared a confused look with her lieutenants - she hadn't expected to catch the rest of the company until nightfall. Her men greeted their comrades while she flagged down Darko and Elbaf to join Arcus and herself as they headed off in search of Major Von Cleigh.

It did not take long to find not only Madrie, but Annabelle, as well. The two were dismounted, both poring over a map and accompanied by a nondescript older man. His clothes were shabby, but well-cared for.

As Talia dismounted and reported with a salute, she noticed a pack mule nearby with the various tools and sundries of a tinker.

"Ah, good of you four to join us," Madrie greeted them warmly. "Come on over. We're just discussing what might shape up to be quite a sporting adventure."

"Ma'am?"

She waved them over, and the group huddled around the map. Talia was more than a little surprised at Madrie's good spirits given the seriousness of their encounter two nights prior, but she knew better than to bring it up in this setting.

"This fellow was just telling us there's *goblin* activity in the area. Isn't that right?"

The man appeared deeply uncomfortable surrounded by so many soldiers, and he gave a funny little bow before speaking.

"Y-yes, m'lady. Tha's right," he wrung a worn leather cap in his hands as he spoke. "They hasn't caused no trouble yet, but we all just stay out tha' way, yeah?"

"One does not allow rats to breed merely because they've yet to cause problems," Annabelle interrupted acidly. "An infestation is an infestation, and it needs to be dealt with." She cast a brief, demeaning look in Elbaf's direction before continuing.

"Goblinkin are notoriously villainous." She raised her chin. "They're too dangerous to leave alone."

"Too right," Madrie agreed. "We'll exterminate them."

She looked at Talia, sizing her up, before adding, "Captain, you'll organize the offensive."

"Ma'am, I'm not sure that I--"

"Are you an imperial officer or aren't you?" Madrie scolded her. "You're better off learning here than when you are pitted against a *real* threat. I want a brief in an hour. Four candlemarks should be more than enough time for something this simple."

Finished with the conversation, she turned back to the tinker.

"You're free to go. And the Empire thanks you," she said as she clapped him on the back and set a golden sovereign in his hand.

"M-m-may the sun never set upon his reign," the man stammered.

With that, Madrie took her leave, handing Talia the map and indicating that Annabelle should follow her.

"One hour," Annabelle warned as she turned to follow the commander.

The four junior officers were left staring at each other as the impromptu huddle dissolved.

"I'm sorry." Darko blinked in confusion. "*What* exactly is our task?"

"Right, ah . . ." Talia tried to organize her thoughts. "There's a goblin fort? Outpost? Some kind of goblin encampment that the commander wants cleared out."

"*Exterminated,*" Elbaf growled, his displeasure evident in his face.

Talia cast him an apologetic look.

"Right, exterminated," she continued. "And we, well *I,* am tasked with providing the commander with our plan to do so within the next hour."

Elbaf, perhaps sensing her hesitation, held his hand out for the map.

She passed it to him and he unrolled it for them to inspect once more. The target, presumably, was indicated by a rough circle drawn in charcoal around a section of forest just off the main road about two miles from their current location. Elbaf and Arcus both seemed to read the dense contour lines and terrain markings of the map easily, speaking to each other almost in code as they worked out a plan before her eyes.

"Right," Elbaf said with a note of finality.

"Agreed," Arcus replied.

"Perhaps you'd like to include me?" Talia asked with exasperation.

"Sorry, Talia, you're right," Arcus began, suitably chastised. "So, we recommend a three-pronged attack, with two prongs serving to drive the goblin forces back and into the waiting arms of the third, which will be here where the road is nearest . . ."

She nodded along as he laid out the plan.

"Ok, but why don't we leave the rest of the archers with the group on the road," she said, indicating a point on the map with her finger. "If the goblins break as quickly as we suspect, we want to make sure they aren't overrun."

"That's a very fair point," Arcus nodded in agreement. "I must say though, I don't envy your conversation with the commander and the ice queen."

Talia let slip an exaggerated eye roll.

"You jest," Talia complained. "But I *really* don't think she likes me."

"Don't worry, Talia. She'll never like you less than me," Elbaf quipped. "That being said, she'll like you less if you're late."

"Right," Talia sighed, rolling the map back up. "Emperor, grant me grace."

Talia stepped off lightly, rehearsing what she'd say in her mind. She felt confident in their plan, but was nonetheless worried that Annabelle would find some reason to belittle her in front of their commander. She wove her way in between men, mounts, and gear until she reached the dome of Madrie's command tent.

"Ma'am, Captain Lorraine reporting as ordered." Talia stood at attention awaiting a response.

Annabelle poked her head out from the fabric of the tent door and waved Talia inside. Madrie was poring over a long roll of parchment, packed margin to margin with dense, neat writing, so Talia waited silently next to her fellow captain. The only other occupant of the tent was an imperial messenger, still breathing hard from his latest delivery. His blue and white tunic and matching leather satchel heaved in time with his labored breaths, but he was otherwise as still and silent as they were.

"Very well," Madrie mumbled as she scrawled a reply at the bottom of the paper. "We'll tend to this next. Please inform Mater Superia Vandrace that I will make this a top priority."

She rolled the parchment back up and handed it to the messenger, who tucked it away in his satchel and promptly exited.

"Now, Soror Talia, let us hear what you have prepared," she said, turning to sit in a small folding chair next to her field desk and indicating that Talia and Annabelle should do the same.

Talia took the liberty of rolling the map out on her desk, but preferred to stand while speaking.

"Ma'am," she began, clearing her throat a little and ensuring that she spoke clearly and with conviction. "We believe the best course of action is to force the goblins into a disorderly retreat. Our initial assault *here* and *here* will drive them back into an ambush *here* where the road is closest to the encampment. They'll take what they perceive as the path of least resistance and find imperial archers instead."

"Annabelle?" Madrie took a questioning tone, inviting her executive officer to speak.

Annabelle shook her head disapprovingly.

"I don't like it. Who's to say the goblins will even break their lines? You would have us commit a third of our men and the bulk of our ranged forces on a bet. We should be mounting a full frontal assault. I--"

"I disagree," Madrie cut her off. "I've fought plenty of goblin-folk and the one thing they have in abundance is cowardice. They'll break alright, and this will ensure they do not slip through our fingers to haunt this land another day."

"But *ma'am*, the risk is--"

"Less than the risk of letting these vermin creep away and go off into the wilderness," Madrie retorted, allowing an edge to her voice. "And I've made my decision."

Madrie stood, took one last look at the map, then nodded to herself in satisfaction.

"It's a good plan." She put a hand on Talia's shoulder and gave it a reassuring squeeze. "Now, see it done. You have command of the company for this operation."

Madrie headed for the door while Talia beamed at her superior's praise, then rushed to speak before Madrie left the tent.

"Ma'am, I'm sorry to linger," she began apologetically. "I wondered if I should debrief you on the details of the incident at the Altimeer Estate?"

Surprised, Madrie glanced over at Annabelle, who was as unreadable as a porcelain doll.

"Captain Montagne already briefed me, unless you have pertinent details I should be aware of?"

"Not to worry, ma'am," Annabelle interjected. "You've been apprised of the facts. I'll ensure that Captain Lorraine files her own report in a timely manner."

"Excellent," Madrie nodded before leaving the tent.

Annabelle rounded on Talia with all the ferocity of a striking serpent.

"How *dare* you," she hissed, jabbing a finger into Talia's chest with a startling amount of force. "How dare you seek to undermine me in front of our commander?"

"I-I-I'm sorr--"

"There is a chain of command, and you would do well to remember your place in that chain," Annabelle continued, unrelenting. "You were, and still are, under strict orders to speak of this to *no one*. It is *my* responsibility to apprise our commander, as it is yours to apprise *me*. Is that understood?"

Talia kept her mouth shut and nodded silently.

"Good. If you'd like to file a report you may do so with me, and given the sensitivity of that report I recommend you do so verbally and *only* verbally. Now, did you have something you'd like to say?"

Talia shook her head.

"I expect an answer."

"No, ma'am," Talia all but whispered.

"Good," Annabelle snapped, turning on her heel and heading out the tent door.

Chapter Seven

"Are you alright?" Arcus raised his eyebrows as his question went unanswered.

Instead, Talia flicked her head, indicating that he should follow her. He took note of her hurried gait, her flushed cheeks, and the thin, angry line of her lips and surmised that her meeting had not gone well. However, he decided not to press for information, opting to simply follow her as she rounded up Elbaf and Darko.

Once the four of them were together, she spoke at last.

"Right, our plan is approved."

Arcus hid his confusion. Why was she so on edge if their plan had been approved?

"With no . . . changes?" he probed gently.

"Correct," Talia snapped.

"Too easy," Elbaf said with a shrug. "When do we move, ma'am?"

"Immediately, gather the men. Take the group that traveled with us these past two days and select another ten, plus the archers in fourth squad. Split the rest in two, they'll form the pincers."

Elbaf saluted and turned on his heel, already bellowing out orders to their soldiers.

Arcus waited, hoping to have a moment alone with the woman, but Darko lingered as well.

"Will I play a role in this operation, ma'am?" the mage asked snidely. "Or am I to tend to the camp? I know our glorious leaders have little respect for my gifts."

Talia was not amused.

"You'll be with us, where I'm sure you'll have plenty of opportunities to utilize your gifts," she turned to walk away, but paused. "And you would do well to monitor your tone when there are so many ears nearby that are less friendly than ours."

Darko let out a long, exasperated sigh and gave her a half-hearted salute before heading off.

"Talia," Arcus kept pace with her as she walked away. "What's wrong?"

He could see her cheeks redden more, and for a moment he worried that he'd done something to offend her.

"It's Annabelle . . ." she finally muttered, her voice as low as she could make it. "I'm starting to think that . . . Ugh, I don't know."

He tried to read her face. He could tell she was wrestling with herself, but over what exactly?

"She's . . . she's my superior and she enjoys reminding me of my place, that's all." She changed subjects abruptly, a clear indicator that she was done discussing the other woman. "Let's focus on the task at hand. Emperor willing, we can be done with this quickly."

Arcus saluted and slowed his pace, letting the distance between them grow.

He watched as she disappeared within the tents and wagons of the camp.

He turned at last to make his way toward his own gear. His eyes caught on a dark shadow, and it took a great deal of discipline not to react. Annabelle, far across the camp and sitting proudly atop a massive, coal-black warhorse, was staring at him with open contempt.

No, he realized a moment later. Not at him, but at Talia.

He felt a chill cross his heart, and goosebumps raised the hairs on his arms as he watched the woman in the corner of his eye. He'd seen that look on the faces of hungry tundra cats as they prepared to strike, and for the first time in many years, he experienced the fleeting dread of a prey animal in the sights of a predator.

He turned away with a shudder, determined to watch her more carefully.

He hurried to retrieve his gear, lest the group be left waiting on him, and was a little surprised to see Elbaf standing by their horses waiting for him.

"How's Talia?" the orc asked, his tone serious. "She looked . . . frustrated."

"She is." Arcus cast a glance back over his shoulder before continuing, but Annabelle had moved on. "And I don't blame her. I think it's Annabelle. She watches her with such . . . such *disdain*."

"Some leaders are good, others bad." Elbaf shrugged with helpless frustration. "In time we'll no doubt be reassigned. Until then, we'll do what we must."

"I suppose you're right, but I must admit that the woman unnerves me."

Elbaf raised an eyebrow at him in surprise.

"You fear her."

"No, I just--"

"That wasn't a question, ranger," Elbaf shook his head. "I can smell it on you. It is faint, but I am not mistaken."

Arcus' cheeks flushed red, his temper flaring with embarrassment.

"I am *not* afraid of her, I just don't trust her."

Elbaf's stare was piercing, and not for the first time Arcus wondered at the depth behind the soldier's eyes. A long moment passed before he spoke again.

"You *do*," he said slowly, but without judgment. "There is no shame in this. I am surprised, but I trust your judgment. We will keep a closer eye on her."

Arcus was torn between insult and agreement. He was finally forced to admit to himself that he *was* afraid, but he didn't resent Elbaf any less for the accusation. He wrestled internally with his pride as he gathered his longbow and quiver and strapped his sword to his waist.

He looked over at his companion who seemed content to wait stoically while Arcus made himself ready for the coming battle.

"Can you really smell fear?" Arcus asked, breaking the silence.

Elbaf nodded.

"What . . . what does it smell like?"

Elbaf turned contemplative, visibly weighing his words.

"It has a sharpness to it, like . . . like vinegar, I suppose."

"And it always smells the same?"

"No," Elbaf shook his head again. "The stronger it is felt, the *hotter* it smells. Does that make sense? It's as though someone is boiling a pot of vinegar for pickling."

"Pickling," Arcus repeated as he tried, and failed, to keep the surprised amusement out of his voice.

Elbaf's brow furrowed with irritation, and his cheeks flushed a deep purplish-green.

"Yes, pickling," he growled. "Mock me if you must, but it was your question I answered."

"Elbaf, wait. I'm sorry. I wasn't laughing at you--"

But the warrior was already stomping away, his shoulders squared.

Arcus snatched up the last of his things then trotted after his friend. Catching up to him, he put a hand on the armored shoulder of the man, garnering himself an annoyed look.

"I'm sorry, I meant no offense. I was merely caught off-guard."

Elbaf huffed a neutral response, but his posture softened.

Elbaf kicked himself internally for choosing such an unusual comparison, but allowed his usual gruff demeanor to cover his self-recrimination. He knew the ranger well enough by now not to be offended, but he couldn't help his embarrassment. He reassured himself with the knowledge that the arena of words would soon give way to his true home - the battlefield.

The pair made their way to the milling mass of waiting troops. Their men, as he had come to identify the troops who'd been at the manor with them, mingled with other members of the company as they awaited instructions. The disordered gaggle frustrated him - it looked sloppy and unprofessional.

"Form it up," he shouted as he drew near. "You look like school children at play, not soldiers preparing to fight!"

The company formed immediately into ranks and turned their collective attention to him. Elbaf looked to Talia, who indicated with a nod that he could go ahead and brief the waiting soldiers. He did so, laying out the operation in clear, simple terms. With his guidance given, he turned control of the two pincer elements over to their respective team leaders and instructed his own men to stand by.

"We're ready, ma'am," he informed Talia.

"Alright, move 'em out."

He saluted, then turned and bellowed the order to the men. The column started off, heading down the road as opposed to following the other two groups into the woods. As they shuffled off, Elbaf maneuvered his way nearer to Talia.

"Ma'am," he greeted her again with what he hoped was a friendly nod.

Either he misjudged the gesture or she was in as foul a mood as Arcus had suggested because she simply nodded in response, her brows furrowed in thought.

Say something.

He was no wordsmith, and it frustrated him that he wasn't sure how to approach the girl. He sensed that she needed reassurance, that something significant weighed upon her, but how was he, of all people, to help her resolve it? No, better that he simply support her from a distance and wait for her to come to terms as she always did.

They kept a good pace and, just shy of two candlemarks later, Arcus was flagging them down from the head of the train. Elbaf glanced around skeptically. Aside from a sparseness to the trees, the woodland surrounding the road looked much the same as it had the whole half hour they were traveling.

"You're sure this is the place, Arcus?" he asked the ranger as they approached.

"I'm sure, Elbaf. The goblin camp is to the northeast of us, and if they break and run this'll be where they come first." The druid nodded to himself, scanning the brush before continuing, "Just there," he indicated a stretch of trees on one side of the road. "Just past that stand of birch, the ground slopes up on either side. Two hills form a bit of a valley a few hundred feet from here which runs all the way to their camp. They'll follow the contours of the ground, and that will lead them here."

"How could you possibly tell all of that? From . . . *this*?" Talia wondered aloud, clearly mystified.

Elbaf, too, was curious. The level of detail was astonishing. Arcus hadn't left their party to scout the area himself, and the map they'd looked at earlier hadn't provided enough context to determine their location that precisely - at least not to him.

Arcus looked bemusedly at the pair of them, then opened his mouth to speak.

"It's rather obvious, I would think," Darko interrupted from behind them. "He's communicating with the forests, I imagine."

Arcus' smile faded as the mage stole the wind from his sails.

"Thank you, wizard," he managed through gritted teeth. "I was incapable of explaining it myself."

"Interesting," the mage mused aloud. "I thought you were having trouble with your magic, or has that issue resolved itself?"

Elbaf watched Arcus' face turn scarlet and his jaw tighten with anger. As amusing as it would be to watch the two of them bicker, they hadn't the time. Although he was troubled by the mage's words, now was not the time or place to speak with Arcus about it.

"We need to organize the defense," he interrupted bluntly. "Darko, you will be with the archers, ready to strike from afar."

Darko glowered at him, mumbling beneath his breath, but did not object.

"Arcus, Talia, will you join me at the fore?"

They both nodded in agreement.

"Excellent," Elbaf concluded with a note of finality.

The warrior turned on his heel and began shouting orders, forming the infantry into a rough semicircle centered on the path the goblins were to take. He left a few swordsmen out to either flank, just in case, but he trusted Arcus' magic enough to commit the bulk of their small force. The archers, with Darko among them, stood in clusters behind the curve of the semicircle, some ten paces back from the line.

The men sobered as they made ready to meet the enemy, most especially those who had seen combat a few nights prior. Elbaf strode the line making on-the-spot adjustments, giving words of encouragement, and acknowledging each man in turn.

Arcus knelt in the tall, rough grass near the center of the semicircle. His eyes were closed and his hands were splayed out on the ground. With the men as ready as they were likely to be, Elbaf moved to Arcus' side and stood quietly over the druid as he meditated in silence. Long, tense minutes passed before the druid spoke at last.

"It begins," he said simply, standing and un-shouldering his longbow.

No sooner had the barbed steel tip of his arrow cleared the intricate beading of its quiver than horns started blowing in the distance. There was no mistaking the clear brass of imperial bugles, nor their meaning.

"Make ready men," Elbaf yelled, un-shouldering his greatsword and cracking his neck in anticipation.

He turned to Arcus, who was standing now with wide, unseeing eyes.

"How's the battle going?"

When he spoke, Arcus' voice was hollow and distant, like an echo.

"The line is breaking. The northern pincer is advancing now . . . They've reached the village."

Elbaf watched his companion nock an arrow and raise it to his eye level. He drew back, preparing to fire as Elbaf's attention returned to the treeline - but he didn't see anything.

"Arcus?"

"Steady . . ."

Elbaf watched as the druid drew slow, calm breaths, his mighty yew bow drawn tight.

"Now," he all but whispered, releasing the arrow with a practiced ease.

Elbaf followed the arrow as it arced outward through the empty trees. The shot passed silently over grass and flowers, but there was no target to be seen. As doubt crept into Elbaf's mind, a squat, greenish figure appeared between two trees just in time to catch the arrow dead in the center of its chest. Elbaf felt his jaw go slack in amazement as the creature crumpled soundlessly to the ground.

It was an impossible shot, one hundred and fifty meters if it was a foot.

Elbaf had little chance to marvel at his friend's skill, however, as a dozen more goblins appeared among the trees ahead of them.

"Archers ready!"

He needn't look behind to know the men were drawing their own beads upon their targets, an ever-increasing horde of clamoring, slavering goblins.

Arcus needed no direction. Arrow after arrow was drawn, nocked, and loosed with lethal accuracy.

The distance closed rapidly, at sixty meters, give or take, Elbaf roared the command that loosed a volley of imperial arrows, clearing the first two ranks of goblins with ease.

Now that they were closer, it was possible to make out details of the onrushing horde. The creatures stood at four-foot or so; an array of muddy brown and mottled green skin covered in ragged, half-rotten hides as armor and wielding pitted, poorly forged blades and short, hardened wooden spears.

Their language, such as it was, was a whooping mixture of barks, grunts, and whistles that assaulted the ears as surely as their stench assaulted the nose.

The leading line of the goblin ranks drew near, and Elbaf lowered his armored shoulder. He readied his blade and with a powerful swing met the foe at last. The heavy blade of his greatsword parted flesh and bone easily, cleaving in half the first goblin unlucky enough to face him. He bellowed a battlecry and waded forth into the enemy as his men, inspired by his bravery, followed. Imperial steel rang out amidst the cries of battle and the clamor of bloodlust. Elbaf lost track of the slain, his focus narrowing as he moved from one unlucky foe to the next.

Wave after wave of warriors broke across the bulwark of their defense as the battle dragged on. Goblin after goblin fell before him and he realized the enemy's ranks were thinning. He took a step back and cleared his head, searching for his next opponent.

Another cluster of goblins, these a bit smaller than the others, tried to break through an opening in the lines to his right, and he moved to intercept them. The first to taste his steel was a woman. She held a spear but was unarmored. He parried her pitiful attempt to lunge at him and severed her head with a brutal swing of his blade. He raised his sword again to strike the next, and realized a moment too late that the goblin he faced held no weapon.

Moreover, it was a mere child.

He managed - barely - to avoid a killing blow, his blade instead digging deep into the earth beside the cowering creature. He blinked to clear his head, totally unprepared for the reality of what faced him.

Suddenly pulled from his bloodlust, he scanned the field. Less than a third of the three dozen goblins standing were armed, and all of them were unarmored women and children.

Speechless with shock, he reached a hand out to the cowering child in front of him, only to pull back when a brilliant, white-hot beam pierced the child's torso from across the field. The beam winked out of existence just as swiftly as it had appeared, leaving behind a ragged, scorched hole through the goblin's chest. The creature tumbled to the ground with a soundless gasp of pain as Elbaf sought the source of the blast.

Darko, some fifteen feet from him, was a thing of nightmares. He stood apart from the archers now, his outstretched hands engulfed in blueish-white fire that was painful to look at. His robes waved as if in a strong wind, though the air was calm. As Elbaf watched, another two beams lanced out from Darko's hands, streaking across the field in an instant and felling two more of the goblins.

Guilt and disgust brought wind back to his lungs as Elbaf pulled his blade from the dirt.

"Hold," he roared. "Stand down, men!"

He lunged forward, blocking one of his soldiers' blades with his own, and catching another against his vambrace. The meeting steel shot sparks, but a goblin woman's life was spared.

The battle stumbled to a halt as the imperial forces held their blades at bay. The remaining goblins froze as well, all eyes on the massive warrior. A guttural cry of pain caused Elbaf to turn on his heel, just in time to see one of their soldiers cut down a goblin woman running past him.

Elbaf saw red, his vision tunneling on the man's wry grin as he looked down at his victim.

The soldier, a man Elbaf didn't recognize, raised his blade to finish off the goblin, but stopped suddenly as the soldier next to him held a sword to his throat. Elbaf was dimly aware that the man who'd stayed his fellow's blade was Private Derrin, but his focus remained on the offending soldier.

"I said stand down," he growled, his greatsword held menacingly in one hand. "And you *dare* to disobey me?"

The man's eyes were wide with fear as Elbaf bore down on him, blade rising.

"Elbaf!" Talia shouted, her voice ringing out clearly over the now quiet battlefield.

Elbaf paused, collecting his thoughts for a moment.

"Bind him and strip him of his weapon," he growled at the soldiers nearest to him. "Now!"

The men moved to comply, and the spell that held the battlefield still was suddenly broken. The goblins, not daring to question the nature of their escape, began again to flee. They ran with single-minded fear, pouring past the soldiers and into the woods on the other side of the road.

"Elbaf, what are you--"

"The next man to cut down an unarmed foe will taste my blade," Elbaf shouted out, cutting off Arcus' question mid-sentence. "You *will* stand down!"

"Reform the line," Talia shouted, taking charge again. "You are to engage armed and hostile enemies only. Lieutenants, a word."

Her tone brooked no argument, and the three men moved to meet her just behind the line as their soldiers reformed their defense. Elbaf watched as goblins continued to appear in the trees, many of them already injured. They faltered at the sight of the imperial lines, but took their chances. As more and more of them made it through, the rest grew bolder and followed suit.

"Elbaf," Talia snapped her fingers in the much taller warrior's face. "What the hell are you thinking?"

"We'll hang for this, I suppose," Darko agreed dryly.

"These are womenfolk and *children*, Talia," Elbaf growled. "Surely you--"

"Do not lecture me on morals, Elbaf," Talia snapped in response. "I . . ."

He watched her wrestle internally with herself.

"Damn it," she cursed aloud. "And damn her. I . . . We can't just--"

"I am with you," Arcus interjected solemnly. "I would not have their blood on my conscience."

"They're *goblins*," Darko said, clearly baffled by his companions' reactions. "Their kind preys upon the weak and innocent the world over, these are not *men* to be pitied."

Elbaf tightened his grip on his blade, bristling with fury.

"And you, *elf*, who are you to be the judge of whose blood deserves spilling?"

"Agreed," Arcus narrowed his eyes at Darko. "Odd that you should be so willing to disregard the spark of their lives for their heritage."

"I am an *elf*," Darko retorted acidly. "Mine is a cultured, ancient race that predates your own by countless eons--"

"And yet you lack compassion," Talia frowned in disdain. "I, too, am appalled by your words, mage. This is no simple--"

"But it *is*! It *is* simple," Darko shouted above the others. "Let not your own sense of justice blind you to the fact that we have the *simplest* of choices here. Disobedience is death, or had you forgotten? Would you all lay down your lives then? You seek justice for these creatures? Fine, so be it. I would *live*, and I desire that for myself just as fervently as do these goblins. There is no great moral quandary here, there is *survival*. Ours, or theirs."

The mage's words silenced them. They could not argue the truth of his words. A long, tense pause lingered between the four friends until at last Elbaf spoke.

"Even so, I will not. Even should it cost me my life."

"I am with you, brother," Arcus agreed.

Darko said nothing, simply shaking his head in disbelief.

Talia as well seemed tormented, torn between her duty and her moral compass.

Bugle calls, much closer this time, prevented further discussion and they all turned as one to the treeline again. The rest of the Brazen Hawks poured forth from the trees, laying low the routed goblins as they came. They met the imperial line with confusion, unsure why their fellows were not fighting.

Annabelle, her black-bladed longsword dripping in blood, pushed her way to the fore.

"What is the meaning of this?" she shouted angrily. "By what right do you allow this filth to pass?"

"On my order," Elbaf roared back, his back tall and proud as he strode to her.

Rage tinged her cheeks with cherry red, and she muscled her way through the men until she was face-to-face with Elbaf. With a flick of her wrist, she brought the tip of her blade to his throat. Elbaf was astonished by her speed, but was unbowed.

"I might have known," she said through gritted teeth. "I hereby sentence you--"

"Stand down, Captain," Madrie's voice carried well in the crowd, and the men parted as she spoke.

The commander waded into the midst of the men, drawing close to her quarreling officers.

"You, men. There," she indicated a cluster of mounted soldiers. "Return to camp."

"Aye, ma'am," the Sergeant leading them responded, snapping a crisp salute before riding off with his dozen men.

"This man has committed treason," Annabelle hissed. "He has disobeyed your direct orders and given quarter to the enemy. He *must* be punished."

"When you have command of this unit you may do as you see fit, Captain," Madrie replied acidly. "Until then, you will do as I instruct."

Annabelle fumed, but lowered her weapon.

"Lieutenant, what do you have to say for yourself?"

"Ma'am," Elbaf saluted. "I cannot kill unarmed women and children."

Madrie mulled his words.

"Soror Talia, have this man disarmed and put in shackles." She waved at four nearby soldiers. "You will escort Lieutenant Elbainsen--"

"Ma'am," Arcus interrupted hesitantly. "If Elbaf is to be bound like a common criminal, then I ought to be as well."

"Is that so?" The woman pondered softly. "Very well then, Lieutenant D'Ari."

She turned her attention back to the soldiers.

"Lieutenants Elbainsen and D'Ari are to be bound and kept under watch. Escort them to my command tent immediately," she paused, glancing around. "Anyone else?"

Darko gave a silent glance to Talia, but said nothing.

"Ma'am," Talia began. "I would speak with you privately."

"I believe that would be in order, yes, Soror Talia," Madire said menacingly. "Captain Montagne, you will relieve Captain Lorraine of her weapon."

Annabelle stepped forward and yanked Talia's mace from her hand.

"Captains," she jerked her head in the direction of their camp. "Let's take a walk."

Elbaf watched the three women leave. A moment later, the men around him closed ranks. Elbaf gripped his weapon tighter, preparing to resist. Private Derrin saw him clench his fist and Elbaf could smell the fear on the young warrior.

"Please, sir," the young man said quietly.

He glanced about, realizing there was no way to avoid bloodshed here, and that these men were not to blame.

"Guard it with your life," he whispered to the soldier, handing him the enormous weapon.

Private Derrin nodded solemnly as Elbaf allowed himself to be placed in rigid steel manacles.

Elbaf looked to Arcus, who was stoically accepting his own bindings, then cast a disdainful look at Darko. The mage met his stare evenly. If he had remorse, it didn't show.

"Sir, if you would, please?"

Elbaf glanced down at the Sergeant who spoke. The man's tone was respectful, almost apologetic. Elbaf simply nodded, and allowed himself to be led back towards the camp.

Ahead of him, Madrie led Annabelle and Talia down the path as well, their heads bowed in heated discussion.

"Ma'am, the fault is mine," Talia apologized as the trio made their way along the packed dirt of the road.

"I am *well* aware, Soror Talia," Madrie replied curtly.

They walked in silence the rest of the way back to the camp, Talia's dread growing with the long and uneasy quiet.

Madrie didn't speak again until they were back in her command tent, half an hour later. She sat herself behind her desk, her two senior officers in front of her, and stared at them over steepled fingers.

"Explain it to me," she sighed, breaking her hands apart and rubbing her temples. "Explain to me how you let this happen."

"Ma'am," Talia stiffened. "There were women, and chil--"

"What I need now is an explanation from you," Madries spoke slowly, deliberately. "Of *exactly* what happened."

"An *explanation*?" Annabelle interjected, outraged. "What explanation? This was insubordination. It was *treason!"*

"Captain Montagne," Madries voice was steely. "You will maintain your composure."

Talia could feel Annabelle's anger like the heat from a raging fire, but the woman remained silent.

"Talia," Madrie continued. "I am still waiting."

"Ma'am," Talia's mind raced. "We engaged the enemy soldiers, as you instructed. The first few waves were soldiers, armed and armored . . . A-after that . . . th-there were unarmed women, and children . . ."

"And?"

"And . . . Lieutenant Elbainsen called the men off, told them to stand down."

"And you countermanded this order?"

"I did not, ma'am. I . . . ." She racked her brain, trying to think of what to say to explain the situation better. "I-I had a hasty meeting with my subordinates and determined that Elba-- er, Lieutenants Elbainsen and D'Ari were correct."

Madrie shook her head, but continued to let Talia speak.

"Ma'am, ultimately it was my decision. I determined that the correct course of action was in fact to refrain from killing the women and children. It goes against the very tenets of our faith, the principles of our--"

"And who are *you* to lecture anyone on the tenets of the faith?" Annabelle shouted.

Talia jumped as the other woman screamed directly into her ear. She hadn't realized Annabelle had gotten so close to her.

Madrie glowered at both of them.

"So," she began. "What am I to do with my wayward officer corps? Annabelle?"

"Ma'am," Annabelle spoke with wicked passion. "I believe an execution would be in order. Protocol dictates that cowardice in the face of the enemy--"

"An execution? Ma'am," Talia would hold her tongue no longer

She wheeled on Annabelle and shoved a finger in her face. "My men did *not* show cowardice. Quite the opposite, in fact! Let us perhaps see the measure of blood upon *your* weapon."

"Mind your tone, whelp," Annabelle growled, her hand drifting to the sword at her belt.

"Enough!"

Madrie stood and slammed her hands down on her desk in one swift movement.

"Annabelle, leave us. Go tend to the wounded."

Anabelle bristled, her jaw clenching visibly. But she did as she was told, storming out of the tent with obvious disdain for the both of them.

"You are so *young*," Madrie said, softer than Talia expected. "But there must be consequences. Elbainsen will receive one hundred lashes, in front of the men. They are to be administered by D'Ari, and that'll be the end of it."

Madrie's face hardened again, all except her eyes.

"See it done, Talia. And he is not to receive any magical healing at the end of it, do you understand?"

Talia could not bring herself to speak, so she saluted and waited to be released.

Madrie walked over to a pile of gear at the other end of the tent. After a few moments of shuffling things around, she straightened up and held out a black, braided leather bullwhip to Talia.

"You are dismissed, Captain," Madrie added as she sat once again.

Talia turned on her heel and left the tent, tears running down her face as soon as she was clear of it. A public whipping - Elbaf would be humiliated. Public punishment in the Empire was rare, but not unheard of. It was generally saved for only the truly craven.

She could see Elbaf and Arcus, still bound, waiting for their fates to be decided at the other edge of the camp. They had a small crowd among them, and as Talia drew nearer she could see that it consisted mostly of those who had fought beside them, not only at the Altimeer estate, but also at the goblin village.

She gestured, and one of the men broke off and trotted over to her before giving a sharp salute.

"Ma'am?"

"Sergeant," she looked at his rank, but didn't know his name off the top of her head. "Gather the men, all of them."

He saluted again, this time with greater hesitation, but turned to do her bidding.

Talia continued forward until she was within earshot of the group.

"Unbind them," she called out, her arm held stiffly at her side and the unfamiliar weight of the whip in her hand.

Elbaf and Arcus rubbed their wrists as their shackles were removed. Their looks of relief turned to concern when they saw the redness of her face, the regret in her eyes.

"Talia?"

"Arcus," she whispered, just loud enough for the trio to hear. "You . . . You're to . . ."

The ranger glanced down at the whip, then back up to his friend.

"It's alright, Talia. I can take it. I'll be--"

Talia shook her head, then took a deep breath and steadied herself.

"No, not you," she said. "You are to give Elbaf one hundred lashes."

"*One hundred?*" Arcus' eyes opened wide in shock. "They've gone mad! That could kill a man. I won't do it."

"Arcus," Talia pleaded. "She could have executed you both--"

"No, ranger," Elbaf interrupted them. "Not here, not now. Do your duty."

Even as he spoke, he was reaching up first with one hand, then the other to unclip his pauldrons. The heavy steel plates fell to the ground beside him, followed shortly by his breastplate, which hit the ground with a dull clang.

Arcus took the whip in his hand as Elbaf removed his shirt and strode to the center of the mass of soldiers. Talia watched him look down at the whip and then up at the broad, muscular back of the warrior. A hush fell over the crowd as Talia and Arcus followed him to the middle of the group.

The men closed ranks, creating a tight circle about fifteen feet across in the center of the camp.

"Lieutenant Elbaf Elbainsen, by order of the commander, you are sentenced to one hundred lashes," Talia's voice quaked, but carried through the ranks. "For the crime of . . . of cowardice before the enemy."

The men, already murmuring in shock at the severity of the punishment, looked outraged at the crime he stood accused of, but they held their ground.

"Lieutenant Arcus D'Ari," she continued. "As a co-conspirator, you will administer these lashes, effective immediately."

With that, Talia took a step backwards and tried to make her face as impassive as possible.

"Elbaf," Arcus called softly. "Are you prepared, brother?"

Elbaf looked over his shoulder at Arcus and nodded sharply, then looked forward again.

The first crack of the whip laid an inch-wide gash across Elbaf's back. Many of the men flinched, and some of the younger ones grew pale at the sight of his skin cut open.

But Elbaf made no sound. He stood steady as a rock under the blow.

Arcus cast a look at Talia, anger written in his eyes.

Again and again the whip cracked, until Elbaf's back was a spider web of angry, weeping red. He refused to break, and the men around him refused to look away.

It took the better part of a candlemark, but at last the final lash fell. Arcus dropped the whip as soon as he'd dealt the last blow and rushed to Elbaf's side. The orc slumped against him, his legs unsteady.

"I'm sorry, Elbaf," he said, an arm around the warrior's shoulders and their foreheads pressed together. "I'm so sorry."

"Talia," Arcus looked at her questioningly. "What are you waiting for? Heal him."

"I can't," she replied, choking back a sob at the sight of him. "I am forbidden."

Elbaf stood in a puddle of blood, his chest heaving. He tried to speak, but couldn't. Instead he managed a slow, weak salute at Talia to reassure her. He leaned heavily on Arcus, and the pair of them walked away quietly. The men parted in silence to let them through, then followed as the pair made their way to one of the sleeping tents.

"See to his wounds as best you can," Talia instructed a pair of their medics. "I'll be in my tent."

Talia turned on her heel and strode away, determined to make it back to her sleeping quarters before she burst into tears. She made it, barely, and spent several minutes quietly weeping before she could compose herself.

Chapter Eight

"You're to send word with one of the messengers in Bethlir as soon as you get there," Madrie cautioned Talia quietly as the young cleric prepared her saddlebags. "The headman there is an old colleague. Track down these insidious terrorists and keep me apprised - especially if the situation is worse than our intelligence suggests."

Talia nodded along, memorizing her instructions as she ensured all of her gear was properly stowed and packed away. She and Major Van Cleigh were standing under the shelter of an ancient elm tree, but the rain pouring from the sky was so thick that they may as well have been out in the open.

A week had passed since the incident at the goblin camp, and the tension in the air among the troops was palpable. Annabelle had yet to say a single word to Talia or the others, and Madrie had been unusually distant as well. The men in the company seemed divided. Many were openly in agreement with the commander, and some even felt that Elbaf's punishment had been too light - a show of favoritism.

But those who had fought beside the half-orc were just as quick to defend him.

There'd been a half-dozen skirmishes within the ranks, fistfights and worse, and the morale was as bleak as the weather. The past two days had brought storms, and today showed no sign it would be different.

The company had been making their way toward Bethlir, but a messenger in the dead of night had changed their plans considerably. A man had stumbled in just past midnight bearing documents with the imperial seal. He was granted an audience with Madrie at once and, as far as Talia knew, the woman had been up since then. The messenger departed just after daybreak, accompanied by a half dozen of their scouts on horseback, and the company had been mustered shortly thereafter.

"Talia, focus," Madrie chided, bringing Talia's attention back to her. "We're redirecting northeast; there's talk of open rebellion near Kent, and the garrison at Polus is largely occupied with raiders in the north. I'm *trusting* you, Captain, just as I am trusting you to tell me if you can't handle it. I can send Annabelle--"

"We've got it, ma'am," Talia interrupted hastily. "We'll handle it."

She couldn't miss this chance. She needed distance to clear her mind.

"Very well, Talia," Madrie's eyes held a peculiar look. Regret, perhaps. "Select the men you need, and leave as soon as you're able."

Talia saluted, then tightened the last strap on her pack.

"Elbaf, Arcus," she called, swinging herself up into her saddle. "Go rouse the wizard and ready the men to move at once!"

"Good luck, Talia," Madrie caught her gaze once more. "Emperor guide you."

"May his light bless your path as well, ma'am."

Talia turned her horse around and trotted off toward Elbaf. The warrior sat like a statue upon his own mount, heedless of the rain pouring down on himself and his armor. She wished, as she often did, that she could read his face. But his expression was truly neutral, with no indication of the thoughts behind his murky brown eyes.

Elbaf saluted as she drew near, but said nothing.

"How are your . . . wounds?" she asked, eyeing the heavy metal plating on his back.

He answered her with a question of his own.

"We have a new mission, ma'am?"

Talia's shoulders drooped. Elbaf had barely spoken to her these past few days, and she could scarcely blame him. Still, his silence was evidence that her course was correct - that they needed distance from Annabelle and Madrie.

"We do." She looked out into the downpour. "We're to investigate the possibility that separatists are gaining a foothold in the region, starting with the town of Bethlir."

He nodded, but said nothing.

"We've been granted wide latitude for the number of men we bring along," Talia posed the statement as a question, but Elbaf didn't take the bait.

"Gather the troops that were at the Altimeer Estate," she told him, dropping her voice low. "We know we can trust them, at least. Anyone else, I leave to your discretion."

He nodded again, his face as unreadable as a mask of steel.

Talia hoped he'd say something, but he simply waited silently until she released him. As soon as she did so, he rode over to one of their men - Derrin, if she wasn't mistaken - and started issuing orders. She watched him as he moved among the soldiers, jealous of the ease with which he interacted with the troops even now, in the face of his public humiliation.

"Derrin," Elbaf flagged the young man down as he rode over. "Gather your things, and pass the word to those of us who were at the Altimeer place, we leave at once."

The warrior watched the young man hurry off, already working on a list of the other soldiers he would speak with. Many of the men who had fought beside them at the goblin camp had expressed solidarity with him over the past few days, and he would have them with him and away from the vile leadership of their company.

All told, there'd be roughly twenty men, Elbaf counted in his head. It would certainly be enough to make an impact, but not so large a group as to compromise the integrity of the rest of the company.

He was relieved to hear Talia's request, that he should select men who had proven their loyalty and with whom they had built trust. He would have suggested it himself if she hadn't beaten him to the punch. He knew she was frustrated with their situation. He was as well, but there was nothing they could do under the watchful gaze of Annabelle and, to a lesser extent, Madrie.

No, it was better that they part ways for a while.

Elbaf turned in his saddle, looking for Arcus near their tents. His breath caught in his chest as several of the half-healed wounds on his back cracked and split open, but he showed no outward sign of his pain. He'd given up trying to keep them from bleeding. It was an impossible task. Instead, he cared for the scores of deep, wide cuts as best he could by keeping them washed and covered with clean cotton at the beginning of each day.

The reminder of his punishment flushed his cheeks with anger, and he turned his attention instead to Annabelle's tent. He found her with ease - her warhorse standing out among the rest - and caught her, as he often had the past few days, staring intently at him.

He matched her gaze evenly until at last she turned away, directing her attention to some other task.

"I don't trust her," Arcus spoke from a few feet away. "I didn't before, but now . . . doubly so."

Elbaf looked over his shoulder to see Arcus and Darko, both on horseback.

"We're moving out," he informed them gruffly. "Headed north."

"We're splitting the company again?"

Elbaf nodded an affirmative.

"What's in the north that warrants such an action?" Darko wondered aloud. "No doubt that messenger in the night brought ill tidings."

"He did," Elbaf agreed. "It seems treason is in the air, and we're to suss it out."

With that, he urged his mount onward to collect the rest of their men.

By the time their small train of horses and men headed out, the sun had well and truly risen. It shone half-hearted behind slate-gray skies and did nothing to warm the deep chill that settled into the men's hopelessly wet gear as they trudged along the muddy swamp that was the road to Bethlir.

"And I suppose you've nothing you can do about this, mage?" Elbaf grumbled, a little louder than he'd meant to.

"Alas," the wizard responded unhappily. "I cannot. Perhaps Arcus can *commune* with the winds or some such nonsense and end this hideous downpour."

They both turned to look at Arcus who, alone of all the men, seemed to be relishing the rainfall. He rode with his arms spread wide, his face to the skies, and his cloak open. He caught their gazes and smiled broadly.

"It's beautiful, isn't it?"

"No," Elbaf retorted, nonplussed. "It isn't."

"I think his mind has been addled," Darko complained, sinking deeper into his robes.

Arcus rode over, shaking his head and wiping his blonde hair out of his face.

"Truly, can't you both feel it?" he asked in earnest. "The *lightness* of it? The . . . the purity of it?"

"I'd settle for a bit less of it, frankly."

"Ah, Darko, take heart! This rain is needed as surely as the sun, as surely as the winds and--"

"I don't *care*," Darko sputtered at the druid. "It's absolutely horrid. Isn't there anything you can do about it? Make this 'much needed rain' fall somewhere else?"

"Honestly, I'm disappointed," Arcus sighed heavily, frowning at the two of them.

"Disappo--"

Arcus raised a hand to ward off the mage's tirade.

"Here, I can bring you some measure of comfort, I suppose," he chided.

Elbaf watched with interest as the druid closed his eyes, his hand outstretched with his palm facing the mage about a foot away. The druid's breathing became slow and deep, his body rocking in perfect time with the footfalls of his horse.

It was difficult to say how it began, but Elbaf noticed suddenly that Arcus was glowing. He blinked rapidly, trying to decide if his eyes were playing tricks on him, but no. A faint, near-invisible aura of gold and silver radiated from him. The aura became stronger and more noticeable near his outstretched hand, where it was flecked with swirling motes of bright emerald green and deep, cerulean blue.

Elbaf watched as the ranger's hand dipped and wove an intricate pattern then, with a soft turn, pointed directly at Darko. The aura flowed from around him to pool in his hand, then jumped the distance to the mage, where it spread to cover his entire body.

The wizard gasped a little in surprise as the rain around him grew softer and softer until it was just a faint mist. He stuck his hand out, smiling in appreciation as the worst of the rain seemed to slip around him as he moved.

"Arcus," he marveled. "I must say, I am *profoundly* impressed."

"As am I, ranger," Elbaf agreed. "That was so . . . delicate. So gentle."

Arcus shrugged, turning his face skyward to enjoy the rain again.

"Nature is loath to heed demands," he replied brightly. "But when one simply asks, she is generous and kind."

Arcus couldn't help but laugh as he spurred his horse onward towards the front of the train once again. His deep and abiding connection with the natural world seemed all the stronger in the midst of a rainstorm. He found himself, for the first time in many moons, truly at peace.

Even the dampening effects of his unnatural collar seemed reduced, and he closed his eyes to extend his consciousness into the woods around them.

Every spark of life blazed brightly in his heart. He could see the whole of the web of life extending out endlessly in every direction. There, just inside an aging beech tree, he could feel the pulsing heart of a slumbering owl; beyond it, a yula spider sheltering from the rain beneath the upturned leaves of a Forsythia bush. On and on he allowed his mind to wander, greeting each creature in turn before moving along to the next.

Kodja came splashing into his mind, the wolf's joy a bright mote of bluish-green among the amber of the trees and the muddled browns of the smaller plants.

Hello, little brother.

Kodja sent him smiles and visions of the mudpuddles he was frolicking in and Arcus' face broke out into a wide grin. He could tell the wolf wanted company, wanted Arcus to join in his silly romping and traipsing through the countless pools of muddy water in the forest.

Sorry, Kodja. Would that I could.

He stayed with Kodja for several miles, sharing in the pure, child-like happiness of the animal and wishing that he could join him.

"Arcus?"

The ranger blinked, returning fully to himself, and glanced over at Talia. She was riding beside him at the front of the group, a look of frustration on her face.

"What's wrong, Talia?"

"You're . . . *spiritual*, right, Arcus?"

Arcus understood immediately the seriousness of her tone, and decided to tread carefully with the young woman.

"I am," he agreed gently. "I would say we all are, in our own ways. Wouldn't you?"

She nodded thoughtfully.

"I would, but I would say that you and I are alike in many ways that outsiders might find challenging to understand, does that make sense?" she asked.

"Well, I think tha--"

"What I mean to say is," Talia cut him off hurriedly, the words tumbling out of her mouth, "your . . . connection to nature - the way that you draw your magic from it - is not so different from my relationship with the Emperor, right? The way we both ask and receive, as compared to, say, Darko's studious taming of the natural magical energies of the world."

He chewed over his response, considering her words carefully before he responded.

"I think that is a fair assessment, yes," he began slowly. "You and I have different ways of accessing power, but I think there is a common level of divinity that provides it to each of us. Wouldn't you agree?"

"I do."

"Talia . . . I have met other clerics, other priests who wield the same divine powers that you do, and they--"

"You have? *Outside* of the Holy Order?" She looked shocked.

Arcus was taken aback, unsure how this information could be so surprising to one of the cloth.

"Well, yes, of course. There are many who are touched by the gods, who walk the same paths as you do. Many of them are conduits of *ideas* and others of one of the gods themselves."

"Ideas? How can one be a priest of an idea?"

"I cannot explain it," Arcus admitted. "But I have seen it. Priests of Justice, of Goodness, of Health, or War, or of Strength. All are powerful concepts, as immortal and as widespread as the worship of any God."

"There is nothing in the teachings about this," Talia mumbled half to herself. "Besides the heathen clergy of the fiends and devils of the Infinite Hells."

Arcus shook his head.

"Talia, there's *so much more* to the world than you have seen," he smiled softly. "More than I have seen. More than any, save perhaps the most ancient of elves, could ever *dream* of seeing in a lifetime."

They rode in silence a while while Talia considered his words.

"If there are so many routes, so many paths to our powers then . . . then how do you know where the power comes from at all?"

It was Arcus' turn to dwell on his answer.

"Hm. I suppose . . . I suppose deep down you can *feel* it, can't you?" he asked. "I know that for me there's simply no question where it comes from. My powers come from nature. They are a gift and, when I die, they will return to nature. Just the way you feel deeply, unquestionably, that your power flows from the Emperor himself."

He watched the young woman's face, paying close attention to the way that her brow furrowed and her eyes, far from relaxing, seemed stormier than they had before. Arcus considered saying more, but he had the distinct impression that she was in a fragile state. Instead, he contented himself to simply ride in comfortable silence.

The road to Bethlir was long, but not particularly challenging. Even in this relatively rural part of the Empire, the roads were well-maintained and fairly safe. Gradually, the dense forests gave way to tall prairie grasses and rolling hills. Arcus was grateful for the easy path and the steadfastness of his mount, as it provided him with ample opportunity to bask in the majesty of nature surrounding him. So it was that he was the first of their party to know they'd arrived on the outskirts of the town. He first felt the presence of a cluster of cattle, then the angry buzzing of two men. He didn't need to see them physically to know they were angry, he could feel it in the tense swirling red of their lifeforce.

"Talia," he announced. "We might have trouble ahead."

She perked up, looking first at him and then ahead at the path which wound out of sight between a line of particularly steep bluffs.

"What? Where?"

"Around this bend, perhaps an eighth of a mile," Arcus said, his voice more focused as he returned to himself. "There's some kind of dispute between a pair of farmers, if I had to guess."

"Finally, a simple task," the cleric muttered aloud before spurring her mount into a trot.

They heard the men before they saw them. They were shouting over each other, both apparently blaming the other for missing livestock, when the group rounded the bend.

Both of the men waved excitedly at the soldiers, confident looks upon their red, angry faces. As soon as Talia and the rest of the group were within earshot, they both clamored for attention.

"Easy, easy," she raised her hands for silence. "One at a time. You there, what's the meaning of this?"

"This bastard - begging yer' pardon, yer' highness - this bastard's been at my livestock. I know 'e has!"

Immediately the other man started shouting in protest.

"Quiet," Elbaf roared, driving them to immediate silence and startling the curious herds in the stony, sloping pastures on either side of the road.

He nodded at Talia, who tipped her head in thanks.

"Thank you. You, what's your name?" Talia asked and pointed at the fellow who'd just spoken.

"Name's Ellard, yer' highness."

"Stop calling me that," Talia sighed wearily. "'Ma'am' will do fine. Alright, Ellard, you've said your piece. Your turn," she gestured to the second man.

The other gentlemen swept his felt cap off his head and did a funny little bow before speaking.

"M' name's Torbin, ma'am," he bowed again. "I've not been in his cattle ma'am, I've got my own troubles. His cattle's been in my pasture! They've scared off my sheep and broken my fence twice just this past moon!"

"That's a boldfaced lie," Ellard shouted. "On the Emp'ror it is!"

"Yer' damn cattle's put tracks all over my field, Ellard. I'll have none of yer' lies--"

Elbaf reached across his shoulder and drew his greatsword with a gentle grace, silencing the men instantly. His impassive, stony glare turned slowly from one man to the other, then back again.

"Please continue, ma'am," he growled.

"Gentlemen, let me make myself clear," Talia said sharply. "I will not have you screaming at one another like children. You'll conclude your business for the day without speaking to one another, and tomorrow you will meet me in the town square an hour after sunrise. Bring any evidence you have, and any statements you wish to make will be considered."

Both of the men looked a little disappointed, but they knew better than to argue.

"Not a *single* word to one another until then," she admonished them. "Am I understood?"

They both nodded and Talia waved her hand at the party behind them, indicating that they should resume their march.

"How much further is the town?" she asked Ellard.

"Not far ma'am, maybe two miles."

She nodded curtly, then spurred her mount forward.

Elbaf sheathed his weapon, then cantered after Talia and the rest of the group. He caught up with Talia and gave her a reassuring nod.

"Ma'am, I think you handled that well, don't you?"

She beamed back at him.

"I do," she agreed with relief. "It's nice to have something *mundane* to deal with. No killing, no battles, no magic. Just somebody's missing cattle and somebody else's missing sheep."

Darko, riding beside them in brooding silence, spoke from beneath the hood of his robes.

"I suppose it's rather banal to us," he cautioned. "But this is a matter of vital importance to these farmers. Their very livelihoods are at stake, after all."

Darko watched his companions' reactions, and noted with pleasure that they seemed to rethink the importance of the issue at hand. He was no altruist, but pragmatically it made very little sense to him that they might endanger the goodwill of the townsfolk by relegating their concerns as 'mundane.'

His point made, he returned to his quiet introspection. His brooding, distant nature was an excellent cover for his true goal - calculating a way out of their current situation.

Darko chafed at the enchantment that held them bound, and every day of servitude thus far had brought him nothing but frustration. He'd be rid of their curse, one way or another.

Master, the town is ahead.

Thank you, Reia. What do you see?

Deep in the shadows of his robe's hood, Darko's eyes flashed a dull silver as he cast his sight to that of his companion. The world around him melted into oblivion and then, just as quickly, was replaced by a swirl of colors that resolved itself into the peculiar telescopic vision of Reia's raven form.

Together they could clearly see the town - a cluster of fifty or sixty structures all surrounded by a strong wooden palisade. The largest building by far was a sort of low stone fort that butted up against both the main gate and the wall. It seemed a defensible structure, and more than capable of fitting the entire population of the village should the need arise. The houses and shops that made up the rest of the town were of simple, durable construction - mostly wooden beams and thatched roofs, with very little stone aside from a few foundations.

Reia wheeled and circled above, watching the people below with keen interest.

None of the townsfolk stuck out as particularly noteworthy, save perhaps the two guards on patrol. They watched the interactions of the villagers as they closed the distance, until the group came at last into Reia's sight. Darko made a habit of not observing himself through her eyes, he'd done so once and had no intention of repeating the unnerving experience.

Instead, he returned to himself just in time to hear the greeting shouted from the gates of the palisade.

"Ho' there," one of the guards yelled, waving. "Open the gates!"

The gate, a tall but narrow barrier of thick pine logs latched together, creaked slowly inward to reveal the muddy town center. The guards saluted as they passed, the fear and wonder clear in their eyes.

Darko thought back to his training. These men saw a Hand perhaps once in every six moons, and generally far less often than that. It was absurd that such a system should work, but here was the evidence that it did. The people of the village ceased their work, gathering instead in gawking crowds as the band of men and horses made their way through the gate to assemble in the center of town.

A middle-aged man in fine black clothing strode down the steps of the fort with his arms wide. About his shoulders he wore a black, fur-lined cloak reminiscent of many of the Black Hand, and on his chest sat a slate gray copy of their own identifying badges - a symbol of his status as a former member of their order.

"Welcome, friends," he hollered boisterously. "Welcome to Bethlir!"

Darko watched the man carefully, studying his movements, and most of all how the townsfolk responded to his presence. He could see that the people respected this man. Their faces showed a mixture of pride and gratitude as he introduced the group to the stable master, the innkeeper, and a few of the other locals.

His concerns with the headman allayed, he turned his attention to the rest of the people gathered in the square.

The wizard paid the ongoing dialogue between Talia, Arcus, Elbaf, and the headman scant attention. No doubt he'd be informed of anything pertinent by the others. His hawklike gaze and sublime hearing instead focused on each of the people in turn, evaluating them all one by one.

One young man, perhaps twenty years of age, caught Darko's eye immediately. His eyes lacked the mirth and excitement of the rest of the crowd and, in fact, he seemed nervous. The boy had a pair of piercing blue eyes and a mop of rough-cut blonde hair upon his head. His clothes were old, but well maintained.

A tailor, perhaps? No, more likely an apprentice at that age. But certainly a tradesman.

His musings were interrupted by Arcus, now dismounted, who walked over and held out his hand expectantly.

"What?"

"Well, as you're the only one still mounted," Arcus spoke low. "I thought perhaps your leg was giving you trouble? Thought I'd give you a hand--"

"I beg your pardon," Darko huffed angrily. "I am perfectly capable of dismounting this horse!"

Arcus' smile faded to a frown, obviously unimpressed by Darko's attitude.

"Suit yourself," he shrugged, dropping his hand and walking away to join Elbaf and Talia, both of whom were staring openly at him in confusion.

In fact, everyone *was* already dismounted, leaving him alone and painfully out of place. He hurried down from his saddle, stumbling a little and cursing his malformed leg. He handed his reins off to a waiting soldier and hurried to join the other officers with the headman.

"My apologies," he lied, "I was attuning myself to the local energies."

The others seemed to take his statement at face value, shrugging off the arcane explanation.

"Welcome, mage," the headman offered his hand to Darko. "I am Ekart Goldrun, lord of this town and a former Hand myself."

Darko took his hand and was rewarded with an obnoxiously firm and enthusiastic handshake.

"Well met, my lord," Darko nodded. "Thank you for your hospitality."

"I should be thanking you," the man said, slapping Darko on the back. "It's been many years since an imperial Wizard graced this town. You've given us something to discuss for the whole of the next few seasons!"

The headman's laugh was loud, but seemed genuine as he led the foursome up the steps of the keep. He also made sure his pace was such that he wasn't outstripping Darko, which struck the wizard as a particularly kind gesture. The group made small talk as they worked their way up to a large, well-appointed dining hall on the second story of the keep. The table there was large enough to seat twenty comfortably, but places had been set for only eight.

"I wasn't sure how many would be in your party," their host explained, indicating with a wave that one of his servants ought to clear away the extra settings. "But I hope you'll indulge me in a brief meal as we discuss business?"

"Of course, sir," Talia spoke for the group. "It would be our pleasure."

"Excellent!"

Lord Goldrun pulled out Talia's chair and waited for her to be seated before he sat down himself. Within a few moments, a pair of servants were pouring wine and bringing out trays of meats, cheeses, and fresh vegetables.

"You'll be wanting to get down to business directly, I assume," the lord said matter-of-factly, helping himself to a plate of smoked sausages.

"Yes, my lord," Talia spoke again. "I'm sure you know that in addition to our regular duties we have been tasked with investigating reports of . . . well, of--"

"Treason? Sedition?"

The table fell into an awkward silence.

"Come now, don't be bashful," he said ruefully. "I sent Madrie a messenger as soon as I found out it was her on the rotation this year. The truth is, there's been *dissidence* of late. No use denying it, and keeping it in the shadows will only make it more dangerous."

The group nodded, hoping he would continue. The man took a deep drink of wine, then looked at them all in turn, very clearly weighing their merits as he did so.

"There's always been murmurs, of course," he shrugged. "It is the way of the governed to question the powers that be, even in a land so plentiful and fair as ours.

This past year though . . . well, it's gotten considerably worse."

"In what manner?" Darko asked, his curiosity well and truly piqued.

"We've been finding literature, pamphlets and such, speaking out against not only the Empire, but the Emperor himself!" The man's tone hardened as he spoke, his brows furrowing. "Outlandish statements of atrocities committed by the Imperial Army," he scoffed with a wave of his hand. "Demi-human supporting drivel, and the like."

Darko nodded along, ignoring the comment about race and hoping that the flush in Elbaf's cheeks wouldn't result in an outburst.

"And you suspect this person is a local?"

"Someone here must be helping them, or else how would their trash have wound up in our town?"

"But no one from the town has turned anyone in or reported anything suspicious?"

"Not yet," he sighed, his shoulders falling. "And to be frank, that's only one of our problems. We've a few backlogged judicial issues we have been waiting on a Hand to rule upon, and then there's the matter of Torbin and Ellard's livestock as well."

Talia pricked up at the mention of the missing animals.

"Of that issue we have some limited understanding, my lord," she chimed in. "We met them both on the way into town. They seemed . . . heated."

The headman nodded gravely.

"It's more serious than you might think," he said somberly. "We've had many a missing product these past two moons. Grain from the silos, fodder from the cattle barns, now livestock, as well. Whatever is out there, it leaves no trace, save the goods it runs off with."

"Have you set a watch on the fields? Guards upon the storehouses?"

"Of course we have," he replied with irritation. "Nothing ever happens at the places where we've men posted. The bandits always strike somewhere else!"

"Bandits?"

"Yes, warrior," he answered Elbaf's comment. "I fear the culprits we're looking for walk upright. No common creature would have need of so much, nor such a variety, of food. I've kept my concerns to myself until now, though obviously I've told the guard to be alert to the possibility. With no evidence however, I'm afraid there's not much else we can do with our limited forces."

"Perhaps these bandits and your dissidents are one and the same," Darko added.

"A possibility that had crossed my mind as well, mage. "

"With your permission, my lord," Talia entreated their host, "we'll take care of the business of settling your backlogged cases and the rest of our usual tasks this evening, and in the morning we'll pursue your dissidents and bandits in earnest?"

"An excellent plan, priestess," he nodded in agreement then raised his glass. "To the Emperor!"

"To the Emperor," they all echoed, drinking deeply of their wine.

The rest of the meal passed swiftly, with all parties interested in rest except, perhaps, Talia. Darko was surprised to see her so conversational, so extroverted, after weeks of watching her settle deeper and deeper within herself. He could only wonder at the cause of her shift in attitude as she smiled brightly and laughed and joked with the rest of them throughout the meal.

When at last the dishes were cleared away and the last glass empty, Lord Goldrun wished them a good evening and made to take his leave. Talia pulled him aside for a moment and held a hushed, private conversation that Darko was all too happy to eavesdrop upon.

"I would take the task of reviewing your legal cases tonight, my lord. Do you have the pertinent documents available?"

"Surely you'd prefer to rest, my dear," he said, his tone as patronizing as the hand he laid upon her shoulder. "Leave the legal work for the morning, no?"

"I'd rather see it done tonight, my lord," Talia gently shrugged out of his grasp and shook her head. "If only so that we might pursue your deeper troubles more swiftly."

"Very well, priestess," the lord smiled and called over a page. "Liam, please see to it that Hand Talia has the documents she needs, and be at her service until she retires for the night."

The page bowed deeply, then turned to wait for instructions from Talia, who began rattling off a list of the items she'd need to formalize their report on the town.

Talia bid the lord a good night, but couldn't help to notice him linger a bit in the doorway as she instructed the page, Liam, to gather the various tax documents, legal paperwork, and other items that she'd need to review and update as part of their usual duties.

Her list complete, the young man trotted off briskly to retrieve what she required. She turned her attention to her companions, who were standing beside the roaring fireplace chatting idly and waiting for her.

"I'm going to work on the sundries this evening so we can focus on the larger job in the morning," she informed them as she walked over. "I'm far too preoccupied to sleep, and it'll be good to set my mind to a task."

She bid the others goodnight and made her way to her room alone.

Her room was simple, but comfortable. It even had a real bed with a straw mattress, which was a far cry from the thin bedroll she'd been sleeping on since they'd departed the Capitol. The bed would have to wait, however, and she turned instead to a small wooden desk.

Liam lit a few candles around the room before bringing in stacks of receipts, rolls of parchment, and a number of dusty, time-worn ledgers. A few candlemarks later, he'd assembled all of the things she'd requested and he turned to ask her brightly if she needed anything further.

Talia glanced around, confirming she had all that she'd asked for, when a thought entered her mind.

"Actually," she mused. "It's Liam, right?"

"Yes, m'lady."

"How do you find Lord Goldrun?"

"I'm not sure I understand, m'lady," he shifted nervously.

"I mean no offense," she reassured him swiftly. "I simply find that the measure of a man can best be taken by the way he treats the people he can afford to abuse."

"Oh, no ma'am, he doesn't abuse us at all!"

"Is he kind? Thoughtful? Does he care about you, or simply see to your needs?"

"He's quite kind actually, ma'am," the young man finally relaxed, convinced that Talia's interest was genuine. "He loves the Empire, ma'am. Misses his days as a soldier, I think. He cares deeply about what happens to our town here, and this business of treachery and bandits has him troubled, if I may say so."

They spoke for another half hour, discussing the mood in the town and the troubles that most often plagued it.

No subject was left untouched.

At long last, however, Talia could tell the young man was exhausted.

"Alright, Liam," she chided. "Off to bed. I've kept you far later than I ought to have, and you've no doubt an early morning. Thank you for the company, and for gathering these things for me."

He bowed and took his leave of her as she turned listlessly back to the stacks of paper on her desk.

"Alright," she grumbled to herself. "No putting you off now."

Chapter Nine

Elbaf knew, in the way that all dreamers know deep down, that his surroundings weren't real. Nonetheless, his heart pounded as he walked, sword in hand, through a dimly lit stone corridor. His footfalls and the creak of his armor were the only sounds that disturbed the gravelike stillness of the long, narrow hallway. He glanced back over his shoulder at the inky blackness, peering into it and seeing nothing.

Less than nothing, really.

He *should* have been able to pierce the veil of blackness with his eyes, as he had his entire life. All those of orcish blood could see well in total darkness. He should have been able to see the stone of the floor, the dull, faded tapestries that hung on the walls, *anything*. But the darkened hall behind him revealed nothing.

Elbaf suppressed a shiver and turned forward. There was a light at the end of the tunnel, faint and flickering, with all the strength of a dying candle. A chill in his spine drove him forward, and the mighty warrior picked up the pace - all but jogging now and no longer caring for the sound he made.

For all that he exerted himself, he seemed no closer to the light.

The hairs rose on the back of his neck and his brow prickled with sweat as he broke into a full sprint. He could hear other footsteps now, besides his own. Dozens of bare feet pounded on the stones behind him, a soft pitter-patter that drew ever closer, grew ever louder.

He could sense the closing distance between predator and prey and cast another look behind himself.

The darkness remained, and he could make out no details of his pursuers.

His eyes forward again, he came to the sinking conclusion that his stand would have to be made here. There would be no end to the cursed tunnel, and no light to shelter in for the coming battle.

With a grunt he planted his feet and spun, his greatsword flashing for a moment in the dying light behind him. He faced the darkness, his chest heaving and his eyes darting back and forth seeking a target. No more than a heartbeat passed before the first of his enemies broke through the curtain of shadow and Elbaf couldn't help but take a step back in alarm.

The creature before him was a horrible, nightmarish amalgam of the undead at the manor, and the goblins they'd slaughtered a few days later. It was a youth, but its mottled green skin had gone pale from lack of blood. The thing's tiny, unarmored body was riddled with imperial arrows, but it walked with the deliberate gait of a thing possessed of life.

A dozen more crawled and shuffled into the light. They all bore mortal wounds and the soulless, dead eyes that had haunted Elbaf since the night at the Altimeer Manor. He recognized the faces of the goblins he'd struck down in his bloodlust, and many of the faces that they'd allowed past.

His blade stayed steady even as his heart pounded in his ears.

The creatures growled and hissed, and he saw that their bared yellow teeth were covered in dark, clotted blood. They shambled closer and Elbaf readied himself as best he could.

Even so, when the wave surged forward, it engulfed him.

He cut, kicked, stabbed, slashed, and punched the onrushing crush of bodies, but there were too many of them. He could feel their claws and teeth scrabbling for purchase in his armor - feel their weight crushing the breath from his chest.

He woke with a mighty gasp of air, sitting bolt upright, drawing the daggers he kept beneath his pillow and taking great, gulping breaths. The sun was barely tinging the horizon with light, but he could once again break through the darkness of his room with his own eyes.

All was as it should be.

The momentary pain of his nightmare faded, and he winced as his wounds, still half-healed, wept blood onto the straw of his mattress. He looked behind himself at the ruined bed, soaked in blood and sweat.

Elbaf shook his head and wiped his sweat-slick brow.

He set the daggers down beside the bed and made his way to the wash basin, where he splashed cool water on his face and tried to calm himself. There was no use returning to sleep - the dreams would be waiting for him should he try. Rather than rest, Elbaf took advantage of his wakefulness and threw himself into a vigorous workout. He lost himself in his exercise as a way to quiet his restless mind, and it worked perhaps a little too well. Before he knew it, it was well past sunrise.

He cleaned himself at the washbasin, grateful for the cooling waters on his aching back and steaming muscles. Refreshed, Elbaf made his way downstairs, and was unsurprised to see Arcus, Darko, and many of their men were already up and about eating cold stew and drinking hot, bitter buttonwood tea.

Several of the men raised their cups to him in greeting as he passed them on his way to the table where his fellow officers sat.

"Good morning," he nodded to them as he took his seat. "Where is Talia?"

"Morning," Arcus replied cheerfully. "Haven't seen her yet, I suppose she's still in bed."

"No one has checked on her yet?" Elbaf asked, his pulse quickening.

"*Checked* on her?" Darko repeated, clearly confused. "What's to check Elbaf? She's probably just asleep."

"Even so," he replied, standing.

"Elbaf," Arcus motioned that he should return to his seat. "She's *fine*. Please, join us for a cup."

"I'm going to check on her," he replied tersely.

He headed to the stairs, ignoring the confused looks he got for his stomping feet. He tried to slow his breathing, but his mind was filled with dark possibilities. Elbaf unconsciously put a hand to the hilt of his dagger as he reached Talia's door.

It was shut, so he knocked gently.

There was no reply.

He waited a beat, then knocked again, louder this time.

"Talia?"

A sound like breaking glass rang out from behind the door and without a second thought he rammed his shoulder into the flimsy wooden portal. The door caved inward to reveal a startled Talia picking up glass from the floor.

Elbaf's blade was already out as he took in the scene. Talia, still in her clothes from the night before, though without her armor on, knelt beside a table covered in books and scrolls. It seemed a glass had fallen to the floor, perhaps disturbed when he woke her.

Her hair was a mess which, combined with her wide, startled eyes, indicated to him that he had in fact disturbed her slumber.

"Elbaf, what in the Emperor's name are you doing?"

He struggled to explain himself. How could he tell her that he was worried for her safety when he had barged into her room needlessly with neither warning nor excuse?

"I . . ." His cheeks burned. "I feared that something had - nevermind. I apologize for intruding."

She looked harder, her expression shifting from alarm to concern.

"Is everything ok? Are the others alright?"

He nodded, grateful for the change of topic and seizing a way out of the awkward situation.

"Yes, ma'am, the others are downstairs. I came to rouse you from your slumber."

Talia opened her mouth to speak, but he had already turned stiffly on his heels and rushed out the door.

Elbaf hurried back downstairs, his face flushed with irritation. The others were right where he'd left them.

"Everything--"

"Yes," he snapped to interrupt Arcus while sitting down beside him and pouring a mug of tea from the large clay pitcher in the center of the table.

Arcus said nothing, and if he noticed Elbaf's trembling hands, he didn't show it.

Arcus had spent a lifetime studying the movements and behavior of animals, and he knew that Elbaf was agitated to a greater degree than he'd let on. What he had yet to suss out was the *cause* for his agitation. He sensed, however, that this was neither the time nor the place to press.

He sipped his tea quietly and turned his thoughts back to the troubles at hand. He was particularly interested in the missing animals. Loathe though he was to admit it, he was quite certain that no animal had taken the sheep or cattle. There simply weren't any creatures native to this part of the world that could have done so without a trace.

His musing was interrupted when Talia finally joined them just shy of a candlemark later. She had dark circles under her eyes and she yawned widely from behind a stack of parchment and books she was carrying.

Still, she greeted them brightly, and the group shared a chuckle at her having overslept.

Talia flagged down one of the pages waiting at the edge of the room and instructed him to take the documents she'd assembled to Lord Goldrun. The young man nodded and hurried about his task, leaving them free to discuss the coming day.

"Right," Talia yawned again. "Where shall we start?"

Arcus and Darko both moved to speak at the same time, then paused.

"Please, after you, ranger," the mage deferred.

"I'd like to examine the fields where the animals were taken," Arcus suggested. "No offense to the farmers, but perhaps I might be able to pick out signs or tracks that they missed."

"I agree with the druid," Darko added. "I will be able to determine quickly if anything supernatural has occurred. Our two methods should compliment each other nicely."

"And you, Elbaf? Your thoughts?"

"I would look into the rumors of treason," he replied. "But I do not think it wise to separate when we know so little of the potential threats we face."

Talia chewed her bottom lip, weighing the courses of action her officers had presented.

"Right, we'll go check the fields," she concluded. "And sort the rest out on the way."

Their plan set, Talia instructed Sergeant Cormorant, the next highest ranking man in their small detachment, to have the rest of the soldiers supplement the town guard and keep a watchful eye out for signs of the rumored traitors.

Without the burden of their company, the four drew mounts and made their way to the town square to meet the two bickering farmers. Arcus rode behind and to the outside of their small group, already contemplating the mystery that lay before them.

He watched bemusedly as they turned the street and caught sight of the square. Both of the men were already present, their animosity for one another clear. They traded ugly looks at one another as Talia and the others rode into sight, each working hard to outdo the other in the warmth of their greeting and their deference.

"Ma'am, I'd rather not stay in this man's comp'ny if it's all the same to you," Ellard complained.

"Why you greasy half-wit, 'ow dare you--"

"Enough," Talia yelled. "Are you children, or men?"

"Ellard." She looked at the man. "What have you got to say?"

"Ma'am," he bowed deeply. "I've had three cattle gone missin' this past month, an' the whole town know's Torbin 'ere--"

"You keep my name out of--"

"I will not say this again," she interrupted. "The next time one of you interrupts the other, or me, you'll be in the stocks."

They fell into a chastised silence.

"He's the only one what *could* have got 'em, m'lady," Ellard explained. "Only one in town with a fam'ly big enough ta eat tha' much!"

"Alright," she turned to the other man, who was busy wringing his hands nervously. "And you, er, Torbin?"

"Yes'm, Torbin, ma'am," he dipped his head. "I'd never steal his cattle, ma'am. More than tha', I've no reason to - we eat plenty well on my sheep, ma'am."

"And what's the issue with your sheep?"

"There's tracks all over my fields, ma'am," Torbin glowered. "*Cattle* tracks or I'm no farmer. This feller's cows have broke my fence and got my sheep ate by wolves or summat!"

Talia eyed the two malcontents, her irritation growing.

"We'll sort out this mystery," she scolded them. "But in the meantime, I am quite certain you can occupy yourselves in a manner that does not require speaking to one another. Tend your herds and keep away from each other or there'll be hell to pay."

She gave a curt nod and their group departed at a trot, leaving the two farmers to fume and fret.

Arcus caught sight of the slight wave she gave him, and spurred his horse to ride beside her.

"Arcus," she said, her voice rising above the din of their combined hoofbeats. "I imagine you'll be taking the lead on this fiasco. Between you and Darko, I assume that Elbaf and I will quickly find ourselves without gainful employment, so we'll go over the crime reports and you give us a shout if anything crops up, alright?"

He nodded and signaled that Darko should join him at the head of the group. Meanwhile, Elbaf and Talia slowed their horses to an ambling walk as she recovered a ledger from her saddlebags.

Darko, still supremely uncomfortable in the saddle, kicked and swore as he tried to convince his mount to match Arcus' pace.

"Easy, friend," Arcus admonished him gently. "Easy. She'll take far kinder to a calm rider, Darko."

He smiled at the mage's glare.

"I imagine she would," he complained. "But she'll have to make do with me!"

Arcus leaned over in his saddle, ignoring Darko's look of alarm as he stood precariously off his stirrups and reached a hand out to the wizard's horse. The ranger calmed himself, his eyes closing and his breathing slowing as he expanded his consciousness into Darko's mount. Within moments the creature was under control and trotting along calmly beside his own horse.

"Now, just . . . don't *do* anything," Arcus laughed. "We'll improve your riding later, but for now she knows what to do, friend. You don't need to show her."

Darko grumbled something unintelligible, but seemed appreciative of his friend's assistance. They turned their focus onward and in short order found themselves back at the scene of their encounter the day before.

"Where shall we begin?"

Arcus turned to see Darko scanning the horizon carefully. He sat patiently as the mage cast his arcane sight to and fro, by now slightly more accustomed to the pale fire in his eyes as he sought out any magical energies that might linger in the area.

"Anything?"

Darko frowned, the flames in his eyes dying down as he shook his head.

"No. Whatever is doing this, it's not of a supernatural nature."

"Perhaps," Arcus said quietly, almost to himself. "Perhaps not."

He clicked his tongue and his horse sprang into a trot then gracefully leaped over the meter-high fence that separated the road from the nearest field.

"Perhaps not," Darko scoffed. "I assure you, I'd be able to detect *anything* out of the ordinary-- Whoa, *whoa!*"

The elf's horse followed Arcus' mount, leaving its hapless passenger clinging for dear life as it cleared the fence and landed with a loud whinny inside the field. Darko prepared to lambast his friend, but the ranger was standing tall in his stirrups, his eyes now glued to the horizon as Darko's had been moments before.

A huge white wolf emerged from the treeline, its head cocked to the side. Arcus waved at the mighty beast and Darko's keen eyes picked out that it was, in fact, Kodja. He was surprised to see the animal here, he'd seen neither hide nor hair of Kodja since their fateful night at the Capitol more than a year ago.

"I-- Wha . . . Did that wolf *follow* us this whole time?"

Arcus looked back at the mage, blinking in confusion.

"Yes? Why shouldn't he?"

"Well, it's an animal. How did you compel it to-- to *stick around?*"

Arcus laughed out loud as Kodja approached them at a full run.

"I didn't *compel* him to do anything," he swung down from the saddle in time to be engulfed by the white, furry missile. "He's a friend, a true and loyal one at that."

He was momentarily silenced as Kodja licked his face excitedly, his tail wagging back and forth like any common hound.

"He followed me because we're friends," Arcus said at last. "Because we're brothers."

Darko seemed both baffled and in awe of the interaction between the two.

"Truly, it seems I have much to learn of your people and their ways."

Arcus nodded without malice.

"I would have thought an elf would have a deeper, ah . . . *understanding* of the bonds between men and nature. I, too, have much to learn."

"We are not so easily categorized, I'm afraid," Darko agreed softly. "Not all of us dwell amongst the forests and play harps for woodland creatures. I have never traveled so far from the Capitol in all my hundred years of life. I have not lived within or even *visited* the Deep Wood of my ancestors."

They regarded each other a moment longer in silence before Kodja interrupted. He nudged Arcus firmly with his snout and trotted back towards the woodline to the north of the field.

Arcus inclined his head, indicating they ought to follow. Darko stayed mounted, but Arcus walked instead, leading his horse by the reins. He searched the ground with a careful eye as they made their way to the edge of the field, narrating aloud what he could see for his less knowledgeable companion.

"There's prints, plenty of them," he began, waving loosely over the ground. "Almost all of them are cattle. Here, the prints of a man, likely the farmer that works these fields. And there, a smaller set, perhaps a son or daughter."

Darko could well pick out the details as he pointed to them, and Arcus could see the wizard's studious face as he carefully committed each item of note to memory.

"How do you know this was the farmer?" he asked, scratching his chin. "And not some bandit or other miscreant?"

"A fine question," Arcus took a moment to construct his response. "You see here, the footsteps wander and weave. They are unhurried, and have the soft outline of worn leather."

He glanced up to make sure the mage followed his train of thought.

"A soldier would walk more directly and would likely be weighed down by armor or gear. A thief, on the other hand, might sulk about with smaller, more timid steps. Whomever walked here did so unencumbered by equipment or fear of discovery."

Arcus followed Darko's look backwards toward Elbaf and Talia and found them lost in conversation over a sheaf of parchment.

"I am unsurprised that this interests them so little," he agreed, echoing the mage's unspoken thought. "They prefer bold action, the heat of passionate decisions. This must surely bore them."

Suddenly, Arcus had a thought that made him feel rather foolish.

"Actually," he said sheepishly, "perhaps I presume too much by assuming you are not likewise bored?"

"Not at all," the mage replied in earnest. "I find your study of woodlore fascinating."

Arcus expressed his appreciation with another small nod and turned his eyes back to the ground. He could see the cattle-prints were especially thick and hurried here, as though they'd gathered in this place and stamped about. Many of the prints were quite deep, but not a human footprint was among them.

He looked expectantly at Kodja, who met his look evenly.

"Well?"

The wolf cocked its head to the side, looked down at the prints and then back at the druid.

Puzzled, Arcus sent feelings of good-natured confusion to his little brother's mind. The wolf returned the feeling, adding deeper levels of sense as he did so.

Arcus followed the wolf's mind, allowing his bond to help further his deep connection to the world.

"What's going--"

Arcus held a hand up to quiet the mage, not willing to break his concentration. His eyes narrowed and his nostrils flared as he allowed his senses to grow more primal, more developed. He breathed deeply, now picking out the individual scents of a thousand separate wildflowers, the hint of dirt and sweat from a rabbit hiding in the bushes, the dry rasp of a sleeping woodpecker's feathers. There *was* something out of the ordinary. It reminded him of a bull, but with . . . something more, the tang of iron and the burn of cured hides.

When Arcus spoke his voice was soft, distant.

"There's something here I don't recognize," he wondered aloud. "It's not a man, but no animal I have ever experienced, either."

His words were perhaps meant only for himself, but even so, Darko had no trouble picking them out.

"Neither man nor beast," he pondered with amusement. "Surely it is too early for riddles, friend."

Arcus returned a rueful smile, noting mentally that the elf's ears were keener than he thought.

"And yet, riddles we are faced with."

He gave a sharp whistle to flag down Talia and Elbaf, then returned to examining the prints on the ground as they approached.

"Have you found something already?" Talia asked enthusiastically. "Perhaps we shall be done with this issue sooner--"

"No," Arcus cautioned, interrupting her optimism. "And yet, yes, perhaps."

"By the grace of the gods, spit it out, ranger!"

Arcus bit back a retort to Elbaf's rudeness, and instead indicated a particularly deep set of prints on the ground.

"See these here, and over *here*," he motioned back and forth, tracing the path of the creature around the field near the fence. "These tracks are much, much deeper than the others, and stranger still they are further apart as well. So much so that it gives me pause."

The three stared blankly at him while he waited patiently.

"So . . ." the wizard began at last.

"So unless you three see a bull out here twice as heavy as any of the others, this was left by no farm animal." He crossed his arms confidently. "Something else lurks about these woods with hooves, and I would wager as well that it walks on two feet, not four."

"You're joking," Talia smiled. "Arcus, you're not *seriously* suggesting this is the work of a--"

"A minotaur, yes."

Elbaf and Talia shared a glance before bursting out in gales of laughter.

Arcus' face turned deep scarlet.

"Well, you wanted my opinion. Now you have it, and I'll say nothing else. Perhaps your own wilderness experience will guide you, and I'll stand idly by as it does!"

"Arcus, wait," Talia called out as he stalked away. "I'm sorry. It's just that . . . Well, it's just that every child has heard the campfire stories of minotaur and dragons and all manner of nonsense creatures made to scare children into obedience. But that's all they are, *stories*."

He turned back to face them, an ugly frown upon his face.

"Oh, is that so?" He looked each of them in the eyes in turn. "Well, as you're so wise and learned, you must be right," he shrugged in frustration. "And yet, I, alone, have traveled the four hundred leagues from D'Ari lands to the rotten sinkhole of Sunset Isle. I, alone, have seen some small fraction of the world you all haughtily claim to know from the pages of some dusty book, no doubt written by the hand of yet another scholar, rather than a woodsman."

They were shamed, and though it did not quell his anger, Arcus could see clearly the apologetic looks on their faces as he reminded them that their sheltered lives were a far cry from the edge-of-extinction living he had endured.

"Very well," Elbaf was the first to break the silence. "Minotaur, then. What do we do?"

Elbaf's straightforward question was echoed in the eyes of his other companions, and so Arcus took the high road and offered his equally straightforward answer.

"We hunt."

He retrieved some supplies from his saddlebags and then sent his horse trotting off by itself in the pasture, indicating that the others should do the same.

"We'll go on foot and as quietly as we can."

With that, he leapt the fence at the edge of the pasture and started prowling around, no doubt seeking signs of the minotaur's passage. Within moments he returned to them, a grin of satisfaction on his lips.

"As I suspected, the minotaur covered its tracks in the immediate vicinity of the pasture but not further out. I believe I've found the path."

He swiftly turned and darted back into the thick undergrowth.

Elbaf brought up the rear as they wound their way through what seemed like miles of twisting and turning thickets. Many times he found himself wondering if the ranger had gone mad, certain that they were re-crossing places they'd already been.

Still, he would not offer further insult to Arcus than he had earlier in the morning by questioning his tracking skills. He felt guilty that he'd been so willing to jest at the ranger's expense and hoped he was less offended than he'd seemed. He was bound, however - both by his reputation and his stubbornness - from offering further apology. No, he concluded, better to simply demonstrate his trust.

Even so, the terrain around them was growing rockier and steeper as the bluffs of town transitioned more thoroughly into windswept hills. He eyed the ranger's studded leather armor with envy as Arcus slipped easily between rock and tree, leaving the steel-encased half-orc to make his way as best he could. Even Talia, who also wore steel, was having an easier time. Her own scale was more supple than his plate, and she was a much smaller person to begin with.

Still, he suffered without complaint. The metal he wore was no burden on the battlefield, and, in truth, it was more the awkwardness than the weight of it that was so determined to frustrate him. He squeezed through a particularly narrow passage with a grinding squeal, the stones leaving thin marks on his polished breastplate, only to find the others already halted on the other side.

"Elbaf, brother," Arcus rubbed the bridge of his nose. "I'm *begging* you to be more careful. If the tales are true, it is not overstating things to say the minotaur are possessed of keen senses and are a deadly threat--"

"I'd challenge you to do better," Elbaf growled. "Let us strap four stone of steel to your tiny body and see how silently you move."

With the sun high overhead and the four companions all sweating in the narrow confines of the rocky passage, tempers were already running hot. Talia raised her hands, determined to ease the tension before it boiled over.

"We should pause a moment," she said, pulling a flask of water from her hip and handing it to Elbaf. "There's no reason we should press like hounds after a rabbit. We have time on our side."

Arcus nodded his agreement, taking a drink from his own waterskin.

The group cooled down for several minutes as best they could, but Arcus' impatience won out after less than a candlemark.

"Hold here," he whispered. "I'll just scout ahead, as I believe we *must* be close to their camp."

With that - and before his companions could object - he slipped silently away.

Elbaf adjusted his breastplate, but resisted the urge to remove it in the field. Talia must have noted his movement, because she left her own sitting place to come and share the boulder he sat upon.

"He meant no offense, Elbaf, I'm sure of it," she reassured him needlessly.

Elbaf stole a glance at Darko, but the mage was deep in thought - or else, perhaps, asleep. Either way, he was sitting quietly, his eyes closed and his hands folded in his lap.

"I know, Talia," he replied softly. "This armor frustrates him because it doesn't belong here, in his world. I will respect his judgment here, just as he respects mine on the battlefield."

They shared several minutes of silence before the cleric broke it once again.

"Elbaf," she all but murmured.

She took the slight inclination of his helmeted head to mean that he had heard her.

"I am sorry for what happened at the village."

She saw the warrior stiffen, then relax a fraction.

"What we were asked to do . . . what we *did*," she hung her head. "It was wrong, and it shouldn't have fallen to you to stop that slaughter - I should have done it myself."

His silence was deafening.

"The punishment should have been mine, as well. You did *nothing* to deserve that. I should have-- I--"

"Talia," he interrupted. "You carry the weight of command in your heart, when it should rightly sit upon your shoulders."

She turned to look at him, puzzled.

"I don't understand . . ."

He heaved a heavy sigh.

"You cannot dwell on the past. You must learn from it, and move on. If you turn away from the challenges ahead to linger on what could have been, you will suffer as a leader, and so will your men."

Talia was taken aback at the unexpected wisdom of her gruff, forbidding friend.

"You never cease to surprise me, Elbaf."

He turned his characteristically unreadable face towards her and gave an almost imperceptible shrug.

"Perhaps because you - like most everyone else in the Empire - view me as something less than, rather than an equal. You judge me for a lineage you do not understand, and you assume the worst of me without a second thought."

With that he turned back to face the pass that Arcus had left through, and Talia found herself at a loss for words. Many times she considered saying something further, something to defend herself from his barbed words, but she could not deny them.

Instead, they simply waited.

Elbaf seemed content to remain as still as a statue, his eyes fixed, presumably, upon the path ahead while they waited for the ranger's return.

But Talia's restless mind wandered, and the more time that passed the more she turned her thoughts to worrying about the ranger.

"Do you suppose he's alright?" she asked no one in particular, casting a glance skyward and noting that nearly an hour had passed.

Elbaf shrugged. He'd clearly be of no help.

"He's fine, Talia," Darko said with surprising certainty. "He'll be back in a moment."

"He's been gone a good long while. Maybe we should go looking for him."

"Truly, Talia, there's no need."

"Yes, you say that," she huffed in frustration, "but how can you be sure?"

"Because he's been following me," Arcus called out, choosing that moment to reappear at the head of the path. "Or these woods have the most curiously single-minded ravens I've ever known."

Talia laughed as the mage's all-knowing expression turned to one of embarrassment.

"Y-yes, w-well Reia is many things," he sputtered. "And a lesser woodsman would no doubt have been fooled."

"Ah," Arcus smiled widely. "Flattery will get you nowhere, friend."

The truth of his words was reaffirmed as a jet-black raven swooped down and landed lightly on Darko's shoulder before cawing indignantly at Arcus.

"It seems I have upset your pet," the ranger said warmly. "For that, I am sorry."

If anything, his words seemed to elicit a stronger reaction from the bird, which hopped up and down angrily before tucking itself inside Darko's hood. The group tried to hide their smiles as the irritated creature glowered at them from the shadows.

"What have you found, ranger?" Elbaf asked, turning their minds again to the task at hand.

"Right," Arcus sighed. "So there is no camp, at least not one out in the woods. Rather, it seems the minotaur has taken up residence in a nearby cave."

"Damn," Elbaf swore aloud. "If the creature is as formidable as you say, it will be difficult to remove from such a defensible position."

"Can we not simply smoke it out or something?" Talia asked. "My father used to hunt the Cypreen Mountains to the northeast, he told me they'd stack green leaves and branches on a fire and fan it into the tunnels when they were driving out cave bears to hunt."

Arcus shook his head.

"No, for one we've no idea if the caves are shallow enough for such a tactic to work, and secondly, you're underestimating the intelligence of these creatures."

"But they are beasts," Darko interjected. "Every treatise and story I've ever read indicates--"

"Minotaur are not mindless animals," Arcus explained softly. "D'Ari lore tells us they are cunning, strong, and a deadly serious foe. They are perhaps simpler than a man, that is true enough. But they use tools, communicate in their own language; I've heard rumors they even have cities in the great deserts past the Koholan Wastes far to the south of here."

The group seemed skeptical, but kept their doubts to themselves.

"Furthermore, they dwarf you for size and strength, Elbaf, and can kill a man with a single blow of their fists. They're no idle matter, and when we enter the caves we should do so cautiously. Huntress help us if the creature has arms and armor."

Elbaf stood and stretched his back.

"Do you think it wise to enter the caves at all then?" he asked. "Why not wait and lay a trap here in the open?"

Arcus shook his head slowly.

"You might think so, at first," he chewed his lip a moment. "But a charging minotaur is an unstoppable force of nature. No, we'll be far better off in the confines of the caves, away from any open ground for it to build up speed."

Sobered, the group followed at his wave and began to pick their way through the rocks once again. In short order they were outside a small clearing at the mouth of a cave. It was here that Arcus gestured that they should remove their extra gear. They did so in silence, forewarned by Arcus of the dangers ahead.

The whole area lay silent, even the birds in the trees seemed unwilling to break the early afternoon hush as the group slowly moved in towards the entrance.

"I'll go first," Elbaf declared quietly. "I don't need light to make out our path."

Talia stepped forward as well. She hefted her mace and shook out her shield arm before taking her place beside Elbaf.

"For now, but if the tunnels allow it I'll be at your side."

The mighty orc nodded at her, and they waited for Arcus and then finally Darko to take their places in the rear.

"I could summon arcane light," Darko offered. "But I will yield to your wisdom, Arcus."

The ranger pulled an arrow from his quiver and laid it gently across his bow before speaking.

"No," he shook his head, then cast a foreboding look at the warriors ahead of him. "Elbaf will guide us. He'll make the call."

Elbaf nodded, then turned back towards the mouth of the cave yawning before them.

He studied the opening. It seemed fairly straight and true, at least for the first sixty feet or so. It was large too, easily a dozen feet across and ten-foot high. He tightened his grip on his blade and started forward.

"Follow me."

Chapter Ten

Elbaf's heavy footfalls were muffled by the thick layer of soft dust upon the floor of the cave, but still they seemed deafening to his straining eardrums.

He'd never been in a cave before, and even the quiet of the imperial sewers was nothing to this - this absolute stillness. The party had been cautiously making its way deeper into the earth for the past candlemark, and in all that time they'd yet to see a single living thing.

Elbaf pondered for a moment how much more terrible it must be for his companions. They were well and truly blind, after all.

He spared a moment to look to his side at Talia. Her eyes were wide but unseeing, and they darted about senselessly in the all-consuming darkness. Her footsteps were timid, but her grip on her mace and shield was iron-strong and steady as the stone beneath their feet.

Satisfied that his friends were safely in tow, he turned his eyes back to scanning the tunnel ahead of them. The stone walls were raw, unfinished, and he needn't be a mason to see that they were devoid of tool marks or signs of an unnatural origin. He supposed the wizard could better explain the reason for the cave to have formed at all - or perhaps Arcus had some insight - but he was not curious enough to ask. As it was, he was simply grateful his fears of a tiny, confining space went unrealized.

The thick cave dust on the ground made tracking their quarry fairly simple; it showed scores of deep hoofprints tracing a path back and forth to the entrance that even a baby could have followed.

Further and deeper in, the caves wound until at last they came upon the inevitable - a fork in their path. Worse yet, it was a four way intersection.

"Damn," Elbaf swore under his breath.

The words were like shouts in the deathly silence, and he saw his companions stiffen next to him.

"What is it, what's wrong?" hissed Talia.

"The path splits," he studied the ground. "And each path has tracks."

"Ranger, I don't suppose you have any insights?" Darko prompted quietly.

"I admit, the deep reaches of the earth are . . . not where I am most at home," Arcus scratched his head. "But I will try."

Arcus knelt in the dust and closed his eyes.

He needn't have bothered, really, considering the impenetrable darkness of the caves ahead and behind him, but it helped him concentrate nonetheless.

He calmed his mind and reached out with his spirit, seeking the vast web of life that he knew extended even here, in this silent, desolate place. The rocks and the earth pressed in on his mind, clouding his normally clear path to the energies of the world. He knit his brows in concentration as he tried to work his way past the obstacles in his mind. Every now and again he would reach some spark of life, a worm or grub or other burrowing creature, but the connection was tenuous and unstable, and it would fail before he could dig deeper.

He gave a frustrated sigh and shook his head, then leaned forward and buried his hands in the dirt.

He resisted the temptation to push back against the stone, knowing that the immutable earth was stronger than him by an unimaginable margin. Instead he drove on with fire and passion, hoping that the earth would yield to the heat of his lifeforce.

It didn't.

He unclenched his jaw, which had tightened to the point that it ached, and tried to center himself. His senses were extended as far as they could reach, his muscles taught with effort from seeking a path. He was wracking his mind for another way when he heard Darko let out a long, drawn out sigh.

He bit back cruel words, aware that despite the mage's simple expression grating at his raw and frustrated nerves, Darko had meant no offense.

"Arcus?" Darko asked quietly. "Perhaps it--"

"Shh," Arcus implored him softly, the wind hissing all but silent across his lips.

Arcus' eyes snapped open wide as he felt the wind move in the cave. Suddenly there was a light of life and energy in the darkness all around him.

He clung to the currents in the wind from his companions breathing, traced their delicate, invisible paths as the air in the cave swallowed the tiny disturbances. The wind faded and Arcus lost track of it for a moment, but felt the current renewed with each breath drawn and released. He all but cried out with joy as he linked at last into the world he knew existed.

On soaring, silent wings he allowed the energy to pull him along the endless winding tunnels of the caves. He relished the eddies and swirls of life, and wondered how he could have missed them initially. Here a cave cricket moved, disturbing for even the tiniest moment the air above its legs. There, a bat shifted in slumber, its rolled wings sending waves that could be felt throughout the whole of the cave system.

He beamed broadly, his eyes blind to the world but his heart linked inextricably with the air in his lungs.

There.

"I've found them," he whispered.

"*Them,*" Elbaf growled. "There are more than one?"

Arcus didn't answer at first.

Instead, he pulled slowly back into himself. He let go of the energy he had ridden through the caves and took a moment to contemplate how much he still had to learn. He'd warned the mage not long ago that Nature was unkind and unresponsive to those who demanded things of her, and yet he had approached this task with arrogance.

Thank you, Eli'Yassa, I have so much yet to learn.

His simple prayer to the earth-mother complete, he stood and dusted his hands off on his trousers.

"Yes," he answered simply. "There are three."

"Perhaps we should reconsider," Darko interjected. "Are we adequately prepared to deal with *three* minotaur?"

Arcus laughed softly as he set his bow across his shoulder.

"There will be no conflict here, not unless we bring it upon ourselves."

Talia chewed her lip, a nervous habit she'd yet to kick.

It had been nearly twenty minutes since they'd stopped at the crossroads, and Arcus had taken the lead ever since. She knew he couldn't see, not *really* anyway, but nonetheless he had wandered unerringly - never tripping or even scuffing his boots against an errant stone.

How? Without the Emperor's guidance, how can this be?

A debate had raged inside her for weeks now, and she had yet to fully acknowledge it. Too much that she had taken as gospel was in question. She couldn't deny that Arcus had powers not unlike her own, certainly more similar than those of Darko, but the fundamental question remained - if not through the Emperor, how were his powers granted? Could what he'd said be true? Were there *other* routes to the divinity she felt flowing through her when she performed the rites of her faith?

"They're just ahead," Arcus whispered, pulling her back to the present.

The group slowed to a snail's pace until at last, after a slow turn in the path, they could see the flickering light of a fire ahead.

"Put your weapons away, friends," the ranger cautioned. "Here blades will not win the day."

Talia hesitated, her instincts screaming at her not to stow her weapon. She trusted the ranger, of course, but anyone could make a mistake.

She had yet to make a decision when she heard Arcus start forward again. She followed as quietly as she could, and compromised by holding her mace low to her side.

They made their way along as stealthily as they could, but even Talia could tell they were making a fair amount of noise. Here the cave dust beneath her boots was thinner, more worn away by heavy traffic, and the scuffling of leather on stone was unmistakable. Even so, it seemed their prey was unaware of their presence - no sound or movement ahead indicated they'd been detected.

Talia caught herself holding her breath and released it shakily as they came to the entrance of a larger cavern. She could make out some details around them now, but the cavern itself was dotted with massive stalactites that obscured most of her field of vision. Many of the rock formations were ten foot tall or higher, and wide as tree trunks at the base.

She stopped watching her feet as closely and looked around more, scouring the room for signs of life. Distracted, she stumbled when one of her feet hit a deep puddle instead of solid rock. Her boot sloshed down loudly, the noise billowing forth into the darkness and drawing the immediate stares of her companions.

She had just enough time to realize what she'd done and to take in the fact that she was standing at the edge of a large pool of water which had been covered by shadows on their approach, before an ear splitting roar shook the cavern. The sound seemed to come from everywhere at once as it reverberated against the stone.

Instincts alone kept her hands on her armaments and not clutching her ears from the din.

She fought rising panic as her eyes darted back and forth, seeking solace in a familiar meditative exercise that the Sisterhood had beaten into her mind during her training.

Silently, she recited the rites of faith. The eleven-line prayer grounded her at once and renewed her nerve even as she repeated it silently over and over. A moment later, her back was again unbowed and her breathing, while still hard, was heavy with resolve instead of fear.

They made a tiny defensive cluster, anticipating an attack that seemed always about to materialize but never happened.

Finally, Talia would wait no longer. She raised her voice in song and every word was deep and rich with power. She called for the divine light of the Emperor to beat back the darkness, and as her voice rang out, a soft white glow grew to envelope her. The light, which clung to her like mists in the fields, grew and grew until its intensity outmatched that of the flickering fire and bathed the cavern in light. Her mace shone brighter than a bundle of torches, and her shield was like the beacon of a lighthouse.

Darko was relieved to see Talia working her magic. It meant that he, too, was free to let loose his own eldritch powers without bringing the ire of the group.

They had no enemy - not yet, anyway - but Darko would not sit idly. He clasped his hands together in front of his chest, feeling at once a small but growing bead of energy beneath his fingers. Within his mind burned the words for his incantation, and he spoke them perfectly into being. With every word he felt the pressure within his closed hands grow, fold back upon itself, and then push against him once again. Electric blue runes of power swirled and circled around his hands, their brightness growing with every passing second.

The shield charm he crafted was simple, in theory, but took mastery to execute well. It was, however, a personal specialty of his. Decades of bullying at the Academy had given him plenty of reasons to practice defensive magic, and this spell in particular was as familiar to him as a musician's favorite instrument.

As he neared the end of the incantation, the force within his white-knuckled fingers started to slip through, looking for all the world like thin pieces of crystal-clear glass.

The final words spoken, he flung his hands outward. The shards spun themselves into a broad, almost invisible disc which flew past Elbaf's shoulder as it grew from palm-sized to almost six feet wide.

Darko kept his left hand outstretched, palm outward, and the runes surrounding it spun and twisted like living bracelets. Invisible to the others, those same runes spun and danced across the face of his shield as well. Where his palm pointed, so did the shield face, and as he searched for threats, he kept it closely orbiting the group.

It was pure luck that he was facing the right direction when the bull charged.

It happened in a heartbeat. The tunnel he'd just looked at was empty, and then, suddenly it wasn't. Ten feet of towering muscle sprinted at them faster than he would have thought possible. His keen eyes barely registered any details at all as the monster closed the 30-foot gap at a full sprint. He saw horns several feet long and as thick as his forearms, rippling corded muscle, and pitted, corroded metal armor.

Darko flinched, his shield sliding in between Arcus' flank and the wicked points of the minotaur's horns just in time. The creature hit the shield like a boulder rolling off a cliff.

For the barest instant the shield held, but it could not contain the monster. A billion jagged red cracks appeared in its surface as the impact of the charge was blunted. The horns pierced it first, sending fragments of the spell out into the air to disappear harmlessly, but the rest was not far behind. The bulk of the creature had caved the shield inward, but the ranger had been spared from what could have been a mortal blow.

The minotaur stumbled backward a few feet, yanking its horns out of the shield, which shattered at last. For a moment the creature was dazed, and Darko could get a good look at it.

It was massive.

It sported a dull red hide with patches of short, shaggy, black fur. The creature's eyes were bigger than he'd expected and full of naked rage. As Arcus had forewarned, the creature wore enormous slabs of pitted cast iron for armor and held in its hands the biggest hammer that Darko had ever seen. To the mage's eye, the armor had very few weak points. Here was an ironclad behemoth, covered nearly as well as Elbaf's full plate, and in armor that looked over an inch thick in places.

Darko saw, from the corner of his eye, another point of movement. He paled when he realized that another minotaur stood off to the right.

No, he realized. It was *two* more!

"On our flank," he shouted, his hands already weaving the complex patterns of spellcraft. "Another!"

He saw Arcus start to move and blinked in confusion as the ranger moved himself between them and the armored warrior, his hands empty and outstretched.

"Hold," Arcus shouted. "Stop, everyone stop!"

Darko knew folly when he saw it, and this was surely it. His hands were already coated in blue lightning, tiny arcs of which danced between his fingers and up his arms. He could feel the static building in his body as his hair, already disheveled from travel, started to raise, as well.

The minotaur in front of them was not dazed for long before it shook its head and stood, ready to assault them again within moments. There was no doubt that it had longer reach over Elbaf, but the half-orc's blade was wielded with skill and the minotaur seemed willing to respect the threat he presented.

"Please, I beg you!" Arcus shouted. "If you lay down your arms--"

Darko didn't wait for him to finish. Perhaps the others had yet to see the threat lurking in the shadows across from them, but he would not be caught unaware.

His pupils and the whites of his eyes were gone, replaced by incandescent blue, and lightning arced across his entire body as the stored energy within him sought an outlet. With a flick of his wrist, three pumpkin sized balls of lightning shot from his fingertips, crackling through the air towards the minotaur across the cavern.

The larger of the two shoved the other to the ground and took two of the three projectiles in the chest, spasming uncontrollably and roaring in pain. The third ball missed, exploding on the wall of the cavern and leaving blackened streaks upon the stone.

The warrior in front of them bellowed a challenge and waded into melee range at last.

Elbaf parried the first swing of the hammer, but it rocked him to his core, nearly lifting him from the ground despite his efforts.

The half-orc pushed his skills to the limit, even managing to drive the monstrous creature back for a moment, but the enormous hammer was too big, too heavy, and too well-utilized for him to retain an advantage for more than a few moments. Arcus' warning had been right, the minotaur's strength, stature, and reach far outmatched his own. It was only through precision and skill that he was able to hold his own at all.

He, Arcus, and Talia danced and fought with the beast, but they could do no better than to keep it occupied it seemed. The armor was too thick, and the feeble purchase their weapons found was only enough to inflict small cuts. Meanwhile, they played a risky game knowing that any blow from the creature might be a deadly one.

Darko looked back to the other pair as he sought a spell that would help his companions.

The larger of the two minotaurs was back on its feet, no small thing considering the punishment that it had received from his spell. It was half dragging, half carrying the smaller minotaur towards the tunnel that the party had come from.

The warrior in front of them disengaged, pulling back and gesturing towards the exit.

"Get her to safety, dearheart!" it bellowed before raising its hammer to strike again.

Darko's mouth popped open as the creature spoke in clear, unbroken Klobratuu.

He was stunned to the point of losing the spell he was working on. His mouth moved for a moment without sound as he reeled from the realization that the monster

134

had *spoken*.

"Wait," he shouted in the dialect, one only rarely heard and, even then, only in academic settings. "Wait, you speak?"

The minotaur's head jerked upwards and it took another step backwards, warding off a wild swing of Elbaf's blade.

"Of course I speak the sacred tongue, sorcerer," it growled at him.

Sacred tongue?

Darko knew of Klobratuu only as an ancient desert-dweller language, similar in many ways to dwarven - and just as extinct.

"I--" the wizard stumbled over the words, but his near-perfect memory served him well. "We are--"

"Hunters," the creature shrugged, its voice booming over the elf's. "You'll not find my horns easy to take. You're not the first or the last to try."

"No," Darko waved his hands. "You misunderstand."

The rest of the group was watching the exchange with growing unease, painfully unaware of what was being said between the two.

"I understand well enough." He hefted his hammer again. "You come to hunt us in our home. There can be no more important truth."

"For the love of the gods, Darko, tell him we mean no harm," Arcus shouted, red-faced and breathing heavily.

He panted from exhaustion as the wizard and the minotaur exchanged heated words, both gesturing wildly as they did.

After several painful moments of arguing, the wizard turned at last to his companions directly.

"He's willing to hear us out before killing us, at least," Darko sighed.

"Ask him if he's been eating the sheep, stealing the grain. If they're responsible for the issues in the town we can resolve this peacefully, I think," Arcus replied.

"Well, obviously they're responsible--"

"Just ask him, Darko," Talia snapped.

More words, followed by an unexpected burst of loud, booming laughter from the minotaur.

Darko made an ugly face and turned his gaze back to the group.

"He says that in his lands the custom is that if one cannot defend his herd, he has no herd."

"Fair enough," Elbaf nodded. "Will they go peacefully?"

Darko shrugged and posed the question.

"They are fleeing from some sort of troubles in their homeland, making their way northward to Brinhille Pass and to the lands beyond," Darko said matter-of-factly. "They need provisions for the journey, but do not intend to stay here permanently."

"Perfect," Arcus said with obvious relief. "Tell him we'll get them provisions if they move along immediately and so long as they swear not to trouble any more imperial lands, holdings, or citizenry."

"Arcus, do you *really* think that--"

He glared daggers at the elf, who shut his mouth, then spoke as he'd been instructed.

The minotaur heard his question, but did not immediately respond. Instead, the creature looked directly at Arcus.

Tense silence grew until the beast reached up and removed it's heavy iron helmet. Beneath the black metal was a wide, bovine face. The eyes were full of intelligence and fire, and the many scars on the muzzle of the minotaur were testament to a hard life. It was difficult to tell, but Arcus took the graying hairs around the nose and mouth of the minotaur to mean the creature was middle-aged or older.

This time, when he spoke, he did so at a much lower volume.

"He wants to know who our leader is," Darko said, carefully addressing them as a group, rather than speaking to Talia directly.

The cleric chewed her lip a moment, then set her jaw tightly.

"Tell him it's me," she said tersely. "I'd rather not hide the truth. If there are to be consequences, they should be mine."

Darko gave a short nod and bit back any warning he might have otherwise given. Instead, he turned back to the minotaur and, while giving his answer, gestured with deference at Talia. The creature remained calm, but it studied her carefully before speaking once again.

"He asks for your, er . . . *honor*, Talia, as leader of our, um . . . 'warband' is the closest translation," Darko said. "He says he needs your honor that his wife and child will not be harmed."

"Talia," Arcus cautioned, his tone turning to that of warning. "We don't know--"

"Done," Talia said without a single moment of hesitation. "I give you my honor that I will do everything in my power to keep you from harm."

Darko translated, but the minotaur shook his head and snorted.

"He says that is not the same, that you must take responsibility for his family's safety."

"Very well," Talia pondered for a moment. "Your safety will be my responsibility, and my honor will guarantee it. So long as you leave peacefully, I offer you my oath to keep you safe and see you on your way."

The minotaur, upon hearing her new oath, raised his head and lightly tapped his throat. Talia mimicked the gesture, and the minotaur broke into a smile. With a bellow, he beckoned over the other two, and began to speak more quickly with Darko.

"He says his name is Vedhellar," Darko translated as quickly as he could. "And this is his mate, Kloriskja, and their daughter Jarhein."

Arcus sighed with relief and slid his scimitar back into its sheath. As everyone in the group began to speak over one another, Darko found it impossible to keep up with the tide of questions and answers.

"A moment, please, friends," he begged, retrieving his spellbook. "I have a solution to this problem."

He bore the curious scrutiny of the assembled group, flicking through age-yellowed pages of fine vellum until he found what he was looking for.

"I will place upon you all a simple enchantment," he advised them. "It may cause you some small measure of discomfort at first, but do not be alarmed. It will allow you to speak freely without requiring me to translate."

Narrowed eyes and slight frowns met his words, but no one objected outright. Taking their silence for agreement, the wizard began to chant softly. As he spoke, a faint chill crept outward from him. It grew colder and colder until his breath fogged visibly between his lips.

Struggling though he might, Arcus couldn't make out a single syllable of what the wizard was saying - it was as though it slipped from his mind the moment it was uttered.

Arcus watched as the elf's foggy breath began to collect, persisting far longer than it ought to have. Soon, there was a thick cloud of mist obscuring the wizard's entire head. Were it not for the raised hairs on his arms, he might have laughed at the sight.

A humming noise interrupted his musing, its volume growing by the second until it was a steady buzz in his ears. He was about to say something, afraid that Darko might be in trouble, when suddenly the fog cloud was shot through with bright golden sparks.

The mist swirled and rolled, shining like flecks of gold in a bowl of quicksilver.

With a sudden pop, all the sounds of the world ceased to be. Arcus blinked, off balance from the sudden and oppressive silence, and shared a startled glance with the others.

"Darko," he cried out, only to realize he couldn't even hear his own voice.

The wizards made no sign that he'd heard, but with another loud, hissing pop, sound rushed back into being.

"Jurr, take the wizard. He has deceived us!" the largest minotaur was shouting, his hand already straying to his ax handle.

"Wait," Arcus interrupted instinctively. "He would not do us harm, give the magic a chance--"

He stopped.

"By . . . by the gods. I understood what you said just now!"

"And I you," the minotaur wondered aloud. "Well met, ranger. It seems I was too hasty."

Laughs of disbelief were exchanged all around for the impressive display, and Arcus noted that Darko's face was bright with a smug, if well-deserved, smile.

"The enchantment *will* wear away eventually," he cautioned. "But it should last most of the afternoon and into the evening."

Talia was the first to fully recover.

"Please, let me tend to your wounds," she implored. "It is the least that I can do."

The minotaur raised his hands in protest and took a step back.

"No, priestess," he said in a heavily accented, but surprisingly rich voice. "It goes against the will of Kullum. To have our wounds tended by an enemy would cost me my honor."

"You would endure the suffering of your wounds for honor?" Talia blinked in surprise.

The minotaur gave a solemn nod.

"A warrior without honor has no seat at Kullum's table; he will be forever denied admittance and loses his place in the battle at the end of times."

Now that they could communicate, it was quickly clear that the legends and tales of mindless monsters couldn't have been further from the truth. The minotaur, for their part, seemed to hold no grudge against the party. It seemed that mortal combat was simply a part of their culture, and it was seen as a great honor to fall in battle against a worthy foe.

The group was invited to share the fire which was already blazing in the heart of the minotaur camp.

Vedhellar sat with them and spoke at great length, regaling the group with stories of great stone temples and cities teeming with thousands of their kind in the deserts far away, beyond the edge of the Empire. They sat raptly listening as the elder minotaur painted stunning pictures of great sand dunes and sunbaked mudflats, blood-red mesas and impossible-sounding arches of natural stone.

"Why would you ever leave such a place?" Talia asked in starry-eyed wonder.

At her question, Vedhellar's expression grew grim.

"An age-old story, I'm afraid. War split my land, and our high priestess was overthrown. I was charged with smuggling out some of our most sacred texts so that they would not be lost when the usurpers tore down the temples."

He gestured to a broad animal-hide backpack sitting beside one of their bedrolls.

"I would have preferred to fight," he sighed. "But my path was set by another. Our way of life lives as long as we do. High Priestess Feljona spoke of a land to the north, past the Empire, where our kind lived in ages past. It is our hope that some remain, that we may continue the Old Ways."

He hung his head and his broad, four-fingered hands tightened into fists.

"I cannot know for certain the fate of my countrymen," he all but growled. "But it is not our way to surrender, nor to give quarter to bested foes."

Talia watched her friends as they interacted with Vedhellar and his family. It was bizarre to her that the histories she'd studied could be so irrefutably *wrong*. She considered, as well, the oath she had taken - it bordered on mutiny, at best. She wagered that when Annabelle found out, there would be hell to pay. But Annabelle was not here, nor would she be. These creatures were not monsters, they were refugees. No, she resolved, she would see them safely away.

They shared several hours chatting idly before Talia could bring herself to remind her companions that they were overdue back at the town. Lord Goldrun would no doubt already be turning out the guards to seek them out.

"Friends, I am sorry to say it, but we should return." She stood and brushed dust from herself. "If we're to make arrangements then we'd best not be thought dead or captured."

Of all of them, Elbaf seemed most loath to leave their new friends. He'd been unusually talkative, and Talia mused that in these warriors he'd found kindred spirits.

It must be hard for one of his kind, she thought to herself. Half-orcs were rarely a product of love, and seldom had a family to raise them. She realized she didn't *know* his history and chided herself for assuming it was such a dark one. After all, it was his unexpected wisdom that had reminded her of the dangers of doing just that.

Vedhellar stood as well, his towering frame dwarfing even Elbaf.

"Friends," he rumbled. "The gods must surely smile upon my family for such an outcome to be born of battle. Travel well, and we will look forward to your return."

With heartfelt goodbyes and well-wishes, her group departed. They made their way back to the entrance of the caves more easily this time with the comforting light of Darko's magic to guide them. They were back out into the waning afternoon in short order and determined to make it back to the town before nightfall.

The young cleric looked back into the darkness of the cave mouth, allowing the others to get ahead of her.

"Benevolent Emperor," she prayed, softly bowing her head. "Grant me your grace as I negotiate for the safety of these creatures, and cradle them with your divine mercy."

"Talia," Arcus called out from ahead of her. "Everything alright?"

"Yes," she called back, her cheeks red. "Yes, I'm coming."

Talia caught up with the others, who met her with curious looks.

"Sorry," she shrugged, strolling past them and down the path they'd followed earlier in the day. "I'm ready. Let's get back to town."

Horsemen met them on the road a few miles outside of Bethlir, a mixture of their own men and some of Bethlir's town guards as well. Elbaf prided himself on being able to pick out who of his men rode amid the half-dozen guardsmen, even at a distance. Garland, Merryl, and Derrin had all accompanied Goldrun's men on what could only be a rescue attempt.

"What's this?" Arcus called to the approaching riders. "Out for a leisure ride?"

"Yes, sir," Derrin called out, smiling brightly. "It's just these last nights of summer are so very tempting and mild."

Chapter Eleven

"You cannot *possibly* be serious," Goldrun asked, his eyes wide with shock.

"And yet I *am*, my lord," Talia's exasperation crept into her voice. "But as I have already said, there's an extremely simple solution--"

He interrupted her with a disdainful wave of his hand, turning and pacing the worn wood of the inn's floor.

Talia and Elbaf, who had insisted he stay with her until her duties were finished, had been talking in circles with Lord Goldrun since their return. The sun had long since fallen below the horizon, but their conversation had barely moved at all.

"Yes, yes, I've heard your solution, Talia," he said, his voice laced with obvious disregard. "And I applaud your kind, if not naive, heart."

Color touched her cheeks but she held herself in check.

"No," he stopped pacing and turned back to the pair of tired officers. "No, it would be absurd. We cannot simply supply provisions to these monsters and send them packing to raid some other hapless town. I won't stand for it."

"I beg your pardon," Talia snapped.

"You, warrior," he gestured broadly at Elbaf. "Tell her it's ridiculous, perhaps she'll listen to you."

"I most assuredly will not," Talia shouted, now red in the face. "I have done my best to respect your authority here, Lord Goldrun, but the decision is mine and it is *made*."

Icy stillness filled the common room and, from the corner of her eye, Talia could see Elbaf stiffen slightly in his armor.

"You must be very tired, Talia," the lord of the town said softly, his words dripping with condescension. "I suggest you take your rest and we resume this conversation in the morning with cooler heads."

Talia's chest swelled but she forced herself to speak calmly.

"This discussion is over," she replied curtly. "In the morning, you will inform me what provisions may be spared and we will make arrangements."

A long and deadly pause followed her words.

She locked eyes with the man, determined to bring him to heel. His gaze was as steady as her own, and though he hid it well, Talia could see that inwardly he seethed.

So be it then, she thought to herself.

"Am I understood, Lord Goldrun?"

His eyes narrowed slightly at her barb, and their staring contest lasted a moment longer before he broke eye contact.

"But of course," he gave a stiff, barely noticeable bow. "I'll see it done, Captain Lorraine."

Without waiting to be dismissed, he turned on his heel and stalked out of the common room; the door slammed shut behind him. Talia at last let her shoulders droop.

"Talia," Elbaf turned to face her more directly. "That man is dangerous, no matter what he says or seems to be. The people of this town love him, and we are strangers here."

"I know, Elbaf," she let out a defeated sigh. "But I gave Vedhellar and his family my word."

Elbaf nodded, but said nothing. His bearing carried more weight than a hundred platitudes, however, and she knew he agreed with her.

"I'm going to bed, Elbaf," she said at last with a broad yawn. "You should sleep, as well. With luck we can be rid of this town tomorrow."

Dawn brought with it stiff joints and sore muscles for Darko, who cursed softly in the darkness of his room as he struggled out of bed. His leg throbbed from the exertions of the day before, and he was much the worse for wear.

You must take care, Master. You were not built for this.

"Yes, Reia," he chuckled bitterly. "I suppose you're right."

Even so, he lifted his battered frame from the bed and stumbled through the motions of getting himself dressed and ready for the day.

Reia watched him intently from her perch upon the low wooden table across the room. At times like this, when they were alone, she preferred her given form to the disguises she took on in the company of others. He was grateful that she felt no need to hide around him, and wished not for the first time that they lived in a more open-minded land.

Still, he thought to himself, if even half of the conventional teachings regarding the rest of the world were true then they were better off within the Empire. He took that thought and ran with it, weighing the newly-acquired understanding that perhaps some of the things he'd learned were not only incorrect, but egregiously so.

He'd stayed up long enough to observe his nightly ritual of recording the day's activities, as well as his own musings and observations. Last night the task had taken longer than usual. In fact, the longer they traveled the more his entries seemed to grow.

"I wonder, Reia," he mused aloud, picking up their conversation absentmindedly. "Just how much of what I learned in the Academy was . . ."

Skewed?

"Precisely," he grinned ruefully. "But I suspect we will have time enough to ponder it on the next leg of our journey. I never thought I'd look forward to riding again, but after yesterday's hike, I will be grateful for the break."

I'm sure Arcus will be delighted to hear that.

Darko knew her threat was hollow, but he glared at Reia regardless.

"Why don't you help me pack, instead of just sitting there?" he grumbled, stuffing book after book into his knapsack.

If you wanted menial labor, you should've bonded with something a little . . .

shall we say, taller?

He wouldn't have bothered re-packing his room at all, but he'd gotten the distinct impression that Talia would prefer to be gone from this town as swiftly as possible. He didn't doubt for a second that his luggage was more expansive than the others in their troop, no matter what appearances might suggest on the road. His knapsack was far more than the aging leather bag it seemed to be. He carried with him a small library worth of notes, books, maps, and other references within its ensorcelled walls. In truth, it was enchanted to hold more than a dozen times its own size, and at a fraction of the weight.

As with much of his capabilities, Darko found it prudent to keep the full extent of his resources hidden until disclosure was required by circumstance. Better to be assumed capable of anything, or else underestimated as he had been his entire life.

He'd nearly finished packing when a commotion outside drew his attention to the window. He peered out from the dusty, leaded glass and was surprised to see what looked like most of the town assembled there. Groups of townsfolk were moving tables, stacking crates, even assembling what looked like a small stage.

Curiosity guided the mage downstairs, where he found the rest of their crew sitting down to breakfast.

"Have you seen--"

"Yes," Talia interrupted crisply. "We've seen."

He waited a beat to see if she'd continue, but the young cleric turned back to the table as if to continue her previous conversation.

"*And?*" Darko pried. "What's going on and why does it have you in a foul mood, Talia?"

"It's best you take a seat," Arcus answered, indicating an empty place on the bench beside himself.

"Lord Goldrun is up to something," Talia hissed. "I don't trust him."

"The good lord of the town is hosting a feast today to celebrate the peaceful resolution of their conflict with the minotaur," Arcus explained.

"I don't understand how that is a problem," Darko observed. "I assume there is some *reason* that we suspect something is amiss?"

"You should have seen him last night," Talia said, thumping her fist on the table, causing the wooden cutlery to rattle. "He was up in arms that we'd even *spoken* to the minotaur, rather than killing them. He was dead set against provisioning them, let alone throwing a feast in their honor."

"And there's no chance he could have had a change of heart? No possibility that you, ah . . . *misinterpreted* how strongly he felt?"

"No," Elbaf chimed in. "They were at each other's throats. For a moment I thought Goldrun might draw steel."

"In the end, I had to order it done, Darko."

"Well, to be fair, the letter of the law provides you the authority to do so, Talia," Darko shrugged. "Perhaps he would rather comply than face any further exercise of your authority?"

"Perhaps," she huffed, unconvinced.

"Ma'am," Sergeant Merryl interrupted the group. "I apologize for the intrusion, but I have news."

"Carry on, Sergeant."

"The guards coming off their shift have confirmed something I was suspicious about. I think we may have identified one of the traitors."

Talia sat back in her seat, scratching her chin and indicating the man should continue.

"We've been logging who comes and goes since we arrived, ma'am, per your instructions. A young man left yesterday afternoon, stating that he was going mushroom hunting in the forest. As of second shift, he has yet to return."

"Did he say he'd be back before nightfall?" Arcus asked the soldier, who turned to address him.

"Yes, sir," the man nodded. "I know for a fact he did. It was my shift when he left, sir. Said he'd be back before it grew too dark, or else at first light if he stayed overlong."

"At last," Elbaf stood. "Something fairly straightforward. Who was he?"

"The name he gave was Thomas Mercane, sir."

"How well supplied was he?" Arcus asked.

"He had with him enough provisions for a single night in the forest, perhaps, but not more. His departure was noted as suspicious, but he was allowed to continue on his business."

"Sergeant, go and rouse the captain of the watch that was serving during your watch, ask him where Mercane lives, and assemble back here within the candlemark."

He snapped a salute and turned on his heel as Talia continued.

"Arcus, you and Elbaf go and let Vedhellar and his family know that there's to be a feast in their honor, and that they'll be provisioned afterwards. Then, track down Mercane's trail as best you can; see if you can get some indication of where he went. Darko and I will take a team and pay a visit to his residence. Perhaps we can gather some insight into what he may have been up to here in Bethlir."

"Are you sure you wouldn't prefer one of us here?" Elbaf asked softly. "A strong sword arm couldn't go amiss if you are correct and Lord Goldrun has something in store for us."

"He wouldn't dare," Talia shook her head. "And you'll be more likely to elicit a positive response from our minotaur friends."

"I agree, Elbaf," Darko added. "Technically, Talia's authority is absolute. She could order him executed in the town square at the height of today's feast and be well within her rights to do so."

"Even so, authority on paper, or in a book of law, is one thing. To challenge this man in his own town, where the people adore him? That is another thing entirely."

"I'm telling you, Elbaf, we'll be fine," she reassured him as Darko took a moment to renew the enchantment upon Elbaf and Arcus, allowing them to communicate with the minotaur once they found them again.

"Go with Arcus. The road is far more dangerous than within these walls. Don't forget we have our own men here, as well."

Within minutes the party had split, Elbaf and Arcus upstairs to gather what they'd need, and Darko and Talia outside to await their entourage of guards.

"I'm surprised you wanted me to join you, Talia."

"Surprised? Why?"

"I assumed you'd stick with the teams of yesterday, given our success."

"A fair point, but I believe your powers will prove more useful here. Arcus should have no trouble tracking Mercane, and between him and Elbaf I believe they have the martial prowess to return safely. We, on the other hand, will be facing the unknown. We don't know how well provisioned the young man was, whether he worked alone, or whether he had any nefarious helpers."

"Do you suspect magical intervention? Perhaps a connection with what happened at the Altimeer Estate?"

"No, I don't, but then again I was blindly unprepared for that. I will not let that happen again. If nothing else, you look at things very differently than I do. I believe that makes us stronger."

"You've been quiet this morning," Arcus reflected as he tightened the straps on his saddle. "More so than usual, in fact."

"Perhaps," Elbaf agreed as he adjusted his own gear. "The truth is that I long to be far from this place."

Arcus stole a glance at his friend's face, but it was covered with steel. He'd been wearing his visor down more and more since . . . well, truth be told, since the incident with the goblins. Nowadays he barely lifted it at all, and then only at meal times or to quench his thirst.

Elbaf either didn't notice his friend's curious stare, or chose to ignore it. Either way, Arcus resigned himself to a quiet morning. Not that he minded, necessarily. Nature was full of voices for someone who knew how to listen.

They made it to the pastures, with Elbaf silent as a statue and Arcus humming softly to himself as he basked in the ocean of life around them, before they shared words again.

"Arcus," Elbaf's low, gravelly voice startled the ranger, but he recovered quickly.

"Hmm? What's wrong?"

"I . . ."

Something in the way Elbaf held himself, perhaps the stiffness in his shoulders, told Arcus that something was, indeed, wrong. His hand strayed to his bow and quiver as he scanned the woodline.

"I am . . . tired, Arcus," he managed, slowly but surely. "This burden placed upon us wears at me."

The ranger paused, then dropped his hands and slowed his mount until they rode side by side.

"What do you mean?"

"This," Elbaf said, gesturing at his throat. "And this badge, this title."

Arcus tried hard to contain his emotions, wary of disrupting the first honest conversation they'd had in some time.

"I *agree*, Elbaf. I did not ask for this. *We* didn't want this, did nothing to deserve this punishment."

"And to have it called an honor--"

"An *honor*," Arcus scoffed, cutting the warrior off. "Indentured servitude, yes. A duty, perhaps. But an honor? Not to me."

The half-orc fell silent, and for a moment Arcus was afraid he'd pushed too hard too quickly.

"If it weren't for Talia," he sighed at last, "and now for the lives of our men, I don't think I could stomach another day of it."

"That aside, what choice do we have?" Arcus remarked. "We are well and truly snared, I'm afraid."

"For now," Elbaf shrugged again.

Arcus saw through his feeble attempt at appearing nonchalant. He could hear the leather pads of Elbaf's gauntlets creak under the pressure of his grip and could practically feel the heat rolling off the half-orcs blazing rage.

He thought about pressing the issue, but decided against it. Elbaf, though his battle-brother, was still something of an enigma to the ranger. No, Arcus decided, Elbaf had opened the conversation, better to let him end it until he was ready again.

They continued beyond the pastures, skirting around the rough wooden fencing until they reached the other side and picked up their trail from the day before. After that, they fell back into a single file. Arcus led the way, guiding his horse through the low-hanging branches and thick brush of the scrubby hillsides. As the path grew more treacherous, the possibility of conversation grew more distant until they were both focused solely on maintaining the rugged path and guiding their mounts.

By the time they reached the entrance to the cave it was well into mid-morning, and the day was already shaping up to be a scorching one. Arcus wondered at Elbaf's fortitude to wear plate day in and day out, even in this blazing heat.

They secured their horses under a nearby tree before heading into the cave. The dark silence of the earth was refreshingly cool, and Arcus found that it bothered him much less than it had the first time they'd come here.

"Do you need light?"

Arcus contemplated his companion's question, jealous yet again that the man could see in the dark. On the one hand, he didn't really *need* to see if Elbaf could, but on the other, he'd never really taken the time to observe the cave. In the end, his curiosity drove him to answer in the affirmative.

They paused in the semi-darkness of the cave entrance to rummage through their packs until they secured a torch, which Arcus lit before holding aloft. The flickering, sputtering firelight accompanied the two into the earth.

The trip through the cave was uneventful, but Arcus enjoyed the opportunity to get a better look at the unique surroundings as they returned to the minotaur camp. He marveled at the smooth ripples in the stone, evidence of some ancient stream or river perhaps. The way the cave seamlessly wove its way beneath the earth like the trail of some great living thing or the root of a mighty tree. Even with torches, the atmosphere was peculiarly somber, and it was evident that they were trespassers in this deep, forbidding world. The light helped them pave their way, however, and the winding trip passed more quickly now that he was sure of every footfall and certain of his destination.

In short order they came upon the cavern where they had first met Vedhellar and his brood. The campfire they'd seen before was dark, and the room was quiet and still.

"Do you suppose we simply . . . wake them up?"

Elbaf shrugged in response, his pauldrons clinking softly.

Their approach had been far from silent, but the earth and stone surrounding them seemed to swallow every sound.

"Good morning," Elbaf announced, his booming baritone echoing off the far walls of the cavern.

"Gods above, Elbaf," Arcus hissed. "Did you have to shout?"

"They're far away," he replied. "I wanted to make sure they're up."

The pair kept their distance, but they could hear the rustling of cloth and stone from the camp ahead. Vedhellar appeared, ax in hand, and waved them forward.

"Good day, friends," he boomed. "You have returned, and so soon!"

"We have, Vedhellar," Elbaf beamed, at ease with the towering soldier.

"We bring news," Arcus interjected. "Lord Goldrun, the headsman of the town, has decided to provision you. Furthermore . . . ah . . ."

Arcus paused.

Should he share his distrust for Goldrun with the minotaur? In the end he decided not to, he didn't want to needlessly poison the goodwill of the celebration.

"Furthermore, he has decided to throw a feast in your honor."

"Why should he want to throw us a feast?" Vedhellar pondered aloud, his broad, shovel-sized hand rising to scratch his chin.

"He says it is to celebrate the peaceful resolution of what could have been a bloody conflict," Arcus shrugged apologetically.

"Very well," the minotaur's suspicion seemed to ease. His broad shoulders lost their tension and a wide smile replaced his subtle frown.

"We've been sent to tell you that the feast is to begin two hours after noon and to request your presence as the guests of honor."

"Hours? What is an hour?"

Arcus blanked, realizing suddenly that there was absolutely no reason that these creatures would utilize the same measure of time as they did in the Empire.

"Ah, right," he stammered. "Elbaf?"

The stoic half-orc returned his stare blankly and without comment. Arcus cast an embarrassed glance down at his hands as he wracked his brain for how to bridge the gap, when suddenly inspiration struck.

"Alright, I've got it," he smiled. "If you place your hand against the sky, like so."

Arcus raised his hand out in front of himself, then tilted it to the side.

"When the sun is," he looked at Vedhellar's hand and compared it roughly to his own, "three fingers past midday, that is the time the feast will begin."

The warrior nodded his understanding, leaving Arcus feeling immensely pleased with himself.

"Will you stay for a meal, friends?"

"I'm afraid we can't," Arcus apologized. "We've other tasks we must attend to before the festivities."

Arcus and Elbaf wished Vedhellar and his family well, promising to meet them on the road outside of town, then returned once again to the tunnels.

"You wanted to say more."

The ranger looked up at Elbaf and chewed his bottom lip.

"Yes, Elbaf, I did."

"Why didn't you?"

"I don't know," he let out a long sigh. "I don't want to ruin this chance we have to do something *good*, you know?"

Silence.

"It's been so long since we did something with which I could find no fault, not since we first took up these wretched badges. This is something genuinely good, that brought only peace instead of harm."

"Vedhellar's family will face enough hardship traveling through the Empire," Elbaf nodded solemnly. "I too wish to make their journey easier. It would bring me some measure of peace, I think, to see them safely away."

Talia fought the urge to tap her foot as Darko continued to examine the sturdy wooden door in front of them. They, along with a half-dozen of the local guards, were standing impatiently outside of the Mercane residence on the far northern edge of Bethlir. The building wasn't much different than many of the neighboring houses, save that it was perhaps a bit further from the nearest homes. The tidy one-floor home was of simple construction. Close-fitting log walls under a thatched roof gave little indication of any seditious activity, and Talia was already beginning to doubt the validity of their concerns.

Even so, Thomas Mercane still hadn't turned up, and no answer was heard when the guards knocked on his door upon their arrival.

"I believe," the mage said slowly, finishing his umpteenth pass over the door frame, "that no enchantments lie upon the door. I think it is safe to enter."

She gave a nod to the guardsmen flanking the door, and the one nearest the handle gave it a turn. The door was locked, no surprises there, but the burly soldiers made short work of breaking it open.

Talia stepped over wood splinters and into the dark interior of the cabin. Inside, it was simply one large room with a few central posts to help hold the framing for the roof. To one end was a rough wooden bed box filled with straw, and at the opposite corner was a stone hearth and a wooden table with a small assortment of cutlery. The rest of the space was occupied with foodstuffs, a few wooden chests of belongings, and other mundane furnishings.

"Search everything," Talia ordered. "Every crate, the bedding, all of it."

As the men snapped into action around her, she pulled Darko to the side.

"I think we may have erred," she muttered.

"I disagree," the mage said, peering around the cabin. "Something about this feels *off* to me."

"How, Darko? This is a perfectly ordinary cabin."

The cleric let out a frustrated breath and moved to join the group dismantling the bed.

"That's precisely my point," Darko sighed to himself. "Why leave?"

The mage ignored the frenzied searching around him and sought out the source of the nagging sensation in the back of his mind. The cabin was simply too normal. There was just the right amount of clutter, everything was exactly where you'd most expect it to be, from the turnips hanging from the rafters to dry to the spare clothing at the foot of the bed. That is what nagged at him most. There was absolutely no reason at all for Mercane to have left.

Rather than occupy himself with digging through crates or sorting clothing, Darko walked slowly around the cabin and allowed his eyes to de-focus, just enough for the background to begin to blur together. It was an old trick he'd learned in school, and it allowed him to effectively expand his field of vision. He lost some clarity and distance, but he found that--

Ah-ha.

A section of wall caught Darko's eyes and drew them back to laser focus. The mage made his way over to the section, which looked nearly identical to the rest of the cabin, and examined it more closely. A set of tools - two hammers, a hatchet, and a file - were all hanging head-down in a neat row. They all had loops at the bottom of their handles, through which nails had been driven to keep them in place.

It was *under* each head, however, that interested Darko. Each of the tools had worn a similar pattern, a sort of half circle where the heads had rocked back and forth and rubbed the woodgrain.

"Talia," he called out, not bothering to look if she responded. "Over here."

He was looking for a latch or catch when Talia arrived.

"What've you found?"

"Look here," he gestured. "The heads of the tools have worn the wall down into a groove."

"Alright?"

"So, Talia, why would they have been swinging? What could have caused them to rock back and forth except the opening and closing motion of a panel or door, no?"

Talia gasped, then shook her head slowly.

"If you're right, I'm twice as glad we came togeth--"

An audible click interrupted her, and a two-foot by two-foot section of the wall popped outward on tiny, whisper-quiet hinges.

"Well, I'll be blessed," Talia laughed, punching him affectionately in the shoulder. "Right under our noses."

"Yes, well," Darko smiled in response, fighting the urge to rub his bruised arm. "Let's just see what we have here before we get too excited."

The panel, which was no more than an inch thick, swung open to reveal a shallow cubby that was set into the wall. Together they took stock of the contents. A few stacks of neatly folded pamphlets, some blank parchment, a signet ring, and a single, jet-black feather.

"Hardly the stockpile of a revolutionary mastermind," Darko remarked.

"I agree," Talia nodded. "I'd mark our man as a follower, not a leader."

She pulled a pamphlet from the stack and examined it more thoroughly. It was a rough sheet of parchment folded into thirds. Both sides were covered in boldly inked writing decrying the Empire.

"Look here," she whispered. "Whoever is writing these is definitely not being subtle. '*The Peace of the Empire is a lie, her true legacy is one of genocide and oppression. RISE and RESIST.*' It's not just some malcontent; they're calling for a full-scale rebellion against the Emperor!"

"Can you blame them?" Darko scoffed, eliciting a sharp glare from his companion.

"Take care, Darko," she cautioned.

Talia flipped the sheet over again, noting for the first time that there was some sort of watermark in the parchment, a design imprinted somehow into the material itself. She couldn't quite make it out in the dingy confines of the cabin, however.

"Curious," she mumbled.

Talia closed her eyes and let out a soft breath, calling forth the divine energies flowing through her body. The spell she cast required only a minimal effort, but, as her hand began to glow a soft white light, she nonetheless prayed her gratitude to the Emperor for his blessings.

With her hand now alight, she held it out behind the parchment to take a closer look at the inlaid design.

Illuminated from behind, the design was startlingly clear. It was a burning sun, with radiant rays of glowing light extending in a circle around its core.

"Talia," he whispered in surprise. "We have seen this mark before--"

She silenced him with a hiss and dismissed the light in her hand with a sharp snap of her fingers. Quickly she folded the pamphlet back up, then reached in and grabbed the whole stack.

"The amulet you wear, Talia," he looked cautiously around to determine if anyone was listening in. "The similarity is beyond chance."

"Quiet, Darko. We may not know the significance of it yet, but I'm *wearing* a symbol of treason."

He opened his mouth to respond but she cut him off again.

"We're done here, I'm confiscating these materials for further study," she announced to the room.

No one argued, though she did receive a few curious looks.

"You all are to finish searching the house, bring anything of note to my room in the inn. When you're finished, set a guard."

"And what of Mercane, ma'am? What if he comes back?"

"Arrest him for high treason and sedition."

With that, she scooped up the rest of the contents of the cubby, turned on her heel, and marched out of the cabin with Darko in tow.

"He'd be a fool to return," Darko observed dryly as they returned to the outside world.

"I don't expect that he will," she agreed.

"What are we going to do about the *sun*, Talia?"

"I don't know," she chewed her lip absentmindedly, worry clouding her mind. "But we agree, it cannot be a coincidence. We must keep this knowledge very close to our chests; I feel this with great certainty, Darko."

"Then let's hope the others can pick up Mercane's trail swiftly, and we shall be gone from this place."

"It's got to be him," Arcus scratched his head. "But he covers his tracks better than most career rangers I know. I can scarcely believe it, Elbaf."

Elbaf, for his part, was still looking for the alleged footprint that Arcus was trying to point out to him.

"Look here, this leaf." The man crouched down into a squat and pointed at some spot in the foliage. "It's bruised just here in a perfect half circle. It's the heel of a boot, I'd stake my life on it."

Elbaf shrugged, trying to cover his irritation.

"Then let's follow it and be done, Arcus. We've been at this for hours."

"Darko said the boy he marked at the town square couldn't have been more than twenty, Elbaf," Arcus shook his head in disbelief. "For someone barely out of boyhood, his skills are incredible. You'd think he lived out here, rather than a cozy bed in town."

Elbaf's heavy sigh must have penetrated the ranger's admiration, because the other man grinned sheepishly.

"Sorry, brother. I know that woodscraft is not your passion," Arcus admitted, giving an apologetic shrug. "I think we can safely say he is headed steadily north since he's barely deviated. I believe, with a map, I could identify the most likely places he'll turn up."

Elbaf nodded along as patiently as he was able.

"Then we should head back," he cast a glance upward to check the position of the sun. "Vedhellar and his family will be waiting for us."

Arcus nodded and reclaimed his reins from Elbaf's outstretched hand before swinging himself into the saddle with a casual grace.

"I'll take point. We should make it to the crossroads with time to spare to guide them into town."

Elbaf nodded and allowed himself to fall slightly behind the ranger. He rode in silence, half-listening to his friend as he explained the differences in the trees around them and named each of the birds who called out in surprise at their passing.

True to his prediction, Arcus had them back on the main road in no time. They even managed to beat the minotaur family to the appointed meeting place, albeit by less than a candlemark.

The creatures were even more imposing in the daylight, and when they finally appeared from within the treeline Elbaf found himself pitying anyone who might meet them in the field. Though he was mounted, Vedhellar's eyes were only an inch or two lower than Elbaf's, and his horns extended above Elbaf's helmeted head.

"Hello, little warriors," the minotaur rumbled. "It is good to see you in the light."

Elbaf bristled, but was forced to admit that to Vedhellar he really was rather . . . small.

"Hello again, Vedhellar," he called back as they approached. "I hope your journey was an easy one."

The creature let out a booming, echoing laugh.

"This land is much more forgiving than the homelands of our peoples, Elbaf. It was a pleasant walk."

They chatted idly, with Arcus steering the conversation as Elbaf led the way towards the gates of Bethlir. The sun was high, and its fiery gaze was unrelenting on the shadeless, hard-packed dirt of the roadways. The minotaur seemed utterly unbothered by the oppressive heat, but Elbaf sighed with relief when they crested a hill and at last the town came into view.

"We'd better hurry," Arcus advised, his hand to the sky. "It looks like they've already set the feast out."

Elbaf let out a silent sigh. If the feast was already prepared then he was unlikely to have a moment to remove his armor and cool himself until late in the evening.

Such was life, he supposed.

Chapter Twelve

"Open the gate!"

Elbaf, Arcus, and the minotaur heard the cry from the high wooden palisade as the wide city gate creaked open at their approach.

Their journey back to town had been entirely uneventful, which was not surprising considering the towering creatures they traveled with, but Elbaf suspected that the rest of the day would more than over-balance the relative quiet of their morning.

"The whole town seems to have turned out," Arcus observed as they cleared the gate and met the unabashed stares of the hundred or so people who lived in the small village.

Elbaf said nothing, but the hairs on the back of his neck began to prickle when a squad of guardsmen approached them. The men were wearing what must have passed for ceremonial gear. Every breastplate had been polished mirror-bright and, thankfully, their weapons were sheathed. Even so, the half-dozen armed men approaching them set off warning bells in his mind. He stole a glance around the square and noted that while the entirety of the town's guardsmen were indeed present and wearing armor, only this squad seemed to be carrying weapons. Their own men were similarly clad in armor, but otherwise unarmed.

"Beggin' yer' pardon, sirs," the leading man, who Elbaf recognized as the captain of the guard, announced. "Lord Goldrun has declared that in the spirit of peace no one is to bear arms today except the guard shift on the walls. We can safely stow your weapons in the armory for you."

Elbaf looked down at the man, not bothering to conceal his scowl.

"I don't think so," he grumbled to the man.

The captain visibly gulped, then looked to Arcus instead.

"Please sirs, I understand you may--"

"My companion here does not part with his weapon except under *very* particular circumstances, captain," the ranger explained, casting Elbaf a stern, frustrated look.

"We'll stow our weapons in our rooms at the inn," Arcus offered gently. "It'll make no difference, really, right?"

"Er . . . well . . . alright, that should be fine, sirs," the man finally replied.

Elbaf caught sight of private Derrin and flagged him down. The young soldier approached at a trot, then stopped to snap a crisp salute.

"Sir?"

"Take my father's sword, see it safely stowed in my room," he said, unbuckling his sheath and handing the massive blade to the young man.

"Yes, sir," the soldier saluted again then made a beeline for the door.

"Here," Arcus said, holding out first his scimitar, then the dirk he wore at his belt, followed by a boot knife, and finally his longbow and quiver. "You can store these in your armory, if you must."

The guard didn't move, instead looking up at the towering, iron-clad behemoths with them.

"I'm afraid they'll need to turn their weapons over, as well."

Elbaf turned to Vedhellar, who was returning the guard captain's gaze stonily.

"I am sorry, Vedhellar, I did not know."

The minotaur glanced down at his family, and Elbaf watched Vedhellar and his partner communicate silently with one another in the manner that all lovers do.

"Very well," the male rumbled at last. "But see to it that my arms are well cared for, for your own sake."

Arcus translated a less threatening version of the creature's message to the guardsmen as the minotaur handed over their weapons. Some of the tension left the air now that they were disarmed, and the guard captain managed a weak smile.

"Thank you, and in the name of Lord Goldrun," he gave a stiff bow, "welcome to Bethlir."

Arcus followed the rest of his group through the gates, noting with a twinge of claustrophobia that the mighty barricades were swiftly closed behind them. He instinctively sought Kodja's presence and felt the reassurance of his brother at once. Though he prowled the forests outside the walls of the town, the bond between them crossed the distance with ease.

He was further reassured when Darko and Talia appeared from within the inn. Arcus dismounted, taking both his and Elbaf's reins, and met them halfway.

"Welcome back," Talia greeted him warmly, her arms outstretched for an embrace.

"Hello," he chuckled, surprised by her gesture. "I hope your investigation was fruitful--"

"We need to talk," she whispered into his ear as soon as she'd wrapped her arms around him.

His concerned glance was met by an unusual stillness in her eyes, a gray glint of warning.

"Talia, what's--"

"Not here," she threw a sidelong glance towards the head table where Lord Goldrun was standing amidst a cluster of advisors. "We'll talk on the road, once we're clear of town."

He pulled back from her embrace and managed a nonchalant smile before letting go. Arcus scanned the crowd of villagers. He wondered whether he'd misread their stares and gawking from the very beginning. Where he'd seen innocence and harmlessness the day before, he now noted too-long stares and threatening scowls on every face.

Darko walked past them and, to any passersby, it would seem he'd barely given them a passing glance. But Arcus caught the mage's eye and took the meaning he found there to heart. If the wizard was anxious then truly there must be a reason for it.

"Calm yourself," he mumbled to himself, forcing long slow breaths in through his nostrils and out past his lips. He sought grounding in the earth beneath his feet and found there the cool, immutable steadiness he needed to relax his over-eager senses.

"I'll join you in a moment, Talia. I'm sure Elbaf will want to catch up with you."

Darko hoped the ranger had taken his nonchalance as a sign of warning, but he couldn't be sure unless he broke his stride and turned back to check. If his nervousness was well-founded then he couldn't afford to tip off anyone who might be watching.

You were right, Master, the gates are sealed once again.

Darko swore softly. Call it paranoia or over-analysis, but Darko was supremely uncomfortable with the idea that the town required sealing for a simple feast. To his mind there was nothing outside the walls to warrant such precaution, which left scant few possibilities except a threat within.

Then again, perhaps Lord Goldrun was simply hedging his bets that the minotaur might turn against them. It wasn't an unforgivable slight, and he could in fact scarcely blame the man for making such a decision.

A trumpet blast silenced his frustrated musings and brought his attention fully to the present.

"To all who shall hear this, greetings," shouted the town crier, a young man in his late teens who was dressed in his cleanest tunic. "Lord Goldrun welcomes our honored guests and bids them take their places at the highest table of honor to commence the feast!"

The crowd cheered and began to move towards the assortment of tables and chairs.

"This feast shall be blessed by the Pax Imperia," he continued. "Let it be therefore known that no man shall draw blade today on pain of death."

The mumbling of the crowd quieted at the invocation of the sacred law. The law was seldom exercised, save when two feuding clans came together over a treaty table, or bloodshed was otherwise likely. Darko searched his memory and could recall less than a dozen times it had been utilized in the past seventy years. He recalled reading of an outbreak of violence between the notoriously proud hillfolk families near Jala that had required imperial intervention, but that was decades ago.

Still, it was a promising sign that Lord Goldrun intended to keep his word.

The crowd was seating itself, and Darko knew that if he remained at the outside of the group his noncompliance would become increasingly obvious, so he made his way to the head table as well.

Lord Goldrun had spared no expense, it seemed, and the tables Darko passed were heavily laden with food and drink. Pitchers of chilled beverages, cool condensation running down their sides, were intermingled with steaming plates of roast and brightly colored vegetables and fruits from the fields and the surrounding forests.

The townsfolk parted respectfully to allow the hobbling mage through, but otherwise politely ignored his passing. All the better, he thought, as he directed his keen senses to the behavior of Goldrun, the guards, and his own party members.

He was the first of his group to make the head table. It seemed Talia and Elbaf were committed to staying at the minotaurs' sides. Still, he had only to wait a few minutes before the others joined him in taking their seats. Their own places at the head table were even more richly decorated, bedecked with real metal plates and cutlery. The minotaur had likewise been honored, though massive pitchers took the place of cups and platters were substituted as plates.

Vedhellar and his family would have obliterated any chair the town could offer, so three large and sturdy tree stumps had been rolled in from the millwright's field for the occasion instead. The minotaur were sat on Lord Goldrun's right, while Darko and the others were on his left.

"It seems no expense has been spared," Arcus remarked as he took the seat next to Darko.

"Indeed," Darko raised his voice ever so slightly, ensuring that Lord Goldrun would hear his reply. "And the reports of the town's stores being *ransacked* were perhaps a bit . . . exaggerated."

Talia stifled a snicker, but Darko's eyes were glued to Goldrun's expression. The man's demeanor changed not one iota, and though Darko knew it was impossible, the man looked for all the world that he'd heard nothing at all.

I do not trust any man who can lie so well.

Nor do I, Reia.

When the last man had taken his seat at the far end of the town square, Lord Goldrun rose once more, picking up a goblet in his hand as he did.

"Men and women of the Empire," he raised the pewter vessel. "Today is a great victory."

The crowd cheered for a moment until he raised his other hand to quiet them.

"It is through the rare and rightly praised wisdom of our own Black Hand," he locked eyes with each of them in turn, but Darko couldn't help noticing that his gaze dwelt on Talia the longest, "that we are gathered here today and that no bloodshed interrupted the peace of our humble town."

The crowd roared approval once again.

"To the Emperor," Goldrun called out, raising his drink skyward. "May the sun never set upon His rule."

All present raised their glasses. Even Darko and his companions were compelled to do so. To ignore a toast to the Emperor himself was tantamount to an insult against the throne, and their situation was already precarious.

He mumbled softly under his breath, calling forth a minor cantrip as he brought the goblet to his mouth. His speech slowed and every word grew heavier until they dripped from his lips as faint, luminous puffs. As he finished the incantation, the liquid in his goblet shimmered briefly, then cleared.

A wise choice Master. One can never be too careful.

Satisfied that it was safe to do so, he drank deeply.

The crowd was cheering again, and Goldrun was wrapping up his welcome remarks, so he expected they would start to eat soon. Just as the lord was about to take his seat, Vedhellar rose, surprising everyone into near-silence.

The minotaur gestured at the mage and indicated he would like to speak.

"A moment," Darko sighed before casting the spell that would allow Vedhellar to speak the imperial tongue.

"Thank you, Darko," the creature rumbled to the shocked gasps of the assembled crowd.

"I am Vedhellar," the minotaur announced, raising his now half-empty drink.

Darko watched as the mighty warrior visibly gulped with nervousness before opening his mouth to speak again. How odd that such a powerful beast should suffer from the same nervousness that many of the assembled would have felt, had their places been reversed.

"My family and I," his words were punctuated by a fit of coughing that elicited further gasps from the crowd. "I'm sorry, I . . . *we* are so very grateful."

Darko's eyes narrowed as Vedhellar's words began to slur, and he turned instead to look at Lord Goldrun. The man had a smug smile on his face as he took another sip of his wine.

Vedhellar staggered, catching himself with one hand pressed against the table, which groaned in protest. He shook his head fiercely, only then noticing that his wife and child seemed similarly dazed, their heads swaying and their eyes unfocused.

"Kloriskja," he called weakly, dropping his tankard and falling to his knees beside her. "Jarhein? My . . . daughter, are you--"

Darko saw the veins in the creature's neck and shoulders start to throb, so he had the barest hint of a warning before Vedhellar surged back to his feet, his breathing heavy and ragged.

"You . . . *swore*," he roared before collapsing into a fit of coughing on the ground.

The other two minotaur slumped to the ground as well, and for a moment there was absolute silence.

Talia watched the events unfold in horror, realizing far too late what was happening. She stood as Vedhellar fell, her voice piercing the deathly quiet of the feast.

"Oathbreaker!"

Lord Goldrun turned, his eyes deadly serious.

"Sit down, Captain."

Talia reached for her mace before realizing it wasn't there.

"Ah-ah-ah," Goldrun wagged a finger at her. "Now I'm afraid you've gone too far."

He raised a hand and the guards around the square began to move in their direction. But Talia was beyond reason.

"You *dare* violate the Pax Imperia," she screamed. "And then you accuse *me* of going too far?"

The man smirked back at her and she felt her skin crawl.

"I declare you a traitor to the throne, *Ekart*," she leveled an accusing finger at him. "Guards, by my command as a Black Hand, you will arrest this man and assemble a gallows."

"So familiar, Talia," he goaded her. "I'm afraid you'll find that a difficult order to execute."

"The Pax Imperia is--"

"It is *intact*," he shouted, his rage suddenly as palpable as her own. "Or rather, it was until you reached for a weapon. Has the Academy truly fallen so far? That young Hands are not even schooled in the most basic principles of law?"

He surveyed the silent crowd, and only then did Talia realize that the angry stares of the people were directed not at Goldrun, but at herself.

"Imperial Law, volume one, chapter one," he sneered, his voice even and mocking. "'These shall be the laws of the Sunset Imperium, as laid down by my hand. By my grace, they shall govern the peoples of our lands, and ensure harmony and justice for all of the *citizens of the Empire* who dwell therein.'"

Talia paled, her mouth moved but no words escaped her lips.

"You endangered our entire village, Captain Lorraine," the man berated her. "For what? Not for the citizens of the Empire, no, for a pack of wild animals!"

He grabbed his goblet from the mess that was the tabletop and lifted it high, his eyes never breaking contact with her own.

"So here's to you, Captain. What could have been your victory is instead your disgrace," he drank a sip and then poured the goblet out. "You shouldn't even *be* a Hand, you don't deserve it. I fought and bled for thirty years alongside real heroes who *earned* that badge you wear. I *served* this Empire."

Talia noted that the honor guard, the only armed men in the entire courtyard, were closing rapidly.

"So no, Captain," he practically spit at her. "You will not be arresting me. As all of these fine people saw, their lives and safety meant nothing to you. I find you derelict in your duties, and you will be thrown in irons until your superiors can be--"

"No."

The word, so firmly spoken, surprised them both.

Darko stood slowly, his face lost in darkness beneath his hood.

"Excuse me?" Goldrun hissed.

"I said, no," the wizard repeated, his voice lower and more dissonant than Talia had ever heard it.

Something in the way he spoke set Talia's teeth on edge, as if his voice was composed of many hundreds of voices, all slightly out of sync.

"You *will* do as I command," Goldrun shouted. "Guards, arrest these pathetic--"

Goldrun's words were cut off by a rumbling, deafening explosion of sound.

Talia squinted her eyes at Darko, who was suddenly at the center of a cyclone of dust and wind. As she watched, motes of black and purple appeared within the winds surrounding the mage until all she could make out was his flickering, shadowy outline.

Her eyes burned and the unnatural wind seemed to suck the breath from her lungs until at last she was forced to look away. Then, all at once, the wind stopped.

She turned back to her companion to find nothing but a pitch black, light-swallowing form of shadow and utter darkness. Specks of painfully bright purple intermingled with his shadowy form and settled onto the ground around him.

Everywhere the sparks landed, the ground cracked and turned black. In fact, Talia noted with horror, the blackness was spreading around him in every direction. The ground was slowly being replaced with inky nothingness that shook her to her core.

"Stop him!" Goldrun screamed, his voice several octaves higher. "Somebody stop him!"

The honor guard, to their great credit, drew their blades and charged. The movement stirred the crowd, and a panic ensued as people screamed and began to run.

Talia looked down at the table and grabbed a carving knife, turning her back to her friend and trusting the instincts of her heart. She and the others readied themselves, clutching pot lids and knives in the face of the charging men.

With a sudden tearing sound, dozens of columns of pure darkness poured forth from the earth. Each was a tentacle nearly forty feet long, and each was shot through with incandescent purple streaks. The guards stumbled to a stop, then broke and tried uselessly to flee as they were all snatched up by the writhing tentacles. Goldrun, his advisors, and many of the other townsfolk who were not swift enough to escape were similarly captured, and soon the town square was clear of everyone but the screaming, panic-stricken people still caught.

"Lord Ekart Goldrun," the booming voice that spoke was not that of Darko, but instead a deep and menacing bass. "You overstep your authority. Do not take us for cheap parlor magicians or petty thugs, or we will be your undoing."

Talia watched as the tentacle carrying Goldrun swung slowly, dragging the man forward until he was face to face with the shadowy figure of the mage.

"You will not impede our departure. You will allow us to leave peacefully and you will remain here, in Bethlir, until imperial justice can be dispensed. You have sullied the customs and laws of our people, and you will be dealt with accordingly."

The once-proud lord was babbling incoherently and tears of pure fear were streaming down his face.

"See that you do not leave the confines of the city, lest your punishment be more severe. Do you understand?"

Goldrun nodded fervently, his arms clamped tightly at his sides by the foot-thick appendage holding him.

The darkness began to recede like floodwaters. The columns returned to the earth and Darko shrank back to his normal height and build. Goldrun landed on the ground, sobbing, and the rest of the now-freed citizens bolted.

"Darko," Talia said in awe. "What--"

The elf held a hand up to stop her speaking, and she could see at once that he was utterly and completely exhausted. Darko put on a brave face, and Talia was confident that the few remaining onlookers, who peered out from shuttered windows, couldn't tell how he trembled.

"I'll kill him," Arcus growled from behind her.

Talia turned in time to see the ranger bearing down on Goldrun's fear-stricken body, a carving knife in his hand.

"Arcus!"

When he didn't respond to her voice, Talia gripped the ranger's shoulder firmly.

"This is not the time nor place."

Arcus spun at her touch, murder in his eyes.

"Talia, how can you say that?" he pointed the knife at Goldrun. "This *monster* killed them. He poisoned them under the guise of friendship."

"Arcus, think," she mumbled, her eyes darting side to side. "To kill this man here and now could be our deaths."

A tense pause followed her statement, and she could see him struggle to contain his anger. At last he turned away from her, back to Goldrun, and for a moment she was afraid he would proceed.

"They will be avenged, Lord Goldrun," he hissed before stalking away. "I swear it."

They gathered their men, their equipment, and their horses and left as swiftly as they were able. Even so, by the time they had all assembled near the gate, the entirety of the town guard was armed and keeping a watchful eye on them.

"We should have his head," Arcus growled. "That *bastard*."

"No," Darko mumbled. "We should leave. Talia, let us be swiftly away."

Talia was gripped by indecision, but ultimately opted to side with the mage.

"No, not today, Arcus," she turned her gaze to the road ahead. "I fear the repercussions of this will be severe enough already."

Without another word, she kicked her horse into a gallop. Their small band poured out from the gate and headed north. They didn't slow down, or breathe easy, until the gates were miles behind them.

Even after they reduced their pace, it was a long while before anyone broke the gloomy silence.

"Did you know he could do that?" Arcus asked Talia quietly, hours later.

The mage had been fast asleep in his saddle for the past fifteen miles with no signs of stirring, but even so they both threw a quick glance in his direction to make certain he was still asleep. He was right where they'd expected, breathing the deep, untroubled breaths of a slumbering man. A jet black raven perched watchfully on his left shoulder, and it would allow no one close without cawing and pecking at them.

"No, I didn't," she replied matter-of-factly. "You?"

Arcus shook his head slowly.

"Seems a bit foolish now," he admitted. "All the fun I've been poking at him. I'm glad he never took it seriously."

Talia shrugged wordlessly, but the thought had crossed her mind. The secretive mage was certainly more than she'd bargained for, yet her heart told her she could still trust him. He was still Darko, still her friend.

"So what now?" he asked her.

"We continue our mission, I suppose."

"But, Talia, *why*?" Arcus asked a little too sharply. "To what--"

"The commander may yet have our heads for this, Arcus," she replied, a hand at her throat. "But we have no choice so long as this curse--"

"Ah-ha," Arcus said, his tone accusatory. "You admit it then, it *is* a curse that holds us captive!"

Talia bit her tongue and rolled her eyes.

"Dammit, ranger, this is no time for wordplay. It is my hope that by finishing our mission - by tracking down Mercane and his fellows - I can still save our miserable lives, don't you see that?"

"Hmph," Arcus replied, his eyes back on the road ahead of them.

"There's a way out of this," Talia admonished him. "For all of us."

"You have such *faith*," the ranger quipped laconically.

"And you have so little," she retorted. "The Emperor will guide us."

"Damn the Emperor, Talia," the druid stared flatly at her, his eyes betraying the depths of his disgust as much as his words. "And damn the Empire as well, the cursed thing."

"Arcus," she tried to soothe their argument before it grew beyond her control. "The Empire has redeeming qualities. Its ideals are pure, I *know* they are--"

"I've yet to see these redeeming qualities, Talia," he shook his head. "Well-intended or not, this way of life is rotten. Any society built upon such casual cruelty is evil."

"And yet you would call *me* the idealist, Arcus?"

The ranger rolled his eyes but said nothing more, leaving Talia to her own thoughts.

Her own doubts echoed those of Arcus, and were it not for her years of training and service to the Order, she might feel exactly as he did. But there was something worth saving in the Empire, there had to be. Half of her nineteen years of life, she'd been taught the grace, the kindness, the gentle guidance of the Empire, and she would not abandon those teachings even after what she had seen.

Instead, Talia turned her attention to their men.

The soldiers hadn't questioned the order to vacate Bethlir, hadn't even batted an eye at seeing their officers stand up for the lives of the minotaur. In fact, Talia could see that many of them were just as angry with the results of the feast as she was.

But none of them were taking their cues from her.

Their conversation and attention was all centered around Elbaf, who rode among them, not out in front with Talia and the other two. A tingle of jealousy crossed her mind - as it often did when she saw how easily he blended with the soldiery - but then again, they were kindred spirits. He spoke their language. When combat grew thick he waded in alongside them. Like them, he had nothing but the strength in his arm and the steel in his hands. No, he was not like her, nor Darko or even Arcus, all of whom relied on gifts bestowed by fate, by the gods, or hard-won through decades of rigorous study.

Talia briefly considered slowing their horses to allow the rest of the group to catch up, but second-guessed herself and kept her pace.

Arcus' mind wouldn't rest, and it was driving him to be uncharacteristically sullen. He knew Talia probably wanted conversation, but he couldn't help withdrawing into himself and riding in silence. If he was honest with himself, he was still angry with her. Nevermind that she was right; executing Goldrun would've likely meant their deaths. Still, it did nothing to assuage his guilt.

Even Kodja's presence at the edges of his mind wasn't helping much. The wolf had been gently prodding him with questions since they'd left the town, sending him the scents and sounds of the forest and inviting the druid to join him in play.

Miles passed, and afternoon turned to evening before the boundless enthusiasm of his unseen friend was able to wear down his frustration enough to let the wolf in.

Hello, little brother.

His companion responded with the comfort of warm sunlight and the unfiltered joy of running through the woodland unencumbered by doubt or worry. Arcus allowed the connection to deepen, shivering at the chilling touch of an ice-cold spring as the wolf padded through it and sharing in the silliness of rolling in mud on the other side. Other sparks began to glow in the woodland around him as he allowed his senses to awaken, and the web of life around him flooded into his mind.

All around him was a frenzy of living things and, like him, most of it was preoccupied with worry. Birds chirped out their mating calls, field mice rustled through fallen leaves for morsels of food, beneath that even the grubs and worms in the earth strove constantly for survival.

Not unlike Vedhellar and his family. They too had sought simply to exist, to . . . *continue.*

The corners of Arcus' mouth turned down as he settled back into his own cycle of worry, his own struggle for survival. He cursed the mark upon his throat for the umpteenth time, wishing he could return to his wild homelands and to the freedom he had there.

Then again, he admitted, life on the tundra was a struggle as well. The D'Ari people lived on the razor's edge of life and death, where the very elements were lethal. Perhaps that was the lesson of the day; to simply live was to toil endlessly.

Kodja prompted his brother with a warm feeling of comfort and confusion, reminding Arcus that he was not alone, not even in his mind.

Just worried, little brother.

Kodja's confusion deepened, and Arcus struggled to convey the complex emotion to his furry friend.

It is . . . it is being afraid of something bad that is not there, but could be someday.

He sent memories of heartbreaks and struggles, hoping the wolf would understand. Instead, Kodja returned with warm memories of scratches and curling up beside fires, of the moonlit nights they'd lain on bare rock and counted the stars together, and of the countless miles of comfortable companionship they had shared.

No, I know it has all worked out so far, little brother. It is the fear that it will not be ok. That it . . . that . . .

Arcus sighed. How could he communicate worry to the wolf when Kodja had never experienced the feeling himself? He framed the question in his own mind several times, tugging at it until he realized that it was impossible, that it would always be impossible.

Kodja struggled, as all living things do, but he spent none of his days worried for the future. He simply lived and reacted to what the fates brought his way. To the wolf, the very idea of worry was alien. Why should he waste his time concerned for the future when life was *now*?

Arcus felt a smile of comprehension form on his face, and immediately the burden weighing upon him began to lift. Nature was, as ever, his greatest teacher. Life was full of struggle, it always would be. However, it was meant to be lived. The wolf knew more about life than he did, it seemed. To worry was to borrow struggles from the future, at the cost of life in the present.

Arcus let go the tension he'd been holding in his jaw, his shoulders, and his upper back. Immediately he could feel the muscles ease and some of the stress knitting his brow flow away. He was still on edge, he probably would be until he was rid of his curse, yet now he was grounded once more.

He let his bond strengthen with Kodja and with the web of life surrounding them, and lost himself in the dizzying, chaotic dance of energy all around.

Thank you, little brother.

Chapter Thirteen

"You're awake," Elbaf noted dryly, drawing the attention of the group to Darko.

They were stopped for an evening meal, though the sun was still several hours from setting, and the mage had been laid to rest near the base of a massive Hollenwood tree at the edge of their makeshift campsite.

A ripple of nervous energy flew through the assembled soldiers and touched the hearts of Elbaf's companions as well. Conversations stuttered to a halt, and all eyes turned to the wizard with a wary new respect.

"I am, and I'm famished," the elf replied with a weak smile. "How long have I been asleep?"

"Just over a day," Arcus added from across the campfire.

Elbaf gestured at an iron pot of soup bubbling away over a low fire.

At first, the men had rotated cooking shifts, but Sergeant Cormorant's cooking had swiftly proven the crowd favorite. When it was discovered that he'd packed with him a small pantry of spices and herbs, he'd swiftly become one of the most popular soldiers in the group. It turned out that he was the son of a modestly successful restaurateur in Leka, a town just southwest of the Capital, and his earthy, spice-filled food was in great demand around the campfire. The other men had all agreed to take on his share of other chores, such as the gathering of firewood, in exchange for his services as the camp cook, and the arrangement seemed to suit him as well.

Darko sniffed the air delicately, and Elbaf wondered to himself if the mage had a strong enough constitution for the hearty boar and vegetable stew. It seemed he did, because the elf gathered a bowl of the stuff, along with two pieces of hard tack, and settled in to eat under his watchful gaze.

Though Darko didn't seem to notice him staring, his peculiar bird certainly did.

The creature made direct eye contact with Elbaf, who returned its steady gaze unblinkingly until the wizard spoke and interrupted them both.

"Reia doesn't trust you," he said, his voice low and velvety in a way that made Elbaf's neck hairs rise. "She says you watch me as you do Annabelle."

"Your bird is observant," Elbaf remarked with deceptive calm.

Darko laughed softly and shook his head.

"Ever the talkative type."

Elbaf said nothing.

"I often wonder what thoughts fill your mind, Elbaf, son of Elbain. What secrets lie behind your closed lips?"

"Do not say my father's name, sorcerer," Elbaf bristled as he had a year ago in the Tilted Table. "To do so is a privilege you have not earned."

"And how does one earn such a privilege, I wonder," Darko mused, pointedly ignoring Elbaf's bruised pride. "We have fought together, spilled blood together, traveled together, and slumbered feet apart for many moons."

Elbaf clenched his jaw, willing himself not to be goaded by the diminutive man.

"You've trusted me with your life. I've trusted you with mine. Well now, one might even say--"

"Enough," Elbaf snapped, baring more of his wide, sharp smile than absolutely necessary. "You try my patience, Elf!"

"And you try mine, warrior," Darko shot back. "If you have doubts about me, then say them. Lay bare your concerns that we may be done with them!"

Elbaf was taken aback and, dare he admit it, impressed. He smelled no fear on the elf, though plenty of it mingled throughout the camp as their confrontation came to a head.

"I mistrust your magic," he admitted. "It seems to me that the powers you wield are not so different than those of Annabelle, or the forces we met at the Altimeer Estate."

Darko regarded him with unexpected calm, and held his tongue. Elbaf had expected laughter, shock, perhaps a sarcastic rebuff, but the narrow-eyed silence of the mage was not something he had counted on.

"I understand, Elbaf, and I cannot fault you for worrying," Darko said with an air of apology. "To the untrained eye, I can . . . see the similarities."

Elbaf watched closely as Darko regarded him, Talia, Arcus, and the rest of the men in turn.

"You all share his concerns?"

"None of your magic feels natural to me, Darko," Arcus shrugged, and laid back against a tree. "But it doesn't set the same chill in my bones as the aberrations we saw at the Altimeer Place, nor does it have the . . . *coldness* of whatever Annabelle did there."

"Elbaf," Talia interjected softly. "I admit, I do not know what powers Annabelle called upon. I do not recognize what she . . . what she did there as a part of any of the teachings of the order. But, there are some mysteries that are not revealed to us until we are ready, until much later in our--"

"Did *none* of you notice that she was using a magical device to work that magic?" Darko asked incredulously. "Truly?"

Silence met his statement.

Elbaf could see genuine surprise on the elf's face. Surprise turned to thoughtful consideration, but the group seemed willing to wait for his next words.

"She utilized an . . . artifact of some kind," he mused. "I saw it only for a moment. It looked like, well, like a stick of chalk, but coal black. It isn't an item I'm familiar with, but it was certainly a device of arcane nature which means she shouldn't have had the training to use it at all, not an artifact that powerful, at least."

"What do you mean, of an arcane nature?" Talia interrupted, her own eyes narrowing suspiciously.

"I mean that it was definitely a powerful form of magic, but it was not divine in nature. When you work your miracles, they are granted to you by divine providence. The same applies to Arcus' magic, after a fashion. The forces of the world grant him his gifts through his special, unique bond with nature and the elements."

"As opposed to?"

"As opposed to my own craft, Talia," Darko's voice hardened. "Mine is a rigorous study, a calculated sacrifice, and a meaningful wrenching of energies from the world around me. I do not suffer reality to dictate my life, but shape it to my will."

Total silence blanketed the campsite as Darko's gaze lengthened and lost focus.

"It is why we are so very different. You and Arcus sail upon the seas of magic with ease. You feel the wind, the sun, the forces that surround us all, and each in your own way you ask and receive the cooperation of those forces." He shook his head softly and absentmindedly scratched the head of his raven, ruffling her feathers. "I cannot ask; I lack the voice that you have. I cannot speak to nature, Arcus. I cannot beg her help, nor does she steer my course."

He scoffed and dropped his voice even lower.

"And the gods do not listen to my prayers as they do yours, Talia," his tone turned rueful and hard once more. "I must *make* the changes I wish to see. I must pull it as ore from the belly of the earth and smelt it to my will. I must shape it in the furnace of my mind until it emerges as a blade, deadly and strong."

"You said she shouldn't have had the training to use the device," Elbaf noted, steering the conversation back to the threat at hand.

"Yes," Darko nodded, once more in the present. "It would take a Master of the arcane to craft a device that powerful and a great deal of training, years perhaps, to use it safely."

"Darko," Arcus announced. "I owe you my apologies. I . . . I underestimated you."

Elbaf was grateful for the druid's words, for though he felt the same, his pride would not allow him to offer an apology so readily nor admit that he had been so wrong.

Darko laughed, but it was not a joyous, happy thing. Instead it was the bitter laughter of insult.

"And I suppose it's my fault you all presumed me an invalid," he retorted, rising to his feet. "I have walked this earth for a *century*. I have spent more time at the Imperial Academy than the lot of you have been alive combined!"

Talia and Arcus shrank under his accusing tone, but Elbaf sat tall and proud. He could see the wizard's breathing was labored and his stance unsteady, and he knew that Darko was still worn out from his unexpected exertion. He surmised that, while the wizard was indeed angry, he posed no immediate threat.

"I have given *everything* for my craft. I have dedicated an entire human lifetime to its study. Did you think of me as some parlor-trick street magician who existed only to light darkened hallways and predict the weather?"

"Darko, please," Talia implored the irate mage. "We know your worth, not only as a wizard but as a *friend*. You're the only reason we aren't all shackled in irons or hanging from a gallows back in Bethlir."

Darko deflated, and his wobbling became more noticeable as the energy from his temper waned. Arcus jumped to his feet just in time to catch the elf as he began to stumble and brought him safely to the ground.

Talia let out a small gasp and began to move to Darko's side, but the mage waved her away.

"I'm fine, Talia," he grimaced as he settled back into a seated position. "I simply overexerted myself yesterday."

"You're sure?"

"Yes, Talia, I am sure," he nodded. "My magic does not simply flow as yours does, and the enchantment I cast was not one I had prepared for."

He took a bite of his stew, before continuing, "I must study and mentally and physically prepare myself for the spells I intend to use. Often, more powerful spells require a series of lesser rituals to be emplaced in order to use them safely. I try to judge what I might need on a given day, and I do my preparatory work in the mornings before we embark. To cast something like that without the proper preparations comes at a steep cost."

"Cost," Talia asked as his voice trailed off. "What manner of cost?"

"It leaves me vulnerable. It drains my reserves of magical energy and leaves me depleted, not defenseless, but certainly less capable. Unfortunately for me it is doubly problematic, as I rely on a number of minor enchantments to help me with my, ah, *mobility* issues throughout the day. I'm afraid I will need some time to recover."

"Darko," Arcus added softly, but clear as a bell. "The strength of the pack is not in a single wolf, but in their ability to compliment one another, to work together, to care for each other. You are not alone. No matter how often you cast yourself as an outsider, you *are* one of us."

Elbaf watched as the group descended once more into quietude following Arcus' words. The ugly tension of the moment had largely passed, and he could see the eyes of the men were less worried, more trusting than they had been while the mage slept away his unnatural exhaustion.

In his own way, Elbaf agreed with the ranger. Though he and Darko did not yet see eye to eye, he would nonetheless defend his brother, as he had done so far.

As he returned to eating his own stew, he wondered at the peculiar turns of fate that had brought him so far from the Brine and gifted him a new family to care for.

The group spent the rest of their meal in relative quiet, with nothing but casual conversation filling the air. They were not so removed from Bethlir that anyone felt completely comfortable, but they'd traveled far enough to be free of some of the nervous energy of the place.

"Well, do we press on or stay the night here?" Talias asked her fellow officers as the last of the stew was finished and the mess kit broken down and packed away.

"I say we return to the road," Arcus chimed in quickly, garnering looks of surprise from the others.

"How much daylight is left?" Talia asked him doubtfully.

Arcus held a hand to the sky and made a quick estimation based on the season.

"We've another three, maybe three and a half hours yet of usable light," he offered. "And tonight the lesser moon should be full and bright by which to set a camp."

Talia still looked doubtful, and Arcus found himself frustrated by her hesitation. Sometimes he longed for the days when he could set his own pace, free of the burden of companions.

"Come now, Talia," he pushed. "None of the tents have been unpacked, the men and horses are yet fresh, and the evening is as fair and fine as anyone could ask. Let's make a bit more progress yet."

"Darko? Elbaf? What do you say?" she asked.

"I leave it to the ranger," Darko sighed. "He knows the woodlands better than any of us, and I'll be tired regardless."

Elbaf simply shrugged by way of answer, which Arcus took as tacit approval with a broad grin.

"Alright, then," Talia's voice rose. "Strike camp, men. We're back to the trail for a few more hours yet."

Her words were met with good natured grumbling, but the group was ready again to depart within a candlemark.

Arcus led the way, his heart open to the splendor of the wide, endless forests around them. He tried to move past his anger, his sadness, and the weight of what had happened to Vedhellar and his family. He knew better than to bury it and chose instead to imagine each hoofbeat of his mount as one step further removed from the pain and one step closer to being at peace. It was not the D'Ari way to cling to grief or to mourn for change when none could be made. Instead, they learned from an early age that sorrow was to be expected, that tragedy was as undeniable as it was unavoidable. They learned to change what they could, and always for the better. To make choices they could live with, to respect the consequences of those choices, and to let go of the things they could not control.

Besides, and perhaps most importantly, Kodja was nearby, the sun was shining, and Thomas Mercane's tracks had aligned with the very trail they rode sometime late yesterday. The ranger had sat in conference with Elbaf and Talia while the mage slept, and together they'd made the educated guess that the fugitive was headed for Gilbad, the only town in this direction within a reasonable distance. Until they arrived, he would relish every moment of freedom from imperial rule, from the reminders of his chains, and from the ugly, unforgivable realities of the Empire's prejudice.

The imperial road, such as it was, was well kept. Out here, in the less populated eastern half of the interior, it consisted of a wide lane clearcut through the forests that meandered and wrapped its way over rocky hills and wide, cool rivers and streams.

Arcus had an easy ride ahead of him and, given they were mounted and their quarry was not, it was likely they'd overtake Mercane in the next day or so. At worst, they'd be just behind him when they got to Gilbad the day after that.

More than an hour passed in quiet contemplation before the distant rumble of thunder and the sweet scent of summer rain turned his mind to the more pressing matter of finding a place to bed down for the night.

The trees here were old, very old, and plenty of space lay between the boles of massive hollenwoods, aspen, and the occasional broad-leafed Yusti. Unfortunately, much of the canopy, though well-established, was fairly thin. What they really needed was a stand of pine, something with good coverage that would not totally rule out the possibility of a warm fire and hot food.

The ranger closed his eyes and cast his mind and heart down through his mount and into the ground beneath her hooves. The rich earth teemed with life and the network of connections all around him was a vibrant, beautiful tangle. He sought the deep browns of the ancient trees around them, tracing their roots back and forth between the mighty beings and searching for the sweet tang of pine in the soil.

As he sought out a place to rest, he was taken aback by a darker energy that drew his mind's eye. An ugly stain of dark reds and deep purples that smelled of copper and smoke lay barely a mile to their northwest. The oily feel of it was all too familiar, and it bore the clear signature of deliberate violence. The way it stained the earth set it apart from the momentary bloodshed of the natural world - the struggle of predator and prey - in the way that it lingered in the air and clung to the nearby plants and animals like stale camp smoke.

"Ambush!" he cried out, instinctively turning his horse and urging the creature into a full-blown gallop.

"Arcus? Arcus!"

He ignored Talia's cries, zeroing in on the fighting ahead. Amid the frenzy of life and death he couldn't tell much for certain, save that the fight was not yet over. They could still intervene for the better.

His horse leapt a small gorge and nearly stumbled, drawing him back to the present, but carried on as single-mindedly as its Master.

"Emperor, grant me patience," Talia cursed between gritted teeth as Arcus disappeared into the trees off the side of the trail.

The young cleric yanked on her reins, garnering a whinny of protest from her surprised warhorse, but was swiftly on the ranger's heels.

"Draw blades, men!" she shouted, pulling her mace from her belt and readying her broadshield as her horse leapt headfirst into the forest. "Be ready for anything!"

The next ninety seconds were a blur of greens and browns. They tore through the underbrush like wild things as leaves and twigs tried to snag their armor in passing. Just as suddenly as they'd entered the woods, however, they broke out into a clearing and found themselves in the middle of a raging battle. Two dozen wagons, several of which were tipped over or on fire, were stalled on a narrow path through the countryside.

Talia could see that Arcus was already locked in combat with a tall, muscular creature she didn't recognize. The beast - one of perhaps thirty in the clearing - stood as tall as a man, but had an elongated canine face. It was covered in rough hide armor, as well as its own thick brindle fur. It fought with the training of a soldier, wielding a wickedly serrated hatchet in each hand, and Arcus was hard pressed to keep his saddle against the monster.

It was immediately clear to Talia that the creatures had ambushed the caravan, and the few clusters of survivors remaining were no match for the well-armed and efficient raiders. Talia's horse shuddered to a halt, rearing up as a stray gust of wind sent smoke and dust into her face from the unexpected chaos. Momentarily blinded, she blinked to clear her eyes just in time to see a barbed half-spear arcing towards her across the battlefield.

"Forward, men!" she shouted, barely deflecting the errant javelin with her shield. "Protect the survivors!"

The words had barely left her lips when Elbaf tore past her, not bothering to slow his mount as he entered the clearing at the head of the rest of their men.

The half-orc let loose a guttural roar, which was echoed in the cries of the men, and Talia thanked the Emperor she would not be on the receiving end of the massive greatsword the man wielded.

Their arrival did not go unnoticed, and a full dozen of the creatures approached at a sprint. Soon Talia found herself blocking additional javelins and facing a growing threat. She took a quick glance around herself, realizing belatedly that she, Darko, Arcus, and a handful of their men were essentially alone. The other twelve, including Elbaf, were cleaving their way through the melee ahead.

"Form ranks," she commanded her small contingent, and the group assembled around her with swords drawn.

Arcus' bow wrought havoc where it could, but these opponents were well-armored and protected themselves from his deadly bowfire to great effect.

"Darko," she asked hopefully, turning to the mage. "We could use a hand."

"I'm sorry, Talia," he replied weakly. "There is little I can do yet, but I will do what I can."

She nodded curtly and returned her attention to the threat before them. Their group was outnumbered two to one already, and the monsters approaching their line were less than half of the total force of the enemy. They took their time, approaching at leisure now that they were inside of fifty feet. The hairy, snarling beasts shifted and moved as a pack behind their shields, and Talia squinted to better observe their movements as the hairs on the back of her neck pricked up.

Realization hit her just in time to see the first of a wave of javelins that rose from the enemy ranks, soaring through the air with terrifying speed.

"Shields!" she cried, raising her own shield to her eye level and watching for incoming projectiles.

The weapons raced across the space between them, but they were not aimed at the men themselves. No, it was at their horses that the monsters leveled their aim, and all of the horses took one or more javelins to the chest. Talia's mount dropped on the spot, one spear in its throat and another which must have pierced its heart.

The heavy beast crumpled, trapping Talias right leg before she could roll free.

She caught herself and watched as most of her men were able to break free of their dying mounts. Arcus stepped from his stirrups and onto the field as though he'd intended to all along, barely even adjusting his hands on his bow, while the others simply scrambled free of their screaming and wounded horses. Corporal Garland was as unlucky as she was, and was similarly pinned beneath a thrashing, convulsing mount, but it was Darko who fared the worst.

The wizard's horse was caught in the haunch and seemed to have gone mad from shock. It bucked like an unbroken stallion and the wizard, already much-abused, was flung to the ground a few feet away from Talia. The horse stumbled off into the woods with most of the wizard's gear, but Talia was far more concerned for the mage himself, who lay in a crumpled heap where he had fallen.

Talia kicked and shoved at her dead war horse until she was finally able to pull her leg free. Already her men were locked in combat with the advancing creatures, who pressed mercilessly while they tried to recover. Garland took an ax to the throat before he was able to pull himself loose. By the time Talia was standing and had recovered her weapon, only four men besides her fellow officers were still standing. Arcus dropped his bow and pulled his scimitar out once more, and Talia could see a resigned grimness to his features that she felt sure was mirrored on her own face.

She stepped up to the line, planting her feet and raising her shield to block a savage downward strike that would have caught Sergeant Merryl in the shoulder beside her.

He grunted his thanks, but Talia spared no energy to respond. Instead, she breathed a silent prayer before sending her mace into an underhanded arc which caught one of the creatures in the knee with a satisfying crunch.

Benevolent Emperor, grant us the strength to defeat our enemies, or else the grace to die valiantly in your name.

The monster yelped like a struck dog, but stumbled to its knees as its leg gave out. Merryl followed her strike with a lightning-fast jab and pierced the monster's neck through and through.

"Men of the Empire," Talia intoned, drawing deeply from the well of power within her soul. "Blessed are those who fight in the Emperor's name."

Talia began to radiate a bright silver glow, her arms and armor gleaming despite the smoke and the dirt in the clearing. Every word she spoke resonated like a chorus, and she punctuated her prayer with vicious blows of her mace.

"Blessed are the blades of the penitent, that they shall cleave the enemies of His divine will."

She felt herself renewed, her muscles fresh and strong, and her resolve bolstered. She could see the men beside her breathing easier, their arms less shaky and their strikes, parries, and blocks conducted with greater strength and surety.

"Blessed is the armor of the devout, that it may turn back the blades of those who would harm the Empire's servants."

The glow from her armor diffused itself, and soon her whole team's arms and armor shared the gentle, cooling silver aura. No longer were they being pushed steadily back to the woodline, now they held their ground against the onslaught.

"Blessed is the will of the Empire, and thus too are those who carry that will into the field," Talia finished her enchantment.

Her men were renewed, certainly, but the situation was no less grim. She tried to see past the flashing metal and snarling faces of the enemies they fought. Tried to catch a glimpse of Elbaf or the rest of their men or at least to take stock of the rest of the field, but the beasts before them were relentless.

Slowly, by inches, they were again being forced back.

Endless seconds stretched into oblivion as the creatures gave as well as they got. The two sides traded nicks and cuts, bumps and bruises, as each tried to beat the other into committing a fatal error.

The monsters made the first slip, and it cost two of them their lives, but just as swiftly poor Elric overextended a thrust and was seized by the monsters. They dragged the young man forward behind their lines in a whirling flash of teeth, claws, and hatchets where his agonizing screams could be heard for a few terrible moments.

"Talia," Arcus said through gritted teeth from his place on her left. "We cannot hold, there are too many."

Talia did not answer. She could feel Darko's body pressed against her left boot behind her, and she knew there was nowhere they could go. Without their mounts they would be cut down like wheat if they turned to run.

"We *will* hold," she grunted finally, bashing one of the creatures in the skull and receiving a ragged cut across her cheek for her trouble. "We have no other--"

She flinched as a massive blade appeared from nowhere, slicing deep into the creature's shoulder and driving downward until it was well past the middle of the beast's chest. Blood sprayed her face as the blade was ripped sideways, exiting the first monster and burying itself deep into the side of the creature to its left.

Elbaf appeared in the space left by the two dead foes, his gleaming platemail slick with blood and his impassive, impenetrably cold visor still firmly over his face.

The beasts broke seamlessly into two groups, one continuing to harass Talia and her band, and the other turning to face this new and deadly threat. With the pressure greatly eased, Talia found she could take in more of the battlefield around her.

The enemy still outnumbered them, but the margin was far slimmer. The rest of their men had formed a protective circle around what survivors still remained from the caravan, and it appeared that Elbaf alone had come to their aid.

Talia took an ax swing to the shield and answered it with a deft strike of her heavy flanged mace, taking more than a little satisfaction with the crack it made as it found the ribs of an enemy. In the time it took to do so, Elbaf had already dispatched another opponent.

He now stood alone against four of the beasts.

She watched his greatsword as it spun brightly around him in tight, unpredictable circles. Every strike the beasts made was accounted for, perfectly deflected with incredible accuracy. On and on the blade spun, its gleaming steel flashing in the last light of day and giving it the look of a thing possessed.

Talia had to look away again to face the creatures in front of her, who were now more hesitant to strike. They, too, were more inclined to look over their shoulders at the unstoppable swordsman to their rear. Between Arcus, herself, and their two remaining men, Tomlin and Merryl, they began to beat back the four creatures they still faced, and slowly they began to make ground again. If they could only join forces with the rest of the survivors, perhaps they could end this.

She shield-checked one of the creatures, sending him stumbling backwards, and looked up just in time to see Elbaf cut down another two opponents. He spun and twisted in time with his whirling blade, and every now and again the singing steel would lash out with the speed and unpredictable path of a lightning bolt. The weapon would cleave through an arm or leg or lay open a chest, and then melt smoothly back into the impervious defensive pattern with terrifying ease.

The young cleric watched half of the creatures who were still facing off against the bulk of their men split off and turn towards Elbaf at a sprint. The warrior almost certainly couldn't see them, as the pack of new foes approached from the rear, and Talia knew she had to warn him.

"Elbaf!" she shouted over the din of battle. "Behind!"

Her warning came just in time, and she watched as his pattern broke out once more into a deadly strike. He brought his massive weapon to bear with impossible speed, and she watched as the three-inch wide blade split one approaching beast in half from its right shoulder to its left hip, and continued on with enough force to sever the leg of its neighbor.

A pair of hatchets shot sparks as they found purchase at last on Elbaf's armor, but if he noticed the blows it was impossible to tell. He roared a challenge and spun on, spilling blood wherever he turned.

For all his might and prowess, the half-orc was now alone against seven opponents. His pattern became more defensive, and he was less able to take advantage of any slips his opponents might make, for fear of overexposing himself.

But his pace was not sustainable. Though he gave an inhuman effort, Talia could see that blood now leaked from between many of the plates in Elbaf's armor.

She fought with a renewed fervor, knowing that if Elbaf were to survive then even he would need assistance.

The four in front of her were seasoned fighters, and they, too, knew the danger behind them was now contained. They redoubled their efforts as well, and Talia was forced back amid a flurry of blows. Beside her, Arcus panted heavily and traded blows with his own foe, and to their sides the two young men were drenched in sweat as well. She could not see a way to swiftly reach her companion.

Talia ducked under a swinging blade and brought her shield up, catching the protruding snout of her opponent with the hardened metal edge of it and breaking its jaw with a satisfying crack. The beast fell backwards, clutching its face and howling in pain.

Arcus pressed the advantage, sliding his scimitar between the thing's ribs before dancing back behind the safety of his own hide shield.

With numbers finally on their side, Talia could again see Elbaf clearly. An enemy hatchet was lodged in the back of his left shoulder, though she couldn't tell how deeply it had bitten beneath his heavy steel plating. His right thigh sported a dagger as well, a long curved thing with a handle of bone that had pierced the flesh through and through.

His enemies were down to five now, and he stood firmly among a pile of fallen foes, but more and more of his opponents' blows were scoring hits against his armor.

As she watched, a javelin arced high and fast from the melee surrounding the survivors, heading directly for Elbaf's tired body. He dodged the brunt of it, but the barbed metal spearhead left a deep groove in the side of his helmet where the steel turned it away. Though he'd avoided a mortal blow, the impact clearly rocked the half-orc, and for the first time, Talia saw him stumble.

"Elbaf," she cried uselessly across the space between them which, though it couldn't have been more than twenty feet, felt like a vast ocean.

The creatures hammered his armor, trying with desperate fear to press their advantage, and soon Elbaf was blocking blows with his bracers as much as his sword.

A shout from the thicket of survivors drew Talia's eyes, and she could see young Private Derrin, his face streaked with blood and his tabard in tatters, shove his way between two of the monsters and charge towards Elbaf's position.

When they'd first left the Capitol, Derrin was the youngest and greenest of their men. Talia knew him only as a boy from the Northlands with no business in battle, who'd never raised a fist in anger in all his life. Or so she thought.

But not today.

Today he looked for all the world like a crusader of myth as he clutched his longsword and shield and charged across the battlefield towards Elbaf and the beasts surrounding him.

Talia saw one of the creatures next to Derrin take a swing at him, but the nimble young man's breakaway sprint carried him out of reach just in time. He dashed across the field and leapt full-bodied into the fray, tackling one of the creatures next to

Elbaf and bearing him to the ground.

The boy threw the fight into disarray, and Elbaf was able to recover his bearings. The remaining creatures tried to pry Derrin loose, swinging wildly with their axes while trying not to hit their companion, but the wrestling match on the ground was growing as each new beast was dragged into the fray.

Elbaf stood tall, roaring a challenge as he raised his greatsword overhead and brought it plunging down through the chest of one of the creatures and pinned it to the ground. Talia watched as the half-orc then let go of the sword and reached his gauntleted hands into the scuffle below.

She took her eyes off of Elbaf long enough to trade blows once more with her more immediate opponents, and when she was able to spare a glance again, she saw that the half-orc held one of the creatures kicking and screaming above the fray by its neck. He snapped the spine of the beast like a dry branch and flung its limp body away before digging back in for more.

Within a few moments the handful of surviving monsters were fleeing, fully abandoning their companions in sheer terror. The last of them, which clawed its way desperately from the grapple surrounding Elbaf and Derrin, finally broke free and sprinted for the woodline.

Elbaf, unwilling to let his prey escape, wrenched free his enormous greatsword and with an overhand throw sent the massive, five-foot weapon sailing across the clearing.

The blade impaled the monster, splitting its chest wide open and driving it to the ground with a wet thud, and the clearing fell into a blood-soaked silence.

Chapter Fourteen

Arcus spun slowly, searching the clearing for more targets, and breathed a long, slow sigh of relief as he found none. He sank to his knees and gave thanks to the Huntress that today was not his day to die. He closed his eyes, acutely aware of his pounding heart, the way each breath he took seemed to roar in his ears, and every drop of sweat that left his tawny hair to fall to the earth.

He reached out for Kodja, who was already busy tracking the monsters on their retreat.

Be careful, little brother.

The wolf sent him the warmth of reassurance alongside the cold clarity of his drive to hunt, a dispassionate violence that stirred Arcus' already boiling blood.

"Arcus, see to Darko," Talia spoke from his right, and he felt her hand give his shoulder a quick squeeze.

Something in her voice made him open his eyes again, and he could see she was already sprinting across the field, heedless of the ache in her muscles or the weight of the scalemail she wore. The object of her concern was immediately obvious. Elbaf was barely standing, his mighty frame trembling like a leaf in the wind, in the center of a pile of bodies.

The half-orc was attended by Private Derrin, but the young man himself was covered in blood. As Arcus watched, the half-orc sagged and sank heavily to one knee. The only thing that kept him from falling to the ground completely was the steadying grasp of the young soldier at his side. Arcus, knowing that the few superficial cuts he had suffered were incomparable to Elbaf's injuries, struggled to his feet and headed over.

"Tomlin, see to the wizard," he said, knowing the mage was in less dire straits. "Get him upright and comfortable, and make sure there's water for him when he wakes."

"Aye, sir," Tomlin saluted stiffly before kneeling beside the wizard.

Arcus rushed over, his shock growing with every step. The butchery surrounding his friend was truly staggering. Nearly two dozen foes, more than half of the enemy forces in the clearing, bore the marks of his signature greatsword. Most of them were in two or more pieces, and all of them had looks of sheer terror marring their faces.

"How is he?" the ranger asked as he approached.

"He's badly hurt," Talia said matter-of-factly, already working to unbuckle the soldier's platemail. "I can't believe he kept on his feet for so long."

Derrin hovered nervously, ignoring his own wounds and wringing his hands uselessly. Talia and Arcus both noticed the young man's fretting, but it was Talia who at last set him a task.

"Go see if the caravan has any clean rags and water, we'll need to staunch the bleeding."

"Aye, ma'am," he said, sprinting away on his errand.

"Help me with this one, Arcus," Talia asked him. "You have to brace him, to keep his body straight. I have to get this ax out of his back."

Arcus nodded and moved around to Elbaf's front. The more closely he examined his friend, the worse the damage seemed to be. The blood of their enemies was everywhere, but it seemed half the seams in Elbaf's armor were draining blood as well.

The ranger helped Talia undo the last few fastenings holding on Elbaf's pauldrons, which fell to the ground with a clank, and then began to work on the breastplate. Every strap and buckle was taught and slick and their tired hands fumbled often, but at last they got the man's chest plate off.

As his friend's armor was stripped away, Arcus could see the shallow, stuttering breaths the man was taking and could practically hear his drumbeat pulse. Every layer of protection taken off seemed to reveal a host of new cuts and splotchy purple impact wounds.

"Alright, Arcus," Talia said slowly. "I'm going to pull this out. Hold him tight."

"You're alright, brother," he reassured the warrior, gripping both of his shoulders tightly and placing his forehead against the half-orc's visored face.

Elbaf's body jerked once, then twice as Talia struggled to pull out the blade jammed in the back of his shoulder. How the hatchet had worked its way under his pauldron was unclear, but it was definitely lodged in his bone.

Elbaf groaned and tensed up, but did not utter a single word as the cleric tugged one final time and pulled the weapon free. Arcus caught a look at the jagged, serrated edge of the weapon before Talia tossed it aside. The ragged gash it left was easily his worst injury, and dark red blood flowed sluggishly from it.

"With this damn curse upon us my own powers to heal his body are limited, but I could gather some herbs from the forest," Arcus offered. "Something to staunch the bleeding, a poultice to help it heal, and maybe something to give him some strength?"

"No," Talia said simply, pulling off her leather riding gloves and removing her helmet. "I will call upon the blessings of the Emperor, and pray that He finds us worthy of His gifts."

She shook her hair loose and scooted closer to Elbaf. Arcus watched as she placed a hand on either side of Elbaf's cut and closed her eyes. She started to mumble, or perhaps sing, but it was too soft for Arcus to make out the words.

He soon stopped caring what she was saying, however, because a soft golden light started to radiate from her. It appeared at first like a ray of sunlight through a gap in the clouds, growing in strength until it bathed the cleric and the injured warrior both in an aura that was as bright as the midday sun.

The young woman's voice rose into a beautiful song, and her hair began to move as though it were touched by a soft breeze. He could not grasp the words, though her volume was now loud enough that everyone in the clearing could hear her clearly. Every sound she made filled his ears with the ringing of soft bells and the blowing of distant horns, rather than words.

He felt a deep and abiding peace flowing from his hands and arms, both of which were still holding on to Elbaf and thus within the beam of radiance. Arcus stared in awe as his own cuts closed, scabbed over, and then faded into smooth unbroken skin.

He then turned his eyes to Elbaf and his jaw dropped as the warrior's wounds began to heal themselves before his very eyes. The smaller injuries disappeared swiftly, but the larger areas were moving much more slowly. Arcus was focused mostly on the gash in the soldier's shoulder, and he watched as the eight-inch long slash began to shrink. The furrow in his flesh scabbed over, then began to scar at an unbelievable pace. He watched as weeks of recovery were accomplished in a matter of moments, until the wound looked no more than a month old and well on its way to a full recovery.

Talia's singing slowed once more and then faded entirely, and with it the glow surrounding her. When the clearing fell back into the late summer afternoon sun, it seemed that all the colors of the world were somehow diminished.

"Talia," Arcus said in soft, sober tones. "That was-- I have *never* seen such a miracle."

The girl managed a wan smile, and he could see that the effort had taken much from her.

"I have done what I can," she took a long breath. "The Emperor's grace is mighty, and He has deemed me a worthy servant to bear His power."

"Talia, I mean it," he pressed. "Even the elders of my people, who are well versed in the healing arts of nature, would be hard pressed to do as you have done here. This is divine work indeed."

Arcus watched the girl's cheeks redden, and wondered at the depth of her embarrassment. "Help me get his helmet off," was all she said in response.

Arcus shrugged and knelt down to undo Elbaf's chinstrap, but the moment he touched his friend's helmet the half-orc reared up as if he'd been stung.

"You're alright, Elbaf. I'm just--"

"No," the half-orc grunted as he rose shakily to his feet. "I'm fine, thank you both. I'm . . . fine."

Arcus shared a concerned look with Talia as the half-orc hefted his blade and headed for the woodline, his blood and sweat covered chest still heaving from his exertions.

Neither of them spoke as the distance between them grew.

Elbaf hoped he wasn't shaking as badly as his mind would have him believe. He focused on making sure each of his steps was as steady as possible, and judging from the lack of intervention from his fellows, he supposed he must have been doing alright.

Inside though, he was a bundle of raw, tangled nerves. His heart was still pounding, and it felt like every breath was catching in his throat before it could fill his lungs. His head pounded mercilessly, and every time he blinked he could see the snarling faces of the beasts he'd been fighting, he could smell their fear and feel their blood washing over him.

Steady, steady, you're nearly to the woodline.

He repeated his internal mantra over and over as he felt the bile rising in his throat and his breathing growing more shallow and less controlled. His eyes were losing focus at alarming intervals, and it was all he could do to keep moving forward.

At last he felt the shade of the trees on his battered flesh and its cooling touch calmed him slightly. He walked through the first several lines of trees, ensuring he was no longer visible to his friends, then set down his greatsword before leaning heavily against a nearby Hollenwood.

As he rested against the sturdy wood, the weight he'd held back hit him at last. It broke through the walls of his self control, and he barely pulled his helmet off in time to fall to his knees and empty his stomach all over the grass. He threw up until his stomach was empty, then retched several times more as black spots popped and danced before his eyes. He remained on all fours, panting heavily, and wrestled with his body for control.

When at last he was sure he wouldn't be sick again, he sat back and wiped his mouth with the back of one of his gauntlets. He shut his eyes to rest for a moment, but was met immediately with flashing images of frantic combat, of blades dancing near his face and snarling teeth.

It had been this way for weeks now. Though he'd been able to suppress it for the most part, he could not help but relive the violence over and over. He could not sleep, and when he did, he got no rest. He could not even sit in silence too long or else he would hear the approaching boots of an enemy, the ringing of blades, or the screams of the dying.

He was no stranger to fighting, but this was not the casual fisticuffs and broken bones of the Brine; here there was senseless death and wanton destruction.

Tears came unbidden from his eyes, and his shoulders rocked as he asked for the ten-thousandth time what right he had to be here, when good men - his own soldiers - had been cut down before his very eyes. They were five men fewer, and each a worthier man than he. He reviewed the hectic, wild charge he'd made and, in hindsight, could see dozens of errors that might have saved their soldiers. Mistakes that he'd made, things he could have done differently, factors that lead to their deaths.

A snapping twig to his left brought him swiftly back to the real world, however, and he snatched up his greatsword and whirled about to face his unseen foe.

His blade halted mere inches from the throat of Private Derrin as the young man stumbled to a halt. All of the color drained from Derrin's face, and he trembled like a leaf as he took in Elbaf's fearsome visage.

Elbaf blinked his eyes clear and turned away at once, his sword tip drooping low. He tried to wipe his eyes without the other soldier seeing and gruffly waved him away.

"Get back to the caravan," he growled. "See to the injured."

"Aye, sir," the timid voice replied. "I am, sir."

Elbaf glanced back when he heard no sound and saw that Derrin hadn't moved.

The young man was impertinent and made no indication that he intended to return to the rest of the group. Elbaf turned to face him once again, aware of how imposing he could look, and prepared to chastise the younger soldier for disobeying him. But something in Derrin's eyes made him change his mind. A kinship, an understanding.

He noted the dark circles under the soldiers eyes and the pieces fell together. Derrin fought the same battles he did, both on and off the field.

"Sit then," he gestured carelessly. "If you'd like."

Elbaf then took his seat and was unsurprised when Derrin did as well. The lad chose a spot against another tree, a few feet away and directly across from Elbaf.

"Sir--"

"Elbaf, please."

"Elbaf, I . . ." The boy seemed choked for words. "It doesn't really get better, does it?"

He spoke with such weariness that Elbaf simply shook his head and dropped his shoulders.

"I don't know, Derrin," he sighed. "I'd like to think it does, but I'm afraid you may be right. I thought perhaps it would after Altimeer, and then again after the goblin camp."

He let out a long ragged breath.

"But now, after those . . . those *things*--"

"Kyush," Derrin interrupted softly. "They're called Kyush. All the worst parts of a rabid dog crossed with a man."

Elbaf cast a curious glance at the young man.

"They make fearsome soldiers, if one is strong enough to command them," Derrin continued absentmindedly. "But they are a savage, unpredictable race."

"How do you know of these beasts?"

"They plague the deeper, wooded parts of the Empire," he shrugged. "They are known to my . . . to my people," he trailed off.

They sat in silence a while until Derrin began to speak again.

"You know," he said softly, "my mother and father were both soldiers." He scoffed derisively before continuing. "I barely knew them, only ever heard of their exploits. They were dead before I came of age, of course."

Elbaf was surprised to hear that, but didn't interrupt.

"That's the way it is where I come from," the soldier shrugged. "We all fight."

Elbaf could sense hesitation, anger, and . . . something else in the young man's demeanor and he seemed suddenly weary beyond his years.

"I didn't know the Northlands were so harsh."

"What do you mean?" Derrin asked, giving Elbaf pause.

"Your homeland, I didn't realize there was so much fighting up there," Elbaf clarified. "We didn't learn about any recent conflicts in the north during our officer schooling."

"Ah, well," Derrin fidgeted with his hands and scuffed his boot in the dirt. "I don't suppose it would be of note to the Empire."

Elbaf thought about pressing, but chose instead to answer the boy's story with his own.

"I know something about fighting, I suppose," he started slowly. "Or I thought I did."

"The men say you were a fighter back in the Capitol," Derrin added.

"Sure I was," Elbaf laughed without humor. "'The Brawler of the Brine' they called me. I was quite a big fish . . . but in a pond smaller than I could imagine. On the streets, your reputation is deadly serious, and we broke bones and split lips constantly to establish who ran what, who owned where. It seems a bit boyish now."

"No, sir, I don't think so," Derrin interjected. "Seems to me that is the way of the world. You fight for what you have, fight for what you want. And to hell with anyone who would take it from you."

"I suppose you're right," Elbaf mused. "I don't know, I wonder at times what my father would have said. Would he be proud that I became a soldier as well, despite my best efforts?"

"Your father was a soldier?"

"Yes, a corporal in the Imperial Army," Elbaf continued. "He was killed far away to the west of here, hundreds of miles from home."

"Oh," Derrin seemed genuinely surprised. "I guess I just . . . nevermind."

"You wonder at my heritage," he spoke with certainty, long used to the awkward dance of people trying to find out just how tragic the circumstances of his conception were.

To Elbaf's surprise, when he glanced up at his companion, Derrin did not look ashamed, rather he was intensely scrutinizing the half-orc.

"Very well," Elbaf said gruffly, unused to opening up so thoroughly. "Before I was born, my parents lived west of the Capitol. They lived a week or so past Fort Gunnhild in a small village, Loxmeer."

Elbaf paused to consider his words before continuing, "Back then, though I suppose you were also too young to recall it, there were dozens of raids throughout the west." He picked at his armor as he recalled the tear-stained cheeks of his mother when she'd finally told him the tale as a youngster. "An orcish warlord, Dramugar, sacked villages, razed towns to the ground, even hit some of the smaller military outposts in the region. His horde, the Splitrock, would strike without warning and vanish without a trace. The armies of the Empire were at a loss and had too many men stretched too thinly, trying to find their stronghold."

Elbaf found himself more appreciative of the dangers those men must have faced now, in the wake of his own experiences.

"My father was in one such outfit. They were far afield searching the hinterlands for the horde's base of operations when Dramugar and his men fell upon our village. My mother told me, once, of the brutality of the orcish warriors in combat and . . . she didn't need to tell me the rest."

They both fell into uneasy silence.

"When my father returned home, my mother was barely alive and five months pregnant with a monster. She was afraid he'd abandon her, but he loved her still and my unborn self as well. They were all but driven from Fort Gunnhild when the garrison discovered her affliction, and it was only my father's sterling record that allowed him to be transferred out of sight, to the Capitol."

"How did he die?"

Elbaf bristled, but chose to answer.

"He volunteered for many missions, always those in search of Dramugar," Elbaf's gaze grew distant and his tone bitter. "I saw him sometimes, as a young boy. I recall him as a strong, proud man. He was the one who taught me what it was to fight and to defend others. But he was gone most of the time, and we had only his letters and my mother's stories."

The warrior's fist balled tightly with a soft creak of leather.

"Then, one day a letter came saying he'd died at the hands of Dramugar's horde," Elbaf hung his head. "The letter came with a few of his belongings, his greatsword and some other sundries, but there was no body to mourn. For my mother, it was the final straw. She wasted away within the year, and I was left with the only family I could find, other half-orcs in the city."

"In the Brine?"

"Yes, in the Brine. I was just a child, five or six perhaps," Elbaf scowled. "The Brine protected me when many in the Capitol would've gladly smashed my head with a boot for the abomination I represented. So, as I grew strong, I protected the Brine as it had protected me."

"Your father sounds like a great warrior," Derrin offered.

"He was," Elbaf nodded solemnly. "And someday, I will finish what he started."

"You mean--"

"I mean that if I must live out my days as an imperial soldier, I will use that title to destroy Dramugar and his horde. I will avenge my mother's suffering and my father's death, though it may take me until my final breath."

"So Dramugar was never defeated?"

"No. After the campaign in which my father was slain, he disappeared," Elbaf growled. "His horde hasn't been seen since."

They slipped into quietude, as neither seemed to know what else to say, and they stayed that way for several long minutes. Slowly Elbaf's heart resumed its normal pace, his breathing eased, and his mind calmed itself to some degree. At long last, however, he could avoid the rest of his responsibilities no longer.

"We'd best be getting back," he sighed as he took his feet and grabbed his fallen helm.

"Aye, sir," Derrin stood as well. "They'll be needing your guidance."

"Derrin," Elbaf's tone caused the man to stop. "You may well have saved my life today, and I'll not forget it."

He studied the young man. He was older than Elbaf, technically, but the difference in the way humans and half-orcs matured still led Elbaf to see him as little more than a boy. The stocky, sunburned twenty-something was more gaunt, more chiseled than he had been when they'd left the Capitol. He'd aged, particularly around the eyes, but Elbaf supposed he would see the same should he look into a mirror.

"It was my honor, sir," the young man said solemnly. "My duty and my privilege."

Elbaf didn't know how to respond, so he silently replaced his helmet and turned back to the clearing.

The pair re-entered the clearing to find the rest of the survivors hard at work. Several of the men stood a careful watch, their blades still drawn and their eyes scanning the treeline. Others were searching and stacking the bodies of the dead for a funeral pyre.

Talia, Darko, and Arcus were all speaking with the few survivors of the caravan, and Arcus waved him over when he noted that Elbaf had returned.

As he approached, it became increasingly apparent to Elbaf that the folks they'd rescued were not from the Empire. Everything from their clothing to their thick, tilting accents was foreign to him.

"Elbaf," Arcus said as he approached. "Meet Reijan and his friends and family."

Elbaf acknowledged the group with a nod, noting the sharp tang of fear in the air from the half-dozen huddled people.

"They're from Tirja," Talia explained. "Away to the far northeast. They must have traveled weeks already to be so deep within the Empire."

Elbaf quirked up an eyebrow, but said nothing. It was unusual for refugees to travel into the Empire, which was notoriously unforgiving of outsiders.

"Well met, sir," Reijan bowed deeply, his balding head bobbing up and down. "We are deeply indebted to you and your companions."

Elbaf turned to face Talia directly and nodded off to the side, indicating he wished to speak with her in private. She caught his signal easily, and they stepped off to the side.

"Talia," Elbaf began matter-of-factly. "The law states--"

"That trespassers to the Empire without a signed writ of trade are to be executed," she sighed heavily, pinching the bridge of her nose between two dirty fingers. "I know, Elbaf. Of course I know."

"And?"

"And we can't do that, obviously," she shot back at him.

"I am not your enemy, Talia," he said. "I am merely stating the laws. Where you lead, I will follow; now how do we save these people?"

She looked back at the rag-top group. They seemed harmless, more than likely drawn to the Empire with promises of an easier, safer life than what they'd found outside her borders.

"If we simply let them go they'll more than likely run into a less forgiving patrol," she chewed her lip. "I don't know how, but they'll get mercy, not damnation from us."

"The only solution I can see," Elbaf offered, "is that we should escort them to safety. No one will raise a blade against them in the company of the Black Hand."

Talia perked up.

"We'll find out where they are headed," she said. "And perhaps, if their path aligns with ours a while, an opportunity might present itself."

Elbaf nodded slowly.

"Right," she nodded, mostly to herself. "Great idea, Elbaf."

He shrugged as she turned away, and they made their way back to the group.

"Reijan," she asked boldly. "Where exactly were you headed?"

"W-we had no destination in mind," he bowed again. "M-my lady, we simply seek a better life, away from the wilds of Tirja. Here in the Empire we hoped to--"

"Then you've no objection to traveling a while with us," she pressed. "I can offer you a guarantee of safety only so long as we are together. You understand you are missing the documents that would allow you to travel unmolested by imperial forces, yes?"

"Yes, m'lady, but I don't understand . . ."

Talia leaned in close.

"We cannot deviate from our own mission, I'm afraid, but if you travel with us we can grant you protection."

"Are we not t-t-to be punished?"

Elbaf wrinkled his nose. The stench of fear was palpable from these poor, brutalized refugees.

"The Empire is mercy, friend." She put a hand on his shoulder. "You and your people will travel with us, and we can see about resettling you somewhere safer."

"M-my lady," the man stammered. "We cannot possibly repay your kindness."

"You'll never need to, Reijan," she reassured him. "Make your people ready to move. We'd best be on our way soon."

Talia took stock of their limited resources. All of the horses pulling the caravans had been slain, and they had less than a half dozen horses left themselves. Many of the surviving refugees were injured as well, and in no condition to continue a grueling trek.

"We'll walk and have our horses pull the wagons from here," Talia told Sergeant Cormorant. "They'll need to reduce the number of wagons to what we can manage, and that likely means leaving a fair amount behind."

"Aye, ma'am," he saluted. "We'll get as small as we can."

They finished preparing the funeral pyres as the evening lengthened on towards night, and by the time everything was ready, the sun had all but set. The survivors formed a small half-circle around the pyres, most with their hands clasped in front of them and their head coverings respectfully removed.

Talia stood at the forefront of the assembled soldiers and refugees, and the clearing fell silent, save for the crackle of the torch she held in her hand.

"Here lie brave heroes of the imperium," she began, her voice low and solemn. "Cut down in their youth to defend the ideal of a land dedicated to freedom, justice, and the virtue of peace."

The group watched as she knelt before the mass of branches and brush that lay beneath the fallen.

"Here, too, lie the innocent. Those whose fall reminds us that no matter the strength of our sword arms, we cannot save everyone, the bitter truth of the frailty of life, and the stark reminder that we must always strive to do better . . . to *be* better."

Her last whispered words faded into the night as she set the torch amongst the branches and brambles, and the spark grew quickly into a hungry flame.

"Benevolent Emperor," she bowed her head as she prayed aloud. "I hope that you hear our benediction, and that you grant the faithful their just reward in the palace of the afterlife."

She finished speaking, and all was still for a moment more. The quiet was broken by the rushing flames as the pyre caught with gusto in a sudden swift breeze, and the flames shot high into the air as the dead were consumed.

The group stayed there until the last fires began to lull, and the bodies of the valorous dead were reduced to ash. Then, at long last, well past the setting of the sun, they were ready to depart.

"Darko?" she asked the mage. "Are you recovered enough to provide us some light? Though it may paint us a pretty target, I would prefer not to fight blind, if it comes to that."

"I believe I am," the wizard replied, his hands already beginning to sparkle with brilliant motes of golden light.

Darko stretched forth his hands, and a dozen softly glowing balls of light shot forth and arranged themselves in a line down the center of the wagon train. Together they provided as much light as twice as many torches, and the mage looked pleased with the gasps of wonder his small feat elicited.

"Men," Talia commanded her tired troops. "We've a long way 'till daybreak, but I'd sooner be away from this place before we bed down. Keep your eyes sharp and your blades at the ready."

Talia caught the eyes of her fellow officers as Sergeant Cormorant took control of the men, and the much-reduced column began to lumber forward into the gathering darkness.

Without a word, the group gathered at the tail-end of the convoy.

"We've yet to discuss the findings at Mercane's place," the cleric reminded her friends.

"I suppose you're right," Arcus replied, a grimace on his face. "Though I would prefer never to think of that wretched town again, so long as I live."

No one was surprised at Elbaf's silence, but Darko's was a bit of a mystery. The mage rode between the other three and was still a bit groggy from his recent efforts, but Talia had expected a comment of some kind.

"Right, well," she started, pulling pamphlets from her pouch for her partners. "Mercane was definitely guilty of sedition and treason, but I think there's more to this. Take a look."

Arcus' eyes widened as soon as he saw the folded parchment.

"Talia, this symbol--"

"It matches the pendant the old man gave me back in the Capitol," she nodded. "I don't know the significance of that, save that it would likely not be in our interests to have that comparison made outside our group."

"I have to say," Arcus said cautiously, his eyes on Talia. "I cannot disagree with the sentiment that the Empire is far from the gleaming example of justice and fairness it pretends to be."

"Arcus," Talia's voice took a tone of warning. "We need to remain objective. We are still servants of the Empire. That makes correcting her *shortcomings* our responsibility and one we cannot run from."

"Only because we are literally bound against it," Darko scoffed from beneath his hooded robes.

Talia stared daggers at him.

"But you're not wrong, Talia," he acquiesced. "For now our only option is to fix this as best we can."

"What about this part?" Elbaf spoke up unexpectedly and began to read aloud. "'The great tree of the Empire is DEAD, *rotten* to her core, but the PROPHET has foreseen the falling of leaves that will fertilize the soil of rebellion.'"

"It's just ramblings, Elbaf," Talia reassured him. "We need to focus on this symbol and these--"

"Wait a moment," Arcus interrupted. "That *could* be a riddle, right? Trees, leaves, soil . . . there's a theme, see? I don't know, maybe it has something to do with the game the old man had us play, remember?"

"I'm more interested in this alleged prophet, personally," Darko chimed in. "Any *true* wizard would have had to go through the Academy. So, they're either a charlatan or there's a rogue imperial wizard out there. Maybe more than one."

"Hang on," Talia tried to rein in the group before their minds wandered too far. "We've also got this ring and feather to consider, as well."

"Feather?"

Talia handed the feather over to Arcus, whose hand was already outstretched. The ranger took a second or two to render his judgment.

"It's from a raven," he concluded matter-of-factly. "A perfectly normal one, from what I can determine, if a bit smaller than most."

"Ravens are extremely intelligent," Darko added. "It could reinforce our rogue wizard theory. Many in the Academy choose to bond with ravens."

"Why would they pluck out a feather then?" Elbaf asked, unconvinced.

"Ah, hmm," Darko furrowed his brow. "I suppose you're right. That would be . . . well, disrespectful and unnecessary."

"Maybe it's just a token," Talia offered. "Like our badges, it simply represents a member of this . . . this resistance group?"

"Then why have a signet ring?" Elbaf asked, again skewering the proposition.

"Right, the ring," Talia frowned and pulled out the small gold object. "This is fairly nondescript, it's just a gold ring with a worn-off design of some kind."

"Let me see," Arcus offered, but he frowned as soon as the cleric handed him the ring. "It's a plant of some kind. It could be a Verulah, or perhaps a willow - it's hard to tell from this engraving, other than that it is a tree, I think."

"May I?" Darko asked, and Arcus handed off the ring.

"This is very, very old," the wizard said. "I would wager this design was once enameled, too."

"Well it's not the sign of any of the great houses," Talia said firmly. "I would recognize it, if it were."

The group went round and round as the hours passed, each testing new theories around the evidence they'd collected so far and each being picked apart in turn. By the time they finally called for the column to halt - sometime around midnight - they were still no closer to understanding the cryptic clues than when they'd begun.

Elbaf and Arcus volunteered to take the first watch, for which Talia was extremely grateful. She made a final round of the campsite, ensuring all was in order and that both their men and the refugees were as well cared for as could be managed, given the circumstances. Finally, the young woman returned to her bedroll beside a low fire and tried to get comfortable.

The stress of the day and her tired bones had her drifting off despite the armor she still wore, and the only thing that kept her from immediate slumber was the dangling question on her mind.

What on earth were they actually going to *do* with Mercane when they found him?

Chapter Fifteen

Dawn broke early, and the forest seemed almost as reluctant to awaken as the bruised and battered company beneath its boughs. Arcus was the only one awake, besides the final guard shift, of course.

The ranger made sure the guards saw him before silently waving off their concerns and slipping into the woodline as the first traces of pink began to grace the skies. He wandered aimlessly, allowing the woods to guide his path as much as anything, and soon found himself in a small gulley. To his surprise, it opened up onto a small creek, which in turn led to a narrow, fast-flowing stream.

He followed the bubbling water to a small cliff, perhaps 60 feet high, that looked out over a larger pond. The view from this precipice was much less crowded, and he found himself facing east just as the leading edge of the sun broke over the horizon. The soft, gentle light spread across the top of the forest below him and bathed him in a growing warmth. Arcus sat there, at the edge of the falls on a patch of soft green Ferelia moss, for what must have been a half hour or more, soaking in the sunlight and listening to the birdsong as the forest began to wake from its slumber.

For a brief, treasured moment he was utterly unconcerned with the events of the day ahead, and more importantly he was able to shed much of the stress and tension of the days and weeks behind him. He meditated quietly, feeling the bounty all around him, the endless cycles of life and death, the water beside him, the growth and decay of the leaves littering the ground.

He opened his eyes to see a massive blue-tailed hawk circling over the trees, no doubt hoping to catch a drowsy squirrel or rabbit for breakfast, and smiled at the majestic bird as it soared effortlessly through the air.

Kodja joined him after a while, each of them silently acknowledging the other, and curled up beside him. The wolf yawned and snuggled closer, his thick fur warming Arcus' leg and his steady heartbeat further grounding the man.

"I suppose, little brother," Arcus wondered aloud, putting a hand on Kodja's neck and giving him a light scratching, "we should return to our companions, no?"

Kodja huffed and stayed put, pulling a laugh from his friend for his stubborn behavior.

"Alright, a little longer then."

Kodja nudged him and then turned his deep, amber eyes to look at Arcus, who caught his gaze.

The wolf projected images, flashes of himself and Arcus as they had made their way alone across the Empire on their way to the Capitol. He could feel the wolf's longing to run free, to return to the colder climate of the tundra, to visit with his own pack back home. The wolf was lonely and tired, and felt the stress of his brother as a weight upon his heart.

"We can't, Kodja," Arcus apologized. "We are bound here, and this new pack needs us, as well."

Kodja put his head back down, a little saddened but just as committed as ever.

They spent the sunrise there together, quietly soaking up the splendor of the morning until the sun was fully above the treetops and they could avoid their responsibilities no longer.

The ranger stood and brushed the dust and dirt from his breeches before heading back to the group, who were no doubt already waiting for him.

"We were about to send a search party," Talia chided him as they trotted back into the campsite. "After what we saw yesterday, what could have possessed you to run off like that?"

"Sorry, Talia," Arcus shrugged. "I was perfectly safe, I promise."

"I'm sure our guests thought the same yesterday morning," she pointed out with a frown.

Arcus shrugged apologetically, and Talia turned away, scolding him with an exasperated sigh.

The wagon train was underway shortly, and an air of cautious optimism began to spread through the group as the morning lengthened and they drew closer and closer to the relative sanctuary of Gilbad.

Arcus thanked the gods that the morning was uneventful. In fact, the most exciting thing that had happened was the group startling a herd of deer that were grazing just off the road. In the back of his mind, however, he could not help but think ahead to the upcoming troubles they were walking into. Mercane was going to beat them to Gilbad, no doubt about that now. The wagon train had them well behind schedule, even if they hadn't been stopped by the ambush or wounded soldiers to tend to.

Whether he would still be in Gilbad when they arrived, or what kind of support he had there, was yet to be determined. Arcus asked himself which would be more difficult, finding that Mercane was alone in his thinking, or finding that the whole town was discontented with the Empire.

"Sir," Corporal Felder saluted as he returned from a quick reconnaissance of the path ahead.

Arcus waved away the formality, putting the short, dark-haired man at ease immediately. He was a capable scout, and Arcus had grown to respect his woodcraft too much to stand on any kind of ceremony.

"How's the route ahead?"

"She's clear enough, sir," Felder grinned from behind his bushy mustache. "Save for there's a town round the next bend, just smack in the middle of the road."

Arcus glanced upward at the sun, then back down to his scout in surprise.

"We're there already? I had us arriving at noon," he scratched his chin. "Well it's a surprise, to be sure, but a welcome one."

Felder's grin was infectious, and Arcus caught the same optimistic smile in moments.

"Alright, you ride ahead and let the guards know we'll be arriving shortly."

"Aye, sir," was all the reply he got before the Corporal turned and jogged back up the path.

"Talia!" Arcus called out over his shoulder. "We're about a quarter-mile out!"

An air of electricity shot through the group at the announcement. Everyone seemed eager to be free of the woods and behind the sturdy walls of town.

Talia felt the surge of energy in her men like the static before a storm, and she hoped their optimism was well-placed. However, even in the best of circumstances, they were here to apprehend and likely execute a criminal, she reminded herself, and so she was a bit more reserved than most of her companions.

She made her way to the front of the column, alongside Arcus, so that she would be among the first to meet with the guardsmen that would no doubt be greeting them. Sure enough, around one final bend in the path, they broke out into a massive clearing cut into the wooded hills.

Gilbad was a frontier town, smaller even than Bethlir and without the mighty keep that the former boasted. Rather, it consisted of a cluster of squat wooden buildings behind a sturdy wooden palisade that sported a single large gate.

Talia could see from her vantage point on the road that the gates were open, and unsurprisingly there were a pair of guards stationed there to challenge anyone who might approach. As they crossed the intervening hundred feet between the edge of the woodline and the gatehouse, she watched as one of the guards headed inside and the other took up a watchful post in the center of their path.

The soldier, judging from his posture, was not quite sure what to make of the ragged band headed his way, and as they got closer, Talia watched his expression turn more confused the closer they got.

When they entered earshot, the young man called out to them to identify themselves, to which Talia returned a shout and a wave.

"Ma'am," the soldier saluted sloppily in confusion when at last he could see their armor and emblems beneath the dirt and blood still adorning them. "We weren't expecting an answer so quickly. I shall have the mayor informed immediately."

Talia turned and raised an eyebrow to Elbaf, who walked beside her, before turning back to the man.

"I see," she proceeded cautiously. "Well, we were met by no messenger, I'm afraid. We're here--"

"About this business with the Mercane boys and young Alicia, no doubt," the guard nodded somberly. "It's a terrible business, a damn shame really, m'lady."

Talia scowled at being interrupted by the man, but was too thirsty for information to correct him.

"Are you the captain of the guard?" she probed. "I would very much like to see him and the mayor immediately."

"Aye, ma'am," he answered, flustered by the authority in her voice. "Er . . .

rather, no, ma'am. I'm just a guard, Kirk Haldrun. I, uh . . . the Sergeant's gone to get the cap'n."

"Excellent," she nodded. "And am I correct in assuming you have an inn here in Gilbad?"

"Sure," he shrugged and hiked a thumb over his shoulder. "After a sort, that is. The Loathsome Stump. She sits right there past the water well, can't miss her. She's the only place in town with proper stables, too."

"Have them meet us there," she said as she brushed past him, already annoyed that they'd yet to be invited within the walls.

"Ma'am," the guard stammered. "These folks that's with ya', I don't rightly know if--"

"They are," she snapped back at him, "*with me*, are they not?"

"Well--"

"And I am a Hand of the Emperor," she pressed, taking a step closer to him. "Am I not?"

"Y-yes, but they're *foreign*, ma'am. Tirjani by the looks of--"

"You forget yourself," she said acidly past narrowed eyes. "These people are my guests, and you will treat them with respect, Soldier."

"Aye, ma'am. Sorry, ma'am."

The lad was turning red in the face and she could see sweat pouring from his brow now.

"You will have the mayor and the guard captain attend to me and my fellow Hands within the hour, and these people are to be treated with the same dignity as any citizens of the Empire in the meantime. Do I make myself clear?"

He gulped and nodded fervently.

Without wasting more of her breath, Talia strode past the man and into the middle of town. She noticed with alarm that another prominent feature sat in the center of town - a three-noosed gallows had recently been erected. It looked brand new - a day or two old at the very most - and its presence made her more than a touch uneasy. Still, she walked directly to the door of the inn.

The Loathsome Stump, whose name was prominently painted above the clapboard siding, was an oddly shaped, lumpy wooden structure that seemed simultaneously to be sturdy as a rock and to be ever-so-slightly leaning off center. The worn-wood and oft-patched roof gave it the appearance of a beloved but ill-used toy, something between a shack and a home.

Smoke rose in a tight curl from its chimney, however, so she pushed the wide double doors in and entered the dim interior.

The inside wasn't much better than the outside, and she could see that habit alone must have kept the place from falling apart years ago. There were no other patrons, not at this hour, but a couple of old, tired sheepdogs lay slumbering beside a wide stone hearth.

"Cedric," a cranky, old voice called out from behind the bar. "E'en fer you it's too damn early ta' drink by the Emp'rah. What in tha hell d'ya--"

A grizzled, paunchy man emerged from what must have been a cellar door and froze mid-sentence upon catching sight of Talia.

"B-b-beggin' yer' pardon, m'lady," he sputtered, hoisting himself up from the depths and coming around the bar to her. "I wasn't 'spectin' no one. I'm afraid we don't have food er nothin' this early in the day, m'lady."

"Food will not be necessary," she reassured him. "I do have need of your common room, however."

"Sure, m'lady--"

"How many rooms do you have available?" she continued. "I'd like to purchase them for the foreseeable future, at least the next few months."

She thought for a moment that the man might faint, his eyes bulged and he seemed at a loss for words. When he finally mastered himself, he bobbed his little head in what she assumed was meant to be a bow before replying, "Ma'am." He bobbed again. "We can sleep 'bout fifteen here in the common room, or we've got six rooms up over the stables. Norm'ly we charge two copper a night, if that pleases ya', ma'am."

"That'll be fine," she waved him off. He smelt of sour tobacco and sweat and she wasn't sure what to make of his obsequience. "We've a dozen travelers with us and, as I said, I'll take the rooms for the next . . . three moons."

She counted out a dozen golden crowns from her belt pouch, placing them into the man's trembling hands.

"We have with us a troupe of travelers who have come here to be resettled, and they'll be needing a place to stay until they can find work and stand on their own," she said, looking behind her to the doorway that Arcus was currently standing in.

She waved him forward, and the rest of their group slowly piled in, drawing confused looks from the innkeeper.

"These people are being resettled by imperial order," she added sternly. "Their custom is to be taken at the same value as mine. I trust that won't be a problem?"

"Oh no, ma'am," the innkeeper bobbed incessantly. "They'll be treated as mine own honored guests, ma'am."

"Good," she nodded, uncomfortable with her lie but relieved at his immediate acceptance. "I expect them to be housed and fed for three moons. From there they'll pay their own way."

"Aye, ma'am," he pocketed the coins and waved to get everyone's attention. "If it please ya', I'll show you lot your rooms, where to find water, and all of that?"

Talia nodded her reassurance to Reijan, and the group followed the innkeeper back out the door towards the stables. With her first order of business complete, Talia sat down heavily at one of the half-dozen long wooden tables in the common room.

"It seems like it's been a long while since we sat in an inn, no?"

Darko's question was met with wry smiles all around as the officers recalled the first night they'd met with varying degrees of fondness.

"Fancy a riddle?" Arcus asked the group.

Elbaf snorted, but Arcus continued in a more serious tone, "Riddle me this, what has three gallows and only one criminal, so far as we know?"

He cast a pointed look outside and the group sobered back up.

"I'd noticed," Talia sighed. "I can only hope the guard captain or the mayor or . . . whoever passes for the leadership of this town can shed more light."

They didn't have to wait long.

No more than a candlemark passed before a huffing, red-faced man in ill-fitting armor and a gaudy feathered cap entered the inn. Behind him, considerably more put together, was a tall, gaunt soldier in an immaculate guard uniform.

Talia stood and resisted the urge to roll her eyes when the overweight official bowed low to her. She was far more impressed with the clean-cut captain of the guard behind him, who rendered her a textbook perfect salute and then stood at attention waiting for her to acknowledge him.

"My most hu-humble apologies, lady," the shorter, squatter man begged. "I had *no idea* we would be graced with the presence of the Emperor's Hands, certainly not so swiftly after we sent word of our . . . problem."

"Please, there is no need to be overly formal," Talia smiled as pleasantly as she could and indicated a pair of seats at the table with her small group. "Sit, and elaborate on your predicament."

"Well . . ." he paused for a long while. "It's hard to know where to start, really."

"May I suggest you start with the night of the incident, sir?" the captain offered.

"Right. Thanks, Terrence." The man adjusted his armor, which he'd obviously not worn in years, and fidgeted with his hands while he spoke. "Two nights past - middle of the night, mind you - there's a commotion at the gate. A holler goes up, and we learned the guard had apprehended a fellow trying to scale the walls."

Talia was curious if it was the heat, his weight, or something more that caused the man to sweat so profusely, but did her best to keep an even expression on her face.

"By the time I got there, we'd already identified the lad," he shook his head in disbelief. "Couldn't believe it . . . It was Tom, old Bill Mercane's boy. He coulda' just knocked on the gate, y'see. He lives in his parent's old place on the east side of town. Well, of course if that'd been it, it would have been dropped. Course he'd had a stern talking to from Terrence, here. But he's just a lad after all . . . But, ah, well . . . "

"But he was in possession of treasonous materials? Pamphlets and the like, right?" Talia eased the man's discomfort.

The mayor's eyes widened with surprise.

"Well, yes'm, but how could you--"

"We were already pursuing Thomas Mercane, that's why we're here," she explained. "I assume you have him in custody?"

"Yes, m'lady, and Dominic and Alicia as well, of course."

"And they are?" She let the question hang, eliciting a confused look.

"Right. Well, we threw Tom in irons, had to really," the man continued. "Frog marched him back to his place only to find his younger brother Dominic and Alicia MacMordan already there. There was a whole mess of evidence all through the house, so of course we . . . we had to take them, as well."

"I see," Talia tried to keep her tone a sort of neutral-serious, but wheels were turning in her mind at a breakneck pace.

The young cleric spared a glance at her companions, and in their expressions she read faith in her judgment. Her resolve fortified, she set a stern look upon her face and turned back to the mayor.

"We'll need to speak with each of the accused, *alone*," she announced. "In the meantime, there is another matter to settle here as well."

"Th-there is, my lady?"

The trepidation in the man's voice was thick, and Talia could sense he wished very much to keep within her good graces.

"Yes," she nodded before continuing. "There is the matter of resettling Reijan and his companions. The people who traveled with us are the Empire's newest *citizens*, and they have great need of a new home."

"And you would choose Gilbad? Do I understand correctly, ma'am?" the captain of the guard surmised.

"I would," she searched for resistance, but found none in the man's features. "They are not freeloaders, and they shall be expected to contribute as all citizens do. Am I correct in assuming that in a town as *remote* as this there are myriad opportunities to work?"

"Yes, m'lady," the mayor cut back in. "We have more jobs than hands to do them, as is ever the case on the frontier. They are, ah, foreign born, yes?"

"They are."

"Very good, ma'am." The mayor turned to his captain. "Terrence, please ensure that our newest residents are educated on the laws they will be expected to follow and abide by."

Talia was pleased, and more than a little surprised, at the readiness of the mayor and his companion to welcome the newcomers. She hoped their intentions were genuine and that the majority of the town reflected their attitudes rather than that of the guardsmen they'd met on the way in. Regardless, this was as close to a fresh start as she could give Reijan without compromising her own safety.

"In that case, I suppose we ought to see about your captives," she sighed and pushed away from the table before standing again.

"Terrence, if you would please?"

"Aye, sir," the guard captain stood and saluted the mayor. "I'll show you to the holding cell, if it please ya', ma'am."

"You're not coming?" Talia asked the mayor, her suspicion roused once more.

"I beg your leave, ma'am. I was going to prepare the town's taxes and other documents for you," he answered.

"Ah, very good. You may carry on," Talia nearly kicked herself and tried to hide her embarrassment at neglecting her other duties. "We'll take your reports while we're here."

The mayor beamed at her compliment and, after a deep, respectful bow, begged his leave of them.

"Ma'am," the captain coughed lightly. "I can show you to the prisoners at your leisure, but I do not mean to rush you. I am at your disposal."

"A moment please," she said with gratitude before waving over Sergeant Cormorant.

The soldier approached her at a trot and stood respectfully at attention while receiving her instructions.

"Have the men rotate between resting and supplementing the town guard, the same as we did back in Bethlir," she ordered him. "Prioritize any injured on the first rest and fit in with Captain Terrence after that. Double rations, if the town's stores can handle the strain, and make sure to pay a little extra."

"Ma'am," Terrence cut in. "That won't be necessary, I assure you--"

"I can handle this, captain," she chided him gently, her eyes sparkling brightly. "Pay extra, Sergeant. The town will benefit from some additional income now that they have new residents."

Cormorant visibly resisted the urge to grin at her nonchalant rebuff of Captain Terrence, but managed to keep his composure. He snapped a salute to Talia and headed over to the rest of the soldiers to begin dividing them swiftly into groups and assignments.

"Right," the cleric nodded, content at the moment that things were as well in hand as could be managed. "Lead the way."

Darko was still nursing a splitting headache, but he was determined not to show it. Instead, he simply refrained from making many of the sarcastic comments that came to mind and tried to keep his head as far back into his hood as he could.

His darkened vantage point had a dual purpose, for it both gave his strained eyes a rest and allowed him to more freely observe both the captain of the guard and the mayor. From his vantage point he came to a series of swift conclusions.

The first, and most obvious, was the observation that the Captain was the true power in the town, not the mayor. From his short observation, it seemed the mayor was a well-meaning but clueless leader, whereas Terrence seemed capable, smart, and reserved enough to remain a mystery.

The second conclusion, which he suspected Talia had not yet arrived at, was that in visiting this town they had somehow stumbled upon a moment of quietude that he had not expected. Of course, there was the matter of Mercane and his apparent accomplices, but for once that was *it*. A mundane judicial task, especially one where the alleged traitors were already in custody, was a welcome change from the consistent mortal peril in which they found themselves.

Finally, he was absolutely certain that whatever level of involvement Mercane had in this rebellion, this tiny podunk was hardly its epicenter. They might find further evidence, but they were hardly closer to solving the case. As there were no grand discoveries to make here, or so he reasoned, he allowed himself to optimistically hope for a short day followed by some much needed rest.

He allowed his mind to wander a bit as their group made the five minute journey to what passed for a jail in this small town. He contemplated how *he* would operate such a dangerous undertaking as trying to produce and distribute rebellious literature in such a lethal climate. Certainly the traditional route - that is, trusting imperial couriers - was out of the question. But how then would a series of mundane, otherwise totally normal peasants find themselves radicalized, let alone deputized into a sort of underground network of traitors and spies?

The town they strolled through was not so different from Bethlir, or Gilmead, or any of the other small rural outposts they'd passed through since setting out on patrol. It had no reliable means of receiving news other than the word of mouth brought in by the infrequent traveler. It also held little to no strategic importance, in fact its most noteworthy feature was the absolute wilderness surrounding it. This palisade sprouted up out of the woodlands utterly alone, days from the next tiny town.

"Here we are," Terrence announced, pulling up short in front of a low, single-story stone tower. "We've only got two cells, so Dominic and Thomas are together and Alicia has been given her own cell."

Darko sighed softly. If the three co-conspirators were able to see and hear one another, then they could coordinate their stories. Now the party was even less likely to discover anything new, but he supposed the captain had done as well as he could.

Terrence pulled a ring of iron keys from his belt and unbolted the iron-banded wooden door of the tower, then held it open for them to enter. Darko proceeded last, and assessed the room within with a critical eye.

The space was well maintained, and the wooden floor had been swept recently. The cells were also well kept, both of solid stone construction with polished iron bars, free of rust or dirt. It was well-lit by a number of small resin lamps that emitted a heavy scent of cedar, and the overall impression Darko got was one of competence and care.

"We didn't want them talking, of course," Terrence noted, gesturing at the cells. "But we didn't want to be cruel either. We settled on fashioning these earmuffs and blindfolds, and Gerry, the smith, made us some locking pins to keep them on."

Darko could see what he meant. Each of the three prisoners had a peculiar headband on that, as evidenced by the fact that none of the three had reacted in the slightest to their entry, seemed to completely obscure their hearing and sight.

"Clever," the wizard remarked with genuine appreciation. "This was your idea?"

"It was, but it was a pretty straightforward conclusion, after all," Terrence waved away the compliment.

"And this door?" Elbaf spoke up, indicating a side door which was not reinforced like the entrance.

"That would be my office, m'lord," Terrence explained, opening it to reveal a simply adorned office with a desk and a pair of chairs. "I was going to offer it as an interview room, if it pleases?"

"That would be excellent," Talia answered gratefully. "You have been incredibly hospitable, and we thank you."

"It is my duty and my pleasure, ma'am," he saluted and handed her his key ring.

Darko noted with an upturned brow that his hand lingered for the barest moment in Talia's before he continued.

"Please make yourselves at home. I do not wish to intrude upon your questioning, and so, by your leave, I will excuse myself to coordinate with your men."

"Thank you, captain," the young woman beamed at him as he departed, and Darko detected a tinge of red upon her cheeks.

When the man had left, closing the door respectfully behind himself, Darko dropped his hood, cracked a quarter smile, and shot a knowing glance at Talia. He was about to remark on her expression, but Arcus beat him to it by a split second.

"Well, we know what you're having for dinner, eh, Talia?" the ranger teased.

Talia's face turned beet red and she sputtered a response.

"I don't know *what* you're talking about, Arcus. You forget yourself!"

"Hmm," was the ranger's only reply, which served only to further redden the cleric's expression.

"Well by the Emperor, Arcus," she hissed at last. "I'm a cleric, not a corpse. Even one as pure as myself is not immune to the occasional *charms* of a passing stranger."

"Is that so?" Arcus smiled back.

"Let's focus," she said, making a face at him. "Shall we?"

"I recommend we speak to Thomas first," Elbaf said, ignoring the romantic comedy of his friends. "We know he is deeply involved, the others are perhaps less so."

"I concur," Darko added, walking up to the cell with the two men. "I think starting with a lead we are familiar with would prove most fruitful."

"I'll get him," Elbaf growled, taking the keys and opening the door to the cell.

The door opening must have caused a vibration, because both of the young men started talking over each other, loudly gesturing and proclaiming their innocence.

Elbaf said nothing, but simply grabbed hold of Thomas Mercane and threw him unceremoniously over his shoulder. He carried the kicking, protesting man out of the cell, shut and locked it, and brought him directly into the captain's office before dumping him into one of the chairs. His job complete for the moment, Elbaf took up a post with his massive arms crossed at the doorway.

"How do you want to do this?" Darko asked Talia, inclining his head at the obviously terrified young man in the chair.

Talia grimaced. She could tell that the mage was as frustrated with their task as she was.

"Let's just get it over with," she frowned, walking forwards and unlatching the man's blindfold and earmuffs.

"Please, this is all a . . ." The boy's eyes widened at the sight of his captors.

"A misunderstanding," Arcus offered, unhelpfully.

Thomas didn't bother answering, instead the young man broke down into tears immediately.

"Listen, Thomas," Talia put a hand on his shoulder. "You know what has to happen here. Make it easy on yourself, and tell us what you know."

"I can't," Thomas sniffled, then raised his head defiantly. "I won't betray the resistance or the Prophet."

"We have ways of making you talk," Darko muttered, already quite certain that the boy was on the verge of breaking down.

He reached within, drawing on the power of his magic to dim the lighting in the room and give his voice an otherworldly resonance. As he did so, he also called forth an eerie sapphire light which blazed from his eyes and emanated menacingly from his hands.

Darko's keen eyes noted the stern, reprehensive look on Talia's face, but couldn't risk trying to signal that it was merely a lightshow, lest the boy see through his intimidation attempt.

"N-n-no, no, please. Please don't curse me!"

"Then speak, boy, or it will be to the icy depths of Carak with you!"

Darko's display had the desired effect, and Thomas wilted before his wrath

"Alright, ok. I'll talk! Just p-please don't curse me or my little brother," Thomas begged. "Please, sir, I'll tell you anything you want to know."

"Who is the Prophet?" Elbaf cut in, growling menacingly.

"I don't know, I swear I don't," the panicked young man blurted out. "I only met her once, sir. I swear it!"

"Her? The Prophet is a woman? What does she look like?" Arcus prodded thoughtfully.

"I-I'm not sure. She wore a heavy cloak made from leaves, sir. I never saw her face."

"Then how do you hear from her? Who gives you your orders?" Arcus pressed, unconvinced.

"They come by messenger, sir. Where they come from before that I do not know."

"Who is the messenger?" Talia chimed in. "Someone here in town?"

"No, ma'am." He shook his head. "It's a crow. It drops off instructions for us."

"Us . . . So the other two, Alicia and Dominic, they are involved as well." Talia frowned, having hoped he would deny it.

"N-no, I m-meant us, like, us in the resistance!"

Darko saw Talia's face fall. She was as unconvinced as he was.

"Thomas," she shook her head. "Don't lie to me. I need the truth."

"Yes, ma'am," he hung his head. "That's my fault, as well. I . . . I was careless, and they found out, and I encouraged them. I filled their heads with stories of freedom and of how someday we would escape."

"We'll deal with that later," Talia sighed. "Tell us more. How did you come to be a part of this *rebellion*?"

"It was shortly after my mother died," he began, his voice growing distant and low. "The tax collector came and we, well, we had nothing left. We couldn't even afford a pauper's grave for her."

The group kept quiet, allowing the young man to speak uninterrupted.

"I was angry. I still *am* angry." His face reddened. "The temple wouldn't heal my mother's sickness because she couldn't pay, and then they wouldn't consecrate her death because she couldn't pay. What kind of benevolent god needs money anyway?"

"The church denied you?" Talia gasped.

"Yes," he practically spat, his face red and his cheeks wet with helpless tears. "We sought the blessings of the emperor, and we were denied."

Darko shot an alarmed look at his much younger friend, suddenly reminded that she was barely twenty. He could see righteous indignation building in her features and feared this one simple statement could derail their questioning.

"Then what?" he interjected, hoping to cut her off.

"I realized that . . . that it had always been this way," he said with a cracking voice. "I looked around and I saw inequity, even in our remote lands. I watched a starving family from Lambir hang because they stole a loaf of bread during the Harvest Festival. Three lives for a loaf of bread. I saw an injured half-orc turned away at the gate for his heritage, only to die alone in the woods."

Darko scanned the room, noting with no surprise that Mercane's testimony was hitting the heartstrings of his companions.

"Go on."

"Years passed, and the list grew beyond counting. Then I . . . I got sick, like my mother," he cried. "I was worried I'd bring it home to poor Dom and that I'd be the death of us both. I couldn't work, and Dom couldn't earn enough to pay for us both and to care for me. Alicia helped for a while, but . . . gods, what have I done? She's just a girl herself."

The sympathetic silence of the party was growing worrisome for the mage.

"I took some rope and stumbled into the forest in a fever daze, ready to end it and give Dom a fighting chance," Thomas explained. "That's when I met her, the Prophet. She knew I would be there. She used magic, *real* magic, and cured my illness." Thomas shook his head in disbelief.

"She sent me home with a sack of berries, wild roots and vegetables, even some silver," the boy snapped back to reality. "How could I repay her kindness? I begged her, and she told me to wait for a crow who would bring me news."

"How long ago?"

"A year."

"And since then you've . . .?"

"We made the pamphlets, like she asked, and she'd tell us where to take them." He cracked a smile. "She always knew *exactly* who to talk to, where we'd be safe and find a sympathetic ear."

Chapter Sixteen

The morning wore on, and the group grew more and more uncomfortable with Mercane's testimony. By the time they'd finished with him it was mid-day, and none of them were particularly enthusiastic about speaking with the two younger prisoners.

Mercane, seemingly at ease with his own death, pleaded for hours for the safety of his brother and Alicia. He clearly blamed himself for their involvement, and for good reason by Darko's measure.

They uncovered links to Bethlir and ferreted out a few more towns in the area that were harboring fugitives with similar responsibilities to Mercane, but nothing substantial. It seemed that each new agent was given instructions directly from the Prophet, and they didn't even know each other's names.

It was beyond dispute that Thomas was guilty, but as the group finished their questions they were left with the hanging question of the other two prisoners.

"This is madness," Arcus hissed when at last Mercane's bindings were replaced, and he was returned to his cell. "These people are not *wrong*. We've seen the very injustices Thomas speaks of, we've lived them."

"Arcus," Talia sighed. "There is not much we can do here. Our hands are well and truly tied."

"You mean to hang them, even knowing what we know? Then again, what *do* we know, really?" Arcus sighed heavily. "We know this Prophet dwells in the woodlands to the north. We know she contacts people who are already disaffected with the Empire. We know she *saved Mercane's life*, not to mention his younger brother's. We know she uses them to distribute . . . *literature*."

"Arcus--"

"No, Talia," he raised a hand to silence her. "What has she done *wrong*, exactly? She's dared to speak out against the Empire. Alright, fine, but who has she harmed? So far all we've heard is the good deeds she's performed and her dissatisfaction with the crown."

"Look, I wish there were another way."

"As do we all," Darko added. "But in this case, the law is painfully clear. Let us discover what we can from the others and be done with it. At least we can spare them further suffering."

"An excuse," Elbaf growled, "has rarely sounded sweeter. But it is an excuse nonetheless."

"And?" Darko asked pointedly.

"And we shall bear the guilt of their deaths for the rest of our lives," the warrior said stonily. "We who traded their lives for our safety."

"My conscience will be clean," Darko muttered.

"Will it?" Elbaf cocked his head to the side, his features, as always, unreadable.

Before the mage could answer, the mighty warrior was already gone. He returned to the room a moment later bearing Dominic, Thomas's younger brother, who couldn't have been more than fifteen years old.

"You'll get nothing from me," he boasted as soon as his blindfold had been removed. "I'll betray no one, least of all my brother or my fair Alicia."

"Your fair Alicia?" Talia probed.

"Y-yes," he stammered. "When we escape from your . . . your *clutches* and I rescue her, she will fall in love with me at last, and we will run away to be married!"

The team exchanged looks of surprise.

"Dominic," Elbaf began, crouching down to the boy's level. "How much of what your brother has been doing were you a part of?"

"You didn't really *know* what you were doing, right?" Talia offered hopefully. "He drew you in with wild stories?"

"No," he puffed his chest up. "I *knew*. I'm a proud member of the resistance, and we'll bring this corrupt and unjust Empire to its knees!"

Darko watched as Elbaf's shoulders drooped.

"Listen, Dominic, we can--"

"I will take no bargain," he boasted from his chair. "My brother will free us yet, and we'll be long gone."

Darko pinched his nose between two long, slender fingers. The boy was determined to dig his own grave, whether he knew it or not.

"Listen," the mage tried. "The odds of your escape are slim. Your brother is likely to hang for treason, but you don't have to hang with him. Just explain to us that you were following his lead, that you didn't--"

"And abandon him?" The boy tried to spit on the ground in a show of bravado, but managed only a weak dribble of spittle down his chin. In lighter circumstances, it might have brought smiles to their faces, but the air in the room was cold and grim.

"Very well," Darko shrugged. "Elbaf, would you return him to his cell?"

The half-orc grunted in annoyance, but moved from where he was leaning against the wall and re-bound the boy before taking him back to his cell.

At last they brought in Alicia, who Elbaf handled with all the tenderness of a fine porcelain doll. The massive soldier set her down with a gentleness that surprised Darko and removed her bindings with similar care.

"Where's Thomas?" she blurted out instantly, her face reddening and her eyes filling with tears. "Please, by the gods, tell me he's not dead."

"No, not yet," Darko answered her.

"Darko!" Talia shot him an ugly look as she interrupted him.

"Alicia, Thomas and Dominic are . . . well . . . Frankly, dear, they're going to be found guilty," the cleric said with a hand on the young girl's shoulder.

She was perhaps seventeen, a few years younger than Thomas, and of a similar ruddy complexion as he was. She was gaunt, as though she were no stranger to the feel of an empty belly, but otherwise healthy. Her dark brown hair was disheveled, but well tended, and her clothes, while poor, were similarly clean and mended.

"I . . . I understand." The girl's face crumpled, but her shoulders and back stayed upright and proud. "Then I shall hang beside Thomas."

Darko narrowed his eyes. Something in her carriage struck him.

"Tell us of your involvement with . . . the Matron," he commanded, garnering a look of confusion from Talia.

"What?" the girl asked.

"You are a member of the resistance like Thomas and Dominic, are you not?"

"Y-yes, of course I am," she stammered, her hands fidgeting and her face going scarlet. "We're . . . we're in this together, always!"

"Then tell us about your leader. How are they called?"

"Thomas?"

"No, the woman in the woods."

"Right, the woman in the woods." Panic and confusion were clearly spelled out on her face. "I-it's as you said, she's the Matron."

"You're sure?"

"Yes."

"You're quite certain she's not called . . . the *Prophet*?"

The girl's mouth popped open and shut a few times before she swallowed the lump in her throat.

"Right, the Prophet. That's what I meant."

"And have you seen her, how she walks in the woods with a cloak of fine velvet?"

"Of course I have. W-we both have, Thomas and I."

"What kind of velvet was it?" Darko pressed, giving her no time between his questions.

"Uh, um, green velvet."

"You're certain?"

"Yes," she nodded.

"And what of your mission? What is the goal of this rebellion?" Talia jumped in, sensing his intent.

"We're, um," she looked around for inspiration. "We're trying to . . . Well, it's just that . . . I can't tell you, that's all."

"Tell us the truth, Alicia," Darko glared at her.

"I-I am," she set her face in a stony frown.

"You're in love with the boy," Talia said quietly, her face softening. "Thomas, you love him."

Alicia held together for a heartbeat more, then broke down into body-shaking sobs.

"P-please don't hang him, please."

"Alicia, oh, you poor girl," Arcus knelt beside her. "This is the cruelest of fates."

"We cannot spare him," Darko stated matter-of-factly. "But you do not need to die beside him. You're lying to us. You have no idea what this is all about, save that you meant to win his heart."

"N-no, that would be a fate worse than death." She left her chair and dropped to her knees in front of the wizard. "Please, please don't make me live without him."

"Alicia, he would want you to live," Talia said, her voice strained. "He's told us as much already."

The girl went into hysterics, begging them to kill her as well, and even Darko's analytical dispassion began to fail him.

"Talia," he caught the cleric's attention. "Perhaps we should all speak outside for a moment?"

Talia nodded, the first signs of tears already in the corners of her eyes as well, and led the party outside the office. They left Alicia sobbing on the floor - she had nowhere to go.

"This whole affair has turned my stomach sour," Arcus admitted, a grimace on his face. "It's sick."

"It is, perhaps, not a total loss," Darko started, pushing through the looks of disgust from his companions as they presumed upon what he would say next.

"I mean to say I believe we can spare the girl," he continued, annoyed at the obviousness of their relief. "I am not a *monster*."

"How, when she seems so intent on throwing herself upon the gallows for this boy?" Arcus asked. "What if we-- Elbaf what are you doing?"

The warrior walked silently to the cell holding the Mercane brothers and entered, pulling Thomas out by the scruff of his neck and yanking his bindings free.

"Do you want Alicia to die, Thomas?" the warrior growled, inches from the boy's face.

"W-what? No, gods, no. Of course I--"

"She sits in that office now, as you did this morning," he interrupted, shaking the boy roughly, "begging us to end her life because you so carelessly forced us to end yours."

"You . . . you've got to spare her! On my life, I swear she knows nothing," Thomas begged. "She's just a girl! She's smitten with me and I . . . took advantage to get her help. The fault is mine."

"*That* is not in dispute, you stupid boy," Darko snapped acidly.

"Get your ass in there," Elbaf snarled. "And say whatever you have to to save her life."

Elbaf carried Thomas to the door, yanked it open, and tossed the lad inside before slamming it shut.

Silence followed the loud bang of the wooden frame for a moment, and they all silently wondered the same thing - could Thomas spare the girl, where they could not?

It seemed a lifetime passed before there came a soft knock at the door to the office. Elbaf pulled it open to reveal Thomas, his head hung low. Behind him, Alicia was sitting stone-faced in the chair where she'd been interrogated.

Thomas said nothing, but brushed past the party and returned to his cell.

They didn't bother to stop him as he removed the blindfold from his little brother and wrapped the young man in a hug.

Darko read Alicia's face and tactfully shut the door to the office once more, catching the barest glimpse of her impending breakdown as the portal shut.

"Thomas, Dominic, are you ready?" Talia asked softly.

"Yes," Thomas answered, his voice strong.

The brothers walked hand in hand to the door, where Arcus and Elbaf took up positions beside them. Talia followed, pausing only when she realized Darko was not standing to follow them.

"You're not coming?"

"No, I will stay and watch the girl," he replied simply.

Talia nodded and left for the gallows with the others.

When the door shut behind them, Darko reopened the door to the office.

"Alicia?"

"Please leave me alone," the girl said softly.

"If that is what you wish, I will do so," Darko nodded solemnly and turned to go.

"The only thing I want is for it not to hurt," she sniffled, wiping tears from her cheeks.

Darko stopped and turned back around. He saw in the girl's face an unbearable pain.

"If you want . . ." he hesitated, then continued. "I *can* make it hurt less. I can take some of your pain and lock it away, or even--"

"Can you make me forget?"

Darko stared into her eyes, searching for even the faintest hint of regret or doubt, and found none.

"I can."

"Please?"

Darko nodded and walked up to the girl. He placed a hand on either side of her head as he began to muster the energies within.

"What do you wish to forget?"

"All of it, every memory of Thomas."

"You're sure? This cannot be undone."

She looked him directly in the eye.

"All of it."

Darko closed his eyes and surged with power. The ripple of deep magic rolled through his veins, blazing down his arms like unseen lightning, and flowed into the girl's mind. His consciousness followed and soon he was sifting through her memories. He did his best to be respectful, not to linger, but he saw snippets despite his best efforts. He directed his magic to the memories of Thomas and was met with the freshest scenes first.

"I never loved you, Alicia. Deep down you know I didn't, and now you're demonstrating why. You're too stupid to know when to quit. You'd hang yourself for a

boy who doesn't love you? Who never did? Pathetic."

He could not blame her for her pain, which dripped from each memory now, but he was at least grateful to Thomas for saving her from death.

The mage set about diligently, burning the memory of Thomas from the girl's mind, and with it the pain of her loss and the devastation of her broken heart. He knew better than to completely remove Thomas, but he sought out and erased those memories that she had once associated with love, relegating him to a distant acquaintance, a relative unknown.

When at last he returned from his trance, he could feel in his aching shoulders that he'd been standing over her for quite some time. His eyes fluttered open, followed a moment later by her own.

"Alicia?"

"Y-yes, m'lord?" the girl answered, looking more than a bit confused.

"Can you tell me about the Mercanes and how you came to be here?"

"I-I'm sorry, sir. I can't believe . . . I must have dozed off in the middle of your questions. I know young Dominic, of course, but Thomas? Well, he seemed nice, I suppose. I never really met him. I have to say, sir, I'm as surprised as anyone at what they were involved in. It's such a shame."

Darko nodded and managed a thin smile.

"It is," he agreed. "Thank you so much for your help. You've done the Empire a great service today."

The wizard concentrated for a moment, summoning forth a small charm, and with a snap of his fingers put the girl into a deep, deep sleep.

He sighed heavily and bent to lift the girl from her chair. The effort was painful, and his weaker leg shot through with splinters of fire as he struggled under her slight frame, but slowly he managed to return her to her cell and place her upon the bed there. His breathing now labored and sweat beading his brow, he sat a moment to rest and recover. It wouldn't have been right, he thought to himself as he massaged his aching limb, leaving her in the chair like that.

After a few moments, his heartbeat slowed and he hoisted himself up once more, taking one last look at the young woman whose face was, for the moment, untroubled.

"I'm so sorry, Alicia," he whispered to himself as he left, closing the door gently behind him.

He walked out of the jail and nearly bumped into Terrence.

"M'lord," the captain saluted. "Lady Talia requested that I fetch you, she said you would have information I needed?"

"Yes, Captain," Darko nodded. "The girl, Alicia, she's innocent. She was bewitched by the Mercane's supernatural benefactor. She has no memory of any of their treasonous activities and should be released when she awakes."

Terrence grew pensive, and for a moment the two stood silently, each gauging the other's intent, until they reached an understanding.

"I see," the captain said at last. "I will see to her safety and inform the mayor of what . . . *befell* her. I am glad she was less involved than it first appeared."

"As am I. It would have been a horrible shame for such a young and vibrant life to end so needlessly."

Darko left the captain there and made his way back to the inn. He considered looking away when he got to the courtyard, but instead forced himself to commit to memory the sight of the two young men—the two *boys*—swaying gently in the afternoon breeze. He stared for several long minutes, then turned away when he was certain he had memorized every morbid detail.

"How long must we stay? There are still four or five hours of daylight left," Arcus prompted for the third time since they'd returned to the inn, drawing an irritated glance from Talia.

"As soon as the mayor is done with us. If we must, we'll leave without another night's rest."

"I'll get no rest here," the ranger grimaced.

The group, who all sat around one of the long tables in the tavern, halted their conversations momentarily when they heard the door creak open, but returned swiftly to their drinks when they saw that it was simply Darko.

"What prompted you to stay behind?" Arcus needled. "Weak stomach?"

Darko said nothing, but took his seat nonetheless.

"Alicia?"

Elbaf's question was left to hang until it was followed up by Talia.

"Well?"

"She sleeps, and in the morning she will be far better off," Darko answered, uncomfortable with explaining the details of the magic he had worked.

There was no telling how his companions would react to the knowledge that he could manipulate their memory or alter their emotions. He would never abuse such magics, of course, he found the very concept sickening, but they had enough reasons to mistrust him already.

He could sense their curiosity, but would not rise to the bait. Instead, he flagged down the bumbling bartender and, in a rare display, ordered whiskey over wine.

He caught a raised eyebrow from Arcus for his choice, but the others had already returned to their conversation.

"We should at least stay the night," Talia picked the thread back up. "If not for ourselves then for the men. They deserve it after yesterday."

"That's true," Elbaf rumbled. "Though I do not doubt they would take to the road this instant if we asked, they do need the rest."

"As do *you*, brother," the ranger prompted, giving Elbaf a pointed look. "Even your endurance is not unlimited."

Elbaf shrugged, leaving the group to wonder what lay beneath his emotionless expression, which was every bit as impenetrable as the steel of his armor.

"Fine," Arcus let out his breath in frustration. "You've made your points. Another night then."

Darko's whiskey arrived in short order, and he downed it without ceremony. The burn of the room-temperature liquor distracted him momentarily, filling his nose with smoke and stinging his eyes.

"I think I will retire," he frowned softly.

"It's barely evening, Darko," Talia blurted out.

"I still need to recover. If you have need of me, I will be in my room."

Without waiting for a further response, Darko lifted himself from his seat and made his way to the stairs. His body still ached and his head still pounded, but above all, his heart was heavy.

Master?

Reia's presence in his mind was soothing, and he wondered at her conspicuous absences of late.

You missed me? How flattering, Master.

She pulled a smile from his tired lips as he managed the creaking, dusty stairs up to his room. His leg was bothering him more than usual, but he attributed that to the rough treatment of the day. Safely within his room, he turned to the simple wooden door. It was a combination of paranoia and habit that prompted him to set a series of arcane locks and wards upon his door, no matter where he slept, and despite the apparent safety of the town, this would be no exception. Flashing glyphs of brilliant greens and purples appeared upon the door, the frame, and the lock. They burned brightly for a moment, shifting and changing with each new layer of protection, and then faded from view entirely.

Only when his spellcraft was complete did Darko truly breathe easy. His room was now a sanctuary, one from which no light or sound could escape without his intention and which most would find impossible to breach.

He shed his robes and cloak, revealing a tailored black satin vest over a cream cotton shirt, as well as his leather riding pants and boots beneath. Reia left her perch within his hood as he removed the symbol of his office. She drifted to the bed and sprawled out like a tiny demonic cat while he folded his robes and set them to the side.

"Well, Master," she said in the soft sultry tones of her spoken voice. "We both know you're not tired, so why are we locked away in our room like naughty school children?"

He rolled his eyes at her playful teasing and sat himself upon the edge of the bed.

"I feel we ought to investigate some of what the Mercane boys said and what they saw," he told her. "And I cannot safely work these magics I intend to use unless I am quite certain I will not be disturbed."

"Then you *do* intend to scry for them." She sat up straighter, the pink flames in her eyes dancing excitedly. "You know how much I love divination magics."

"Close," he smiled. "How do you feel about working on our tether spells?"

Darko couldn't help but copy the small demons wide, toothy grin, and he was glad to find her so excited to work on what had been his latest project before he unexpectedly left the Academy a year ago. Although his studies had been interrupted, he'd had plenty of time to practice and theorize while he prepared his spells each night. His forays into combined consciousness and astral travel had progressed considerably from the first scribbled notes that were no doubt still cluttering his old room in the tower.

"Yes, Master. When can we start?"

"Patience is a virtue, Reia," Darko chided her playfully.

"Master," she pouted, her flaming arms crossed and her bottom lip puffed out. "What in all the realms of existence would lead you to believe, me . . . virtuous?"

Darko chuckled, but had to admit she was correct. Rather than answer her directly, he retrieved a number of reagents from his satchel. He carefully collected a soft leather pouch filled with ashes, a jet black shard of onyx, a small and perfectly polished mirror, and a handful of deep blue candles before returning to the center of the room.

The pain he felt as he knelt to the ground to arrange his materials was minor compared to the excitement building in his mind at the prospect of exploring new and untamed magics.

The ashes were spread carefully into a pentacle approximately seven feet across. Around this he placed a smooth, unbroken circle, which was then surrounded with runes and other words of power.

As the sun wheeled through the sky, he toiled endlessly, placing dozens of enchantments, wards, and other protective spells in place, each more powerful than the last. Many would have called him paranoid or overly cautious for the number of charms upon his bedroom door, but no wizard would begrudge him the obsessive level of detail he put into this new venture. Opening doorways was a dangerous gambit for any caster, even in the mortal realm. To do so unprepared was to invite disaster.

His work at last finished, he surveyed the scene. Each point and intersection of the pentacle now bore a candle, and the ashes glowed with a faint silvery sheen. Within the very center of the diagram sat the onyx. It faced upward from its place in the middle of the mirror, awaiting his use.

Darko took a moment to inspect the circle with arcane sight, admiring the dozens of overlapping layers of scintillating magic. The effect was a prism of elegant, vapor-thin barriers capable of protecting his vulnerable body and mind from anything in this world or the next. Or as close as he could manage, at least.

"Ready?"

Reia said nothing, but the flames around her were blazing so brightly that motes of fire kept flickering up into the air above her.

"Right then," Darko said under his breath. "Here we go."

Darko and Reia stood at opposite ends of the diagram on the floor, their eyes locked in concentration. Without a spoken word, the two walked in unison to the center, their every step matching perfectly with the other. When they reached the middle, they sat with the onyx and mirror between them.

Darko could feel the air humming around him, and he stole one last look at his most precious companion before settling in and closing his eyes as she had already done.

In his mind, Darko could still see every detail of the room. He would need to maintain that crystal clarity and sense of place to ensure his safe return.

Reia?

I'm here, Master.

In his mind, her voice was always so much deeper, so much more vibrant and rich, and now with their bond magnified by the circle, it was as though she were standing right next to him.

The wizard began to chant, softly at first and then with rising bass. He knew that the wards he'd placed around himself would prevent anyone from overhearing him, and he tried to ignore the fact that he was effectively yelling into the void. He felt his robes swirl about him, moved by a wind that was not of this Earth. Slowly, as the power of the circle burned brighter and stronger, he began to feel the floor beneath him fall away. The utter darkness behind his closed eyes was filled with pin-pricks of light, a vast, endless sea of stars all around him as far as could be imagined. Just as suddenly, the circle appeared in his mind, the various bars and rings that made it up expanding. The flat drawing he had made became a sphere of rotating, swirling patterns and lines.

Next to appear was Reia, though she was difficult to recognize.

Where she normally stood less than a foot tall, she appeared before him now as tall as he was. Her fiery form was perfect, dangerous, and seductive. From her hooves to her hair, she was clothed only in fire and a fine, short coat of scales.

He almost lost his concentration as she opened her eyes to reveal stunning violet pools, endlessly deep and without an iris or pupil.

Steady, Master. We stand on the edge of a void I cannot pull you from, should you fall.

Darko redoubled his concentration and willed the mirror and onyx to appear next. They did so, manifesting into existence with a loud, crackling boom.

The spell was nearly complete, and the entire world seemed to be holding its breath in anticipation. Sweat dotted Darko's brow, though his companion seemed unfazed by the spectacle around them. With a hesitant, trembling hand he reached toward the shard of onyx in front of him, Reia mimicking his every move perfectly.

The instant they touched the onyx, the world turned inside out in a swirl of color and energy, then went pitch black. A sound like rushing wind hit his ears, followed swiftly by a sudden jolt of light.

He could see.

He could see?

No, that didn't feel right. Something was wrong about that.

They could see. *They* could hear. *They* could smell and taste and . . . move?

Darko felt *different*, that much was certain. As their vision swirled into focus and the sound and smells around them resolved into the familiar, they became more aware of what they had become.

Hmm, your mind is even more comfortable than I thought it would be, Master. And, of course, it's surprisingly roomy in here.

Though the voice spoke within them, Darko could feel it in their ears as though Reia had spoken aloud.

Reia?

They felt a warm, satisfied feeling in their chest, and it spread throughout their body as Darko and Reia confirmed that they had indeed successfully melded their consciousness. Their experiences and minds were as blended and inseparable as their bodies had become. For a few moments they simply sat, still in the position they had been in at the beginning of the ritual. Their minds slowly but surely unscrambled into one distinct entity and it was *more* than either of them had been to begin with.

Darko's old body sat unmoving in front of them. It towered above their own small form, the body that Reia was used to owning. It was a strange sensation to observe himself, made more so by the peculiar perspective and the decidedly *other* quality of their current being.

Reia's eyes were more keen even than Darko's, and it took some getting used to. What's more, colors were just a bit off from what Darko was used to.

Do you always see like this?

I do, why? Is something wrong?

No, no . . . It's just so much more than I'm used to.

Everywhere they looked, Darko was missing something. But, what? Then it struck them. There were no shadows anywhere. Any place that might have held a darkened corner or sat in shade, it was as clear as a midday sun. As a matter of fact, though it was certainly early evening, the light coming in from the windows was enough to see quite clearly to every corner of the room.

It was not unlike a spell Darko knew, which would allow the user to see in the dark. But unlike that enchantment, which allowed only black and white vision, Reia's eyes provided true sight no matter the amount of light available. How many other incorrect assumptions had he made about her senses and abilities?

More than a few, I would guess.

Sorry, I suppose my thoughts are not my own here, are they?

They're still yours, Master. It's just that you can no longer keep your secrets from me. Not when we're bonded like this.

Darko wished very much to continue to explore their abilities, but reminded themself of the urgent matter that had prompted this transformation in the first place. Thomas Mercane's confession had yielded a surprising result, one which further confirmed Darko's suspicion that a rogue wizard was out here in the northeastern wilds planning treason against the crown. If that were true, Darko wanted to confirm it beyond doubt.

Then we are to assume the form of a crow, correct, Master?

Correct, and we'll find this wizard's familiar, track it back to its master, and deal with this 'prophet' one way or another.

Darko looked down at their tiny body. Reia's form was slender and supple, but also quite strong. The flickering flames that adorned them seemed to cause no harm, and Darko was surprised at how comfortable they felt in the small, unclothed form.

How do we . . . shift?

Allow me.

Darko felt their body pulled gently from their control, and he became almost a passenger as Reia pushed to the front. Reia's will was incredible. Darko felt a fleeting moment of concern as they realized that, should Reia choose, Darko had no doubt that her personality could dominate his own, at least in this body.

The knowledge that Reia could at any moment assume command of them was less threatening than Darko expected. The wizard was surprised at his level of comfort with having their lives so closely linked, but then again, they reasoned, they had been through so much together over the past century that it was only natural they should fit together so well.

Ready?

The wizard set aside the theoreticals running through their mind, secure in the knowledge that there would be ample time to record their findings later when the situation was less pressing.

Ready.

Darko had never utilized any transfigurative magics before, at least none that would alter his own form, so when their skin began to tighten and stretch, and their bones shift and tumble about, it was all he could do to keep from crying out in surprise. There was no pain, not even really discomfort, but it was nonetheless extremely disconcerting. Thankfully, the process was swift, nearly instantaneous, so they didn't have much time to dwell on the shifting flesh and sprouting feathers. The only part that truly threw Darko was when their face stretched and morphed into a beak, and their vision split and sharpened.

Are you alright?

Yes, but I will admit that was a . . . novel experience.

The wizard felt Reia relinquish her full control of their shared body, and as they did so, Darko could suddenly feel all of the strange and wondrous new details of this tiny avian form. The experience of having feathers, and wings, was bizarre, but Darko quickly adapted.

The sun was nearly down now, and according to Mercane's testimony the scheduled rendezvous with the messenger crow was fast approaching. They didn't have time to experiment with the new body, or to practice any other shifts, if they wanted to make a move to intercept.

So, rather than explore in careful, studious detail, they simply hopped to the ledge of the open window and made ready to take a leap of faith.

Don't worry, Master. I've done this hundreds and hundreds of times.

Without waiting for worry or doubt to take hold, they hunched down, then leapt out into the open air. Instincts granted by the power of the magic, and Reia's experience, guided them on silent, shadowy wings out into the gathering night.

It should be here by now, Master.

I think so too, but Mercane did say sundown, and the sun has not fully set . . .
yet.

They weren't wrong, but the faint sliver of sun that still graced the horizon did little to inspire hope that the messenger was going to make an appearance this evening. What they would have called sundown was now essentially past, but stubbornness kept them firmly rooted in the branches of a broad-leafed oak some fifty feet above the ground.

Minutes ticked by, and night began to truly fall. The clearing, just north of town, was now heavily shadowed, and mortal eyes would have had a very difficult time seeing in any detail. Darko found themself grateful that Reia's night vision seemed to carry over to their current form, it made it a simple matter to maintain watch over the area in minute detail.

It was a good thing, too, because just as they were preparing to depart, there came a nearly imperceptible flutter from an elm tree across the clearing. Peering through the leaves, Darko could make out the sleek black form of a smallish crow perched expectantly on one of the lower branches. It stood stock still, and Darko was amazed that Mercane was ever able to see it at all.

Do you see the messenger tube on its left foot, Master?

Sure enough, a tiny silver tube was tied to the crow's leg.

I do. How do you propose we get it?

That depends, do you want to follow them for a while first, Master?

Darko considered for a moment. The bird was extremely well camouflaged, and even with Reia's senses being what they were, there was no guarantee they could follow the creature successfully in the close confines of the forest. They may well end up losing both the bird's trail and whatever clues the message held.

I think that the message is more important.

Then allow me, Master.

Reia took back control of their form without further permission and leapt silently skyward. As they flew, Darko again felt the transformative magics being worked, and within seconds their form had changed to that of a deadly falcon. Their senses sharpened, and their eyes locked on to the unsuspecting bird below.

In the darkness they cast no shadows, and the messenger bird had no warning as they pulled their wings in and began a steep dive. Wind rushed past their head as Reia made tiny, critical adjustments of their tail feathers, ensuring they would be on target.

Darko could feel Reia's bloodlust, the thrill she got at the prospect of making a kill, and wondered how often she felt the powerful desire for death that he could feel now.

He didn't have long to ponder it as they fell faster and faster, talons outstretched. Together they hit the crow with all the force of a hammer blow, and Darko felt its spine snap as razor sharp talons dug deep into its feathered body.

Reia's pleasure was intoxicating, and Darko felt their own mind begin to cloud with the unfiltered joy of killing that they were experiencing.

Reia.

They felt a jolt as Reia reigned in her instincts.

Sorry, Master. I didn't mean to get carried away.

No harm done, Reia, but it seems we'll have to be cautious of the emotional bleed-over when we are linked like this.

They lifted the crumpled body of the crow and soared back to their room, where they were met with the sight of Darko's body exactly where they'd left it.

I suppose we ought to shift back.

Yes, Master, I suppose you're right.

The ritual to split their being once more was similar to the magic used to bind them, but Darko found it easier to separate himself from themselves, as well as easier to navigate the odd void between the two states. In short order, Darko was back within his own body and diligently deconstructing all of the myriad layers of protection surrounding them.

By the time his work was done, Darko was exhausted and the night was half over. If he wished to be useful in the morning, he would need to prepare his magics for the coming day and take rest.

The message, Master?

"We'll see to it in the morning, when the others are present."

As you wish, Master. Have you further need of me tonight? If not, I think I'll go take another flight.

Darko cocked his head in surprise. Reia rarely left him alone by her own volition, usually only when something important pulled her away.

"Are you alright?"

I am, Master, but it is good to be . . . by oneself after such a connection is severed.

"Be safe, then," he shrugged, worried that something might be bothering her or that he had upset her somehow. "Will you be--"

Yes, I'll be back by sunrise, Master.

She transformed into a raven once more and was gone before he could say another word.

Chapter Seventeen

Arcus woke to birdsong and sunlight filtering in through the open window and took a moment to bask before opening his eyes. He'd specifically chosen a room facing the dawn, and he took great pleasure in the warmth on his skin.

He stood and walked to the window, enjoying the soft breezes and the sleepy sounds of the slowly waking town and the forest surrounding it.

Already he could see smoke rising from the blacksmith's chimney and the baker's next door. A laughing group of lumberjacks were just disappearing into the brush to the north of town, followed by a wagon and a pair of aging mules.

The ranger took a deep breath, enjoying the crisp air of an early fall and the promise of cooler days ahead. He felt so much more at ease here, deep in the heart of the woods and far from the menacing scrutiny of their imperial overseers. He found himself anxious to get on the road, not to bring them closer to returning to the Brazen Hawks, but because the forest called to him and bid him take his place among the trees.

Unseen at the edge of town, Kodja nudged his mind with an offer to play, or else to wander the trees in the early dawn until the rest of the group arose. He had to admit, he was sorely tempted; he wanted to put some distance between himself and the grisly deed they'd had to do the day before.

Arcus was grateful, too, that his window did not overlook the gallows in the square. As his thoughts turned to the two boys they'd put to death, his carefree face pulled into a deep frown. The boys' fate was unavoidable, really, as they'd been caught red-handed committing a Capital offense.

Still, it didn't sit well with Arcus. While he was glad they'd managed to save the girl, it still felt like far too little, far too late.

No, the longer he walked the path of the Hand, the more certain he became. This life was no privilege, no great honor, as it had been sold to him. It was a curse, and he was determined to be rid of it. Every step they'd taken since leaving Sunset Isle had brought him grief, frustration, or downright anger, and he was sorely tired of the neverending swath of injustice they were forced to leave behind them.

Kodja could sense his unease and sent him reassurance and the oft-repeated question, why not simply leave? It was impossible to explain to the animal the concept of perpetual servitude. Kodja had always been free. Even now he stayed with Arcus of his own volition, and he would remain so or die, as was the law of the wild.

A knock at the door alerted the ranger to the fact that he was no longer the only one of their party awake. He moved to open it and was surprised to find Darko on the other side.

"Good mornin--"

"We have a problem," the mage interjected, his tone deadly serious.

Darko held out his hand, which held a small, neatly rolled strip of parchment. "What's this?"

"I intercepted the messenger crow Thomas spoke of," Darko held a hand up to cut off Arcus' questions. "And it was carrying this message . . . for us."

Arcus blinked rapidly and felt his pulse quicken. Suddenly the idea of a 'prophet' in the wilderness seemed less a far-fetched fairytale and more a potentially fatal reality.

"Go on, read it," Darko insisted. "From what I can tell, it's addressed to all of us, anyway."

"What do you mean?" Arcus asked as he reached for the scrap and unrolled it. "*Addressed* to us?"

Darko said nothing, but nodded his head toward the paper.

Arcus bent his head to read. Whoever had written the note had beautiful, sprawling handwriting filled with loops and swirls, delicate as a spiderweb but clear as crystal.

My dear children,

Yours is a story of faith and sacrifice, and though I wish it were not so, none may choose the trials one must endure. And endure we must.

The winds whispered to me today; they spoke of a soldier, a student, a servant, and a savage. They breathe the sounds of broken chains and whispered dreams. The birds in the trees sing songs of hope, an unseen glimmer in a vast spider web of darkness and despair. A hope that rises like the sun.

My heart is heavy for memories not yet come to pass and for the recent passing of my faithful Thomas and young Dominic. But the scales must be balanced; this you have seen with your own eyes, and you know it to be true in your hearts.

You may regard me as an enemy, lurking in the wilderness beyond your reach, but I am not what I seem, just as you are not the faceless arbiters of the Empire that you appear. The cracks in your facade are laid bare to my sight, and I can see upon you the desperate bonds of servitude.

But your course has long been set, and even now you draw nearer to a destiny of light and shadow, joy and grief, victory and loss. Take heart, for strong winds guide you northward, and then, home.

Beware the spider, for she too senses the struggles within the web, and as you come closer to your freedom, you will court death unseen.

The day will come soon when we will meet, but until then I beg of you, do not lose hope. For though the night may seem dark and cold, the promise of daylight is never far away.

Yours,
Lilliana

Arcus narrowed his eyes, mistrustful of the document but unable to deny that it did seem to be addressed to them specifically.

"What do you make of it?" the mage asked, genuine curiosity on his face.

"It . . . it doesn't seem possible," Arcus allowed. "That she should be able to describe us is no surprise and, honestly, our discontent has been more obvious than we should like, I presume. But this business with the boys, how could she know so quickly?"

"My thoughts exactly," Darko nodded. "Unless, she has excellent spies."

"Or else is very close by."

They shared a silent moment of deliberation before Arcus spoke again at last.

"We should leave this place, and soon."

"I'm already packed," Darko gestured at the few belongings still scattered around Arcus' room. "You finish here, and I'll go alert the others."

It didn't take long for Arcus to get his room in order and head down to the common room, but Darko had apparently already broken the news to Talia and Elbaf. All three of them were visibly uncomfortable, and judging from the redness of Talia's face, she was angry - very angry.

"Arcus," the young cleric called out as soon as she saw him on the stairs. "Did you know Darko was going to look for that bird last night?"

Arcus blinked in surprise. Her tone was scathing.

"No, but I think--"

"So you didn't consult *anyone* first?" Talia turned on Darko, interrupting the ranger. "You--"

"Talia, it was an excellent plan," Arcus interjected, redirecting some of her ire. "But I suspect that something more than our wizard has you so worked up. What's wrong?"

Talia closed her eyes and took an even, measured breath.

"We've been summoned back to the Brazen Hawks," she admitted at last. "An imperial messenger came just before dawn and left this *request*."

She gestured to a neatly folded packet of parchment bearing a broken blue wax seal. From her tone it was evident that she was disgusted with the contents.

"Annabelle is summoning us," she explained. "Effective immediately."

Arcus picked up the packet and skimmed it quickly. It seemed that Madrie had been injured, critically, in fact, in combat with a band of brigands. Annabelle had assumed command of the company and was instructing them to rendezvous south of Kent at some sort of temporary encampment.

"This is dated eight days ago," Arcus wondered aloud. "It must have happened very shortly after we left."

"Yes, and apparently this messenger has been hot on our trail ever since," Talia sighed. "But it also means we're far behind, and Annabelle will no doubt have our hides. I can only hope the commander has recovered in the meantime."

"How far is it to this . . . camp?"

"Three days hard ride," Elbaf chimed in grimly. "That is, if we push our mounts each day and rest as little as possible."

"That certainly puts a damper on pursuing this *prophet* Lilliana. But then again, I suppose she should have . . ." Darko paused for effect, "*seen* that coming?"

Arcus rolled his eyes and headed for the door. His hackles were well and truly raised, and the peace and excitement of the morning was ruined. Returning to the Brazen Hawks meant crawling back under Annabelle's thumb, and he chafed at the very thought of it.

"Where are you going?" Talia asked, piqued.

"To ready the horses, Talia," he grumbled. "I'd hate to keep our mistress waiting."

The horses were standing by in the courtyard, and their gear was stowed securely within the hour. The column itself was ready to depart shortly thereafter. Arcus spent the time avoiding his companions and speaking as little as possible. The morning had turned as gray and sour as his mood, and by the time they rode out the gate, a drizzling mist had taken up residence over the town.

Arcus and his scouts rode ahead of the column, but the cheerful banter that usually filled the air was conspicuously absent as they plodded along the worn muddy trail through the trees.

"Something wrong, sir?" Private Tomlin finally asked after over an hour of silence. "You're unusually quiet."

"I'm . . . frustrated, Tomlin," Arcus admitted, leaning back in the saddle and running a hand through his rain-slicked hair.

"Word is we're linking back up with the company, sir." The thin, lanky man scratched at a half-healed cut on his cheek absentmindedly. "I suppose that means a little less freedom for all of us."

Arcus cast a sidelong glance at the man, one of the shrinking number of soldiers that had been with their small band since the Altimeer estate. His features had grown more gaunt, and his eyes had hardened over the past weeks. The ranger saw in Tomlin a kindred spirit, a man who shared his love of the wilderness and disdain for confinement. He also chided himself for assuming the frustrations of his fellow officers went unseen in the ranks.

"I think it will," Arcus agreed. "I'll admit freely I have little love for Captain Montagne, and if she's assumed command of the company I expect that feeling will only grow."

The soldier nodded his understanding, and Arcus considered the risks of openly speaking ill of his new commander in front of him. Judging from the thoughtful look in the scout's eyes, however, Arcus' sentiment fell upon sympathetic ears.

"Sir," Tomlin allowed at last. "It never sat right with me - hell, with most of us - what happened after . . . well, you know. Don't think I didn't see - *we* didn't see - who made the call to dishonor our dead. To forget them, and their sacrifice . . ."

Arcus felt a great weight in his heart as he contemplated the soldiers who had fallen to the abominations during their trip to the Altimeer estates.

"Loyalty is earned, sir," the man frowned stoically. "Some of our leaders have it, and some don't."

Arcus was hit with a wave of validation and gratitude. His struggle was not his alone, and their men were with them. The two rode on in silence at the head of the column as they pushed their way eastward through the forests.

Time passed and the trees grew denser and older, until the company could no longer ride even two abreast. As the distance from Gilbad grew and they plunged into the wild heart of the forest, there was less and less visibility, fewer felled trees, and fewer worn footpaths.

A few hours into their journey, they were deep inside the muted greenery of untouched woods. Here the rain trickled in streams from gaps in the canopy far above, and a deep and abiding silence accompanied them as they picked their way between massive trees heavy with moss. Something about the ancient trees and the soft, low bird calls that filled the air drove Arcus and the others into silence. Here the voices of men were an unwelcome intrusion, and the branches overhead seemed to cast a watchful gaze upon their column as they disturbed the peace.

A whistle from the rear - three short chirps and a long low note - signaled to Arcus that the group was stopping, but they were so spread out now that he couldn't tell why. Still, the signal was clear, and he pulled back on his reins, gently bringing his horse to a halt. Looking over his shoulder he tried to catch sight of Tomlin, who should be next in line. But the other scout was nowhere to be seen. The whistle hadn't sounded far off, and if he'd given his group the slip it *must* have been recently.

Swearing at his carelessness, Arcus coaxed his horse to turn around in the tight confines of the forest and made his way back along the path, such as it was. So close together were the nearby boles that he couldn't turn in place and, instead, had to loop off of the trail to circle back.

He had nearly made his turn when, upon turning his eyes back to where the trail should be, he let out a short gasp of surprise and pulled up on his reins. His eyes told him the forest had shifted, though it could not have been possible. His memory of how the woods had looked was crystal clear and yet, now - now, he couldn't have picked the direction he'd come from if his life depended on it.

The whistle rang out again, and Arcus was startled by how distant it sounded. He tried to pinpoint the direction, but found himself turning this way and that to no avail.

He forced himself to remain calm and to extend his senses outward into the forest. This was no grave threat. Here in the wild he was more than capable of finding his lost companions, he reassured himself.

The ranger sank into himself, sending his mind downward into the ground and there into the web of life surrounding him with practiced ease. But he was unprepared for the intense, dazzling vibrancy of the forest all around him. He was nearly blinded by the power thrumming under the surface of the serene woodlands and felt his eyes begin to water instinctively.

It was not simply the overflowing abundance of life that disturbed him, but the *feel* of that life. It had a texture and an aura that he had never felt before. It was warm, inviting, intoxicatingly familiar, and - at the same time - it was undeniably alien.

"*Arcus*," a woman's voice whispered.

He swore he felt a soft breath on his neck and smelled the warm scent of summer rain on a field of wildflowers. The ranger whipped around in his saddle, heart pounding, but his darting eyes saw no one.

"*This way, child of the tundra*," the voice came again, this time accompanied by a gentle breeze across his chin that felt like the slender fingers of a woman directing his gaze northward.

The ranger's heart stirred at the woman's voice, and he felt driven, *compelled*, to heed her.

With a gentle squeeze of his thighs, his horse began to pick its way through the trees, and the path almost seemed to clear ahead of them. Certainly their travel was swifter and smoother, and the roots and brambles that had plagued his riding were conspicuously absent as he drew nearer to . . . something.

Sunlight began to peek more regularly through the branches, and the forest thinned, revealing what must be a clearing ahead. The closer he got, the more intense the pull upon his heart and mind, until he was drawn like a magnet through the woodline and into a lush, grassy meadow.

Wildflowers swayed in a cool breeze, and plump, care-free bumble bees buzzed from one brightly colored perch to another. High above, a pair of blue-tailed hawks circled, their calls no doubt scaring field mice into hiding below. Arcus took a deep breath and leaned back, the warm, clear sunlight falling softly on his face.

Longing hit him like a gust of wind, and he slipped from his saddle without a second thought. The waist-high grass was shockingly soft, and he wandered aimlessly with his hands outspread, feeling the waving stalks.

"Welcome."

Arcus spun around, only to be confronted by a woman so astonishingly beautiful that he completely lost his sense of self. For a moment even his name escaped him, and he could not have strung two words together.

She was tall and slender, but with the well-muscled body of an athlete. Warm auburn hair with hints of pure gold fell below her shoulders, and within it were braided chains of stark white lilies. She wore a simple, shoulderless dress of intricately beaded leather which halted mid-thigh, light green leggings, and a pair of soft brown knee-high leather boots. She wore a headdress of deer antlers as well, which gave the appearance that they were her own rather than the remnants of another creature. But perhaps the most interesting garment she displayed was a broad cloak of feathers and leaves. A turquoise clasp held the item about her shoulders, and it looked to have been sewn of feathers and leaves from every species imaginable.

Arcus had nearly recovered enough to speak when the woman smiled at him, driving him to speechlessness once again as he fell into the molten gold of her eyes.

The woman gestured broadly around them, her smile every bit as radiant as the sun.

"This is Nizhóní, and I am Lilliana."

Arcus finally found the courage to speak, but bowed deeply before he did so.

"My lady, Nizhóní must certainly mean paradise in the language of your people."

Lilliana's laughter was a sound so rich and vibrant that Arcus wished he could live within its echoes.

"You are a flatterer, Arcus." She turned and began to walk slowly away. "Follow me, druid."

Arcus did as he was instructed, hurrying to walk beside her instead of behind. He felt it impossible to describe the *rightness* of her presence, and could not imagine returning to a life without her in it.

"My lady--"

"Lilliana," she chided gently.

"Lilliana," he smiled. "What . . . *is* this place? Who *are* you?"

"This is Nizhóní, my grove," she explained as they walked. "She is one of the oldest groves, one of the last of the Primordials, and she has been my home for *many* years."

Arcus cast a sidelong glance at her. He couldn't see her ears, but she had the fine features of those with elven blood. Then again, she lacked the delicacy of the fey people. At least, no elven woman he'd ever seen had possessed such musculature. The closer he looked, the less certain he was of her heritage; she seemed a perfect blend of all the races of men.

"Your stare is not unnoticed, ranger," she advised him, with the faintest hint of irritation in her voice.

"I-I'm sorry," Arcus stammered, his cheeks flushing a deep red. "I meant no offense."

"Of course not," she smiled. "Nonetheless, there are mysteries more beautiful than my ancestry in this grove. I would suggest you focus on them."

Something in her words made him look ahead just as they crested a low hill and gained a better view of the paradise they walked through. A wide, glittering sapphire lake stretched out before them, its edge ringed in delicate reeds and soft, sandy beaches. He could see the shore on the opposite side, across some hundred yards of smooth, glassy water, and to both sides the crescent-shaped body stretched further out of sight behind a series of low hills to the north and a grove of silver-leaf aspens to the south.

Beyond the meadow, in the far distance, snow-capped peaks reached up to fluffy clouds. A distant thunderstorm raged miles away, and an endless swath of trees blanketed the raw, untamed landscape.

"It's unbelievable," Arcus whispered under his breath. "How can this be the Empire?"

The ranger smelled the familiar tinge of ozone that comes before a lightning strike, and the hair on his arms stood up as he spoke.

"This is *not* the Empire," Lilliana said with unexpected disgust, catching Arcus by surprise.

Lightning flashed in her eyes, as well as across the hills in the far distance, before she turned away and continued towards the lake.

"What do you mean?" Arcus pressed, lengthening his stride to keep up. "Where are we if not, er, there?"

"This grove sits outside of the plane you call home," the woman explained, her temper fading like a summer squall. "You no longer walk the soil of Scera, druid."

Arcus froze.

How and when had he crossed into this place, and how would he ever find his way back? His understanding of the planes was limited, but D'Ari lore spoke of them enough for him to understand his predicament - there was every chance he would never set foot on Scera again.

"Nizhóní, like all of the Primordials, connects many realms and yet belongs to none but herself," the woman explained. "At her heart, she sits closest to the Endless Green, hunting ground and home to Alia'anara herself."

"And you . . . brought me here?"

"I did." She turned to look at him with curious melancholy. "It is long past time we spoke, I think."

The pair were nearing the water's edge now, and Arcus could hear the hum of dragonflies and see the momentary ripples in the surface as the winds played across it.

"Come here," she beckoned. "Tell me what you see."

Arcus took the last few steps to the lake and looked down, only to recoil in shock at what he saw. Instead of himself, he saw a dark, twisted, distorted version of his own face. His skin was sickly pale, his eyes black and hollow, and his armor an inky mass of blacks and grays. Utter blackness with specks of poisonous green poured forth from the insignia on his chest, and the band around his necks reflection pulsed with an unnatural energy. He felt a growing tightness in his chest and around his throat and brought his hands to his neck as he backed away, the image burned into his mind's eye.

"What *sorcery* is this?" he asked, eyes wide and heart pounding.

"You bear a dark and terrible burden, Arcus," she announced solemnly. "A sickness that the grove will not long abide. Already its poison works within your mind, your heart, and your blood to mute your connection to the natural world and to twist you away from the balance."

"I do not want it," Arcus shook his head. "I would be free of this burden, this slavery that keeps me beholden to an unjust crown."

Lilliana half smiled at his words.

"Then you would be cleansed? Born again free of the yoke placed unfairly upon your shoulders?"

"I would," he nodded firmly. "I would see myself freed so that I might save my companions."

Her smile drooped.

"I hope, in time, you may." She gestured towards the water. "But I cannot save them, not now. Their paths are . . . too *different* from yours."

Even without clear direction, Arcus felt his body move of its own accord. He stepped, fully clothed, into the sunlit waters of the lake. The cool water electrified his skin, but was not so cold as to be uncomfortable as he waded into the shallows. The shore dropped off quickly, and in short order he found himself waist-deep and looking back at the woman.

To his surprise, she had followed him in and was only a few steps behind. She gave a small wink and a reassuring smile.

"Right there will do, ranger."

Arcus swallowed the lump in his throat, unsure what might be coming next as the woman approached and stood directly in front of him. Less than a foot separated the two, and he felt mesmerized by her closeness.

"Observe the stillness of the water," she said, her voice even and low. "Observe the lie that is the clarity and the quiet."

"The lie?"

"Yes, the lie. Stillness is not the natural order of things, and though it appears to mortal eyes to represent balance, it is in fact only the illusion of control and symmetry that we see."

As she spoke, she dipped a single slender finger into the water, sending a perfect ring rippling outward. The ring grew and grew until it hit the reeds, the beach, and all the jagged edges of the pond, cascading off into random and unpredictable directions. Soon, the entire surface of the lake was distorted by overlapping, interlocking lines.

Arcus marveled at the chaos of the surface of the water and saw that, even as the ripples faded away, the surface was not as still as he had first thought. Tiny, imperceptible breezes skated across the surface, the movements of fish and insects disturbed the water he had thought to be mirror-smooth just minutes ago.

"It was never still at all," he murmured under his breath.

Lilliana smiled again and shook her head.

"No, ranger, nor should it be. Balance is not stillness," her voice was firm and her brows knitted together. "Nature is not a cleanly ordered machine, not a series of levers and pulleys to be carefully charted and calculated."

"I understand, I think," Arcus chewed his bottom lip.

"You will in time." She sighed heavily. "The Empire has grown fat on the promises of order and justice, it has provided the illusion of control that feeds the minds of the masses."

Arcus scoffed, drawing a wry smile from Lilliana.

"You are right to mock the Empire, but you may not yet truly understand the terrible peril it has placed you in." She locked eyes with him. "The danger it represents to us all has yet to be realized, save by a few. This Empire, though birthed in hopeful light, has fallen into shadow and darkness."

"I struggle to believe there was *ever* a time when the Empire truly represented good and justice."

"It did, ranger." Lilliana's gaze grew distant. "I was there when its laws were written. I watched and nurtured it as best I could. I was . . . *naive* enough to set aside my doubts, and I feel terrible shame at the harm that has already been done because of it."

Lilliana regarded Arcus with a curious look, a mixture of hope and sadness, and her features hardened into a scowl.

"But no longer," she shook her head softly. "I will abide it no longer."

"How can I be of service?" Arcus asked grimly, eliciting a small but genuine smile from the woman.

"Take heart, young ranger." She placed a hand on his shoulder. "Do what you know is right. Serve the balance."

"I--"

She held a finger to her lips, stopping him before he could even start.

"This will be a painful process, like drawing venom from a serpent's bite." She gave him a gentle squeeze as she spoke. "Are you prepared?"

Arcus drew a shaky breath, suddenly afraid. His heart pounded and his jaw tightened, but he managed a curt nod and steeled himself against the unknowable.

"Arcus, child of the tundra," Lilliana intoned, stretching her hand out to place her palm upon his chest, covering the emblem of the Hand. "Today you cast off the chains that bind your life."

Searing pain erupted under her palm, and Arcus grit his teeth but did not cry out.

"Today, you reclaim the life that was taken." She placed her other hand on the side of his neck where it, too, began to throb. "You return from a cursed life, a half-life."

Arcus gasped as he felt the woman's fingers dig into his chest and his neck. He tried to move but found himself utterly paralyzed. A brilliant mixture of emerald and golden light erupted from her hands, and Lilliana's eyes, only a few inches from his own, swirled with a bottomless maelstrom of purples, blacks, and deep blues.

Her voice rose and deepened, resonating in his lungs as she spoke, "To undo what has been done, to return you from the clutches of great peril." The woman's fingers dug deeper, and Arcus felt them penetrate his flesh and reach inside his body. "I call upon you, Alia'anara, keeper of the balance and hunter of darkness, to heed your servant's call."

Arcus felt the woman grab hold of his still-beating heart, her slender fingers as strong as iron, and felt an electric fire run through all of his veins. At the same time, the hand on his neck was wrapped firmly around his artery and he could feel every beat of his pulse caught between her fingers.

It wasn't until she started to squeeze, however, that he truly knew pain.

The ranger called out as she began to push her hands, still clenched in fists, within him. He felt spasms of horrible, sickly burning in his neck and chest, as tendrils of caustic fire were sent throughout his whole body.

"Take strength, Arcus. *Find your Elawei.*"

As she spoke, Lilliana's eyes suddenly cleared, and in them Arcus saw the endless night sky, complete with billions of stars, swirling, spiraling galaxies, and a thousand more unnameable wonders. He wept openly at the beauty of her gaze and followed it into infinity.

Something within her called to him, and he yielded unquestioningly. As he did so, he found himself falling backwards in a sort of slow motion.

He managed one last, deep gasp of air as his back hit the water, and an instant later was plunged entirely beneath the surface. He didn't struggle at first, but as the moment dragged on his lungs began to ache, and he felt his body's resistance growing.

Lilliana's hands were still holding him firmly below the surface, and even as he began to buck and push against her, she was immovable as an ancient tree trunk. His eyes widened as his lungs burned, and he began to panic at the realization she intended to drown him.

Harder and harder the woman squeezed his heart and neck, and he could feel what seemed like a roiling mass of snakes in each of her fists. Though that frightened him, it paled in comparison to his impending death. He grasped at her arms and found them as unyielding as steel. With all of his strength he could not make her budge, and he began to feel his strength waning as he started to black out.

At last his body betrayed him and he let slip the last ghost of breath he had left, allowing the unforgiving water surrounding him to pour into his lungs. He felt his limbs grow weak as he kicked and struggled, and soon he could not move at all.

Arcus felt Lilliana pull her hands from his body at last, but the pain had been replaced by a crushing numbness, and he sensed that he was sinking deeper and deeper below the water's surface.

His vision blurred as he fell, but not before he saw the two masses of swirling, writhing black tentacles in Lilliana's hands. He watched them as they struggled to be free of her grasp, and were overcome with blinding golden light. He witnessed them being incinerated, shredded down to the smallest of particles, even as he plunged downward in the cool weightlessness of the lake.

"*Find your Elawei.*"

Arcus sank for what seemed an eternity, half-aware of himself and strangely unconcerned that he hadn't breathed in what felt like a century.

He pondered the druid's words. He'd never heard of an Elawei, but the word clung to his mind and his heart the way a mother's love clings to the warmth of an embrace. He repeated the word over and over in his head, sinking deeper into a state of absolute peace and serenity, before it suddenly hit him.

His elders had spoken of a trance, a state in which one was in perfect harmony with the world around them. *Elwa* they had called it. It could be achieved by perhaps a single druid in a generation, if that.

No sooner did the thought cross his mind than did his eyes snap open.

He was not dead, or even beneath the surface of the water as he had assumed, but was instead floating perfectly still upon his back, staring at the night sky. Arcus knew at once he was not back on Scera, as three moons hung suspended in the sky instead of the two he'd known all his life. Stretched out before him was a field of endless stars, but they paled in comparison to his sudden awareness of the life force all around him. He realized now how blinded he had become by the curse he'd borne, how very isolated he had become by it.

Every tiny mote of algae, every buzzing insect and even the planet, the air, and the water around him glowed with energy, with power, with life.

He floated a while longer before the soft notes of a flute broke his silent introspection. He put his feet down and, to his surprise, found himself able to touch the bottom with ease. He waded to shore to find Lilliana leaning against a low berm, her eyes skyward and a flute on her lips.

He recognized the tune as one from his childhood, though it was subtly different from the version he was used to hearing. *Odinamn* it was called, a song of darkness and of light. He wracked his brain for the lyrics as he approached, hoping not to disturb her playing.

He stumbled to a halt as the creature he'd mistaken for a berm raised its head, revealing itself to be a massive savannah lion. True, unmitigated fear gripped him. The lion was five feet at the shoulder and three times that in length. It let loose a low, ground shaking rumble and revealed teeth longer than Arcus' own foot in the process.

"Easy, Kismat." She smiled brightly, waving Arcus over as the cat settled back down. "Come, Groveborn. Sit a while."

Arcus eyed the big cat warily, but made his way next to the woman.

"Am I . . ."

"Yes, Arcus." She smiled at him, and he noted her eyes had returned to normal. "You are free of the hold of the Black Hands. Though to them you must still return, for now."

Arcus let out a relieved sigh, only to tense back up again.

"Right. We're meant to return to the Hands," he frowned. "How will I hide that I'm no longer cursed?"

"The mark, you'll see, is permanent, I'm afraid," she gestured at his throat as she spoke. "And the Hand won't know the curse is broken unless they attempt to activate it. If you give your superiors no reason to murder you, then you should be safe enough."

Arcus caught sight of her wry smile before it disappeared, and he found himself mimicking it.

They shared several hours more of conversation before eventually falling into a comfortable silence. Arcus lay down on the soft grass and enjoyed the majesty of the stars while Lilliana added her soft, somber flute to the symphony of the night.

Chapter Eighteen

Arcus woke to a puff of hot, steamy air in his face, and when his eyes snapped open he was staring his beloved horse, Trajo, directly in the snout. He was not where he'd fallen asleep, rather he was surrounded by trees and the deep silence of an ancient forest once again.

He realized with concern that his friends must be looking for him and worried sick, or else long gone from here, as he'd been gone for almost an entire day now.

He jumped to his feet, grateful that Trajo had stuck around, and hopped back into the saddle. Looking himself over and dusting himself off, he realized that aside from a crick in his neck, he was none the worse for wear. He sent a silent thanks to Lilliana, wherever she was, for no doubt watching over him.

"Talia? Elbaf? Darko?" he asked into the darkness.

Arcus only half-expected an answer and was mightily surprised when none other than Tomlin called back to him.

"Arcus," he called. "Where are you, sir?"

"Here," the ranger called out, urging his mount between the trees in search of his companion.

A few moments later, he found himself confronted by the entirety of the column, packed as closely together as the trees would allow.

"See?" Elbaf was saying, gesturing at the ranger. "I told you he wouldn't be far. He was probably staring at a bush or something."

"Where were you?" Talia frowned. "We were worried when you didn't answer right away."

"I . . ." Arcus paused, surprised at the nonchalance of his companions. "Really? That's it?"

"Yes," Darko sputtered. "What, you wanted us to be in a panic because you were gone for a few minutes? Please, we're not *completely* helpless without--"

"*A few minutes?*" Arcus blinked in shock. "I've been gone overnight, and then some!"

Silence fell and many in the group exchanged nervous glances at the druid's bizarre claim.

"I think," Darko began in a conciliatory tone, "that perhaps Arcus may have been exposed to Noexum pollen, a powerful and dangerous herb which can alter the senses--"

"*Noexum pollen?* How dare--"

"The two of us can bring up the rear," Darko shot Arcus a look of warning. "I'll tend to him with some curatives in my bags and he'll be right in no time."

"I, um . . . I think that would be best, yes." Arcus managed a weak smile and, despite Talia's look of concern, the column began to move again.

The ranger waited until all but he and Darko had left, and sidled up alongside the mage.

"There's no such thing as Noexum pollen, Darko."

"And you weren't gone for an entire day," the wizard frowned back. "But, here we are. I lied to cover for you, obviously, but unless you've lost your mind completely, I haven't the foggiest idea why *you* did."

"Darko, I swear on my life it wasn't a lie."

"Alright, I'll bite."

Arcus explained the events since his disappearance, and, to his mild surprise, his wizard friend barely interrupted at all, and then only to ask pertinent questions before allowing him to continue. He decided at the last minute to leave out being freed from the curse, though he couldn't have said why. When he'd finally finished, more than an hour had passed.

"I see," Darko pondered aloud. "And I suppose this Lilliana is the one who gave you that?"

The ranger returned a puzzled look.

"Unless you've taken to wearing a flower in your lapel, that is."

Arcus looked down where, sure enough, a seven-petalled lily was pinned to his leather armor.

"What in the--"

He plucked it from his chest, pulling free a long silver pin that had been used to secure it. The pin was inscribed, but it was too fine a script for him to read given the lighting of the forest.

"Here," he handed it over, minus the flower. "Can you make this out?"

"It says, 'Wear well the seven-star, and shed her petals in direst need, no matter the distance I will take heed,'" Darko read with a smirk. "Cute."

"It's not *cute*, Darko," Arcus growled protectively. "It is a badge of honor. A treasured gift."

"I'm far more interested in how you managed to travel the planes before me," Darko laughed cynically. "Truly, the greatest of ironies. Perhaps *I'll* discover a new species of tree frog."

Arcus could tell the wizard's bravado masked a certain frustrated pain at having missed out and decided not to rise to his jabs.

They rode a few minutes in silence before Darko spoke again.

"You *truly* walked another plane . . ." the wizard mused. "And right under my nose."

"For what it's worth," Arcus said with an air of apology, "I didn't exactly *mean* to."

"Honestly, I'm more frustrated that I didn't *sense* anything." Darko shook his head. "Magic that powerful, I should have sensed it a mile off."

Talia cast a glance skyward.

They were two days out of Gilbad, and they'd been pushing the horses and the men to their limits. The trees were much sparser here, and they'd been able to ride two, or even three, abreast in places. Even so, she had no idea how far it was to the meeting place Annabelle had provided them. It didn't help that the encampment wasn't on any maps, but Arcus had proudly proclaimed that he'd be able to find it if they only got close enough.

Thinking of Arcus, she realized eventually that she was going to have to have a few words with him. He'd been a perfect model of respect and a role model of good behavior since his run-in with the pollen in the deep woods, but that wasn't what concerned her. No, what knit her brow with worry was his apparent, and sudden, *romantic* interest in her.

"Talia," Elbaf called from ahead of her. "Something you should see."

The young woman gave her mount a kick and pushed past the soldiers between herself and Elbaf, pulling up when she arrived beside him. The warrior was dismounted and kneeling beside a stump, and the object of his attention was clear. A dead orc, wearing a hodge-podge of armor, was leaning against the rotting wood, his notched longsword at his side.

"Well," she said, nodding at the imperial arrows in his belly, "at least we know who killed him."

"I suspect that means we're close," Elbaf said. "Though we've no idea if this one's companions survived whatever run-in they had with the Brazen Hawks."

"I think I can answer that," Arcus announced, riding into sight from ahead. "And the answer is no, I don't think they did. There's quite a battlefield ahead. It looks like an orcish war camp was razed, but I don't think it was our company that got them."

"What makes you say that?" Darko called out, just now arriving, as well.

"There's far too many horse-prints. I suspect a cavalry company of some kind," Arcus answered.

"That would support the notion we're close to the encampment." Talia removed her helmet and ran a hand through her long blonde tresses. "Do you think you could follow the trail of the horsemen? That'd likely lead us back to the camp."

"I think it would be harder to *lose* their trail than it would be to follow it," Arcus winked, bringing a flush of embarrassment to her cheeks.

She avoided his gaze, but in doing so her eyes caught on the flower he wore, and she blushed even harder. She was definitely going to have to speak with him in private.

"Very well. We'll follow your lead, Arcus."

Arcus turned with a smile, and the group set out, newly emboldened at the idea they might soon be clear of the forest at last.

No more than a few minutes passed before the air began to smell of cold smoke and decay, and less than a candlemark after that, they broke into a wide clearing strewn about with burned huts and slain bodies. The entire clearing reeked of days old corpses, and blackflies buzzed in thick clouds through the air. Little effort, if any, had been made to honor the dead. Gutted corpses lay strewn about with arrows and broken lances still protruding from their flesh.

Talia's nose wrinkled in disgust, and her stomach churned as she looked away. True, this was a war camp, of that there could be little doubt. All the bodies here were of soldiers, but the grisly massacre before her gave her no joy, and the cold dead eyes she met were sure to haunt her dreams.

True to the ranger's word, the entire area had been trampled by horses. There were no imperial dead, which left little doubt as to who had won the day. The path out of the clearing couldn't be missed, all the grass was churned to dirt, and even the branches and brambles between the trees had been torn down by the passing horsemen.

Hot on the heels of the imperial soldiers, the group was able to make excellent time. The trees continued to thin, and the terrain began to slope softly but definitively downward. As more and more bare rock dotted the ground around them, and the trees gave way to bushes and shrubs, Talia got the distinct impression that they were approaching the end of the woodlands and that they might soon be in a better position to get the lay of the land.

She found out how right she was when they crested a small rise and found themselves atop a broadly-sloping bluff. From here they were overlooking a valley of rolling grass which was cut through the middle by a wide, snaking ribbon of blue. Arcus, at the head of the column, was waving at her from the edge of a limestone cliff.

"I'd say we found them," he called out, pointing to the center of the valley where a mass of tents rose from the prairie like a small city.

"You lot go ahead. Elbaf, you're in charge," Talia instructed her newly inspired men, who shared smiles and relaxed laughs at the thought of safety and a warm meal. "Arcus, ride with me for a moment."

Elbaf saluted and led the rest of the group down the slopes, making a beeline for the encampment.

"Everything alright?" Arcus asked, riding up alongside her as they made their way much more slowly.

"Arcus," she felt her cheeks already starting to redden. "We really should talk."

"Okay . . ." he replied a bit hesitantly.

"We *can't* be romantically involved," she blurted out. "I'm very flattered but I, um . . ." Talia gulped, sure that her cheeks were hot enough to cook upon. "I'm not, erm, looking for that . . . right now," she finished as firmly as she could.

Glancing over at Arcus, she saw the look of complete bewilderment in his eyes.

"Talia, I think there's . . . something I'm missing."

All the color drained instantly from the young woman's face as she came to the realization that Arcus had no clue what she was talking about.

"I . . . but you're . . ." she sputtered. "But you're *wearing my family crest*!"

"I'm what?" Arcus looked at her blankly.

"The *lily*, Arcus! The seven-petal lily. It has been the crest of my family for a thousand years," she pointed in exasperation. "You've been wearing it for two days!"

"So . . ."

His blank look confirmed her worst fears.

"It's just . . . I'm . . ."

Talia closed her eyes, mortified, and prayed that when she opened them she'd realize this was all a bad dream. She grimaced when, upon reopening them, she determined she was not so lucky.

"I . . ." She tried to find the words but couldn't, so she turned her head in embarrassment.

"Talia, I'm sorry," Arcus said earnestly. "I never meant to give you the impression . . . Well, you're . . . I mean, you're *beautiful*, o-of course--"

"Arcus," she groaned. "You don't have to say that. My gods, I am so embarrassed."

"Talia, listen," he said firmly. "You *are* a beautiful young woman, it's just that--"

"It's just that I'm an idiot," she groaned. "Right there on your chest, that's where young noblemen wear the signet of their beloved and betrothed, and I'm an absolute *buffoon* for thinking you knew that." She bit her lip and sighed heavily before adding, "Can we . . . can we *never* speak of this again?"

"Yes, Talia," Arcus was clearly stifling a laugh. "Yes, I promise, not a word."

Elbaf led the men downward into the valley, and was unsurprised to hear bugles from the camp announcing their presence. The warrior studied the banners and pennants flying above the makeshift battlements, breastworks of earth with a wooden palisade, and searched his memory for the crest of the various regiments in the Imperial Army.

There were a number of smaller elements he didn't recognize, but the largest banner was that of Fort Jala, a lancer rampant on a gold and purple background. He didn't know the commander by name, but the silver trim around the banner indicated his status as an important member of one of the Noble Houses.

Elbaf frowned, then restored his face to passivity. He was not particularly enthused about having to deal with yet another haughty highborn. Then again, anyone chosen to lead the auspicious 7th Regiment would have to be a battle-tested commander so perhaps he was in for an officer like Talia, rather than one more in line with Annabelle.

Jalan horsemanship, as best as he could remember from his history lessons, was renowned the world over. These men, and those who bore the same banner, had perhaps the most decorated military history of any of the Seven Regiments of the Empire. They were notorious both for their heavily armored lancers and their fast, hard-hitting skirmishers. Time and again, throughout the long life of the Empire, they had risen to an impossible challenge, whether the invasion of the endless legions of the Sulura Lizardmen tribes a century ago, the demonic incursion in Feanren before that, or in any other major conflict the nation had faced.

The real question, though, was why the Empire had seen fit to bring the famed cavalry of the far southwest all the way up here, to the eastern reaches of the realm.

The gates swung outward at their approach, and a double column of twelve horsemen in bright, shining armor approached them at a trot. They bore longspears, but their visors were open and their steel shields remained on their backs.

"You must be Lieutenants Elbainsen and Branislav," the leader said as he saluted. "Welcome to Camp Vengeance."

Elbaf watched the man's friendly, welcoming smile fade as he looked over the weary troops.

"Is this . . . everyone?"

"It is, Sergeant," Elbaf replied gruffly. "Save for a pair bringing up the rear."

"I see, sir. I'm sorry." He gave them a melancholy look. "I can see your men fed and housed, sirs, and Roderick will take you to the command tent to debrief the General whenever you're ready."

"Thank you, Sergeant," Darko smiled thinly. "But we'll wait here for the last two before meeting with the commander, if it's all the same."

The soldier saluted again and led the rest of the troops, all save one, inside the compound. The last soldier, a scrawny young man with a youthful, patchy mustache, waited nervously on his horse. Elbaf noted the boy's discomfort and wondered if it was simply the nerves of being in the presence of an officer or if the boy was intimidated by his appearance.

The trio waited in awkward silence as Arcus and Talia made their way towards them. Thankfully, they were only a few minutes behind, and so the group was together again in short order.

"Captain," young Roderick saluted. "I can show you to the commander whenever you're ready."

"We'll go now," Talia sighed. "We should get our briefings over with before we find meals and racks, or else I'm afraid we won't manage to get out of bed until tomorrow."

Her warmth, in contrast to Elbaf and Darko's coldness, seemed to bring new energy to the boy, who spurred his horse forward and led the way into the mass of tents and soldiers.

He pointed out various places of interest - the chapel, the mess tent, and the like - as they rode. Elbaf tried to memorize the pertinent details, but found himself much more interested in the one thing the man seemed to be ignoring completely.

Everywhere he looked there was evidence of *digging*. Tools, piles of rubble, wheelbarrows, and all manner of carts and wagons were everywhere around them. Large areas had been marked out with colored string and wooden stakes, and dozens of workers occupied dig sites all over the camp. In some of the pits he could see the stacked stones and bricks of ancient ruins, where others seemed to sit empty.

"What is all this?" Darko asked, gesturing at one of the larger pits as they passed.

"Hmm?" The young man turned, then followed Darko's outstretched finger. "Oh, the excavation? The Sisterhood sent a bunch of historian types out here shortly after we arrived, and they've been digging like leopard moles ever since."

"Digging for what?"

"Couldn't tell ya, sir. But they get awful' excited every time they find some new building." The boy shrugged helplessly.

Elbaf was glad the wizard had asked, but further speculation was cut short as they neared what he assumed must be the central command tent. The structure, which in truth appeared to be multiple smaller tents all assembled around a larger central pavilion, was massive. It looked as if it could hold fifty people or more in the central room and double that in the adjacent spaces.

An honor guard of a half dozen soldiers, each bearing golden trim on their platemail, closed ranks at their approach.

One of the men stepped forward and, though he rendered a salute, remained wary.

"State your business."

Roderick opened his mouth to respond, but Talia cut him off.

"Captain Talia Lorraine, reporting for Major Von Cleigh and the camp commander, as ordered."

The guard cocked his head to his side and seemed ready to say something, but apparently decided not to. Instead, he stood to the side and offered a clear path forward.

"Roderick," Darko said, dismounting along with the others. "Can we entrust you with our horses?"

"Aye, sir," the boy saluted and took their reins all together. "I'll get them stabled for you, sir, and registered with the quartermaster."

Elbaf watched Talia adjust her uniform, brushing the dust off as best she could before raking her hands through her hair. He suppressed a smile as she did her best to not look like she'd spent the better part of ten days riding through the wilderness and fighting for her life, and he simply waited patiently for her to lead the way inside.

Talia took a deep breath to steady her trembling hands.

She wanted to look behind her, to check on her fellow officers and to take strength from their presence, but she forced herself to step forward instead. They needed her to be strong, and she wouldn't let them down.

The ten feet to the door of the pavilion filled her with a sense of dread, but she did her best to shake the feeling as she pushed forward confidently.

"Captain Lorraine," she announced as she entered the dim confines of the building. "Reporting as instructed . . ."

Her words trailed off as she took in the scene before her. A half-dozen members of the Sisterhood were in a rough horseshoe around a large sand table. At the head of the table was Annabelle, resplendent in her ebony armor, and at its foot was a trio of men in military gear. One among them, an older gentleman of perhaps forty years, seemed mid-sentence when she interrupted.

Talia noted with trepidation that Major Von Cleigh was nowhere in sight.

"Captain Lorraine," Annabelle snapped. "Small wonder *you* have chosen to interrupt us. I will be finished in a moment."

"That's not strictly necessary, now is it?" the older man asked, his deep baritone contrasting starkly with her acidic voice. "This young captain has been through hell, if the reports are accurate. I think we can forgive the intrusion."

As her eyes finished adjusting, she realized with dismay that Annabelle had been promoted. Sometime since they'd parted ways, she'd been bumped up to Major, and she wore the shiny new insignia proudly on her breastplate. Talia scowled, then paled as she realized the only way that could have happened was if Major Von Cleigh had fallen on the battlefield.

"Duke Boric," Annabelle protested. "We're not--"

"It can wait, Major," he waved her off. "The situation in Kent will not resolve itself this afternoon, even if we talk ourselves blue in the face."

Annabelle made a face like she'd drunk a tablespoon of lemon juice, but checked her tongue.

"I'm so sorry, sir," Talia stammered to the Duke, her cheeks red. "I didn't intend to--"

"Nonsense, Lady Lorraine," he chuckled. "Your presence is a cool breeze in this stifling tent. Walk with me?"

"Yes, my lord. I would be happy to." Talia blushed again at his use of her formal title, an honorific she'd not heard since joining the clergy years ago.

"Begging your pardon, Duke Boric," Annabelle interrupted Talia, "but I need to speak with Captain Lorraine regarding the former commander."

Boric turned back to Annabelle, and the two locked eyes in silence. Tension mounted until Boric finally shrugged with apparent nonchalance and turned back to the rest of the group.

"Very well, Major," he drawled. "Lady Lorraine, I would be most honored if you would meet me for dinner this evening, and you may, of course, bring your friends as well."

"Yes, ma'am," Talia forced a pleasant smile onto her face as she responded to Annabelle's demand, and shot her friends an apologetic look. "And, sir, I am humbled by your offer."

"See that you take me up on it, m'lady," he winked. "Gentlemen, let me show you around!"

Talia watched helplessly as her companions were steered away by the Duke, leaving her alone with the rest of the Sisterhood and, worst of all, Annabelle.

Elbaf tried to think of an excuse, any excuse, not to leave Talia alone with Annabelle and the other Sisters, but Duke Boric was already ushering him away.

Boric was a mystery to him. He wasn't a Hand, at least not judging from his apparel, but he wore the rank of a General on his shoulders, and his title alone made him a member of the Council of Lords. By rights, he had no reason at all to be in the field, living in a tent, no matter how nice it might be.

According to their teachings with the Hand, each of the thirteen Noble Houses was represented on the council. It had taken Elbaf and Arcus quite by surprise to learn that their very own Talia belonged to one of them, House Lorraine. Boric belonged to another: House MacMordain, if Elbaf was recognizing the bear and willow crest correctly.

"You boys have had a hard few days, I'm told," Boric said as he led the way through the tent city. "I'm sorry for your lost companions."

"Yes, m'lord," Darko acknowledged. "It's been challenging, but the Emperor protects."

Elbaf's eyebrows raised when the Duke scoffed at Darko's words, but he seemed to be the only one that heard it.

"You'll need to eat," Boric said, pointedly ignoring his duty to repeat the traditional response to any mention of the Emperor. "There's a mess tent some of my officers and I like to use here on the north wall."

Elbaf noted at least three dining tents during their ten minute walk across the encampment and was left to wonder why they weren't good enough to stop at.

"Here we are."

The oblong tent that sat before the group was large, capable of fitting a few dozen soldiers at least, and the heavenly smells of roasted meat drifted from within. Inside they found a small contingent of cooks dutifully preparing and doling out roasted boar, braised greens, and a hearty brown stew of root vegetables.

Long tables were arranged around a flat, cleared circle of sand in the center of the tent, and the diners were all captivated by a wrestling match taking place there while they ate. Two men, both well-muscled and wearing nothing but their boots and pants, were grunting and sweating as they tried to pin their opponent to the ground amidst the cheers of their fellows.

"This tent is generally avoided by the Sisterhood." Boric gave Elbaf a sidelong glance. "Apart from those who double as Hands, the Sisters of the order tend to shun violence as a matter of principle."

At Boric's insistence, each of them collected a tray of food, along with a slab of the thick, durable, and ubiquitous trail bread the men referred to affectionately as shovel-bread. Their loot in hand, they made their way to one of the tables closest to the ring and took seats.

Elbaf noted with respect that Boric sat among the soldiers, and, in fact, there seemed to be no distinct dining area for officers as he had often seen in other dining halls during his year in the army.

"So you," the Duke nodded at them as he broke a chunk of shovel-bread off to use as a spoon for his stew, "you're a bit of an odd bunch."

"Ah, yes," Darko interjected smoothly. "Allow me to introduce my companions, Lieutenants Elbaf Elbainsen, Arcus D'Ari, and myself, Darko Branislav."

The Duke acknowledged each of them in turn with a smile and a small nod.

"I know who you are. The men *do* talk, you know."

Elbaf felt a bead of sweat form at the base of his neck. Depending on who the Duke had spoken with, his communication with the men could be very good, or *very* bad.

"Oh, don't worry, warrior." The Duke smiled at Elbaf, reading his expression. "Many of them offered you high praise."

Elbaf sighed softly.

"I find that speaking to the soldiers, to a man's subordinates, is the second best method of knowing a person," he finished, taking a swig of dark, sweet lacho tea.

"What's the first?" Arcus wondered aloud.

"A fistfight," Elbaf growled, taking a deep drink from his own rough wooden mug.

"That's right," Boric chuckled and nodded. "Combat tells you everything you need to know about a man."

"I'd have to respectfully disagree," Darko scoffed. "I don't see the reasoning behind that at all."

"I didn't say it was the only way," Boric laughed, clapping the mage on the shoulder with a broad, heavy hand. "I will say I find it the swiftest, though."

Arcus cracked a wry grin at Darko's discomfort, but spoke in his defense.

"I'd agree with the wizard, actually," he chimed in. "Seems like a hot cup of tea and a low fire would be a much more comfortable option to me."

"Hmm . . ." Boric smiled even wider. "Seems you and I are the only two who see eye to eye on this, warrior."

Elbaf returned the man's wide, easy smile and raised his glass to toast the idea.

Boric returned his toast, drained his cup, and then set it roughly on the tabletop.

"What do you say, Elbaf?" He raised a brow. "Shall we get to know each other?"

"Elbaf," Darko cautioned. "You should perhaps recall that striking a superior officer, let alone a member of the Council of Lords, is a Capital offense--"

"Yet *another* ridiculous law," Boric rolled his eyes.

Elbaf assessed the man in front of him. The Duke was fit and healthy, but much older as well. He moved with a powerful grace and, as he stood up to stretch, Elbaf noted he was still as broad shouldered and powerfully built as a much younger man.

"Come now, Elbaf," he entreated. "Humor me, no?"

Elbaf drained the contents of his mug and pushed back from the table to stand as well.

"As you wish sir," the younger soldier shrugged. "But I'll not hold back."

"I'd be insulted if you did," Boric chuckled. "Besides, you know what they say about old age and experience."

Elbaf saw Darko pinching the bridge of his nose as he often did when he was irritated, but chose to ignore his companion's warning. He turned back to the Duke even as his elven friend stood to leave.

"What are the rules?" he asked, already unclipping his pauldrons and breastplate.

"We'll fight to submission, pin, or knockout," Boric explained, removing his own tabard and the armor underneath. "Nobody calls the match but one of us."

Elbaf nodded again, stretching his shoulders and rolling his neck before pulling his shirt over his head. He was not ashamed of his body. In fact, he was proud of the physique he'd built throughout his young life. His rippling muscles bulged under ruddy greenish skin marred by the scars of battle and a misspent youth. His back drew a number of stares, though. The layers of thick striped scars started a low murmur in the audience.

"Corporal Vanger, you'll give us a signal to begin and officiate any disputes."

"Aye, sir," the man he named said as he jumped to his feet and took his position beside the ring.

"You've led a hard life, warrior," the Duke noted solemnly, his attention returning to Elbaf as he took off his own shirt.

Elbaf kept his surprise in check, but only just.

Duke Boric's clothing had concealed a dozen or more large, intricate tattoos of differing designs, all painted artfully across muscles sculpted from steel. The tattoos varied, and it was easy to see which ones were oldest from the fading. Elbaf looked them over as he loosened up his shoulders and headed to the ring. A Jalan lancer, a rearing stallion, a broad-bladed spear, a brilliant golden dragon, and other martial designs decorated his shoulders and pectorals. But the tattoo that most captured Elbaf's eye was a faded - but still crystal-clear - sun emblazoned over his heart. It was carefully distinct, separated from the rest of the artwork. It would have drawn his attention even if it hadn't been an exact replica of the symbol they'd seen, but the fact that it could have been a carbon copy made it all the more interesting.

He noted as well that the Duke bore his own share of scars, many of which were very clearly earned on the battlefield. Judging from the fading pink and white of the scars on the man's body, he'd taken more than one arrow in his career and perhaps a spear or sword as well.

"Dead man walking," one of the soldiers in the crowd called out to gales of laughter.

"Don't worry, lieutenant," another answered. "The sisters will patch you right up."

The crowd of men continued cheering and joking as the two made their way ringside, even going so far as to chant 'fresh meat' as he walked past, and Elbaf was surprised at the level of energy and their absolute confidence in Boric. A few moments later they were both in the ring, a dozen feet or so separating them. Elbaf was bare knuckled, where the Duke was wearing a thin pair of leather gloves, but aside from that they were both stripped down to the waist and completely devoid of armor.

The half-orc searched his opponents bright blue eyes, analyzed the way he stood, his breathing, anything he could to gain an edge against the other fighter, but the Duke was an unreadable statue of emotionless calm.

From the corner of his eye, he could see the third man at the edge of the ring, Corporal Vanger. He was a seasoned fighter in his late thirties, with scars across his face and a dark leather patch over his left eye. In his lips he held a small bone whistle, and he was carefully watching both of the fighters before him.

"Sir," he looked to the Duke, who nodded his readiness.

"And you, sir?" He looked at Elbaf. "Ready?"

Elbaf gave a curt affirmative nod and braced himself.

The sharp blast of the whistle broke the stillness of the tent, and the two soldiers moved as one. Elbaf charged ahead, sand spraying behind his boots, while the Duke danced left and right, his feet barely seeming to touch the ground, while his hands were both raised and ready.

Elbaf noted the careful stance and the relaxed confidence of the man as he closed the distance, but he was already committed to his attack. He knew that Boric likely had the upperhand in a boxing match, but flattered himself by assuming that in a down and dirty ground game he could best the older man.

Elbaf saw the man tense up as he neared striking range and decided to take a more cautious route than he'd planned initially. He turned his charge into a dive and roll, sweeping with his arms at his opponent's legs.

His left hand caught the Duke's ankle as he tried to sidestep from the unexpected maneuver, but by the time he regained his feet the Duke was rock-steady and waiting.

Elbaf had barely stood when a flurry of blows rained against his instinctively raised arms. Every impact felt like a sledgehammer, and Elbaf was taken aback by the power behind the careful, precise strikes.

The half-orc gave ground, pulling back in the hopes that he could make an opening for himself, but the avalanche of strikes was relentless. The Duke worked his arms until he was nearly certain he could predict the next strike, then would unexpectedly transition to his sides and his gut, never keeping the same pattern for more than a moment. It was all Elbaf could do to avoid a blow to his face or head, and he came to the swift realization that in a standing game he was rapidly losing a path to victory.

He needed to change the dynamic.

The Duke's rhythm was a steady but unpredictable staccato, but he attacked with his arms alone. The man's feet shifted back and forth, allowing him to step rapidly from side to side to make good use of any opening that Elbaf left, but he seemed to view them only as support and not as an additional weapon.

Elbaf gritted his teeth against what he knew would follow and allowed an opening to appear in his defenses on his left side. Boric saw it instantly and leaned right to hammer him with a wide haymaker. What he failed to anticipate, however, was Elbaf's knee, which shot up like a piston and caught him in the lower ribs as he moved into it.

The impact was heard in the audience, and Elbaf gave a savage grin as he heard the Duke's breath leave his body in a painful grunt. As one, the crowd fell instantly silent, leaving only the sounds of their labored breathing and the pounding in their ears as the half-orc followed up with a savage roundhouse kick to the Duke's thigh, buckling the man's leg as he tried to recover.

Smelling blood in the water, Elbaf pressed on, bringing his right hand crashing down toward the Duke's jaw while he was momentarily thrown off guard. He barely made contact with the Duke's face, as Boric squirmed away at the last second, but nonetheless landed the heavy blow on the man's chest and drove him a half-step back.

Boric tried to recover and build distance with a lightning fast jab, and Elbaf's head was rocked back from the viper-like strike. But the half-orc was already twisting to the ground, lashing out with a kick and tangling the Duke's legs in a corkscrew motion that dragged him to the ground.

By the time the Duke hit the ground, Elbaf was already turning to grab hold of him. The man was flexible - and *strong* - and Elbaf received a booted kick to the face for his trouble and saw stars.

But a lifetime of fighting gave him the instincts to drive through the disorientation. The Duke was warding him off better than expected, and after another kick to the jaw loosened one of Elbaf's teeth, he decided to pull out all the stops.

The next time Boric attempted a kick, he received a staggering punch to the knee-cap in response. Elbaf heard a crack that meant a fracture or worse, but was too busy ducking the roundhouse that followed it to care.

He had the Duke on his back, and now he just needed to capitalize on his superior position. He began working his way closer and took a great deal of punishment for it as he did. Every kick and punch that came his way was answered with a brutal strike to the offending limb and at a joint whenever possible.

The warrior spent the next several seconds trying to get atop the Duke, and when he finally did so there was a mess of blood and sweat covering both of them. As he established his position straddling the Duke, Elbaf was rocked again by a powerful uppercut and nearly lost his balance. He managed to hang on and slipped his hands around the Duke's neck.

Boric kicked and squirmed, then turned his focus to trying to break Elbaf's grasp. He hammered on Elbaf's wrists, and the warrior felt his left wrist break from the onslaught. But he held tight as Boric's face started to redden.

Realizing he wouldn't break Elbaf's grasp, Boric changed tactics again and caught Elbaf in the temple with a broad haymaker. Elbaf's vision blurred, but he did his best to hold on as the two of them raced to see who would black out first - Boric from lack of air or Elbaf from blunt force trauma.

Elbaf's vision darkened and swam until he felt his fingers begin to loosen of their own accord. His right eye was swollen shut, and the Duke's blows, although feeble, were still landing with surprising force.

He felt himself falling into darkness, but refused to let go even as he blacked out.

Chapter Nineteen

Arcus was sitting beside Elbaf when he woke up and offered the warrior a good-natured chuckle and a look of disbelief. He replayed the final moments of the fight he'd witnessed in his mind and still couldn't believe the narrow margin by which the Duke had bested his friend.

"Welcome back," he smiled. "You know, you *almost* had him."

He watched as Elbaf tried to speak, but winced in pain instead.

"I wouldn't talk just yet, brother," he laughed. "You're rather worse for wear."

He looked across the medical tent to where Duke Boric was being attended a few beds down.

"Don't worry, you're up next," he said.

True to his word, a few minutes later a pair of young Sisters, both of whom reminded him for all the world of Talia the night they'd met, appeared at the bedside.

"Good afternoon, Lieutenant. I am Neela, and this is Falawaii," one said, her bright green eyes sparkling with amusement. "Let's get you taken care of, shall we?"

"Be gentle with him," Arcus teased the girl, bringing a flush to her cheeks. "His mind wasn't that strong to begin with."

"Easy," Elbaf growled, his voice cracking.

"Please hold still, sir," Falawii said, as she placed a hand on either side of Elbaf's face. "You may feel some tingling, but you shouldn't experience any pain."

Arcus, having never really had a chance to study the healing magic of the Sisterhood up close, watched intently as the young woman worked. The girl's dark skin clashed pleasantly with the soft cream of her clothing, and her deep amber eyes were every bit as captivating as the magic she wove.

He felt waves of calm and serenity wash over him as the woman began to softly sing. The words lost their meaning as her hands glowed with a soft silvery-blue light and brilliant motes of energy danced between her fingers. The druid watched as the mess of bruises, cuts, and swelling between her hands began to soften and resolve itself back into the face of his good friend.

Neela was giving the half-orc similar treatment, but focusing on the rest of his body. She worked on his broken wrist, his ribs, and a few of his fingers as well before she was through. The two of them finished one after another, and there was nearly no trace left of his wounds, save for the sweat on their brows and the heaviness of their breathing.

"You have my gratitude,Sisters," Elbaf said solemnly, bowing as best he could from his hospital bed.

"Not to worry, warrior," Falawii smiled. "Duke Boric and his men keep us fairly busy with their fighting pit."

"It's not a *fighting pit*," Boric scoffed, drawing attention to the fact that he had moved to join them. "My gods, you make it sound like some sort of slave arena."

The man was stretching out the kinks in his shoulders as he spoke, but he had a bright smile on his face. The Sisters gave him fleeting looks of disapproval as he bordered on blasphemy, but his smile was infectious.

"Will that be all my, Lord Boric?"

"It will. Thank you, Neela. Thank you, Falawii," he bowed graciously to them. "I'll try to keep my men out of your hair for a few days."

Arcus eyed his two companions as the Sisters departed. An hour ago they'd been at each other's throats, literally, but now they exchanged open grins like old friends.

"You nearly had me, you know," Boric smiled, offering a hand to help Elbaf to his feet.

"I don't know about that," Elbaf shrugged, taking Boric's hand and pulling himself upright before swinging off the bed. "You hit like a loaded wagon rolling down a hill."

"Well," Boric laughed. "That's true enough."

"Where's Darko?" The half-orc asked, doing some stretching of his own.

"He's at the Duke's tent, reading or . . . I don't know," the ranger shrugged. "Doing something mystical, I suppose."

Elbaf's skeptical look prompted him to continue.

"He said he was retiring until you two had recovered," Arcus said apologetically. "I got the impression he thought this whole exercise was a little foolish."

"Ah, well." Boric nodded. "Not for everyone, I suppose."

The older man noted the growing darkness and clapped Arcus and Elbaf on the shoulders.

"Why don't we go and pester him? Talia should be finished with Annabelle soon, if she isn't already."

I'm bored, Master.

"I know you are," Darko sighed, turning a page in the book he was reading. "You're pacing. You never pace."

Reia stopped long enough to glare at him, then resumed walking circles around the edge of the small end table she was perched upon. Darko chuckled at the pink flaming hoofprints she left as she walked the dark grain of the wood. She paused and turned to the doorway, then smiled broadly at him.

Finally, we have company.

The tiny demon disappeared in a puff of black smoke, then flew over and perched upon the wizard's shoulder in the form of a jet black raven once again. She made a great show of preening her feathers as she kept careful watch over the room.

Darko looked up over the top of his book in time to see Elbaf, Arcus, and Duke Boric enter the confines of the breezy canvas tent. Both the nobleman and the half-orc were splattered with dried blood.

"I presume your bout was as effective a communication tool as you expected," he remarked dryly, shutting the tome he held.

"It was," the Duke boasted. "Elbaf here is a formidable fighter, he nearly had me."

And yet . . ." the warrior growled good-naturedly.

"Well," Boric shrugged with surprising humility. "As I said, it was a good fight."

The Duke took a seat in one of several camp chairs all arrayed around a folding table which held maps, scribbled notes, and several sloppily stacked sheafs of parchment.

"Don't mind the mess," the man said, indicating the others should seat themselves as well. "This whole business has me and my men spread fairly thin."

"What exactly *is* this whole business?" Arcus chimed in, looking over the map. "What's the prestigious 7th doing out here in the northwest, and what on Scera are you *digging holes* for?"

"A fair question," Boric nodded, only to be interrupted by a page entering the tent.

"Yes, Ollie, we'll have some wine. And go ahead and tell Lasario that I'll be taking dinner here, in the tent. Enough for five and plenty of wine," he told the page before dismissing him.

The young man bowed low and promptly exited again.

"I was on my way back from visiting an old friend up in Fort Kyber, the commandant at the Advanced Officer School there, when I was roped into this nonsense." He sighed heavily. "What was supposed to be a routine sweep for bandits led into a series of skirmishes against a local orcish warband, and that somehow turned into garrison duty in the middle of nowhere a fortnight from home."

He gestured dismissively at the tent and the camp beyond, his disdain impossible to miss.

"To be honest with you, I'm more than a bit irritated that my men are being used as glorified babysitters," he scowled. "The Sisterhood has *archaeologists* crawling all over these hills, digging up ruins. Old forts, the remains of a town, I guess, and a couple of doors no one can seem to open." He chuckled. "I offered to build a battering ram, but they wouldn't have it."

"But they gave you no reason?" Darko pressed. "Nothing at all to indicate their importance?"

"No," Boric frowned. "But this is no business for soldiers. Hell, even with this trouble in Kent there's no reason at all for me to have over three-hundred horsemen standing by."

"About Kent . . ." Arcus spoke up again, gently probing. "What exactly is going on there?"

"*Apparently* there's talk of open rebellion." Boric rubbed the bridge of his nose. "The town itself is sizable, and fairly self-sufficient, but there's been no demand or attempts to negotiate, either."

"So . . ."

"So, they sealed the gates the last time an Imperial messenger came through." He smiled ruefully. "Naturally, he reported it. Then, *somehow*, Major Von Cleigh found out about it. Now, instead of peacefully resolving this, Major Montagne is foaming at the mouth to raze the whole city to the ground."

"I see, sir," Darko nodded. "We happened to be on the trail of some . . . dissidents, ourselves. I believe that the imperial messenger simply happened upon us in his haste to return to the heart of the Empire."

"Dissidents, eh?"

Something in Boric's tone put Darko on edge. The wizard noted the threads of steel under the man's nonchalant tone. His keen eyes picked out the tightness in his muscles as Boric sat seemingly at peace.

"Thomas and Dominic Mercane," Darko announced flatly, hoping to pull an unconscious response from the warrior. "A pair of boys that were distributing literature, fomenting rebellion, back in Gilbad."

"I see."

They were interrupted by the page, Ollie, returning with a tray which held three bottles of red wine and a half dozen wooden tumblers.

"Thanks, Ollie," Boric smiled. "That'll be all until dinner."

"Yes, my lord," the young man bowed low and moved swiftly out again.

"So what became of the boys?" Boric asked, pouring wine for each of his guests.

Darko marveled at the mask the man wore, his attention seemingly consumed by the dark red liquid in his hands.

"We hanged them," Darko said, ignoring the glares of Arcus and Elbaf.

Silence filled the tent after his announcement, and the hairs on the back of Darko's neck raised as the tension mounted. Boric set the wine bottle down with a soft clink, but his eyes stayed focused on the glasses.

"What Darko is trying to say," Arcus interrupted, his voice dripping with irritation, "is that we were *forced* to hang them. We couldn't have saved them, they were . . . gods, they were sloppy. Too thoroughly guilty to pardon."

Boric looked up, staring each of them in the eye in turn.

"And what *would* you have done?" he asked softly. "Had you the power to do anything in the world, what would you have done?"

"They'd have lived," Arcus said without hesitation. "They would have had their grievances addressed and . . ."

"And?"

"And, I don't know," the druid cast about helplessly. "Maybe something could have been done. We could have *fixed* the problem in the first place, instead of murdering two boys whose only crime was pointing out the . . ."

"Pointing out the *sickness* in the Empire," Elbaf prompted, his eyes firmly locked on Boric's.

Silence fell with Elbaf's statement; for a moment, no one breathed.

"Some might call such a stance . . . treasonous," Boric replied, his voice even, despite the threat.

"Perhaps *that* is the problem," the druid shot back, to Darko's alarm.

"Arcus," he chastised his companion. "That is perhaps too far--"

"Is it too far?" Arcus raised his voice. "Is it?"

"You're right though, druid," Boric interrupted the exchange with a frown. "More right than you know. There is a growing sickness in the Empire, and those of us who love her are fearful for the future."

"How can you love such a wicked, ugly thing?" Arcus asked caustically.

"Arcus," Elbaf growled, speaking up for the first time in several minutes. "Many would call the Brine a wicked, ugly thing, but I love it nonetheless."

Silence again descended upon the tent, and it seemed to grow colder for the lack of words.

"The Brine is more than the crime, the crushing masses of the poor, and the brawling in the streets. It is also *people*. People who live, raise their babies, work hard, do everything they're supposed to do. Those people need someone to believe in them too, every bit as much as the stuffy mansions of the Altimeers, the Lorraines, the Montagnes, and all the rest of the nobility," Elbaf continued, his voice quieter than before.

Elbaf's words were followed by another, longer silence that went unbroken until Ollie returned, a candlemark or more later. He appeared with a pair of porters, who set up a second folding table and arrayed it with more wine, wooden plates, iron silverware, and sumptuous foods that filled the tent with the smells of roasted venison and steamed vegetables.

While the porters made ready the meal, Ollie trimmed the wicks around the tent to fight back the growing darkness and, perhaps sensing the tension in the room, left without speaking as soon as the porters were ready.

"You know," Boric said when they were alone again at last, "there is much of the Empire that was good, and much that still is. The poison that creeps through its heart is not yet a fatal dose. If I can just seek it out - if I can cast light upon that shadow - perhaps it can be saved."

Darko considered what they had learned of the Duke, weighing the dangers of pointing out the man's sun tattoo, and sussing out as much information as he could from the only potentially receptive person they'd met that might actually *know* something. On the one hand, to draw attention to it could put them in a precarious position if the conversation turned sour. But on the other hand, Arcus had all but admitted to his own treasonous thoughts and the Duke *had* seemed to share his sentiments.

It is perhaps best not to press, Master.

Reia's caution was not something he often ignored, but neither would he leave her motive unquestioned.

You have concerns?

A man in Boric's position is infinitely better suited to rooting out whatever corruption he sees than we will likely ever be, Master. It is perhaps wiser to practice .

246

. . discretion.

We could--

Whatever he is planning, Master, it will not be subtle. We do not have the same protections, the same loyalty, or the same fallback plans as he. Should we be implicated in some botched plot, we could swing from a hangman's rope for our troubles.

"Sit, please," Boric said, his tone lighter. "I'm sure Lady Lorraine will join us when she is able, and it would be a shame to have the food go cold."

As if summoned by his words, Talia burst through the opening of the tent without ceremony. On her face was written all the rage of a tornado, and her steps were heavy with anger.

"Talia? What's wrong?" Arcus' adrenaline spiked.

He could sense from the moment she blew into the tent that she was angrier than he had ever witnessed. The emotion radiated off of her like a heat wave, and for a moment she seemed beyond words.

The group in the tent stood uneasily as she paced a moment, opening and shutting her mouth several times as she searched for the words to speak her mind.

"Talia--"

She held up a hand to ward off the question, but stopped her pacing.

"I've been reassigned, effective immediately," she snapped, taking all of the air out of the room with her announcement.

"You're *what*?" Arcus was floored. It was an outcome far worse than the worst his mind had cooked up since realizing they were to return to Annabelle. "Why?!"

"Talia, my dear," Boric's voice cut through the tent. "Sit, I insist."

He poured her a tumbler of wine, all the way to the brim, and handed it to her as she reluctantly sat.

"It's . . ." She massaged her forehead and took a deep drink. "Major Von Cleigh is dead, slain in battle by a poisoned arrow, or so that *harpy* says."

"Dead," Elbaf repeated grimly. "Then we are firmly in Annabelle's grasp now."

"It will not stand," Arcus thumped the table. "And what the hell good does reassigning *you* do for anyone? Should you not take her place as second in command?"

"I'm to accompany Madrie's body back to the Capitol to be interred in the Catacombs of the Sacred Martyrs," she bowed her head and teardrops dotted the table, but none dared say a word.

Her hand clenched with rage, and the tumbler in her hand shook with the effort she made to not throw it across the room.

"It's all very *proper*," she managed softly. "I'm to resume my training, to take on the mantle of Soror Superia when I return to the Capitol."

"Talia," Arcus put a hand on her shoulder. "You'll be a capable Sister superior, you can continue your good works--"

"Do not patronize me, Arcus," she retorted, knocking his hand away. "That *wicked* woman had something to do with Madrie's death; I know she did. And now she means to do the same to you. She's sending me away so I can't protect you."

"Take caution, Lady Lorraine," Boric warned her gently. "Your voice, though beautiful, may carry to unkind ears. My men are sworn to me, and your secrets will be safe with them, but there are others here I cannot vouch for."

"He's right," Darko nodded. "Moreover, if you're right and Annabelle is up to something--"

"She is!"

"*If* you're right," he continued, "then we need to be careful. To kill her commanding officer and get away with it is a bold stroke, and one she would not make if she was not certain of her position."

An uncomfortable pause followed his words.

"Let us not forget ourselves," he cautioned. "We are still the flies, and she is still the spider."

Arcus raised an eyebrow at Darko's metaphor, curious if he had intended to lift it from Lilliana's note or if the comparison had been unconscious.

"Speak plainly, dammit," Elbaf growled.

"We have no choice, Elbaf," Darko rolled his eyes. "We are still *bound* to obedience, and until that all-important fact changes, we are under her thumb and there we will remain. Without Madrie to protect us, we are vulnerable, and we must therefore watch our backs all the closer."

"All is perhaps not lost," Boric wondered aloud. "But I would like to know the history of your discontent with Annabelle, if you have time to tell me of how this hatred of her formed."

"Time, alas, is something we are short of." Talia shook her head. "I am to leave at first light."

"All the better that you'll spend your last night with friends." Boric raised a glass. "To the beauty of the road. The road that leads us ever on to new adventures and yet, on looking back, reminds us just how far we have come."

They raised their glasses to his toast, then, at his insistence, they sat to eat. The food they shared was superb, and every detail seemed sharper for the weight of the moment. Arcus tried desperately to commit each moment to memory, as a nagging sadness filled the back of his mind. He dwelt in the moment, relishing the time spent with his companions as the night drew on towards midnight. Ollie returned twice more to trim the candle wicks, and still the wine flowed and their spirits filled the tent with warmth and the bittersweet melancholy of the coming dawn.

Sometime near midnight they told Boric at last of their adventures thus far. They left nothing out, not even the happenings at the Altimeer estate, and his stony silence spoke volumes. By the time they'd finished, they reasoned it must be sometime in the early morning, and Arcus figured there to be only a handful of hours left until daybreak.

"You should all get a few hours rest," Boric announced at last, nodding at Talia as she snored softly in the chair where she'd fallen asleep. "The dawn will soon chase the darkness out of the skies, and you'll all be the worse for wear if you get no sleep."

"The dawn," Arcus snapped his fingers, drunkenness giving him courage. "Surely this is too great a coincidence."

"Do tell," Boric smiled.

"You bear a mark we have seen not once or twice but *three times* now." Arcus pointed at the man's chest. "You bear the mark of the sun, and I would like to know its meaning."

Boric took a sip of wine and sat deeper in his chair, looking Arcus over and visibly considering his response. He held the attention of everyone in the room as they all sat in anticipation of his answer.

"It is the mark of the Dawn Martyr," he said at last.

Arcus noted with suspicion that Boric's gaze lingered on Talia as he continued.

"The Dawn Martyr offered her life for the Empire early in our history," he explained. "Her origins are shrouded in mystery, but she dedicated her life - and her death - to safeguarding the Empire against a growing darkness."

"Hmph," Elbaf grunted. "A convenient enemy, one which can neither be confirmed or denied."

"Make no mistake," Boric shook his head, "there are forces abroad that would see an end to the Empire."

"And what of threats *within* the Empire?" Darko muttered, louder perhaps than he'd intended.

"A threat from within is every bit as dangerous, if not more so," Boric agreed darkly. "But there are yet those of us who seek to carry on the Dawn Martyr's work."

Arcus tried to decide whether he found the man's answers satisfactory, but the wine and his exhaustion worked to overthrow his senses; he agreed at last that perhaps Boric was right and that they should turn in.

"What of our fearless leader?" He pointed to Talia.

"We could carry her back to her quarters?" Elbaf offered, rolling his neck and flexing his shoulders.

"Better to let her sleep, I think," Boric offered. "I have a spare cot I keep here for the times when I stay up too late working."

He retrieved a folding cot from amidst the clutter in the tent, and in short order they had it set up and Talia tucked safely under a scratchy wool field blanket.

Talia woke to the clear, piercing notes of a bugle call. She sat up with a start, caught momentarily in a flashback to her days as a trainee when that note signaled the beginning of another day of endless physical punishment and screaming drill instructors.

She blinked through bleary, crusted eyes and licked her chapped lips as she tried to piece together where she was. Her mouth tasted of ash and stale wine and there was a decidedly uncomfortable crick in her neck from the unforgiving cot beneath her.

She spied a waterskin with a handwritten note on it beside her and took a deep drink of the cool, refreshing beverage before she examined it.

Lady Lorraine,

I hope this water finds you rested. Considering the amount of wine you drank last night, you'll no doubt be grateful for it. See me before you leave, if you have time.
~Boric

The memories of the night before came rushing back, except a few erased by sweet red wine, as the water roused her fully from slumber. Setting the waterskin down, she sighed deeply. Talia did her best to ignore the well-deserved pounding between her ears and hung her head in frustration. She really was leaving, and from the light creeping in under the edges of the tent, she hadn't much time left at all.

Unwilling to waste her final moments moping, she stood and stretched. She'd slept in her armor, and her body was worse the wear for it, but being only twenty she retained the flexibility of her youth and knew she'd limber up soon enough.

"Duke Boric," she called out into the semi-darkness, unsure if her host was still asleep.

She received no answer, and decided that if he had indeed slept through the bugle then he likely needed the rest. More likely, she decided, he was already up and about tending to his duties around the camp.

She had very little to do to make herself ready to leave, since she'd scarcely had time to unpack anything in her own small tent. Still, she knew she'd better be prepared. She made her way through the breaking dawn to her tent, where her few bags had been supplemented by a pair of saddlebags she didn't recognize. Upon closer inspection, she found that they were filled with foodstuffs, minor medical supplies, and a host of other useful things she might need for her return to the Capitol.

That'll be Boric again, she reasoned with a smile, before hoisting the gear up and heading for the stables. She passed a pair of guards coming off shift who, upon seeing her arms full of gear, stopped short.

"Ma'am?" The leader, a short, stocky corporal, called out, "Would you like some help there?"

"No, no." She smiled around the baggage. "You two are headed to your beds, and deservedly so. I can manage."

They seemed loath to leave her without helping, but her insistent smile fended them off.

Talia made her way to the stables where her mount was being kept and set about preparing her horse for the journey home.

"It'll be strange for you, as well," she joked with the large gray mare. "Leaving your friends, too."

"I thought I might find you here," Boric announced from behind her just as she was finishing up. "I knew better than to think you'd have a stablehand readying your gear for you."

She grinned sheepishly.

"You know, Talia, they have a job to do as well. The stablehand is every bit as important as the cavalryman or the commander." He put a heavy hand on her shoulder and locked eyes with her. "We all have a role to play." His smile turned sad. "Though it might not be the role we wish. Do you understand?"

Something about his tone threatened her eyes with tears, but she fought back against them valiantly.

"Listen, Talia," he mulled over his words carefully. "You're not doing anything wrong, you hear me? You're not leaving your men behind, you're not abandoning them, and you're no less a leader or friend for returning to the Capitol."

Talia lost her battle at last and hung her head in shame as a pair of tears worked their way down her cheeks.

"It . . . it feels like I'm abandoning them, sir," she shook her head. "I should be with them. I should be looking out for them."

"Talia," he said firmly. "You didn't ask for this."

"I should say something to Annabelle," she countered. "Perhaps if I try again she would--"

"Talia, enough!"

She shut her mouth again, frustration boiling behind her sealed lips.

"Talia, you have before you a *sacred* duty."

"But, sir--"

"Talia, escorting a fallen sister to the Catacombs of the Sacred Martyrs is one of the oldest and most solemn traditions of our nation," his voice was low and earnest. "It is a tradition that dates back to the founding, and you do Sister Madrie Von Cleigh a *disservice* by downplaying the sacrifice she made."

Talia's spine stiffened, and she felt suddenly ashamed.

He was right, of course. Every initiate into the Sisterhood knew the importance of the Catacombs, the final resting place of every Sister who had died in the service of the Empire. It was a place more sacred than the throneroom of the Emperor and holier than any relic. The teachings of the church held that deep within the catacombs lay the first martyr, a person whose name had long ago been lost to myth and legend, who had laid down their life to save the Emperor's, and thus laid the very foundations of the Empire.

"You're right, sir." She took a shaky breath and held her head high once again. "I will do my duty."

"That is all we can do, Talia." He smiled back at her. "Now go, you'll have all the way back to the Capitol to dwell on your future. Live *this* moment in your present."

Talia fought the overwhelming urge to give the man a hug, and instead bowed her head respectfully.

"You honor me with your wisdom, my lord."

"Please," he scoffed. "Ask your father about my *wisdom* some day and he'll bend your ear for a fortnight with tales of our reckless youth. Make your peace with your friends before you leave, as I have no doubt Annabelle will have you swiftly on your way."

Talia bowed again, suppressing a mirror of Boric's infectious grin, and left him there holding her reins.

It took her a few minutes to find her friends, but circumstance conspired in her favor, and she met the three of them exiting a dining tent in a group.

"Talia," Arcus smiled, flagging her down. "We feared we had missed your departure."

He let out a huff of air as she wrapped him in a bear hug, then patted her back with a smile.

"I'll miss you too, Talia." He smiled. "But you act like we'll never see each other again. You'll be back to us soon, of that I have no doubt."

"I wish I held your certainty," she shook her head, turning to Elbaf and giving him an equally big hug. "If the Emperor wills it, I will be grateful to see you again soon."

She pulled back and turned to Darko, who grinned and tried in vain to fend off her embrace.

"Yes, *all* of you, old man." She held him tightly for a moment and laughed as she released him. "Even your stuffy sarcasm and that little bird of yours."

She winked slyly at the small shadowed form hidden in his hood and would *swear* she saw a pair of eyes gleam pink with delight.

"You are prepared to depart, I *presume*?" Annabelle's voice cut through the moment like a dagger made of ice. "Since you are . . . frolicking about?"

Talia felt her shoulders tighten like a bowstring and resisted the urge to let slip the first harsh words to cross her mind.

"Yes, ma'am," she managed through gritted teeth. "I am ready to depart as soon as Mater Von Cliegh's procession is prepared--"

"It is prepared, Captain," Anmnabelle interrupted with poorly concealed glee. "They await you at the southern gate."

Talia tensed up, her irritation growing in proportion to Annabelle's apparent pleasure at her departure. Her superior officer sat astride her signature warhorse, a jet-black beast of nearly impossible size, and therefore towered over them.

Rather than offer a verbal retort, Talia gave Annabelle a salute that would meet every textbook requirement, but which fairly dripped with disdain. Annabelle's face turned sour, but Talia knew she could find no fault with her, and so her own joy rebounded by some small measure.

"Go report to the gate," she hissed. "It is unprofessional to have those soldiers waiting on you--"

"Not to worry," Boric's booming voice carried over the group as he appeared with Talia's horse in tow. "I've got your horse *Lady Lorraine*. And we'll escort you to the gate, of course."

"That won't be--"

"My dear Major," Boric forced a laugh. "Of course I know *you'll* be escorting her, as would any commanding officer of worth, but I must insist we come as well. It would only be fitting to watch a friend depart."

Annabelle smiled in a manner that could curdle milk, and nodded in deference to the Duke.

"But of course, my lord." She turned her gaze to Elbaf, Arcus, and Darko. "You three will report to me immediately following her departure. You have new assignments."

"It is hard to believe you have time to manage your holdings, Lady Montagne," Boric noted dryly. "Given how *busy* you keep yourself tending to your soldiers, that is."

"I manage, my lord." Annabelle gave another funny little bow from the back of her horse. "I regret I will not be able to see off Soror Talia, as I have urgent matters to discuss with the Sisters here before we move on."

With that she cantered off, much to the relief of the group she left behind.

"What did you mean, sir?" Arcus chimed in. "What holdings does Annabelle tend?"

"She comes from nobility, as well," he explained. "The Montagnes, like the MacMordains or the Lorraines, are among the ancient Noble Houses."

"But why should she be tasked with caring for those states unless--"

"You have the right of it, ranger," Boric nodded. "She is the sole bearer of the name Montagne."

"They bear a curse," Talia interrupted darkly. "A curse centuries old, or so my father told me."

"Curse?" Elbaf's ears pricked up. "What kind of curse?"

"A terrible one," Darko surprised the group by chiming in. "I read about it, years ago. News of it makes the rounds about once every human generation and, when I was quite young, it swept through the Empire and captured my interest."

Talia watched as Elbaf and Arcus stared in rapt attention to the elf, and she wondered if she, too, would learn something from the much older man.

"Every generation there is a born but a single child to House Montagne," he began, "and always a girl. That girl is, without exception, called to join the Sisterhood--"

"To atone for some ancient, unknowable sin," Talia pointed out, drawing a glare from the wizard.

"Ahem." The wizard quirked up an eyebrow. "The girl joins the Sisterhood and generally makes a fair name for herself before she meets and falls in love with a man. They are happy, for a time, and perhaps they even believe they may be the ones to break the curse. But then, tragedy strikes. As soon as the couple finds out they are with child, the man's days are numbered. Lord Montagne is dead within six months, and the lady, perhaps grief-stricken, does not survive childbirth. The child, a daughter, survives. She is raised by the staff, the estate, or a steward, and the cycle continues."

Arcus let loose a low whistle.

"No wonder she's so . . . *cold*."

"Some of the Montagne women attempt to alter the course of events, of course," Darko mused aloud. "They'll swear not to fall in love, only to fall head over heels for a man out of the blue. Some have taken many lovers in an attempt to have more than one child, but they never bear children until they find themselves smitten. A few of them, in times before I was alive, were rumored to seek out mystics and soothsayers. But one thing unites them - they are always searching for a way to end the curse."

The group quieted as the elf finished speaking, and Talia found herself reluctantly admitting that perhaps *some* of Annabelle's icy demeanor could be chalked up to the horrible burden of the curse. Even so, she could not fully forgive the woman's relentlessly cruel attitude.

"Let us dwell on happier things," she said as cheerfully as she could muster. "I would not depart amidst bitterness, if I could have my way."

She followed her words by stepping off brightly to the south, her horse in tow. The rest of the group followed, and by the time they reached the edge of the camp they were laughing again, reliving the brighter moments of their journey so far. As the southern gate loomed large in front of them, they found themselves at a loss for words, and Talia wished she could muster words as wise as Boric's.

There waited a trio of wagons and an honor guard of twenty cavaliers, all arranged and ready to depart at a moment's notice. The leader, a lieutenant in brightly gleaming armor, saluted the Duke as the group approached

"At ease, men," the aging warrior called out. "You depart at Lady Lorraine's command. And let me not hear of a single hair on her head coming to harm, or you'll have my wrath to answer to."

"Talia," he said in lower tones for just the group to hear. "I have selected these men specifically; they will see you safely to the Capitol, my dear. Go with the Emperor's blessings."

He gave her a warm smile and then walked over to talk to the men, leaving Talia and her fellow officers some privacy.

"My friends," she announced. "I will not say goodbye, because I leave a part of myself with you. In so much as I walk in the Emperor's favor, I hope his blessings protect you and see us together again on some not-too-distant day."

"Well said," Arcus smiled, opening his arms for another hug. "May your journey be swift and blessed with fair weather and easy roads."

Talia could swear the sun shone brighter and the breeze warmer with his words, and she marveled for a moment that perhaps she'd never truly appreciated his powers.

The second she let go of Arcus, she was wrapped in a mighty bear hug as Ebaf unexpectedly lifted her from the ground.

"You stay safe, Talia," he said, a roughness to his voice she hadn't heard before. "Promise me, little sister."

"I promise, brother."

She returned his hug with a desperate fierceness as he placed her back on the ground amidst stares of surprise from the group.

Talia lingered a moment more, and then at last took to her saddle. She caught the eye of the lieutenant, and with a nod of her head the column began to move out, Madrie's wagon in the center, draped with the ceremonial silver cords and black velvet of mourning.

She considered looking back as she passed through the gate, but chose to treasure the smiles of the past few minutes, rather than face the sadness in her friends' eyes. Instead, head held high, she trotted to the head of the column and began the slow journey eastward towards Sunset Isle.

Towards home.

Chapter Twenty

"You're engineering a *massacre*, Major," Boric roared, slamming his fists down on the table in the center of the command tent, sending charcoal sticks, maps, and small tactical markers flying.

"The Brazen Hawks are *mine* to command, Duke Boric," Annabelle retorted coldly. "And it is our duty to seek out traitors to the realm."

Darko stood quietly, as he and his two companions had been doing for the past several minutes, while the two raged back and forth. It didn't really matter if he had a different idea; both of the two commanders in front of him were beyond reason. What had started out as a briefing by Annabelle to inform them of their next mission had descended rapidly into a shouting match over her choice of tactics.

"The Brazen Hawks may be yours to command," Boric pointed a finger in her face, "but you'll be hard pressed to clear the walls with light infantry. And if you think you'll have the backing of the seventh, you're out of your mind."

"I am a *Hand of the Emperor*," Annabelle screamed, finally fully losing control. "And your men are mine to command if I see fit!"

"You'll find that that badge on your chest means precious little should you try to turn my men against me, *Major*," Boric dropped his tone to a low, icy threat.

"I could have your--"

"You could try, certainly," Boric interrupted. "But know this, you are *far* from the only Hand I know, and I assure you a confrontation would not go the way you seem to expect."

"Begging both of your pardons," Darko chimed in at last, drawing looks of alarm from Elbaf and Arcus beside him. "But perhaps a compromise could be found."

"Go on," Annabelle hissed.

"Elbaf, Arcus, and I could take some of our men ahead. We could . . . assess the situation and see if a diplomatic solution exists," he offered. "Then, your forces combined could follow the trail we blaze. Should negotiations fail, you will be able to take the appropriate actions in Kent to bring it back under Imperial control."

The wizard watched as the Duke and Annabelle locked eyes once again, both clearly evaluating the solution and both unwilling to weigh in on it first. Tensions mounted until Annabelle at last relented and, with an expression that left little doubt as to her displeasure, gave a curt nod of agreement.

"You'll have a two-day head start, lieutenant," she warned him. "Seek out your *diplomatic solution*, if you wish. But when we arrive, anyone who has strayed from the light of the Emperor will be dealt with accordingly." She then turned on her heel and stalked out of the tent without bothering to wait for a reply.

"I'll be hearing about that, I'm sure," Boric sighed, rubbing his temples. "She is worse than her mother was, and that's saying something."

"You knew her mother?" Arcus noted with surprise.

"I did," he nodded. "I was twenty-two when Annabelle was born, and I had the dubious privilege of working with the late Lady Montagne until shortly before her death. She was every bit the coldhearted witch that her daughter is. Hell, their family is half the reason I avoid this area of the Empire."

"What do you mean?" Elbaf prompted.

"The ancestral seat of House Montagne is up here, a few days' ride to the east."

Darko filed that information away in his mind, should the need to recall it arise.

"Of course," Boric chuckled darkly, "it doesn't help that she's the spitting image of her mother, either."

"Forty-eight hours is hardly enough time to negotiate peace," Arcus rolled his shoulders, changing the subject back to the matter at hand. "We'd better head out and hope the situation is more under control than we've been led to believe."

"You're right," Boric nodded. "And I'm sorry if I have caused you greater hardship. There's precious little she can do to me, but she may well take out her frustrations on the three of you. For that you have my genuine apology."

"No apology necessary, my lord," Darko soothed.

"Still, I may yet regret my temper," Boric sighed. "She does have the legal right to requisition my forces for legitimate cause, and I'll be hard-pressed to stonewall her bureaucratically if it turns out that Kent has truly seceded from the Empire."

"But your men?" Arcus asked. "Would they follow her if . . . if it came to a confrontation?"

"Not a chance." His lips drew a thin, prideful line and his chin lifted as he spoke. "These men and I have bled together; we are a family born of battle. They would not betray me."

"That they would face the gallows for you is impressive," Darko nodded. "But I fear they would face it all the same should you refuse to aid Annabelle in her assault on the city."

"Sadly, you might be right," Boric nodded darkly. "I cannot risk a sundering of the Empire, and I will not shed Imperial blood and sacrifice the lives of my men to satisfy a decades-old feud."

They were quiet a moment longer before Boric sat down in one of the few chairs that was not knocked over.

"We're wasting time," Elbaf prompted suddenly with his characteristic gruffness.

Darko watched as the warrior shook his head softly, his eyes still glued to the map on the table.

"Annabelle will not delay, neither should we," he added with a note of finality.

"Elbaf's right," Boric let out a heavy sigh. "You'd best be off."

With no clear line of succession, there was a moment's pause while the trio looked at each other and tried to read one another's stance, but it was Elbaf who broke the moment.

"I will notify our men," he said. "You two make yourselves ready and we will meet at the North Gate in half an hour. Two candle marks ought to be plenty of time to depart with so small a force."

Funny, I thought Arcus might take charge, Master.

Darko did not voice his agreement, but he was certain Reia could feel it nonetheless. He had no desire for the spotlight of leadership, and in truth, both of his companions would make capable leaders. Instead, he nodded with deference to the half-orc and exited the tent. While thirty minutes may be enough time for the soldiers they traveled with, he had considerably more delicate items to pack and would need every second if he were to be ready in time.

Elbaf surveyed the assembled men. As he looked out over the small band, he saw there also the faces of the fallen in the back of his mind. Their specters haunted him, reminding him of his failures as a leader.

"We're going to Kent."

His voice carried easily over the handful of soldiers before him. There were less than a dozen now who had been with them from the beginning.

"Word is that the city is in revolt, and it's up to us to bring them back to the fold," he said firmly. "If we fail, every man and woman in the city will be put to the sword as traitors."

Looks of concern and disbelief crossed the faces of the assembled men, but they kept their composure.

"I would not have their blood on my hands," Elbaf frowned.

As Elbaf spoke, Arcus and Darko approached from the rear of the formation with their loaded mounts ready to go.

"Captain Lorraine has been reassigned," he continued. "I'm sure you've heard as much already."

Grim looks filled the crowd.

"I am not the leader she was, and I will not try to be." He saw no objections in the eyes of his men and took heart. "I will tell you plainly what I know, and I expect you to do the same. We will carry on as we always have, accomplish our mission, and conduct ourselves as soldiers of the Empire should."

Elbaf ignored the beaming smile he was receiving from Arcus, feeling much more comfortable with the politely attentive stare he got from Darko.

"Questions?"

He waited a beat, but no one spoke.

"Good," he nodded. "Move out."

The column of weary horsemen headed out single file, the dark circles not yet faded from beneath their eyes, but their bearing proud.

Elbaf waited on the side while the troops passed, making sure to meet each man's gaze and give them a nod of encouragement as they passed the gate. Arcus and Darko brought up the rear, and he fell in step between them.

"Well now," Arcus ribbed him gently. "Who knew?"

"Arcus," Elbaf frowned. "Don't start."

"Elbaf the *orator*," Arcus shook his head softly. "Truly, the *people's* General. A soldier's soldier. A leader of peerless--"

Elbaf glared at his friend, halting him mid-sentence.

"Come now, brother," the ranger prodded. "In all truth, your words were well spoken. They deserve praise."

"I . . . concur," Darko chimed in. "I believe your words had an impact, and your leadership filled the void of Talia's absence well."

At the mention of Talia's leaving they again fell quiet, and as the low din of the camp faded behind them, they were left only with the slow, determined hoofbeats of their troops.

The rain started some three hours into their journey, and the downpour swept away any shred of cheer from the group. Elbaf and Darko had taken up residence in the heart of the column, while Arcus forged ahead of the men by a few hundred feet.

The land here consisted of low, rocky hills for the most part, so they would sometimes go several minutes without seeing the ranger through the gloom, only to have him reappear from the east or west with news of an easier path or a copse of trees to rest beneath.

It was past mid-day, and Elbaf was just starting to wonder at his absence after a particularly long period, when he saw the familiar form of the ranger crest a ridge ahead. He was unsurprised to see Kodja's stark white form padding alongside the ranger's horse and was reminded just how *big* the animal was, nearly the size of a small pony. The pair gave a wave and a long, high whistle, indicating to the column they should make their way over. Elbaf waved back, acknowledging to the pair that their signal had been received and brought his horse to a trot to take the lead.

He topped a hill halfway to Arcus and saw what the druid's reason for pausing must be - a wide, fast moving river crossed the path ahead of them. The rains had swollen the normally calm water and it had jumped its banks on either side.

"Is there a bridge?"

"There was," Arcus frowned. "What's left of it sits just over there."

Elbaf followed the druid's pointing finger to a curve in the path, where it circled behind a rocky outcropping and disappeared out of sight.

"It's been destroyed," the druid said, confirming Elbaf's fears. "I'd wager the folks in Kent did it to cut short an Imperial response."

A few minutes later the group was all assembled beside the wreckage of what had once been a sturdy bridge of felled logs and stone pilings.

"Now what?" Cormorant mused aloud, drawing a look of irritation from Elbaf.

"It's too wide and too deep to ford," Arcus submitted. "Even if our mounts kept their footing, we'd be begging the waters to claim a life or two."

"Darko?" Elbaf asked. "Can your magic help us across?"

"Not with the horses," the wizard replied with a frown. "There's every chance they would panic and bolt."

"Hold on," Arcus said, taking the others by surprise. "Give me a moment."

Arcus was nervous, he'd be tipping his hand if he wasn't careful. He hadn't worked any but the most basic of magics since he was freed of his bindings by Lilliana, but his powers were returning to him and his bond with the natural order had been restored. He could feel the power of the planet returning to his heart and the magic of nature flowing unhindered through his veins once again.

He could not risk his freedom being discovered, but with only their trusted few men present, he felt confident he could make a brief exception to remove the obstacle they currently faced.

The ranger slipped from his saddle to stand beside the river. He closed his eyes and took a deep breath of the heady, stormy air. He could hear in the far distance the rumble of thunder, and the beating of the rain all around him spoke to his soul.

Arcus stepped forward to the very edge of the stream and took a knee, placing his hands below the surface and burying his fingers in the mud below. Immediately he felt a cool, icy magnetism from the river. It called to him, and he felt the power in its flow. The river was a channel of energy, carrying the power of the storm down through the plains.

He expanded his consciousness, feeling his way along the bottom of the river, over flooded grasses and through swirls of debris and flotsam. He'd hoped to sense the presence of the logs that had once spanned the river, but the floodwaters must have drawn them downstream.

"Make ready to cross," he said aloud, his voice strong but distant. "We will not have much time."

He was vaguely aware of movement behind him, and he could sense the others climbing back into the saddles of their nervous mounts and standing ready.

Digging deep within himself, he summoned his will and tightened his grip on the mud in his hands. As he did so he opened his eyes, turning his gaze to the space between the half-submerged stone bases that had once held the bridge.

He felt the strength in the earth, the unimaginable power and the incredible, silent, stillness of it. Sweat beaded on his brow, mixing with the rainwater as he coaxed the ground to hear his call. He heard soft gasps of surprise as his arms began to darken, the skin slowly turning a deep brown as his energy mixed with that of the ground below them. His veins ran dark under his skin, and motes of dark browns and grays began to radiate from his still-kneeling form.

Slowly, steadily, nature began to respond.

The bottom of the river began to twist and move, disturbing the surface and kicking up silt. A murmur ran through the group as dirt and mud began to push upwards at either end of the missing bridge. The mounds of dirt grew and grew until they were large piles, taller than the mounted men observing them.

Arcus slowed his breathing and began to push his hands together beneath the muddy water. The dirt responded, and from either side of the river the ground reached out until it linked the middle with a crackling thud. The dirt smoothed itself out, becoming flatter and wider until it was unmistakably a bridge.

"Go," Arcus managed through gritted teeth. "Quickly now."

Fortunately, the earthen crossing was wide enough for two horsemen abreast, and the group was swiftly across. Kodja lingered a moment beside Arcus, but the druid shook his head insistently.

"You, too, little brother," he grunted.

The wolf cocked its head to one side briefly, but did as he was told and was on the other side of the bridge a few moments later.

The effort of holding the bridge together would have been tremendous even without the downpour. With the added weight of the rainwater, and its efforts to erode his creation, Arcus was quickly tiring.

"Come on, Arcus," Elbaf called out over the roaring waters. "It's only you now."

Arcus took one last deep breath and gauged the distance he would have to travel. He tensed his body like a bowstring, knowing he would really only have one chance.

With a sudden heave, he pulled his arms loose from the ground and sprinted towards the bridge. Instantly the discoloration in his skin drained and the motes of energy flickered in and out before dissipating entirely. Chunks of rain-soaked dirt began to break off of the bridge almost immediately, and it started to crumble before his very eyes.

By the time his feet hit the surface of the bridge, it was smaller by half, and by the time he reached the midpoint it was barely wider than his shoulders. He was still almost ten feet from the end when he felt the ground beneath him start to give way. He summoned all of the strength he had and dove for the far bank. The bridge broke apart behind him, tumbling in great ragged clumps into the surging waters just as he hit the ground beside the river in a clumsy roll.

He rolled to a stop on the flat of his back and relished the cool rain on his tense muscles. He felt like he'd just run a mile, and yet there was an undeniable high as well. His blood was pounding - he felt ten feet tall and deeply, utterly connected to the moment and to the world around him.

Arcus couldn't contain himself. He laughed out loud, bringing on looks ranging from concern to confusion from his friends, as he sat up.

"Oh, come on now." The ranger smiled widely, gesturing at the river behind them. "What an adventure life is, no?"

"If you say so." Elbaf cracked a grin as he held out a hand to pull the ranger up from the muck.

Something has . . . changed with him, Master.

Curious.

Do you disagree, Master?

Darko was uncertain, a state of mind he absolutely despised in himself. He thought back to his previous interactions with Arcus and could not avoid the obvious conclusion - either something *had* indeed changed in his friend, and with no clear explanation, or he had inexplicably been holding back throughout their journey.

I'm not sure yet . . .

The wizard was so deep in thought that it took the prompting of one of their soldiers, Corporal Rennault, to pull him from his reverie as the column began to move out once again.

"Sir?"

Darko shook his head and realized they were the last two to get moving. He nodded his grateful thanks and was taken aback by the warmth of the man's returned smile. Something in his expression must have called for reassurance, because Rennault spoke again as they started moving.

"S'alright, sir," the man chuckled. "I find myself lost in thought every once in a while too."

Darko searched the man's words for sarcasm, but found only genuine humor. They trotted after the others to catch up, a maneuver that he would have desperately struggled with a year ago, and he contemplated the ways in which they'd *all* changed.

Upon catching the others, Darko thanked the soldier once again for rousing him and headed to the front of the column as the other man took up his post at the rear.

On this side of the river, the rocks grew more plentiful and the hills turned more to bluffs. The party found themselves traveling through shallow gullies in single file with trickling streams of water underfoot and scrub brush to either side.

"Arcus," he called out as he neared the ranger. "I would--"

The ranger raised a hand for silence and cocked his head to the side a moment, cutting the mage off mid-sentence. By now accustomed to the ranger's cautionary ways, he shut his mouth and slowed his horse, pulling up beside the other man.

Darko strained his ears, but the rainfall and the sounds of hooves scrabbling over gravel and river-rock was too muddled, and his senses revealed nothing untoward.

The moment stretched into eternity, and still Arcus' hand was raised in alarm. Darko could see the tension in his friend's shoulders, and on instinct he began to harness the energies within, just in case. He took a deep breath, filling his lungs with air as the nerves in his fingers began to tingle with the electric energy of his magic. It took more concentration and greater effort, but he kept the usually colorful display of the protective magic he worked to a minimum, and only the keenest of eyes would be able to pick out the shimmering field around his clenched fists, or the way the rain seemed to drip off his hands without touching them.

When the attack came, there was only a fraction of a second to react. Darko's inhumanly sensitive ears picked up three stray sounds in quick succession - the light scuff of a wet boot over a loose stone, a soft grunt, and a whisper-silent whistle.

"Ambush!" Arcus shouted, shattering the calm air and twisting around to pull his longbow from his back.

Time seemed to slow for Darko who saw with sudden clarity the figures of a dozen men appear on the crest at the top of the gully above them. The men, dressed in a ragtag combination of leathers and make-shift armor, burst from the bushes amid a volley of javelins and shortspears, which were even now arching down towards the party in a deadly wave.

Darko's training kicked in, and he flung one of his hands forward, stretching his fingers out toward Arcus and projecting his power in a sudden burst of violently blue radiance. The light, which sprung forth in a thousand tiny strands, wove itself into a complex and ever-tightening lattice of electric, humming lines of energy.

By the time it reached Arcus, the shield was a circle roughly three feet across.

The shield slipped into place just as the hardened iron point of a broad hunting javelin impacted it, showering white-hot sparks as the tip glanced off and ricocheted down and to the left, where it found a home in the flank of Arcus' mount and sent the horse to the ground. An arrow swiftly ended the horse's suffering, catching the noble creature between the ribs and only narrowly missing the ranger's leg.

Darko had to take his eyes off his friend as he lifted his other hand, haphazardly emitting a shield for himself as best he could. He deflected two spears with his own shield, silently cursing the limitations of his powers amid the screams of injured horses and the grunts of his companions as projectiles struck true all around him.

Worse yet, a tremble in the ground revealed an additional complication. The ambushers above were well prepared, and the whole edge of the ridge gave way as they triggered a broad, tumbling rock slide.

Darko pulled his shields together and poured energy into them, barely expanding it enough to deflect the rocks rolling towards them. He managed to cover their small group from all but a shower of smaller stones and rubble, but the gully was a wreck in both directions.

They were trapped.

Darko's temper flared, and with a savage twist of his hand, the shield he projected spiraled together into a crackling blue cord of energy that blazed with white hot sparks. He summoned the powers within himself, and his eyes glazed over with a deep swirling purple. The smell of ozone pervaded the air as the hair on the wizard's head and arms started to raise. The tangled braid of raw power in his hand coiled and wrapped around itself like an injured viper, twisting around his hand in a mesmerizing swirl as he scanned the ridgeline.

One of the attackers peeked over the ridge, exposing himself for a moment as he leveled a javelin at one of the soldiers below.

Darko's hand shot forth and the writhing cord burst outward like a lighting bolt, zigzagging through the intervening space before impacting the man square in his chest. Electricity crackled and the man immediately started to convulse, his skin smoking and crackling as the energy tore its way through him.

The cord left Darko's hand completely, drawing itself up into the warrior above before branching out in great arcs that, judging by the screams of agony over the ridge, were finding their homes in other members of the ambush.

"We're too exposed," Elbaf shouted from the middle of the column. "But we'll never clear those rocks on horseback."

The half-orc leapt from his saddle, gesturing to the others to do the same.

"Dismount, shields up," he cried out. "Form a shield wall!"

"Julias," he grabbed the shoulder of the nearest man. "Lead them back over the rock slide, I'll be right behind you with the others."

Elbaf scrambled past Darko, headed towards Arcus who he was struggling to pull himself free of his mount.

"Can you move?" the half-orc called out as he sprinted across the broken ground.

"No," Arcus shouted back, grunting under the horse's weight. "My leg is caught."

Darko cast a glance at his friend and was taken aback to see the ranger's eyes glaze over with a reddish brown haze. Though the air in the gully was still, the man's hair moved as if he was in a breeze. The raindrops that hit his body and his armor defied all logic, streaking off of him as mud instead of water, and the ground had risen up around him in a small mound surrounding him and his fallen mount. Power radiated from the man in great trembling waves that Darko could feel through the ground under his own mount, and he recognized the tell-tale rumbling treble of transmutative magic.

Darko was unsure what the ranger's plan was, but he agreed wholeheartedly with Elbaf - they were far too exposed in this gully. He also knew that Arcus could not move in his current state and that trying to move him could result in the disastrous unraveling of the spell he was working. He didn't know how long the ranger needed, but he knitted his brow and decided to attempt to buy him time.

The elf clapped his hands together and sparks of fire emitted from his palms, blasting outwards like the slag from a blacksmith's hammer. He took a deep breath, holding his hands together and drawing power in through his lungs and diaphragm. As he filled his chest with air, the fire between his palms blazed brighter, and it waned slightly as he breathed back out. He took a second breath and then a third, filling breath; each time the fire blazed as if stoked by mighty bellows.

When his chained lightning spell finally ended, and the first brave fools poked their heads over the ridge, Darko was ready. Between his hands he held a brightly blazing inferno, so hot that the raindrops in the air around him sizzled. He saw his enemy dare to breast the ridgeline and raised his palms overhead. He took one final breath and blew it out, hard, between his palms. His breath blossomed upwards in a massive cloud of flames. The fires spread as they rose, and by the time they reached the ridge above they were a towering wave twenty feet across. The rocks blackened and cracked under the onslaught, and the men were driven back once again.

A great rumbling filled the air, and Darko turned to see that the ranger beside him had finally moved. His arms were outstretched, reaching back down the gully where their men were struggling to overcome the rockslide while under a constant hail of arrows and spears. Darko gasped as the rocks and stones sanks into the earth before his eyes, clearing the path for their men at last. At the same time, earth from the walls of the gully projected outward in a jagged shelf, covering the men below from sight and danger.

"There are more down the ridge," Arcus gasped as Elbaf arrived at his side. "I can feel them, thirty or more."

"Easy, brother," Elbaf grunted, gripping the druid's saddle straps with both hands and straining to lift the dead weight of the horse. "We'll get you out of there."

He groaned with effort, and the horse's belly lifted under his straining muscles. A moment more and Arcus was able to pull himself free. Elbaf dropped the horse with a thud and offered his shoulder to Arcus even as a white-fletched arrow ricocheted off his pauldron.

"Can you walk?"

Arcus put weight on his leg and nearly collapsed.

"It's no good," Arcus shook his head. "I don't think it's broken, but I can't move quickly."

Arcus judged the distance between where he was, leaning heavily against Elbaf, and the shelter of the overhang he'd created for their men. The 70 feet separating them was a yawning maw of open ground and the people above were growing bolder once again. Options slipped away before his eyes until he was left with only a single, inevitable conclusion.

The druid glanced down at his chest where the seven-star lily was still pinned, seemingly impervious to the dirt, the water, and the chaos around them. With trembling hands, he reached upward and grasped a single, milky petal between rain-slick fingers. It offered only a whisper of resistance as he plucked it from the base, and the world around him descended into an instant and abiding silence.

A split second later and the silence was drowned in a deafening tsunami of rain and rushing winds. In the space of a few heartbeats, the rain clouds overhead became a swirling cyclone. Hurricane force winds whipped raindrops like tiny stones and the ground trembled underfoot, driving everyone to their hands and knees.

The funnel cloud above lengthened, driving downward like some steely gray serpent. The cloud drew nearer, and there could be no mistaking that it would engulf Arcus and his companion. Helpless to move, pelted by the stinging rain and held motionless by the roiling earth, Arcus held his breath as the cloud descended over him. Against his will, he closed his eyes, unable to force them open in the elemental onslaught of the storm.

Then, suddenly, all was calm.

Blinking back tears from his watery eyes, he opened them at last to see Lilliana standing before him. She was every bit as magnificent as he remembered. She stood with her cloak cast open, her arms wide, and a stern, disapproving look upon her angelic features.

"Groveborn," she spoke in a light, clear voice like a birdsong. "Rise."

The woman extended her hand, and Arcus accepted. She pulled him easily from the mire, and the ranger realized the rain had stopped altogether. He stared in awe at the sky. Where they stood, and for a few hundred feet in every direction, the skies were clear and the sun shone brightly. They were an island amidst the endless gray skies that had been their constant companions throughout the day.

"You summoned me?" She quirked an eyebrow in a manner that was both charming and regal. "Why?"

"To avoid further bloodshed," Arcus resisted the urge to bow to her. "And to save my friends."

She broke into a soft, genuine smile.

"A *good* reason then." Her eyes twinkled. "I'm glad."

Lilliana closed her eyes and took a deep breath, then slowly let it out. When she opened her eyes again, Arcus was surprised to see them replaced by deep pools of amber flecked with traces of gold, brown, and the deepest black.

Liliana raised her hands softly, effortlessly, and as she did the entire floor of the gully they stood upon rose up like the crest of a wave. Arcus, Elbaf, and all of their companions rose with the swelling ground until it merged seamlessly with the cliffs that had been above them. They stood now on a flat plain, as though all memory of the ravine they had been trapped in was erased completely.

Arcus could see now the damage that Darko's spells had wrought, and nearly a dozen of their attackers lay slain and strewn about the wet grass. Still, there remained a sizable force to oppose them. The thirty or so fighters that faced them were pale as sheets, cowering behind their makeshift armor and clapboard shields at the raw power Lilliana so casually displayed.

They stared at one another in silence, twenty feet separating Arcus and his Imperial companions and these rag-tag warriors who had so clearly held the upper hand, but who were now hilariously ill-prepared to defend themselves.

"Stand down men," a leader spoke as he emerged from the clump of cowering men. "We've no fight to win here."

Arcus narrowed his eyes, taking in the man's fiery orange hair and beard and the soldierly bearing about him. His armor fit well, his shield was steel, and the blade in his hand carried with a practice ease until he tossed it on the ground in front of himself.

"We surrender," he sighed, his head hanging low. "These men are faultless. They followed my orders and mine alone. I will answer for my treason."

A rumble of dissent flowed through the crowd and was just as quickly silenced by a sharp cutting motion from the leader's hand.

"You," Elbaf called out. "You're in charge of these men?"

"I am Kirrel Forthnin." The man raised his chin defiantly. "Commander of the garrison of the Free City of Kent."

"And you are a fool," Darko muttered next to the ranger, "to think you can withstand the hammer's blow that is coming for you."

"Easy, now," Arcus mumbled back, knowing the elf could hear him. "Perhaps they'll be willing to--"

"Speak with me in private," Elbaf hollered out, his gruff bass cutting the clear air like a blade.

"What would--"

But Elbaf was already walking away, confident that the man would follow. He did, to Arcus' surprise, and the two were swiftly deep in conversation. He wished desperately to join his friend, to know what the two grizzled warriors were saying, but he did not want to intrude on the delicate peace.

"I cannot stay, Groveborn."

Arcus flinched at the unexpected voice inside his head, and turned to Lilliana in alarm.

"Yes, child, it is I," the voice announced within his mind.

The woman made no movement, and to all appearances she, too, had turned her attention to the two fighters. But her voice was clear and rich within his mind, and the twinkle in her eyes confirmed it was no trick. He turned his gaze back to Elbaf and Kirrell, but his mind was focused entirely on the lady at his side.

"Can you . . . hear me?"

"I can," she managed to convey laughter tinged with sadness. *"And I am sorry, Arcus. My attentions are called elsewhere, and the need is pressing."*

"What do you mean? I--"

"So much hangs in the balance now, Arcus," she interrupted his train of thought. *"I cannot stay and I cannot explain, though I wish dearly that I could. Instead, you must trust that the threads of fate are pulling you northward for a reason. Follow the light of the Sun, as you have already done, and you will find those who can help you."*

"When will I see you again?"

"Soon. But first, this business with Kent. You must see it swiftly done, or else be left helplessly complicit in their destruction."

He turned again to face Lilliana, and was surprised to see that she'd disappeared. He glanced around, looking for any trace of her, but the only sign of her presence was a tuft of wildflowers that seemed to have sprouted beside him.

"What are you doing?" Darko asked, nudging him. "You've done your part, now just stand still."

"Where did she go?" he hissed back. "Did you see her leave?"

"See *who* leave?" the mage whispered. "Who are you talking about?"

"*Her*. She. Lilliana. By the gods, the woman that just reshaped that entire ravine, you dolt," Arcus huffed in disbelief under his breath. "How did--"

"You mean, *you* didn't do that?"

"W-what?" Arcus sputtered. "I appreciate the vote of confidence, but no, I- I *couldn't* have done that."

Chapter Twenty-One

"You're not executing me?" Kirrel asked, disbelief written across his features. "Is this some kind of trick?"

"No trick," Elbaf shook his head.

"Then . . . what is it you want from us?"

"My men need medical attention," Elbaf looked back over his shoulder at his assembled soldiers.

No one, save a few horses, had sustained a life-threatening injury in the bombardment, but many a body was battered, bruised, and bleeding from falling projectiles.

"And you'll take me to your leader back in Kent," the half-orc growled.

"Ah, then you mean to execute the Governor, Findral." The warrior shook his head. "I cannot betray him--"

Elbaf's flat stare silenced the man.

"I do not mean to execute anyone," he sighed. "I would save your lives, if I can."

"Even after we ambushed you and your men?"

"Especially after." Elbaf's gravelly words hit home. "You fight for what you believe in. A warrior should aspire to such honorable conduct."

He looked again at his weary men, and measured them against the tattered ragamuffins they faced.

"These people are not warriors," he gestured broadly. "They're civilians. Unless you want them, and the rest of Kent, to be slaughtered like livestock then we must speak with this *Findral* and negotiate a peace."

It was hard to tell who was more surprised by the tentative ceasefire, Kirrel or his men. For their part, Elbaf's retinue took his unorthodox decision in stride. The most severely injured, those sporting broken limbs or deep gashes and puncture wounds, were given preference on the few remaining horses while the rest of the group walked.

More than an hour passed before the groups were comfortable enough together for conversations to spring up, but eventually the ice broke. Their pace was quick, but fell short of a forced march. Even so, the civilians' energy lagged behind the sturdy discipline of the professional soldiers who accompanied them.

"This is taking too long," Arcus offered unprompted. "We'll have no time at all to come to terms."

"It'll be fine," Elbaf replied, doubting his own words and estimating the waning daylight on the horizon.

"Surprisingly, I'm with the ranger on this," Darko chimed in. "There's got to be a better way . . . Perhaps we could ride ahead with Kirrel and--"

"Enough," Elbaf snapped. "The weight of command was not a burden I took with pleasure, and if you want it, then have it. Otherwise, we stay together, and that's the end of it."

Darko and Arcus exchanged looks beside him, both chafing at his rebuke.

"Well?"

Arcus shook his head and sighed, but said nothing.

Elbaf turned to Darko's still-silent form.

"Magician? Shall we turn to you for guidance, then?" he asked.

"No, Elbaf," Darko relented. "You're right, it would be unwise to split our dwindling forces further."

Elbaf gave a nod and adjusted the gear on his back.

The men had become something of pack animals in the wake of most of the horses being killed in the gully behind them. Still, they'd had to leave behind plenty of supplies. Thankfully, the villagers that Kirrel had cobbled together into warriors were willing to help.

Elbaf was surprised at Kirrel and grateful that the man seemed as eager to avoid bloodshed as he was. He suspected, however, that as the battlefield was traded for a negotiating table they were still likely to find themselves on opposite sides of a sword blade.

"You seem troubled," Kirrel stated through labored breaths some time later. "A strange sight from the man who bested us."

"I did not *best* you," Elbaf shrugged. "My companions wield magics I do not understand. I cannot take credit for their power."

"Hmm," Kirrel raised his eyebrows. "And humble enough not to claim the glory of your men? You surprise me again."

Elbaf said nothing, and the friendly smile faded slowly from the lips of the man beside him.

"Don't mind him," Arcus huffed from Kirrel's other side. "He's like that with all of us."

Elbaf snorted and resisted the temptation to grin.

"And you, ranger," Kirrel looked him over with a careful gaze. "I daresay you're of the Tundras to the east, are you not?"

"I am," Arcus noted with a small nod and a broad smile. "Well spotted, sir."

"We've had dealings with some of your kind before." Kirrel shook his sweaty locks and his smile turned rueful. "Learned quick that your mastery of the land is peerless. Not to mention your proclivity for befriending giant, man-killing animals like ice-bears and yunna cats and . . . wolves."

Kirrel cast a pointed look at Kodja, then met Arcus' gaze again.

"Nature is a kind teacher and a staunch protector," Arcus admitted. "Though to outsiders our ways seem strange, I am sure."

"It always sat ill with me that the conflicts of our fathers are so easily passed to the sons," Kirrel frowned. "I was young when I assumed command. I was still hungry, still convinced that the Imperial way was the only way, the Divine Right . . ."

"What happened?"

Kirrel let Arcus' question hang in the air, unanswered, for a moment.

"I found that . . . Well, I found that when I stopped looking for fights, stopped leading with a blade . . ." He hung his head. "I found the true aggressor had been us all along."

Elbaf noted a growing redness on his cheeks, though from anger or shame he could not tell.

"I stopped pushing, stopped trying to dominate our perceived enemies, and together we ushered in nearly two decades of peace."

"Two decades? How did you get away with it?"

"What do you mean, ranger?"

"He means, how did the Empire not grind you into dust for stepping out of line?" Darko injected flatly. "I have found it to be utterly uncompromising."

"We lied," Kirrel shrugged. "When Hands come through each year, we put on airs. We'd swear up and down to pacify the countryside, to spread the laws and rid the land of the faithless." He chuckled softly. "They saw what they wanted to and moved on."

"Then why now?" Elbaf barbed. "Why break the peace?"

"Because," he sobered. "In our hour of need we were cast away."

Curiosity burned in Elbaf, but he loathed to seem overeager. Thankfully, Kirrel continued without prompting after a moment of angry silence.

"We started losing wagon trains." His face drew tight. "Merchants were raided in the countryside, farms burned with the families slaughtered, and never a trace of the enemy."

A dread feeling, like a tickling at the base of his neck, began to rise in Elbaf's mind as the man spoke.

"Whoever they were, they were well-equipped and coordinated." Kirrel spat in the mud below their feet. "They cleared our outposts one by one, and they didn't care who was at the end of their blades."

"The Empire refused to help you?" Derrin's voice, so soft and unexpected, intruded on the conversation and drew the looks of the other three.

"Sorry, sirs," he shrank into himself. "I didn't mean to eavesdrop."

"You're alright, son," Kirrel reassured him, seemingly grateful for the breath of fresh air the young man brought to the conversation.

"Yes, they refused us. I, myself, personally wrote to the Regional Commander and was advised to 'sit tight' until the next rotation," he shook his head. "Even though there were more than a hundred dead or missing in the past six months alone."

"Tell me about the raids," Elbaf directed. "You said there were no traces of the attackers?"

"Aye," the man nodded. "They come without warning, kill everyone, burn everything, and leave nothing but boot prints and the mangled bodies of our people. Most times they didn't even take much before they set it all ablaze."

"And the tracks, they--"

"Disappeared within a few dozen yards of the site of the attack, every time."

"What are you thinking, Elbaf?"

Darko's question was an unwelcome intrusion, and Elbaf silently cursed the elf's keen observations. He had no desire to speculate on his suspicions, at least not until there was more evidence.

"I'm not sure," he replied diplomatically, hoping the wizard caught the hint.

"Perhaps I could examine one of the sites," Arcus offered. "I could take a look around for--"

"No," Elbaf sighed. "I'm sorry Kirrel, but there's no time."

"What do you mean?" Kirrel's features were burdened with sudden worry.

Elbaf considered how to break the news that they were but a small forward element of what amounted to an army. Kirrel seemed a good enough man, but for his dissidence, he was without a doubt going to be executed. In fact, all of the men here were likely to hang, and that wouldn't necessarily guarantee that Kent would be spared either.

"Better to discuss it with your governor, as well," Darko prompted, meeting Elbaf's eye. "Talk it over all at once."

Darko spent the next few hours lost in thought. Too many loose ends were going unanswered for his liking, and he felt his focus splitting in too many directions.

He dwelt on Kent and wondered how he might help his companions make peace with the inevitable conclusions he had already drawn. There was very little point, at least in his mind, to convincing these people to surrender. Annabelle, for whatever inscrutable reason, seemed to fuel her zeal with an unquenchable bloodlust.

That, of course, was another mystery. Annebelle's excessive cruelty and apparent lack of empathy, compassion, or even the faintest trace of humanity was a constant worry. It was only a matter of time before the woman found a way to rid herself of him and his companions. He flattered himself to think that if he could only be rid of this damnable curse, he could make short work of the woman, push come to shove. In fact, for several minutes he allowed himself to think fondly about banishing her to the icy depths of Carak, or perhaps transmuting her into a housecat - a form where her homicidal tendencies would be more appropriate and less dangerous. Then again, Annabelle's implausible ability to utilize a powerful arcane artifact was another source of worry, and of danger.

On the subject of danger, it seemed that they'd managed to stumble across yet another perilous mystery. The idea that magically assisted raiders – for he had no doubt that magic alone could have covered up the movements of a substantial number of troops so thoroughly and for so long – were prowling the hills and valleys around them was disconcerting, to say the least. Their forces had long been dwindling, and Darko had precious little trust to spare on newly acquired friends and lackeys. No, he convinced himself for the thousandth time, better to trust only these few who had borne out his faith in them.

But it was Arcus' unlikely new powers that featured most prominently in his mind. It gnawed at him, driving his mind down tunnels of possibility until his jaw clenched with frustration and his eyes were sore from scouring his companion's appearance for some sign or hint of what had changed.

"Alright, what did you do?" he prodded just before sunset. "And how did you do it?"

"You'll have to be a tad more specific," Arcus laughed as he readjusted his pack, which was more than double the size of the few small bags Darko had shouldered.

"Your powers," the mage insisted. "You either thoroughly fooled me for months - an unlikely answer - or you've somehow . . . *grown*."

His keen eyes caught the momentary lapse in the ranger's carefree expression and noted with interest the sudden hardness in the man's eyes.

"I've . . . I've found a way to renew my connection to nature, to some extent," the druid mumbled. "You might recall an earlier conversation we had, about the *limitations* I was experiencing?"

Realization hit Darko like a runaway wagon.

"You've slipped the curse," he accused quietly but earnestly. "How? How did you do it?"

"*Quiet*," Arcus hissed, looking around to make sure no one else had heard the mage's assertion.

Darko narrowed his eyes, but did not speak further until the druid answered him.

"Lilliana broke it," he apologized in a voice so low it would be unintelligible to anyone without Darko's keen elven hearing. "I tried to tell you before, I--"

"You lied to me," Darko snipped quietly, anger turning his tongue to barbs.

The elf worked a simple enchantment while they walked, his whispered words and subtle hand movements going unnoticed by the rest of the group around them. A moment later, a nearly invisible haze had surrounded his head, and that of Arcus beside him. In the lingering daylight it would be all but impossible to spot, and when darkness fell it would disappear entirely.

"Now you may speak plainly," he announced to the druid, who cast him a furtive, uncertain look.

"It's alright," he reassured him with exasperation. "I've charmed the air around us, no one besides the two of us will hear, and any attempt to read our lips will fail."

"There's a clever cantrip--"

"I am not *interested* in my own cleverness, Arcus," he cut him off acidly. "I am *interested* in when and how you broke the curse, and, quite frankly, what possessed you to keep it a secret from the rest of us."

"Darko, I don't *know* how she did it," Arcus explained, a pleading expression on his face. "It was never my intention to keep it from you. I was waiting for an opportunity to--"

"You said you saw her again this morning," Darko interjected, chewing his lip in contemplation. "But I couldn't see her, couldn't even *sense* her presence."

"I . . . guess not--"

"It makes no sense."

"Well, I don't know--"

"This woman, she must be more than she seems," he muttered to himself. "An extraplanar being, or some kind of demi-god, perhaps."

"Darko, I *swear* I'd tell you if I knew how to break the curse."

Darko waved the ranger's concerns away, already fixating on what to do next.

"How did she know to come to our aid? Do you have some way of communicating with her?"

"I do, sort of."

Arcus' cagey response set his nerves on edge again.

"Well?"

"It's complicated, Darko," the ranger shot back, his own irritation evident. "I can't just call her for no reason. Besides, she already told me my circumstances were different, told me she wasn't able to remove the curse for the rest of you."

Darko's hopes were dashed like waves on a rocky coast.

"I suppose that's to be expected," Darko sighed none too gently, "given the manner in which my life has unfolded for the past year."

Darko dismissed the spell with a gentle wave and spent the next hour deliberately refusing any invitation to converse further, nursing the stinging wound that was his continued servitude.

"Lights!" The shout rang out just after moonrise. "The city is just ahead!"

Word spread backwards through the group of weary travelers, and sighs of relief were heard all around. The land had grown wooded again and they were all tired of tripping on unseen branches and loose stones.

Elbaf had insisted, with Kirrel's surprise agreement, that they travel into the night. Lanterns had been lit, but ordered to remain mostly hooded so as to prevent their passage being noticed as they slipped through the countryside. Elbaf had begun to question this wisdom of forcing the group onward, but he was reassured by the second wind that flowed through the column at the news they'd nearly arrived.

He was confused, however, when it seemed the head of the column was bunching up instead of pushing onward. By the time he got up to the fore, nearly half of the men were standing idly in a horseshoe around Kirrel.

"Elbaf," Kirrel greeted him in the gloom. "This hillside leads down to the city itself."

He gestured broadly, and Elbaf could see that they were just at the edge of the forest and looking down over a quarter mile or so of open, rolling hillside. Judging from the clean-cut line where the forest met the grasslands, he assumed it must have been logged in ages past, but for now it was every bit as clear and defining as a fence or a low wall would have been. At the bottom of the hill sat a broad city, its walls illuminated at regular intervals by torch-laden towers and its bustling heart filled with glowing taverns and houses. It was bigger by a fair sight than any of the towns they'd stopped at so far and likely held several thousand residents. Moreover, the sturdy walls of stone spoke volumes of its past as a retired frontier fortification.

"Then let us press onwa--"

"I'm sorry, Elbaf," Kirrel interrupted, shaking his head. "I cannot allow you and your men into the city."

"We discussed this," Darko injected quickly, possibly taking note of Elbaf's souring features. "We need to speak with your governor. It is a matter of extreme urgency."

"Even so," Kirrel stood his ground. "I cannot allow potential enemies past the gate."

For what little it was worth, Elbaf did note the apologetic, genuine expression on the man's face.

"Am I to assume you have an alternative plan, then?" he asked as calmly as he could.

"Yes, I've given it some thought," Kirrel nodded. "I will take my men into the city, released as a token of good faith. I will awaken Findrall, and we will return to speak with you here, pending his approval."

"And if he doesn't *approve*?"

"Then I will return to deliver the news personally, regardless. You have my word."

"And what good is your word," Arcus scuffed his boot in frustration, "when you have already altered the deal we struck?"

"I understand your frustration, ranger, and I--"

"We let you live," Elbaf growled. "I could have had your men's lives."

"And I am grateful, Elbaf, I really am." Kirrel raised his hands pleadingly. "But, on my honor, I cannot allow you in without the governor's leave. I am asking you to trust me, to put your faith in me as you did when you spared our lives."

"I'm sorry, Kirrel," Elbaf shook his head. "I can't--"

"A compromise, perhaps," Darko cut in. "Kirrel, you are more than capable of writing a letter to your governor explaining the situation, are you not?"

"I . . . suppose so, yes."

"Well then," Darko offered, "you write a missive to be carried by your men, and they will be released to the freedom and safety of the city. We'll keep you here until your governor decides to join us."

Elbaf nodded his approval, then turned back to Kirrel. He could see beads of sweat on the man's brow and did not envy the man for his position. Certainly he must still fear that his life hung on a thin thread, made all the thinner now that it would be his alone.

"Very well." The man extended a hand, his face set like stone. "The safety of my men is worth it, and I have confidence in Findral that he'll do the right thing."

Elbaf grasped the man's hand in a firm handshake, and the tension in the group dissipated somewhat. Darko produced an inkwell and quill and sat down with the warrior while they crafted instructions to send to the man who would, ultimately, decide the fate of the soldiers and citizens of Kent.

Elbaf moved throughout the camp, ensuring that the men were rested, their wounds tended, and their bellies full. Trail rations were hardly an exciting meal, but dried jerky and salted meat turned to bubbling brown stews with the addition of a few local native root vegetables and mushrooms, courtesy of Arcus and the other scouts.

The half-orc allowed himself a moment to relax over a crude wooden bowl of soup, enjoying the camaraderie of a wide, low fire and the brotherhood of the sword around him.

"You said we were short on time." Kirrel sat down beside him, holding his own bowl of stew. "And I get the feeling that you wanted to say more."

Elbaf put his spoon down and met the man's hardened gaze.

"There's an entire army a day's ride from your gates," he said bluntly. "Led by Duke Boric and accompanied by a small but powerful group of clerics from the Sisterhood."

Kirrel's jaw popped open and his eyes filled with alarm.

"Your walls will be breached," he shrugged, "regardless of how well fortified you think you are."

"But, we can . . . I mean, certainly we can work out--"

Elbaf shook his head sadly.

"I know the woman who leads this force," Elbaf frowned, his gaze distant. "She has no mercy."

They'd been waiting for hours, and many of the men had long since grown restless.

Arcus had produced a bag of ripe, purplish berries that seemed to have incredible restorative powers, and had given them to the most severely wounded among them. Those few were now sleeping soundly, their bleeding staunched, and their breaths even and restful. The rest of the men, though strong and hearty to Elbaf's eyes, would not be enough to counter even a modest offensive.

Not for the first time, Elbaf wondered if he had made a mistake. With the fort so near, they could be ambushed and killed without ever being able to warn the rest of the Brazen Hawks. Moreover, the leadership in Kent now knew of the impending assault and could plan accordingly.

Had he done anything but waste more lives in the inevitable siege of the town?

"You worry for your soldiers' lives," Kirrel interrupted his musings from a few feet away where he, too, stared at the dying light of the campfire, lost in thought. "As all commanders do."

Elbaf nodded thoughtfully.

"Good commanders, anyway," the aging warrior sighed. "I'm worried, too. If this army is real--" Elbaf started to speak but was waved away.

"I trust you, warrior," Kirrel reassured him. "I simply fail to see how our people can survive the coming storm. I wonder if I was too rash, too quick to support Findral's dream of independence."

Elbaf tried to put himself in the man's shoes, finding it easier than he expected. They were not so very different, after all.

Movement on the hill below caught his eye, some hundred feet out or so at the edge of his nightvision. A trio of men were approaching with what certainly struck them as great stealth, but to the bright black and white of Elbaf's vision it was almost comical. He observed them a while as they slipped from rock to rock, hugging what must be the deepest and darkest shadows they could find.

"Arcus," he nudged the sleeping druid with his boot. "We have company."

Kirrel looked surprised at his words and turned back towards the city.

"I don't see any torches, are you sure?"

"I'm sure," Elbaf said, matter of factly.

"Save yourselves the effort," Elbaf called out in a booming voice that startled most of the men in the clearing.

The trio flattened themselves against the ground, sharing obvious looks of alarm that he could make out even from where he stood.

"You there, in the grass," Elbaf called out again. "Time is short. Continue to creep through the grass from rock to rock if you wish, but there is no need."

To his relief they stood, brushed themselves off sheepishly, and approached the camp by a more direct route. He took the time to study them, muttering a clear description to the now-alert Arcus and Darko on either side of himself.

"Three men, the one in front bears armor. Chainmail, it looks like. He has a sword at his hip, but no shield--"

"Findral," Kirrel sighed with relief at the description.

"And he's flanked by two in platemail, both who carry greatswords."

The three officers in the camp looked down at Kirrel, expecting more names.

"Don't look at me," he raised his hands. "That could be almost anyone. We here in Kent are hearty stock, known for our mastery of two-handed blades and our stature."

Elbaf watched as the men made their way into the firelight. They stopped at the edge, and the man in the center gave a sort of half-wave.

"You're Findral," Elbaf called out, more a statement than a question.

"I am," he called back awkwardly across the thirty feet or so between them. "Governor of the Free City of Kent, and Lord Commander of--"

"Enough," Elbaf waved him closer. "We have no *time* for formality here. Come, sit. Let us try to find a way to save your lives."

Findral's displeasure was written on his face, but he and his two bodyguards approached cautiously.

"Your weapons," Darko called out. "Leave them there."

Findral and his men stumbled to a halt and shared a look.

"You can trust him, Findral," Kirrel called out, drawing the man's attention and eliciting from him a relieved sigh. "He's treated me with dignity, my lord, and I believe you need to hear what they have to say."

"Very well," Findral agreed, unstrapping his sword and placing it gently on the ground.

"We would prefer to remain armed," one of the guards advised him. "Perhaps our hosts are willing to allow us to remain here, at a distance, and keep our blades?"

Darko looked ready to answer, but turned instead to Elbaf to defer to his decision.

Elbaf was less than thrilled with this new burden of responsibility, but he was determined not to let it show.

"Fine," he nodded, taking his seat once again and gesturing that Findral should join them.

Findral approached and Elbaf studied the man's features, evaluating him as best he could.

He was younger than Elbaf expected, maybe in his mid-thirties, but at the same time his features were worn and worried. He bore streaks of gray hair that clashed with his apparent youth, and lines of worry were already beginning to crease his brow.

"My men told me you treated them fairly." Findral nodded respectfully as he approached. "For that I am grateful."

"You sent boys and old men to fight hardened soldiers," Elbaf frowned. "To kill them would be cruel."

Findral hung his head and took a seat beside the fire.

"My choices were limited," he frowned back. "And our *resources* are . . . limited."

"So are your options," Darko noted dryly to a glare from Elbaf.

"I think you'll find our defenses quite--"

"Irrelevant," Darko needled.

"Easy, Darko." Elbaf raised a hand to quiet him.

"You travel with a wizard," Findral raised an eyebrow. "Is that how you plan to defeat our walls?"

"No," Elbaf's voice was flat and humorless. "The bulk of the Seventh Regiment is a day's ride from here, and, at their front, a squad of battle-Sisters."

Findral paled in the flickering light of the fire.

"They have no intention of taking any of you alive," Elbaf continued. "The woman who leads them, Annabelle, is as heartless as she is devoted to the Emperor."

Silence fell, and the two locked eyes, each measuring the other and weighing their options.

"We'll surrender," Findral announced suddenly. "I will turn myself in, to save my people."

"I don't think that will slake her thirst," Arcus said.

"I agree," Darko added softly. "I find it unlikely that your head alone will be enough to atone for the sin of rising up against the Empire."

"Meaning . . .?"

"If we are fortunate," Darko tried to hide his disgust, "she will be satisfied with the lives of all of your officers, as well."

"And if we are unfortunate?" Findrel asked.

Darko looked again to Elbaf.

"She may well raze your city, regardless."

"What, then, do you propose?" Findral shot back. "What are you even offering me, besides a preview of a gruesome, genocidal fate?"

"Well," Arcus tried to soothe the growing frustration. "If you present yourself and Kirrel here, there's a chance that--"

"A chance," Findral spat into the fire. "What do I care for a *chance*? We would be better served fighting to the death." He stood, his anger flaring. "Why did you invite me here at all?" he asked, gesturing widely. "To gloat? To tell me of the impending execution of my men, the letting of innocent blood?"

"Calm yourself," Elbaf growled.

"How dare you," Findral snarled. "Calm myself? By rights--"

"By rights we should have killed your men where they stood," Elbaf roared, standing with clenched fists.

Nerves frayed, and the whole clearing seemed ready to explode.

"But we *didn't*," Elbaf bit off each syllable one-by-one. "And your gratitude means *nothing* if you are still determined to spill their blood."

The two were locked in a silent contest, a battle of wills, until at last Findral broke. His shoulders dropped and he brought a hand to his face, rubbing the bridge of his nose with a defeated sigh.

"I have yet to hear a plan that doesn't involve the wholesale slaughter of my people." He shook his head. "I pray you have one."

"Sit," Elbaf said, his voice lower and calmer. "Let us try to find a way to spare your men."

A few candlemarks later and they had at least the framework of a plan in place. With Annabelle still a day away, Findral would return to the city and organize the bold undertaking of a total evacuation. Elbaf and his men would remain behind, doing their best to confuse the trails left by Findral's people and waiting to inform Annabelle that they had discovered the town abandoned and her people missing. Duke Boric would, having no immediate mission, presumably turn his forces back towards the far southwest of the Empire. This would leave Annabelle with only the Brazen Hawks, an insufficient force to defeat Findral's forces even should she choose to pursue him. Meanwhile, Findral and his people would be well on their way northeast to the Tirjan border, where they would either be allowed across or turn southeast and head into D'Ari lands and out of easy reach of Annabelle and her crusade of vengeance.

Findral departed with the hopes of all those assembled pinned to his chest, and Elbaf felt a swelling hope that perhaps, just maybe, they would be able to pull off the impossible. With their supposed enemy gone, Elbaf roused the entirety of the camp and assembled them together.

"Men," he started, solemnly. "I want you to understand what I have chosen to do."

He explained the situation to them, leaving nothing out, and addressing his actions in his trademark bluntness. None of the gathered men batted an eye at his announcement that they would be committing treason, and to his great pride not a single hand was raised when he asked them for objections.

"In that case," he announced, "rest well. Tomorrow we will have a great deal of work to do."

Arcus was restless.

The winds blowing across the fields below were filled with a melancholy dread that kept him awake and staring at the stars as they wheeled slowly through the skies. He tried everything, from the mind-clearing meditations of Shaman Ku'La back home, to the breathing practice he'd learned on his first hunting trip with his father across the ice floes as a youth.

Even so, time stretched into the void and the twin moons Lici and Ati danced towards the horizon together. Finally, tired beyond words and having exhausted every idea that had come to his mind, he decided to at least enjoy the night. He sat up with a tired sigh and crossed his legs, taking as comfortable a place as he could and looking out at the frenzied movement of torches and men in the city below.

All through the night, below in the distant flicker of torchlights, the citizens of Kent swarmed like tiny ants. Wagons were loaded, crying children roused from slumber, and belongings either packed or cast away for lack of room. By the time dawn was starting to tinge the sky with the first hints of pink, the first wagon train was lining up at the gate, making ready to depart. A hundred wagons, all laden with gear and men, stood ready to leave as soon as the roads were lit enough to travel. The trains would head to the north, and Arcus would use his mastery of the elements to cover their tracks and restore the ground to make it harder to track their progress.

The flickering lights and the stillness of the dawn conspired to grant him rest at last. Arcus finally started to drift fitfully to sleep and resigned himself to a few short hours of rest. He wouldn't be needed until the wagons left, which wouldn't be before midday.

"Did you stay up all night, brother?"

Arcus started, and looked over at Elbaf in surprise. He wondered a moment how long the warrior had been awake, but nodded with a frustrated shrug.

"Get some rest, if you can." Elbaf patted him on the shoulder as he stood and stretched joints stiff from sleeping in armor. "I'll wake you when it's time."

Arcus nodded his gratitude and slipped, finally, into unconsciousness. Though he slept, his sleep was far from restful. The druid's dreams were filled with darkness, with visions of black clouds and green lightning, burning fields and the cries of wounded men.

Chapter Twenty-Two

Arcus awoke with a start, covered in sweat and breathing like he'd run a mile.

"Something's wrong," he gasped, still in a fuzzy half-dream state. "Very wrong."

He couldn't quantify it, but something, some presence, was sweeping over him like a wash of cold oil. He felt it in his bones and in his very breath.

Darko, who was sitting next to him quietly reading, snapped his book shut and cast an uncertain look at his companion.

"Wrong?"

But Arcus was already reaching into the web of life surrounding them. He felt the grass, the trees, the rocks, and the creatures of the fields around him. But above all he felt a sort of quiet fear pervading the natural world. He reached further and found the vast clumps of life from Kent below them in the valley, the trains of evacuees making ready to depart.

Some gentle nudge in the back of his mind reflexively turned his senses southward, and he felt himself shiver with unnatural cold.

"No," he blurted out. "She's here."

"What?" Darko shot back. "Annabelle?"

Arcus stumbled to his knees as a wave of nausea passed over him, and he returned to his senses just in time to see Darko's mysterious raven take to the skies from the shadows of his hood as the wizard's eyes and hands begin to glow.

"We have to warn them."

"We're too late," Elbaf said as he appeared out of the trees, breathing hard. "She's minutes away, at most."

Arcus took in the sight of his friend, who had clearly just run in full armor to warn them, and knew the truth of his words.

"Darko--"

"I'm working on it."

The mage was deep in concentration, so Arcus simply watched with growing impatience as he raised his already glowing hands and clasped them together. They pulsed with a deep crimson light like a heartbeat, faster and faster as he whispered into his clasped hands, too low for the ranger to hear.

The light intensified until it bathed the campsite in an ugly red.

Darko took a deep breath and slowly, deliberately, pointed his hand up at an angle towards the city.

A sudden bang echoed through the campsite and a great ball of red energy launched itself from his outstretched fingers.

The orb shot out with the speed of an arrow and arced out across the plains towards the city itself, where it exploded in a shower of red-orange sparks and a distant boom. They watched as the distant men and wagons immediately began to scatter, trundling out from the gate amid a sudden terrified burst of energy.

"That's all the warning I can give," the wizard exhaled heavily. "Anymore and we would risk--"

A bugle call cut him off and announced the arrival of Annabelle and her army.

"Come on," Elbaf said, turning on his heel and heading back towards the woodline.

He pulled up short as Annabelle, flanked by Duke Boric and another officer, rode through the trees with an entire rank of cavalry just behind them.

"Y-you're early, ma'am," Arcus stammered. "We weren't expect--"

"The Emperor's justice cannot wait." She waved her hand dismissively.

"We need more time, ma'am," the ranger replied, in an obvious attempt to stall. "We--"

"I have altered our agreement, *lieutenant*," she snapped at him before drawing a cruel smile. "As is my prerogative as your *commander*."

She didn't bother to stop, instead riding past him on her massive, coal-black warhorse. The animal's gaze lingered on the druid as it passed, and he felt a chill run down his spine.

He started to reach out with his mind and found himself utterly unable to perceive the creature, a fact which shook him to his core.

"Ready the line," Annabelle announced from the rocky edge of the bluff overlooking the city below. "We attack immediately."

"But--"

She cut the druid off with a glower.

"Duke Boric," she shouted, not even bothering to look behind herself as the man approached atop his own horse, his armor a shining, gold-trimmed contrast to the ebony of her own.

He rode up beside her, but chose not to answer. His silence turned her cruel smile to a frown of disgust and insult, and she pointedly refused to look at him.

"You were *unsuccessful* in your attempts to negotiate with the city, I see."

"Well, ma'am--"

"You have clearly failed. Even now the city is being abandoned," she cut him off with a raised hand.

She glanced at Arcus and regarded him with such disdain that it made his blood boil.

"Boric, order your men into the valley," she grinned.

"Of course," he answered crisply and emotionlessly. He turned to his side, where one of his officers sat quietly on a roan mare. "Sir Aaron," he gestured towards Kent. "Surround the gates, order the citizens to return to their homes under martial law, and detain the guardsmen and the city garri--"

"No."

"No, Sister?"

"No," Annabelle repeated. "By fleeing the city rather than face my justice, they are complicit in the treason of their leaders. You are to execute them, and set fire to the city."

"You can't be serious," Boric scoffed. "My men won't murder an entire--"

"Your men will do as I command," she replied with casual confidence. "As will you."

"No."

Annabelle turned to Boric, a look of unfiltered hate in her eyes.

"You dare defy me?"

Duke Boric set a thin, humorless smile on his face, but did not immediately respond.

"Answer me," she growled.

"I have contacted The Imperial Cathedral." He frowned. "Mater Prima Superia Crimwell *assures* me that an Arbiter has been dispatched to assess your conduct."

Far from backing down before him, Annabelle's temper flared visibly. Her cheeks took on an ugly purplish tinge and a vein bulged in her neck.

"If your men will not fight on behalf of the Empire, I will do it *myself*." She yanked savagely on her reins, wheeling her horse around and trotting away from the edge of the bluff they stood upon and back towards the woodline.

Arcus took an impulsive step back as she rode past, momentarily stunned by her visage. Her eyes, already possessing deep black irises, were bloodshot and the whites were flecked through with specks of black and gray. Her lips were drawn back in a lock-jawed snarl and her focus was singular as she made her way across the short stretch of grass back to the treeline.

The feeling of *wrongness* returned with such strength that he barely resisted the urge to shudder.

The mighty war horse she rode upon whinnied and stamped its feet as it made its way across the clearing, and the further away it got the more the ground shook beneath its ironclad hooves. Before Arcus' eyes the horse's mane turned hazy and began to emit tendrils of blackish smoke until, by the time she turned back to face them, horse and rider both were half-obscured in a roiling cloud of black.

Arcus tried to make sense of what he was seeing, but a deep and primal fear had him rooted firmly in place. He watched as the horse stamped again, this time shooting bright, poisonous green sparks as it did so. The beast huffed angrily, tossing its head side to side as noxious smoke and flickers of green flame spewed forth from its mouth and nose.

A rushing, crackling sound filled the campsite, blowing embers from the fire up into the air and driving the horses and men into a terrified frenzy. Well-trained mounts bucked their riders and battle-hardened soldiers cowered in terror as Annabelle and her steed were, for a moment, consumed by the smoke and flashing green.

An ear-splitting roar thundered forth from the cloud, draining the color from the men who heard it and sending the few remaining horses bolting into the woods. The explosion of sound made Arcus go cross-eyed, and he fell to all fours uncontrollably.

A hot, heavy wind, reeking of ammonia and decay, hit him in a wave and burned at his eyes. He managed to pull himself upright in time to see the clouds around Annabelle dissipate at last, but his mind refused to believe what was before his eyes.

A massive black dragon, its shimmering, onyx scales a compliment to Annabelle's armor, sat coiled where her warhorse had stood moments ago. It was the size of a small tavern, at least three times taller than Arcus on his own mount, and yet its rider seemed to perch between its shoulders with a practiced ease. Broad wings sat curled at each shoulder, and its four limbs were tucked up beneath it like some massive, deadly cat. A thirty-foot tail lashed back and forth, a trio of meter long blades of bone at the end of it gauging the earth and felling trees absentmindedly behind the monster. The head, easily six feet wide, swayed back and forth like a desert cobra, attached to the body by a long, almost delicate, neck. Foot long spines, wickedly sharp and curved like scimitars, ran the length of its neck and culminated in a crown of spikes and horns at the base of its skull. The face held jaws that could swallow a horse whole and yellow-green eyes as big as dinner plates and every bit as intelligent as a man. Green smoke coiled upwards from flaring nostrils, and the entire creature seemed deceivingly relaxed, not unlike a panther preparing to strike.

Despite the monster before him, Arcus was drawn to its rider once again. Annabelle's eyes were pitch black now, and the veins under her porcelain skin ran in a dark spider web of blackish gray. Her breathing was heavy, but the manic smile on her face was firmly plastered for anyone who beheld her to see. She drew a long black blade from her side and, without visible command, the dragon stood up and unfurled its wings with a crisp snap.

The rush of wind from this simple motion knocked several men flat and shredded what was left of the tents in the campsite. The wings were huge expanses of leathery hide and bones, as broad as the sails of the trading galleys to the south, and they shadowed the entire clearing.

The dragon crouched like a cat, and then, without warning, it took two great bounding steps and leapt into the sky with a powerful downbeat. It roared again as it soared out over the valley. It took all of Arcus' willpower not to cower at the sound. They watched helplessly as the monster covered the quarter mile to Kent in less than a minute, and that helplessness swiftly turned to horror.

The men at the camp pulled themselves together and, within a few minutes, they found themselves standing at the edge of the cliff staring at the unfolding wreckage in the valley below. The dragon swept in low over the town and they watched as it let forth great blasts of flickering green. Whole houses disappeared under ugly clouds of greenish gas, and within minutes the city was covered in smoke, fires, and ash.

"By the gods," Darko gasped, tears streaming down his face.

"What is it?" Elbaf prompted, turning to the wizard. "What do you see?"

Darko, looking through the eyes of Reia as she flew high over the battlefield, was too disturbed to answer. The dragon's breath was a hellish combination of poisonous gasses, flickering green flames, and thick molten droplets of acid. Back and forth it swept, turning broad swaths of fleeing, terrified civilians into smoldering, dissolving corpses.

"It's a slaughter," he whispered.

The mage fought the urge to vomit.

Steady, Master.

But he was not reassured. He stumbled to the edge of the clearing and emptied his stomach behind a bush, wishing desperately to erase the images burned into his mind. Even so, when he could stand again he forced himself to look back.

Men, women, and children screamed and writhed as their flesh melted from their bones and their skin was covered in caustic, sizzling boils. Wagons, homes, and stone walls melted into slag beneath the heat. Even those fortunate enough to be missed by the flames and acid, fell to their knees choking on poison fumes, their eyes, ears, and noses bleeding until their pain-wracked bodies stopped twitching.

Master, there is nothing for you to gain by seeing this.

Someone must witness this. Someone has to know what happened here.

He watched as long as he could, but after the first few passes it became apparent that Annabelle meant to make good on her promise to slaughter the entire population, so he pulled back into himself with a revolted shudder.

"Darko," Elbaf repeated. "Tell us."

"We have made a terrible miscalculation," Darko managed weakly.

"But what of the *people?*" Boric interrupted, grabbing the mage firmly by the shoulders. "What's happening down--"

"My lord Boric," Darko interrupted him softly. "I . . . It is a slaughter."

Boric took a single, unsteady step backwards, yanking off his helm and running a hand through his hair.

"What have I done?" he said, half to himself. "By the gods, what have I done?"

Boric and the others watched in silent disbelief from the hilltop as Annabelle began to steadily reduce the entire city into a smoldering pile of death and despair.

"Listen to me," he said with sudden urgency, snapping out of the stupor they found themselves in. "You three need to make your way further north. I've been in touch with the Prophet and--"

"*You* know Lilliana?" Arcus blurted out with surprise.

"I-- Who?"

"Lilli--"

"It doesn't matter now," Boric waved him off. "I forced Major Montagne's hand by contacting the head of her order. I knew she was dangerous, but this is . . . far beyond anything I thought she was capable of."

"Forced her hand?" Elbaf frowned. "You suspected something like this, and you didn't tell us?"

"I didn't know she had a *dragon*," he spat back.

"It must be spellcraft then," Arcus offered. "Dragons are legend, *myth*, not--"

"No, Arcus," Darko shook his head solemnly. "How she kept up her illusion as long as she did is beyond me, but what we see before us is real. Deadly real."

"The threat we face as an Empire was never going to come from the outside," Boric said grimly. "I mistook Major Montagne's intentions, and now I fear we are beyond recovery." His face fell as he continued, "I meant to disabuse a needlessly cruel and ambitious young officer of her poor habits." His gaze grew distant. "Instead, I've awoken a viper."

"You couldn't have known," Darko replied. "Even I couldn't see through her spellcraft, and I--"

"I threatened her," Boric disagreed, turning away. "And I counted on the pressure of the Order to keep her in line."

Darko sat down heavily.

"How in all the infinite hells are we supposed to escape her clutches *now*?"

Boric was filled with a sudden nervous energy.

"There is a colleague of mine, Colonel Harrold Redding. He's the commandant at an advanced school for field-grade officers up north in Kyber."

"And what good will leaving do," Darko pointed sarcastically to the cursed magic band around his neck, "if she can simply end our lives the moment she decides we've 'betrayed' her?"

"That curse requires you to be visible to the caster," Boric waved away his concern. "Though the Sisterhood keeps that a jealously guarded secret."

As he spoke, he was removing his gauntlets, unbuckling them hastily and looking over both shoulders to make certain no one was watching them. He pulled off the thin leather gloves he'd worn for the boxing match and handed them to a surprised Elbaf.

"What's this?"

"May they serve you well," the Duke said, already putting his armored gauntlets back on. "Now put them on quickly, before Major Montagne returns, and get out of here while you still can."

Darko took silent note of the twin suns tattooed on the backs of Boric's hands, but he was far more interested in taking a closer look at the gloves. He found himself suddenly wishing he'd attended the brawl of a few days ago, as the thin, unremarkable leather screamed 'enchantment.'

A whispered word and his eyes glazed over with blue flame, revealing to him the various magical energies swirling throughout the air around him. The gloves shone with a bright silver aura and, despite the circumstances, he turned up a wry smile as he recognized a simple but highly effective strength spell. It was not so very different from the spell he'd cast on Elbaf months ago, though it was infinitely more elegant.

Unless he was mistaken, it would be more than enough to win the bearer most any contest of strength.

Darko watched as Elbaf donned the gloves and his veins were shot through with the faintest of silver sparks. They mixed with the same blackish, reddish haze that had so caught the wizard by surprise the first time he'd tested his magical gaze against the half-orc and, not for the first time, the mage wondered at this innate *otherness* of his companion.

"You must meet up with Colonel Redding," Boric insisted. "He's a good man, brave and true, and his heart is loyal to the Empire. Those who truly love our land are not yet gone from this world. However, we are dwindling and our window of opportunity is swiftly closing."

"Boric, slow down," Elbaf shook his head.

"I wish there was more time, Elbaf," Boric frowned sadly. "But I was a fool, and I have perhaps been too cautious. Now is the time for bold action, lest we all--"

Annabelle's dragon roared with savage delight, drowning out his words and cutting him off from nearly a quarter-mile away. He looked again at the destruction she wrought before turning back to Elbaf.

"Get your men out of here," he ordered. "My men will give you fresh horses and as many supplies as we can spare. Go north to Kyber, and, at least for the first few days, steer clear of the Imperial Highway."

"And this Colonel," Darko raised an eyebrow. "He's just . . . expecting us?"

"No, but he will be. I'll send my swiftest messenger ahead," Boric frowned, then paused. "On second thought, take this with you." He reached beneath the neck of his breastplate and pulled forth a silver chain with a ring threaded onto it. "This is my signet ring," Boric told them, a peculiar sadness in his voice. "A symbol of my inheritance, my station, and, above all, my duty to the Empire. It has been carried by the head of my family for nine centuries and has never left our side."

"Surely you should keep it then," Elbaf shook his head, thinking of his father's sword. "I know the value of such an heirloom."

"As I said," Boric repeated firmly, putting the ring into his hands. "Above *all*, my duty to the Empire."

When at last Annabelle and her nightmare of a mount wheeled back towards the hilltop, they were miles away. She appeared as a dark, terrifying blot against the incongruously clear blue skies.

"Darko," Elbaf called out." We have to--"

"Keep moving," Darko pulled himself back to the present, realizing he was once again the last horse in their small column. "I know."

The wizard had been taken by surprise when the rest of their men had elected to join them in their escape. Now they were well and truly on their own, Brazen Hawks no longer. Tomlin and Kardon had both been injured during Kirrel's ambush, but with some creative field medicine they were capable of moving. Poor Kardon's leg, pierced through with a javelin, was now bandaged to the point of immobility.

Still, despite the danger of Annabelle's wrath, not one man had hesitated to make their decision.

Their plan, such as it was, consisted almost entirely of hugging the deepest and darkest cover they could while following the generally northward meandering of the Imperial Highway.

According to Darko's recollection, they were now well beyond the point of any but the most rustic of Imperial outposts. He thought back to the maps he'd studied during the strategic analysis portion of his military education, studying the images he recalled with perfect clarity. Nothing of note populated the hilly expanse between Kent and Fort Kyber, save for a few firewatch stations and those, while staffed with teams of wildland rangers and foresters, had no military function to speak of.

He reassured himself that if they could break free of Annabelle now - when the chance of success was at its absolute peak - then they might yet survive.

Anxiety hung over the men and horses as they slipped furtively from one stand of trees to the next, navigating deep, overshadowed gullies and crisscrossing shallow, icy streams. Every bird that flew over, every tiny shower of pebbles knocked loose by an errant hoof, caused the men to flinch and turn skyward.

Even as morning turned toward midday, and the sun at last began its slow descent into evening, the air remained tense. Darko, generally unaffected by the emotional states of the soldiers he accompanied, began to fray at the edges as quickened pulses and shallow breathing of the soldiers around him started to wear at his over-keen senses.

And, of course, none of this has to do with your own anxiety, Master.

He bit back a retort to Reia's offhand comment in his mind, but couldn't help his perspective shifting and his analysis turning inward.

Allow yourself the chance at introspection, Master. The things you saw would be difficult for any mortal to . . . process.

But not for you?

He was not yet ready to discuss the events of the morning, and so he clung to the only thread in the conversation that might steer him clear of them.

I have lived a thousand lifetimes and seen more death than you could comprehend, Master.

She seemed to sigh inside his mind, and he was once again reminded of how much more natural this form of communication was to her and of the nature of her life and how it differed so greatly from his own. He wished he could convey more feeling, more emotion, when they talked this way. He feared his thoughts had none of the nuance of Reia's, and that represented to him just another barrier he had yet to overcome.

Your avoidance will only delay the inevitable, Master.

And yet I cannot help it. I have no wish to relive the memories of this morning, Reia. Let that be the end of it for now, please.

Silence met his request, but he could sense the disapproval in the small creature's mind.

Reia, I--

As you wish, Master.

Reia fluttered forth from his hood, unseen by Darko's companions, without another word. Her sudden departure stung, but Darko would not allow himself to reach out to her first. He sulked a while instead before realizing dejectedly that he had no stomach for that, either.

"How do you know what she did down there, sir?" Cormorant asked him softly.

Darko practically jumped out of his saddle, and both his hands were wreathed in sparkling purple flames in an instant. Cormorant flinched as well, yanking on his reins so his horse would side-step a few paces. Darko's heart felt like it was going to beat itself out of his chest, and he had to force himself to breathe again.

"Sorry, m'lord. I--"

"No," Darko croaked, clearing his throat. "No, I apologize, Sergeant. The fault is mine."

The flames flickered and died, and Cormorant sidled back over, though not so closely as before.

"It's Eric, by the way, m'lord." Cormorant nodded politely, "Eric Cormorant."

"Eric," Darko said warmly, realizing with shame how little he'd asked about the lives of the men who had fought and died beside them for the past several months. "I have the ability to . . . augment my senses magically. This is especially true when my companion Rei-- er, *raven* is with me."

"Can . . . can anyone learn magic, sir?"

Darko tried, with great difficulty, to hide his surprise.

"Er, well," Darko studied the man's earnest eyes. "Not *anyone*, exactly."

He watched the man's expression fall.

"It takes many, many years of study and discipline," Darko tried to comfort him. "For the younger races, it is a difficult and demanding life. Often, wizards spend thirty years before they are deemed worthy of the red robes."

"*Thirty years,* sir?"

"At least," Darko nodded, thinking to his own studies. "I graduated in twenty-eight years, and I was considered a prodigy. I studied in the tower another fifty years and made something of a name for myself, researching and pushing the boundaries of magic. I was a professor, actually."

"You taught magic, sir?"

"I did, yes." Darko studied the furrowed brow and the lost-in-thought eyes of his fellow soldier. "May I ask why you are so curious?"

"It's nothing, sir," he smiled ruefully. "Nothing that matters now, anyway."

"Really," Darko prodded. "What?"

"My daughter, sir." He shrugged. "She just turned four and . . . there's something very strange about her."

He must have mistaken Darko's surprise for disbelief, because he quickly followed up his declaration.

"She can do *amazing* things, sir." He frowned. "We were . . . well, to be honest, sir, we were starving. And she *made food* out of thin air. Turned a pot of bone broth to a soup filled with meat, vegetables, all of it."

"Well--"

"And more, sir, she killed a rabid dog just by looking at him!"

"She--"

"Had my poor wife cornered," Cormorant said. "I was at the recruiting station, I, um . . . I joined up because it was our last chance, I'm not proud to say. I told her not to go out."

"Down in Low-East," his cheeks burned as he continued. "That's where we live in the Capital, sir. There're plenty of them strays, starving and desperate. Wife told me, she said, 'Eric, your girl looked at that dog and I swear on my life it keeled over dead,' and I believe her too--"

"Eric, Eric," Darko raised his hands. "Calm yourself, friend."

"But, I--"

"It sounds like your daughter *is* gifted," Darko explained. "And when she turns five, she'll be picked up by the Academy. Her schooling will be paid for, she'll have a wonderful, meaningful, productive life. All her needs will be met."

"And . . . and my wife?"

"The Academy will see to her, as well," Darko smiled. "In fact . . ." He trailed off, lost in thought. "I'll reach out to an old colleague." He shuffled in his pocket, pulling out a fine silver chain with a handful of strange silver coins fastened to it.

"What's that, sir?"

"These are *keys*, Eric." Darko smiled at the look of confusion. "They allow magi who have exchanged them to communicate, albeit in a limited manner."

"And you're--"

"I'm sending someone to find your daughter." He smiled. "You said she's four?"

"Yes, sir."

"Then what use is having your wife and child suffer another year before the Academy scouts find her?"

"Thank you, sir. I . . ."

Darko could see the beginnings of tears in the man's eyes but said nothing, focusing instead on sending a brief but clear message to a friend he'd entered the Academy with, a man who now oversaw a portion of the talent scouting offices as the Undersecretary of Recruitment.

"I'll never see them again," he shook his head, wiping his eyes. "But at least now I know . . . now I know they'll be ok."

They rode on in silence, leaving Darko with the deepening discomfort of knowing that the families of the men they'd lost would be expected to live on a pittance of a salary from the crown. Moreover, they'd likely never even learn the true fates of the men they'd sent off to fight.

"How did you know?" Elbaf asked Arcus as they rode at the head of the column with Merrly and Tomlin.

"Know what?" Arcus asked, his eyes scanning the sparse, birch-wooded hills on their western flank.

"About Annabelle," Elbaf shook his head, leaving Arcus to feel embarrassed at missing the obvious.

"I'm not sure," the druid replied. "I *felt* her, I think."

"You . . . felt her?"

"I know," the druid sighed. "I know it sounds . . ."

"Stupid?"

"Not the word I would have chosen," he frowned. "But fine."

Elbaf tried not to let his frustration show, but he was growing very weary of the convoluted, secretive ways of his two fellow officers. He missed Talia, who at least had usually tried to be straightforward with him, and he missed even more the days when his life was never more complicated than a street brawl and lukewarm alcohol.

"Why couldn't you 'feel' her before?"

"I don't know for sure," he wondered aloud. "But I think it has to do with Lilliana. I think, perhaps, that when she broke the curse--"

Elbaf yanked up on his reins, pulling his horse to a stop and staring in total shock at his companion.

"When she *what*?"

"Damnit." The ranger rubbed his eyes. "I . . . Look, Ebaf. I *was* going to tell you. It's just, ah, well, we were still so close to Annabelle, and I didn't have a chance to pull you to the side, um . . . yet."

Elbaf's whole body was tense. The desire to punch Arcus in the face was almost too much for him to control, and with every syllable the ranger drew closer to a fistfight, whether he realized it or not. He turned his head and cracked the muscles in his neck, a habit he had from his days as a brawler, and he could feel his pulse in his fists, so tightly were they curled.

"Elbaf, brother," Arcus pleaded, turning his horse towards him. "Say something."

Elbaf held a hand up, not trusting himself to speak as the rest of the column bunched up behind them.

"Problem, sirs?" Derrin's small voice spoke up as the whole group instinctively looked back over their shoulders towards the ruins of Kent.

Elbaf was even less inclined to have this fight in front of their men, so he slipped from his horse and, handing his reins to Derrin, stepped off the road and into the brush on the hillside.

"Elbaf? Elbaf," Arcus called. "Where're you going?"

Elbaf didn't look back, but he heard the ranger slip from the saddle and follow after him.

"Set a camp," the ranger called out. "No fire, and half of you man the watch at a time. We'll be back in a moment."

Elbaf walked a few dozen yards into the woods, out of sight and earshot of the column at least, and turned around to wait for the ranger. He crossed his arms to keep from drawing a blade and tried to control his rising temper as the ranger strolled into sight, a sheepish look on his face.

"Listen," he started, hands up in apology. "I *was* going to tell you."

Elbaf could feel a vein in his forehead throbbing, and he worked hard to master himself in the face of the anger he felt.

"You lied to me," Elbaf shook his head. "You found a way out, and you *kept it from us?*"

"Elbaf, it isn't like that at all. As I already told Darko, it--"

The ranger, already within easy arm's reach, had now crossed the line of Elbaf's patience. He grabbed the man by his collar and lifted him from the ground like a child, slamming his back against a tree with enough force to shake the branches above.

"You told the *wizard?*" Elbaf roared. "And you--"

"Elbaf," the ranger's voice turned deadly serious. "Take care, my patience has limits."

"I would worry yourself less with your patience," Elbaf growled, shaking him roughly, "and more with my good graces."

The ranger's eyes flashed and he reached his hands up to Elbaf's wrists. His eyes took on a strange, yellowish tinge and his pupils narrowed into slits. His body, at first light as a feather, doubled and then tripled in weight, straining even Elbaf's magically enhanced muscles. Course grayish fur started to sprout across the druid's shoulders and the backs of his hands, and his face began to push forward into a snout as he spoke.

"I'm warning you," the ranger snarled again, revealing teeth that were lengthening into fangs before Elbaf's very eyes.

"Damn you, ranger," Elbaf said as he allowed the druid to slide down the tree trunk until his feet touched the ground once more. "And damn your sorcery, as well."

He let go of the man's collar and took a step back, looking up to the druid for the first time in their lives as Arcus now stood over seven feet tall, his muscles bulging beneath his armor.

"Of course," Elbaf spat on the ground between them before turning away. "Why keep one thing secret when you can keep many."

"Elbaf," Arcus' voice was rough and guttural, as though his vocal cords were more than half animal. "It isn't like that! Dammit, man, *listen to me.*"

"I just want to know how you did it." Elbaf turned away. "You owe me that. How do we rid ourselves--"

"It doesn't work for anyone else!" Arcus yelled back, his voice returning to normal as he shrank back into the man that Elbaf knew and recognized. "Don't you think I would have told you? Do you *truly* think me so selfish?"

"I don't know anymore," Elbaf said, his hands raised in frustration. "We long ago passed out of the world I understood."

Arcus looked ready to speak, but held his tongue.

"A year ago, this world of grand sorcery," he gestured wildly, his pulse quickening, "of walking dead and shape-changing druids, it didn't exist for me! There were no *dragons*, there were no *wizards*. They were nothing more than tales spun in taverns by hungry bards."

The few feet between them seemed, for the moment, an uncrossable gulf.

"I don't know anything, it seems."

They fell to silence as Elbaf turned his gaze down toward his clenched fists.

"Fine," Arcus sighed. "Fine. You're right, and I apologize. I should have told you."

Ebaf said nothing, nor did he meet the ranger's gaze.

"Elbaf, I swear I'll help you find a way out." Arcus took a step closer and put his hand on the half-orc's shoulder. "All of you. We're in this together, bound by far more than this curse."

"Don't lie to me again." Elbaf jammed a finger in the man's chest. "Not after the things we've done, the things *I've* done."

"Elbaf--"

"Damnit, Arcus," he swore. "My hands are filthy, covered in bloodstains I'll never wipe clean. We've bled together, I've *killed people* for you. So you of *all people* don't get to lie to me."

"*None* of us is innocent, Elbaf--"

"How am I supposed to protect you?" Elbaf blurted out at last, his arms wide. "If you hold back the information I *need* to know, then how in all the hells can I protect you? These men? Even that blasted sorcerer?"

"Elbaf you don't have to--"

"I do," he cut the ranger off again. "I do."

Silence fell again, and Elbaf's heartbeat seemed to him as loud as a pounding drum. He shook his head, fighting back the panicky tightness in his chest and forcing himself to breathe slowly and evenly. He lost track of how long they stood in silence.

"I swear it," the ranger said solemnly, extending a hand to the warrior. "I'll never lie to you again."

Elbaf looked at the outstretched hand, a million thoughts racing through his mind, but he chose at last to grasp his brother's hand and was unexpectedly drawn into an embrace. He stiffened, and it was only because he was so surprised that he didn't immediately push away.

"I'm sorry, brother," Arcus said, turning him loose again. "I should've trusted you. Forgive me?"

"I'm tired, Arcus." He backed away again. "I'm so very tired of . . . *all* of this."

Arcus' features spoke volumes, and Elbaf knew he felt the weight of their fates, as well.

"And yet," Elbaf looked back towards their men, "when I think of our future, I cannot help but think the bloodshed is just beginning."

Chapter Twenty-Three

The two received a few over-long looks from several of the men when they returned, but Darko was the only one who commented aloud.

"I wasn't sure you'd both be coming back," he remarked with genuine surprise.

"A disagreement," Arcus said with a sideways glance at Elbaf's expressionless face. "Nothing more."

Darko looked from Arcus to Elbaf, and then back again, but made no further comment. Even so, the air in the camp was tense, and all of the men surreptitiously sized up the two men.

"So," Arcus turned back to Elbaf, his tone conciliatory and his voice cutting through the air clear as a bell. "Do we strike camp, sir, or press on?"

"We'll camp here," Elbaf answered, grateful for the druid's nod to his continued leadership. "Three watches. Between us we ought to be able to manage that."

"And fire?"

"No fire," he shook his head to a low grumble. "I'm sorry, men. I'll not be any warmer than the rest of you, but that's a low price to pay for staying out of Major Montagne's gaze."

The mumble turned to a murmur of frustrated agreement, and the men settled in for a miserable night. That is, until Darko, perhaps looking to score some goodwill with the soldiers, revealed that he could enchant a pile of stones to emit the same warmth as a roaring campfire.

This development, along with Cormorant's continued culinary prowess and Arcus and Corporal Felder's luck in finding wild edibles, served to turn the evening fairly cozy.

"D'you suppose she's looking for us, sir?" Derrin chimed in some time later, a warm bowl of rabbit stew between his hands and starlight in his young eyes. "The Major, that is."

"I don't know," Elbaf allowed. "But I think Duke Boric risked a great deal to speed us on our way like he did."

"Duke's an important man, though," Tomlin chimed in from across the rock pile. "He'll be a'right, I suspect."

"I hope so," Elbaf agreed, relaxing a little as the talk turned to less serious matters and the camaraderie of the evening began to chase away the chill of autumn. The sun set, the moons rose, and he allowed himself to unbunch his shoulders, to unclench his jaw, and even to share a few laughs with the soldiers in his care before his shift at watch.

Arcus' sleep was troubled, again.

Never one to lucid dream as a youth, he was nonetheless beginning to develop the skill against his will. He awoke sitting at the edge of a forest, his legs crossed and his hands resting on the longbow across his lap. He knew immediately that he was dreaming, or else that the events unfolding weren't quite real at least, but he couldn't shake how vivid it felt nonetheless. Something within him compelled him to stand, and he squinted into the moonlit wilderness before him.

There, between the trees, he could see a flicker of reddish orange, a sure sign of a fire. A big one, from the size of it. He felt a deep, primal need to preserve the woodlands and, without a thought for his own safety, he stood and sprinted into the trees. Twigs, branches, and leaves seemed to slide effortlessly out of his way as he ran, and neither root nor stone troubled his steps despite the darkness.

The firelight grew and, as it did, he began to hear the crackle of the flames, an arrhythmic rumbling, and another, harsher sound. The sound was known to him, but tonight it struck him at his core: the sound of axes biting wood.

He slowed; he could make out shadowy forms backlit by a massive bonfire ahead of him. Harsh, guttural voices shouted back and forth across the darkness as tree after tree fell to the onslaught of axes. He couldn't count the shadowy forms, but they numbered thirty or more and each stood well over six feet tall. They wore armor covered in serrated edges, spikes, and horns, and they walked with a slight hunch as they swung axes taller than a man and with blades to match.

In the middle of the clearing stood an ever-growing pile of trees, cast carelessly upon the fire with no purpose or respect. Arcus felt each falling tree like an arrow in his back, and a burning rage filled him.

He nocked an arrow, drawing a bead on the closest figure. He took a breath, pausing at the height of it, and the arrow had nearly slipped from his fingers when the ground trembled and the blazing inferno took on new life. He was blinded for a moment in the flash, and when he looked again the heart of the fire was a black and shadowy portal.

He re-positioned himself, aiming at what he instinctively recognized as a doorway, and sure enough, a heartbeat later, a truly massive figure emerged from it. The monster before him walked like a man, but had to be eight feet tall. It held in one hand an enormous ax, bigger than any man could carry.

Without hesitation, Arcus let his arrow fly.

The shot traveled across the distance in a heartbeat, the silvery fletching catching the moonlight in a flash too brief for any but an elven eye to see, and arced unerringly towards the neck of the creature stepping from the flames.

Arcus let loose his breath with all the noise of a whisper, trusting the truth of his aim, and began to reach for another arrow. His eyes, still locked on his prey, widened with surprise as the creature flinched with unnatural speed. His arrow, which should have found its home in the slit between the beast's helmet and his breastplate, shot sparks as it glanced off of the creature's pauldron instead.

He couldn't see the creature's face, but its helmet turned directly to face him and the ranger took an unwilling step backwards, his fingers fumbling with his quiver, as the being lifted its weapon and leveled the blade directly at him.

The ranger woke with a start, his hand going immediately to the hunting knife at his side. Elbaf was crouching next to him, a look of deep concern on his face.

"You stopped breathing," the half-orc hissed. "Are you . . . ok?"

"I don't know," the ranger gasped, sitting up and clutching at his chest, which was inexplicably sore. "I . . . I don't know what's happening to me."

"Try to describe it," Darko's soft voice rose over the whistling night winds from where he sat cross-legged by the warmth of the rock-pit.

"I have these, these *horrible* dreams," Arcus began, embarrassment clear in his voice. "But they feel so . . . so *real*."

"I wish you could see what I see, right now," Darko muttered to himself. "You have around you a most peculiar . . . *aura* of magical energy. It isn't *possible*, and yet I see it now with my own eyes."

"What does it mean?" Arcus pressed. "What *aura*?"

"You are covered in *aestra*," the wizard continued, holding his hands out for warmth. "It's . . . fluff, *dust* if you will, and a hallmark of those who travel the planes."

"But I don't travel the planes." Arcus rubbed his temples. "And unlike you, I need more than a few hours rest each night."

"You may not mean to," Darko allowed, "but the evidence would suggest that you're doing *something* . . . ah, extraplanar?"

"Do you think that's how I--"

Arcus paused as the wind was knocked from his chest. He doubled over, his mind ringing with the echoes of axes on hardwood, and placed his hands over his ears.

"Arcus," Elbaf stood, one hand on his sword-hilt and the other helplessly clutched in a fist. "What's wrong?"

The pain stopped, and Arcus stood and faced the woody hillside to the northeast. His vision blurred and refocused, and for a moment he thought he saw a flicker of firelight in the distance.

"Tell me you see that, Darko," Arcus said, pointing along the ridgeline to a faint but swiftly growing orange glow.

"I do," Darko said in a forced, even tone as he tried to ignore the tooth-beared growl coming from Kodja at Arcus' side. "I think perhaps--"

"Everyone up!" Elbaf called out, pulling his blade free from its sheath.

The camp awoke like a well-oiled machine, each man rolling swiftly from their sleeping sack at full alertness. Within a moment the entire group was mounted and ready to move.

"We'll head straight west," Elbaf ordered. "Cross the Imperial Highway and--"

"No," Arcus whispered in a voice not quite his own.

The ranger felt the heartbeat of the world, soft at first but rising like a symphony. It cried out in pain that echoed in his mind and resonated in the chambers of his heart. He would not leave, he *could* not leave.

"Arcus," Elbaf shook his head. "There's *no* reason for us to engage this threat. We should leave."

"I'm sorry," Arcus said, wrestling with himself but unable to turn away. "I can't."

"*Arcus*," Elbaf tugged the reins of his restless mount. "Get a hold of yourself, we need to *go*."

"You're right, you should go," Arcus set a stern look on his face. "I'll catch up with you if . . . well, I'll catch up with you after. Push north and I'll follow your tracks."

With that, he turned his horse towards the firelight and with a mental nudge sent the creature barrelling into the woods. True to his dream, the forest seemed to slip away from him and his horse as well, and they rode as easily through the dense trunks as they would have through a sunny field.

"Damn you, ranger," Elbaf growled, pulling his mount around.

He looked to his men, all of whom were waiting unquestioningly to follow his orders, and after a split second he spurred his horse forwards after his friend.

"Blades out, men," he roared. "And follow me!"

They tore through the trees after Arcus, Elbaf praying with every hoofbeat that his horse wouldn't fall or turn an ankle. Somehow, some way, they caught the ranger a hundred paces or so from the edge of the firelight.

Whatever he'd expected, it wasn't a gigantic bonfire and a small army of armored, ax-wielding soldiers. It was impossible to count the enemy accurately as he rode through the trees, but Elbaf was certain they were outnumbered.

Their hoofbeats betrayed them, and as they rode down a gentle slope towards the fiery clearing ahead he could see a half dozen of the massive warriors forming a rank, their axes poised to strike. Elbaf raised his greatsword in response, taking his hands from the reins and trusting his mount to carry him true.

He could feel the now familiar tingle of magic behind him, and it took all his trust in Darko not to turn. A sizzling sound filled the air as he rode and ozone set the hairs on his arms and back on edge as, with a crackling boom that shook the ground, a bolt of thick red lightning arced towards the enemy. It shot between Elbaf and Arcus, missing him by less than a foot, and impacted one of their enemies in the center of his broad breastplate. Sparks danced and lightning arced across his body as he writhed in pain. That same energy then radiated outwards, driving the two soldiers on either side of him to the ground with grunts of pain.

Elbaf hit the line with a precise double handed swing of his greatsword. The impact of his weapon caved the breastplate of his target before dragging upwards and sliding alongside the creature's neck in a spray of blackish blood. He took the rebound of his blade and spun it full circle, removing the head of another from behind as they broke through the line.

Another crackling boom and a massive flare of light appeared above the clearing, shedding light as bright as a midday sun as Elbaf's troops poured through the hole they'd created.

He wheeled his horse around, looking for an easy target and did a quick count. They were outnumbered almost three to one, and severely outclassed.

"Arcus!" he called out a warning as one of the creatures they fought took aim and launched its heavy battleax in a wicked double-overhand throw.

The ranger and his horse moved as one, but he could not quite dodge the flashing blade of the ax. It caught his horse in the ribs, just behind his calf, and the poor beast skidded face-first into the dirt.

The druid, however, rolled with startling grace, and Elbaf gaped as he transformed mid-roll. He watched as his friend completed his transformation from earlier in the day, emerging from his tumble as some terrifying hybrid of a man and the largest bear Elbaf could have imagined. In a few heartbeats, the familiar form of his ranger companion had become a terrifying eleven-foot tall beast with limbs the size of tree trunks and a snarling, roaring maw.

Arcus lumbered forward on all fours, backhanding one of the creatures and caving its entire chest in like the blow from a battering ram. The druid and his snowy white companion moved in deadly harmony until both of them were soaked in the blood of their enemies - but there were too many. Arcus roared, sending shockwaves through the air in the clearing and giving pause even to the helmeted, platemail-wearing enemies that now had them encircled.

"To me!" Elbaf shouted, rallying his men into a tight defensive circle and taking stock.

Five mounts were down, and poor Felder was missing his right leg from the mid-thigh. He paused for a moment to survey the battlefield. He and his cluster of men had their backs to the pile of burning trees that dominated the center of the clearing, and they'd formed a tight circle of shields. There were still about twenty of the enemy remaining, and they were now well organized and approaching with caution.

He took a moment to appreciate the innovation in the armor they wore. Each man's right shoulder plate extended out and down, creating a sort of oversized buckler they could lead with that covered most of the precious few gaps in their already impressive armor. What's more, when a group of them stood shoulder to shoulder it created an effective shield wall.

"Dismount," Elbaf ordered, sliding from his saddle and slapping his horse on the haunch. "The horses leave us--" he was interrupted by another ax, thrown overhand with alarming speed, that he barely managed to deflect with his sword. "--exposed," he finished. "Form a line, we need to close." He sized up their enemies and took the best odds he could gamble on. "If we can close, those axes will be less effective."

His soldiers, to their great credit, faced down the armored giants across from them with steely resolve.

"Darko," Elbaf looked to his friend. "I pray you're not out of tricks just yet."

Darko said nothing, but the half-orc watched the mage's hands begin to glow with an eerie blue-white light. He widened his stance, moving his arms in a slow, deliberate figure-eight before bringing his feet together, straightening his back, and resting his two fists against one another at his waistline. The glow intensified, and a chill wind overshadowed the blazing fire behind them as the mage took a bounding step forward and then slammed both of his fists directly towards the enemy.

From his hands a cone of pure white light blasted forth with the howling, screaming force of a hurricane. The temperature in the entire clearing dropped precipitously, and frost formed on the armor of the soldier to Darko's left and right.

But the true horror of his spell was not realized until the light faded.

A cone of devastation emerged outward from his fists and extended all the way across the clearing and into the woodline. All of the vegetation was gone, coated beneath several inches of ice, and a thousand razor sharp spikes of ice had shredded and impaled everything in their path. Four of their enemies now hung as limp as ragdolls, impaled a dozen times or more and imprisoned by the same thick hoarfrost coating as the ground and the trees behind them.

Elbaf watched the wizard slump back, supported by Cormorant on one side and Julias on the other as they kept him in the shelter of their shields.

"Arcus," he called. "We're running out of options, brother."

Arcus was bleeding from a dozen wounds of varying severity, the least of which were foot long gashes that seeped blood sluggishly into his matted gray fur. The form he'd taken, that of an Arctic Kursa bear, was strong beyond reckoning but vulnerable without his armor, which melded seamlessly into his body when he was fully transformed. He drew long, ragged breaths and looked to either side of himself.

He'd driven these men into a slaughter, and for what? To answer some compulsion they could not feel?

His musing was interrupted as the whole of the enemy host suddenly charged, axes raised.

Their line held as best it could, but the initial impact of these well-seasoned and well-armored shock troops broke them. Shields were splintered, swords shattered, and men's screams mixed with the primal yells of battle.

Arcus battered his foes, peeling one open like a can of meat and smashing another's helmeted head beneath his paw, yet more and more axes found their homes in his flesh as the enemy focused on the clearest threat.

As his blood flowed, his magic waned, and he felt his enchantment beginning to end.

"Elbaf," he growled, his voice heavy with pain as he took two stumbling steps backwards. "I must return to my form . . ."

His words trailed off as he began to shrink back into himself and he momentarily lost sight of the battle around him. He blinked as his vision returned a few moments later and saw Elbaf standing over him, his greatsword in one hand and a scavenged steel shield in the other.

"If you've any more tricks," Elbaf grunted as he deflected a wild ax-swing with his shield, "we are well past the time."

He saw Elbaf deflect another blow with his sword and then raise up and jam the pointed bottom of his shield into the neck of the man who swung. A wet gurgle emanated from the beast as it fell backwards, dragging his shield away as he fell.

He was at least renewed, a side effect of the shape-change being that his body underwent incredibly accelerated healing. He was fully invigorated as he raised up and drew his bow in one solid motion. He let fly a flurry of arrows, driving the enemy back behind their shoulder-shields and giving what was left of their men a brief reprieve.

Their men were separated now; he couldn't see Derrin, Tomlin, or Julias at all, and it was only Elbaf's stalwart presence that kept some semblance of a line in front of him.

"This isn't working," Elbaf yelled, as he, Cormorant, and Rennault held the line as the last visible men still on their feet, besides Arcus and an unsteady Darko.

He looked to his chest and saw with relief that Lilliana's flower was still there, all six remaining petals glowing unsullied in the firelight. The druid reached up and plucked one in desperation as he dodged a wickedly barbed hatchet that flew lightning-fast from the enemy line, praying Lilliana would answer his call again.

As before, the world seemed to buck and roil as the magic of the petal was unleashed. Lightning flashed overhead and the trees swayed in a sudden gale force wind.

But almost as soon as it began, Arcus could feel something was wrong.

The fire at their backs sparked and flurried, growing and shrinking dramatically in fits and spurts. He turned in horror to see the core of the fire turn to flickering black flames, and for a brief moment he could see *through* them.

The ground beyond was red sand, barren and hot, and filled with a war camp that put Duke Boric's to shame. A whole host, *thousands* of soldiers like the ones they fought now, were arrayed in neat, organized lines, training at pells and drilling in parade fields overseen by officers.

The skies turned ugly and lightning seemed to strike at random, tearing up great chunks of ground as the sky unleashed a torrent of arcing electricity throughout the woodland and all over the clearing.

Whether by chance or Lilliana's blessing, the lightning didn't hit any of their men, but two of the enemy were not so lucky; they were reduced to smoking husks by the columns of energy from above.

The remaining warriors, defying all expectations, gestured wildly at the fire, then broke and ran. They lifted up as many of their dead as they could and dragged them swiftly towards the fire.

The warriors seemed suddenly unwilling to engage, and rather than draw within the range of the group's blades, they pulled their dead companions around to either side and then straight into the flames.

Elbaf, Arcus, and their men watched in wary disbelief as the soldiers disappeared into the flames one after another, until, just as the last warrior disappeared into the heart of the fire, the flames extinguished themselves in a sudden whoosh.

Lilliana appeared in the same instant, a crackling peal of thunder announcing her arrival as a cascade of lightning filled the skies.

Arcus wanted nothing more than to fall to the ground and weep, but he could not, not with Lilliana here.

"My lady--"

"I couldn't reach you," Lilliana scowled, her gaze lingering on Arcus for only the briefest moment before turning towards the ashes of the fire. "Something was . . . interfering with me. Someone *else* was opening doors in a way I haven't felt since . . ."

She turned from her musings with sudden concern.

"How did you know of this place, Arcus?"

"I-I don't know," he stammered. "But these men, they need aid--"

Lilliana grimaced and seemed to flicker in and out of existence for a moment, alarm written all over her features.

"I . . . can't stay long," she managed through gritted teeth. "Take these berries, they will heal the wounds of your brethren." As she spoke, she knelt and placed a hand upon the ground. When she stood again, a broad berry bush, bearing fruit the size of apples, sprouted from the ground.

"Go north. Find Lorehammer at Fort Kyber," she flickered in and out again as she spoke. "Heed your dreams, but be cautious; other forces are at work now."

"Lorehammer," Arcus repeated, confused. "I don't understand."

"Find him." She gripped his shoulders. "Tell him what happened here. We will meet again, Groveborn."

With that, she faded entirely.

Arcus stood frozen a moment, utterly unprepared for her sudden disappearance and deeply afraid of anything that could make her react so strongly.

But men were bleeding out at his feet, and he could not leave them to die.

Arcus sorted through the wreckage, finding what was left of their missing men, including young Derrin who, apart from being unconscious and sporting a nasty gash on his forehead, was shockingly uninjured some twenty feet away. Then he plucked a double handful of the berries and started to distribute them to the injured, helping those who were too hurt to feed themselves. Cuts and gashes healed, bleeding stopped, and even life-threatening injuries scabbed over and stitched themselves together as his patients ate.

Arcus worked through what was left of the night, adding in as much of his own power as he could apply and wishing desperately that Talia was still with them.

By the time dawn broke, the bulk of the work was done, and they were left to survey the gruesome scene of the battlefield around them.

When their labors finished, Arcus and Elbaf sat together, both exhausted beyond words and tired to the bone. They were the only soldiers still awake. Darko had cast a spell of sleep on their men that he said would help them recover further, and in Elbaf's frank assessment it was worth the risk.

"Why, Arcus?" Elbaf asked him softly, looking out over their slumbering troops. "Tell me there was a reason."

Elbaf stood, his knees and back aching from the constant weight of armor and the exertion of combat.

"I *know* there's a reason," Arcus answered him, his voice cracking with guilt. "Something here called to me, though I don't know why."

Elbaf looked over the field. The pile of ashes and half-burned logs still smoking from the night before, the sparkling, slowly melting sheet of ice that still held several of their foes suspended, and the bloodsoaked ground all around them. Something nagged at him, dwelling in the back of his mind like a thing forgotten. Restlessness took hold of him and he strode over to the nearest enemy soldier, looking down on the man's broken body. Mud and gore was smeared across the man's breastplate, but half an emblem lay beneath.

Even the corner of it caught his gaze instantly and his blood ran cold.

He dropped to his knees and wiped the dark steel with his bare hands, smearing the grime around in an attempt to reveal the markings underneath and yet, when at last they became clear enough that there could be no mistake, he recoiled as though bitten by a snake.

The breastplate was emblazoned with an upside down ax embedded in a cracked mountain, the chosen heraldry of Dramugar, warchief of the dreaded Splitrock Horde.

"Impossible," Elbaf managed between shallow breaths.

The half-orc rubbed his eyes, steeled himself, and then looked again, but the symbol did not change. He stumbled to his feet and rushed to another soldier, then another, each time further confirming the truth he could not reconcile with reality.

"What's wrong?" Arcus struggled to his feet and joined Elbaf. "Do you . . . know these men?"

"They are not men," Elbaf growled, kneeling to rip off one of the helmets and revealing the dark green skin and long fangs of a gigantic orc.

"By the huntress . . ." Arcus' eyes widened. "Orcs? Of this size?"

"They are not of this plane," Darko added menacingly from behind the two, surprising them again with how stealthily he could move when he so chose.

"These are Ohryics," he explained, spelling out the difference and turning up his nose. "So called, *true* orcs. They are the pureblooded of their race, not diluted by eons of intermingling with goblin, giant, and ogre folk."

"They are more than that," Elbaf tried to keep his voice steady. "They are of Dramugar's horde."

"Impossible," Darko shook his head. "He hasn't been seen in nearly fifteen years, and before that Dramugar pillaged the far western reaches for a decade or more."

"So," Arcus said. "Is it not possible--"

"Dramugar *must* be in his twilight years by now," Darko insisted. "No orc, trueblood or not, would still be fighting in their forties or, god forbid, their fifties. And that's *if* they were to live that long."

"Well, what if--"

"No *orc* has ever mastered planar travel," Darko shot back. "It's simply not possible. More likely he has an heir who has taken up the mantle of warchief. More likely still, some powerful wizard directs them from behind the scenes and enables their movement for their own nefarious purpose."

"But they're *here*," Elbaf gestured at the fallen bodies. "They're here *now*. We have to warn people, we have to warn--"

"What would you have us do, Elbaf?" Darko raised his hands in frustration. "We are fugitives in all but name. We have no standing to warn the Empire. We have no Duke Boric, no audience in the halls of power. We should do as we were told and push northward to Kyber and pray that Colonel Redding will hear us when we arrive."

"Darko," Arcus said, his voice low but earnest. "There's more." He waited a beat, ensuring he had the full attention of his companions. "I saw something in the flames," Arcus explained as clearly as he could. "At the end, when they were retreating or falling back or . . . whatever they were doing."

"What did you see, Arcus?" Darko narrowed his eyes. "Be as specific as you can."

"I saw a war camp and thousands of soldiers just like these."

They all fell silent.

"If they have a host that large," Elbaf chewed on the revelation, "they have the power to threaten the Empire itself, or at least to occupy the bulk of her armies for a few seasons."

"Tell me," Darko prompted. "Tell me about the skies, the ground. Were there animals? Plants or trees?"

"I saw red sand and bare rock," Arcus shrugged. "The skies were a hazy purplish color, I think. There was smoke from a thousand fires, but no, no vegetation at all."

"*Red* earth," Darko mulled. "Purple skies and no plants? That's like no plane I've ever heard of."

He pulled a tome from his bag, one that seemed far too large to have fit in the first place.

"What does it mean, Darko?"

"I'm not sure, Elbaf," the wizard answered darkly. "I need to do some research . . . By the gods, I wish I had access to my materials back at the Academy."

After a great deal of bickering, the party finally reached an accord. They opted to burn the bodies of their fallen foes and bring with them a breastplate and an ax emblazoned with Dramugar's crest. They would continue northward as Darko had suggested, but would insist upon an audience with the Colonel when they arrived and warn him at once of the danger this incursion represented.

They rested as long as they could, but by midmorning they began to feel the same paranoia that had driven them to travel so far the night before. At any moment they expected Annabelle to appear overhead on her dragon, or for another pack of Dramugar's men to assault from their extraplanar holdout.

When Elbaf finally roused the men who were still asleep and ordered the soldiers to strike camp, there was a palpable feeling of relief to be back on the move and away from the scene of the frenzied combat of the night before.

Arcus had managed to recall their horses, a blessing which Elbaf could not overstate, and the bulk of the gear was separated out among the five remaining animals.

Corporal Felder rode as well, to his embarrassment, but there was no getting around the fact that without his leg, he would otherwise slow them down considerably. Elbaf tried to console him by giving him charge of the baggage train, but he knew in his core the frustration the man must feel.

They'd set out fairly early, and he hoped by nightfall to be far away from this place.

He shouldered his own gear, which he ensured was more than any of his men would have to carry, and headed to the middle of the column. He found himself next to Derrin and found the boy uncharacteristically quiet. His eyes had a hardened, hyper-vigilant focus and he studied each of his fellows as they marched beside him.

"Sir," he said simply as Elbaf approached.

The boy's formality stung, but Elbaf attributed it to the fresh scar along his forehead.

"How are you holding up?" he asked.

"Fair enough, sir." The boy shrugged again. "I'll be alright."

Elbaf raised an eyebrow at the young man's nonchalance, surprised beyond his ability to suppress.

"It's alright, you know," Elbaf reassured him. "You took a nasty wound last night. If there's anything you--"

"I'm fine, sir." Derrin smiled unconvincingly, his eyes showing nothing of the carefree youth that had been his hallmark.

"Alright." Elbaf shrugged, adjusting the weight of his pack.

Elbaf stayed alongside Derrin for a while, hoping the young man would open up again and kicking himself for not checking in more regularly, but eventually it became obvious that Derrin had nothing more to say. Determined not to let such a gulf grow between himself and the rest of his men, Elbaf made sure he checked in personally with each of his soldiers as they walked. He spent most of the day dropping back and forth along the short column to hear from every member of their party. Most of them were grateful, confiding in him their doubts, their frustrations, and their fears.

The last of these, their fears, Elbaf treasured most. These were not soft men, they were strong of back and of resolve, and for them to trust him enough to reveal the thoughts that kept them from slumber in the dark of night only furthered his determination to see them safely to the end of their journey.

Chapter Twenty-Four

One day turned to two, which rolled into a week before the party at last began to breathe easily. With every uneventful day that passed, they recovered their morale and their health. The dark circles that hung under the eyes of the men began to fade, and their sunken, hollow cheeks filled back in on a steady diet of rabbit, venison, and anything else they could harvest from the surrounding wilds.

At eight days, Elbaf began allowing for a small fire at night, and the effect it had on the mood of the party was considerable. By fifteen, the group had regained much of its humor, and boisterous laughter accompanied the fires each night.

Elbaf's mind grew more at ease with each new sunrise, and were it not for Private Derrin's continued distance, he would feel almost normal again.

By the end of their third week on the trail, the scenery had begun to change, as well. Autumn had well and truly fallen, and the further north they traveled, the more rugged the hills became. Mountains grew in the distance and loomed unspeakably high as they approached.

"The northern edge of the Krishta Range," Arcus informed him one afternoon as they hiked a bare ridgeline against a blistering wind. "If you followed that down to the southeast you would find yourself in my homeland."

"Is that where this cold is blowing in from?" he retorted. "If it is, I think I'll pass."

Three days later, they got the first glimpse of their destination.

Fort Kyber, nestled at the mouth of the infamous Kyber Pass, was a fortress unparalleled. It was fed by not one, not two, but three underground streams that bubbled up from different parts of the mountains surrounding it, and many high pastures were nestled within its walls to keep its people fed in times of siege.

It was the oldest military installation in the entire Empire, and legend claimed that the Emperor himself had seen to its construction a millenia ago.

Walls thick enough for four men to stand abreast surrounded the city in three concentric circles, and each with only two gates: south to the Empire, and north to her ancient enemy, Tirja. The outer wall was fifty feet or more, and the gates, as they saw on their approach, looked to be of solid iron. Each of the two wide swinging doors must have weighed several tons. When they were fully opened, as they were now, three or four wagons could likely ride side by side through the opening.

All of the trees, as well as any bush above waist height, had been cut down for a quarter mile around the walls, so there was no use trying to hide their approach.

Elbaf caught the glint off a spyglass from the wall, and was therefore unsurprised to find a welcome party of two dozen men-at-arms. One man with stark white hair and a wide billowing cloak of black, stood out as much for his onyx platemail as for his regal bearing. If he wasn't mistaken, this would be Colonel Redding.

"My lord," he called out from the head of the column as they approached the at last. "Lieutenant Elbainsen, reporting for duty with Lieutenants D'Ari and Branislav, as well as our . . . er, security retinue." He ended his statement with a precise salute, just as he stepped within the prescribed ten paces.

"Is that supposed to mean something to me in particular, Lieutenant?" The man returned his salute, but otherwise didn't budge.

"Ah, sir," Darko cut in. "Perhaps we could have a more private word with you?"

The Colonel continued to look nonplussed.

"Duke Boric sent us with--"

"Aha." The man broke into an immediate smile. "You must be candidates for the schoolhouse."

"Yessir," they said in unison.

"That old bastard is always sending me his *handpicked* candidates," he laughed again, waving his men forward to relieve the soldiers of their burdens. "You and your men look like you've been through hell, twice."

"It's been a rough go, sir," Darko agreed politely.

"Well, let's see them fed." He gestured to the three officers, "You three come with me; we'll get them set in the infirmary and bedded down with full bellies."

They bid farewell to their men amidst reassurances from the Colonel that they would be well cared for, and he led them through the gates ahead of the rest of the group.

"Welcome to Fort Kyber," he gestured as they emerged through the first and thickest wall.

The space between the first and second walls was a patchwork of small but carefully managed pastures. In all, it was perhaps three hundred feet from the one gate to the next, but that space was packed densely with low stone walls, livestock, and well-tended fields of hay and other fodder.

"We've outlasted many a siege here," Redding explained, noting the analytical stares of his newest recruits. "And if the Empire requires it of us, we'll weather more."

The next set of walls was closer together and far older. The space between held a warren of houses, three stories high. The streets wound off in unpredictable ways, and despite the distance between the walls being half the previous set, it took twice as long to traverse it.

"An invading army would be absolutely at your mercy," Elbaf noted dryly after their fifth turn.

The innermost ring was a single massive castle, its towering parapets overlooking both the city and the pass from which it drew its name.

"You'll have to get used to it," Redding chuckled. "But don't worry, it's much easier to memorize the streets from up in the keep itself and you'll have plenty of time to familiarize yourself over the next six months."

"Six months?" Arcus mouthed at Darko, who glared back and shushed him silently with a finger to his lips.

"First though," Redding announced as they mounted a wide stone staircase just past the third and final gate. "You'll meet the rest of your class."

Thirty minutes later they entered a wide plaza, ringed with a low marble railing that overlooked the city.

"You've arrived just in time, actually." Redding walked to the railing and looked out over the city below. "The last class graduates next in four days, and you'll start the day after that."

"Sir?" Elbaf asked. "I am ashamed to admit that Duke Boric wasn't able to give us much of a briefing on what this course would consist of."

"It's not like old Boric to send folks unprepared . . . I'm here to build you into a better leader, son," Redding turned back towards them. "I'm here to teach you how to fight with your heads, not just your swords, your bows, and your spells. To elevate your thinking above the immediate battle and to keep your eyes on the *campaign*. In short, gentlemen, I'm here to teach you how to win wars."

Elbaf tried to size up the rest of the people in the room, but he found himself with more questions than answers. Three straight-laced looking captains eyed their group with similar interest from the far corner of the room. Elbaf judged them to be open-and-shut military types - regular officers though, not Hands - and judging by the quality of their armor and the matching longswords at their hips, they were likely noble-born.

Arcus was ten feet away, towards the center of the room, chatting up another woodsy-type fellow. They'd done all but compare longbows at this point, and, at last listen, they were discussing the finer points of identifying mushrooms on the trail.

A few minutes ago, a lithe shadow of a man had slipped silently through the door and immediately posted up with his back to the darkest corner of the room, just inside the door and to the left. His sparkling blue eyes contrasted magnificently with the inky blackness of his skin and the charcoal gray of his leather armor. He wore a rapier and at least three knives that Elbaf had marked, but he found it challenging to get a read on him. Was he a spy? An assassin? He wore no rank, and his outfit screamed of custom tailoring and costly materials.

As he pondered the stranger, he turned his attention to Colonel Redding and the two individuals quietly flanking him at the far end of the room. To his right, a bronze-skinned man in a cream colored vest and odd balloon-like pants of sapphire blue. His shoes - which looked more suited to dancing than to combat - had upturned, pointed toes. About his waist he had the most extravagant blade Elbaf had ever seen. The scabbard was ivory studded with topaz, and the platinum hilt was engraved in soft swirling patterns reminiscent of a cluster of seashells. The man's broad smile was disarming, and he shared it freely with the students arrayed before him.

To Redding's left, a man who could not be more the first fellow's opposite. He was small and frail, his gray hair cascading down his bowed back and organized into neat braids. He wore simple robes of deep, rich brown and leaned heavily on a tall wooden staff. He read as some kind of spellcaster, but if appearances were to be believed, Elbaf couldn't see why he was here except that he seemed as old as time itself. That said, Darko hadn't taken his eyes off the ancient fellow since the moment he entered the room, so Elbaf made a mental note to ask him about it later.

He was spared from further musing by the Colonel, who glanced at the light outside one of the large bay windows and, after a slight frown, stepped forward and waved, silencing the low murmurs filling the room.

"Welcome," Colonel Redding announced, raising his hands and smiling warmly at the unusual assortment of characters before him. "I rather expected we would--"

The door behind Elbaf flew open just as the man began to speak, but rather than angry, the Colonel seemed relieved and even, perhaps, amused.

"Ah, here we are," he smiled. "Our *exchange* student, so to speak."

All eyes turned to the newcomer, and Elbaf couldn't help it as his mouth popped open with surprise. The woman in front of him, from her polished steel breastplate to the flowing, muted yellow priestess' garb she wore beneath it, shone like an angel. Golden hair and bright green eyes swept the breath from his lungs and a nervous, crooked smile set his heart stuttering.

The woman gave a short bow and tucked a wild strand of hair behind not-quite-elven ears as she shuffled closer to the rest of the group.

"My apologies, sir," she apologized with a voice that sounded like a chorus of songbirds. "A pair of *brigands* sought to profit from my apparent helplessness in the pass."

"Which they no doubt paid for, my dear." He smiled warmly. "This is my god-daughter, Sami Herzsteller. She's a visitor from Tirja, and I expect that won't be a problem, right?"

Aside from a few widened eyes, no one said a word.

"Good." He nodded sharply. "Then I'd like to introduce you to your two primary instructors, Archmagus Varin Lorehammer and Swordmaster Razael, Bahram of Maraan. Between them, they will elevate your understanding of warfare."

The education offered so far at Fort Kyber, at least in Darko's estimation, was superior in nearly every conceivable way to his initial training. Even now, while he awaited Archmagus Lorehammer, he couldn't help but compare the vast, floor-to-ceiling library he stood in with the barren classrooms of the Capitol's Battle Magic Basic Course he'd been forced to endure.

"Magus Branislav," Loreammer announced his arrival with a warm smile and gestured that Darko should sit. "I have been looking forward to meeting with you directly."

"As have I, sir," Darko bowed respectfully at the waist.

"Your companion," Lorehammer looked pointedly at Darko's hood, "might be more comfortable out in the open, but I leave that to the two of you."

"I, er, thank you, sir." Darko was impressed; he hadn't detected any spells, but there was no way that Lorehammer could have seen Reia without augmenting his sight.

Reia fluttered down to the table and, perhaps to see if she would get a reaction from the old man, transformed abruptly into her natural form in a cloud of pinkish smoke.

"Welcome, Q'Jralli," Lorehammer nodded respectfully. "Thank you for joining us."

"Why thank you," Reia smiled broadly and performed a quick and only slightly sarcastic curtsey. "Charmed, I'm sure."

"Sir." Darko chose his next words delicately. "I'm not sure what I am supposed to *learn* here, sir. Is there specific spellwork I should--"

"No," Lorehammer laughed. "No, not at all, my elven friend. You are nearly as old as I am, I presume, and so I do not intend to teach you any specific spells. This library is *full* to the brim with knowledge, and if you choose to seek out and learn new spells or enchantments, then I both applaud and support you."

"Then I'm not sure I understand my role, sir."

"I'm here to teach you about the *application* of magic." Lorehammer winked. "To teach you the utility of understanding the battlefield and how a seemingly irrelevant spell could determine victory or defeat." While he spoke, the old man produced a map from within his robes and placed it on the long cherry-wood table between them.

"Study this map," he said. "And tell me, how best you could apply your magic to provide your men an advantage."

Darko looked at the map, which depicted a stranded unit of infantrymen with their backs to a broad river. They faced an overwhelming force to their front and an impassable river behind them.

"Sir," Darko scratched his chin. "Am I to assume I am the only wizard in this formation?"

"You are, yes."

"And the enemy numbers . . ." He counted tactical symbols. "*Two hundred* or more?"

"They do."

"I . . . I could not possibly defeat so many with my magic alone," Darko shook his head. "And with only twenty five men to support me . . . I'm sorry, I don't see a way to--"

"What's limiting you?"

"Well, the *river*," Darko laughed nervously. "Crossing it is our only hope."

"So, get to the other side."

"If we *could* cross it our survival would be assured," Darko continued. "But there's no way I could move that many men that quickly."

"How then," Lorehammer leaned forward, "do you propose to get them to the other side?"

"Well, that's what I'm saying," Darko repeated himself, frustrated already with the exercise. "I can't move that many men with any kind of speed."

"What *can* you move?"

"I-- What?"

"What can you move?" Lorehammer smiled. "And how can you get your men to the other side, if you can't move *them*?"

"I can't move an *entire river*," Darko scoffed. "If that's what you're suggesting."

"Can't you?"

"It's impossible, no one could possibly move that much water." Darko shook his head, his chin up with confidence. "And even if you *could*, the water is already moving on its own!"

Lorehammer stared at him with a soft smile, and with one gnarled old finger, traced a steady line across the river and in front of his imaginary soldiers.

"The water *is* already moving." Lorehammer sat back. "A simple wall of stone or force would change its course. The water becomes your *opponent's* obstacle, and your men are safely behind it, not having moved an inch."

Darko sat straighter and looked at the map more closely. The wall in question would be a fairly simple construct. It was deceptively easy to shape earth and stone, and it was a series of spells that every new mage learned early in their career. More advanced casters could create walls of other materials - ice, fire, or even pure energy - but it took a great deal of effort to do so.

"Proper application of force is everything." Lorehammer tapped the parchment, his face suddenly serious. "One need not be the greatest sorcerer of all time to win a war, only the most *useful*. The most *effective*."

"I am . . . humbled."

"Then you are learning." Lorehammer stood and turned back towards the door. "Your lessons begin in earnest tomorrow, and you may expect every day to end with a similar exercise. The only right answer is success, and the only wrong answer is failure. Do you understand?"

"I do, sir," Darko stood. "And, er, the library is . . ."

"Available for use at your leisure," Lorehammer smiled warmly and bowed again before showing himself out.

Arcus was resting, his breath heavy and sweat dotting his brow as he stretched out the kinks in his sword arm. He sat on a low bench at the edge of a sparring room and sipped some tepid water from a flask.

"Your large friend," one of his fellow students tapped his shoulder, prompting him to turn around. "He fights like a demon."

The man, Captain Kristoff MacCadal, was one of the three swordsmen they'd met on their first day in Kyber. He was a better swordsman than Arcus, but he too was resting after being soundly beaten.

"He is, I think, the best swordsman I have ever met," Kristoff said, his funny lilting accent giving away his heritage as being from Soelves in the far northwest. "Except, of course, Swordmaster Razael himself."

Their instructor was a tornado of steel and silk, and of the fighters in the room, only Elbaf could last more than a minute against him.

Razael never tired, he never sweat, and he never rested between matches. But every afternoon he would cycle through every one of his students in one-on-one combat. No matter the order he fought them in, they all wound up bruised and exhausted on the bench.

After the first three weeks, he'd taken to saving Elbaf for last, and though some might have thought it favoritism, none of the warriors in the class disputed Elbaf's primacy. It didn't hurt that it was a genuine pleasure to watch the two of them spar. Wooden training swords blasted a frenzied staccato, and all eyes were glued to the two dancing, swirling fighters.

Today, the fight was particularly intense and had lasted longer than ever before. Elbaf surprised the crowd by turning an overhand swing into a feint and sweeping his opponents legs with a swift kick, and a collective gasp ran through the small crowd. Razael rolled left, narrowly avoiding a wicked downswing, then he pulled himself into a somersault backwards to dodge another, rolling to his feet and narrowly deflecting a third blow.

But the balance had irreversibly shifted, and Razael gave ground over the next few swings. All of the other students were at the edge of their seats as the two traded blows until, in a surprising twist, Razael executed a particularly superb parry and riposte, knocking Elbaf's larger sword away and closing fast for a finish. But Elbaf wasn't out yet. Instead, he met the instructor's advance with a haymaker to the gut, impacting the much smaller man with a sound like a sledgehammer and an audible grunt.

Razael slid back several feet, and it was Elbaf's turn to close, hoping with a vicious side swing to end the fight. The Swordmaster caught Elbaf's sword swing on the blade of a dagger in one hand while he thrust with his saber in the other, and the fight came to a close at last.

The students stomped and cheered, breaking out in spontaneous applause as the two were locked momentarily in a frozen tableau. Razael's blade was barely touching Elbaf's throat, and the half-orc's sword was barely held back by a thick-bladed dirk, just a few inches from the Swordmaster's neck.

Both were panting, and for the first time since beginning their lessons, Razael seemed winded.

"Very good, Master Elbainsen," Razael huffed, flashing a broad, brilliantly white smile. He dropped his arms and, while stretching his shoulders out, turned to address the rest of the class, "An early day today, I think." He gave a short bow, as he always did, before continuing, "Thank you for your attention, your dedication, and your trust. Have a wonderful evening. I will see you at sunrise."

The class, having expected a few more hours of drills, was ecstatic to be leaving so early, and they promptly began their afternoon clean-up ritual of sweeping the rough wooden floors, polishing the wall-length mirror that ran down one side of the sparring room, and all of the other sundry chores required to maintain the space.

"Master Elbainsen," Razael stopped him before he could go join the others. "I would like a private word with you."

Elbaf glanced at his companions, uncomfortable with the idea of them cleaning while he talked to their instructor, but nodded and returned to the Swordmaster's side. Razael led him across the room where a set of wide folding doors led to a balcony overlooking the pass.

"After you," Razael waved at the doorway.

Elbaf passed through, followed by the Swordmaster who turned and shut the doors behind them.

"You are a mystery to me," Razael mused aloud, leaning against the railing and staring into the falling dusk. "In all my years, I have never met another Bahram in the Empire, and yet you are raw, and seemingly unaware of your--"

"Sorry, sir," Elbaf interrupted, trying to keep up. "What *is* a Bahram?"

Razael paused, a look of genuine surprise on his face, and then broke into a fit of laughter. His laugh was soft, kind, and not at all demeaning, but Elbaf still felt uncomfortable not being in on the joke.

"Sir?"

"You have answered my questions already." He put a hand on Elbaf's shoulder. "Most of them, anyway." Razael grew serious once again. "Bahram are what we call spirit-warriors in Maraan. They harness energies within themselves to become one with their weapon, invincible in battle. *I* am Bahram and, perhaps more importantly, *you* are Bahram."

"I'm sorry, sir, but you're mistaken," Elbaf shook his head. "I have no magic, no *energies,* within me. Certainly none I can use, or I wouldn't have grown up a street urchin too poor to eat most nights."

"Trust me, Master Elbainsen," Razael urged him. "This I know for truth. You have the gifts within you, and with training you *can* be Bahram. You were born to be."

Elbaf hesitated, unsure. Something about what the man was saying rang true to him, but he could not reconcile his simple life with the idea of possessing some kind of mystical powers.

"Your parents," Razael changed the subject abruptly. "Tell me about them."

"My father was Imperial Army, and my mother a basket weaver," Elbaf said, his trademark expressionless facade falling over his face at the mention of one of his least favorite subjects.

Razael seemed to sense his frustration, but he didn't shift topics again.

"The man who raised you," he nodded. "He was a soldier, yes, but what about your *father*, do you--"

"My father, *Elbain*," Elbaf growled, his hackles well and truly raised, "was a soldier who died serving his Empire and, above that, a good man."

Razael relented, raising his hands in surrender.

"As you wish, Master Elbainsen," he frowned.

Neither spoke as the uncomfortable moment lengthened, and Razael turned back to staring off into the distance. Elbaf stood awkwardly, unsure of whether to stay or go, until Razael broke the silence at last.

"Master Elbainsen," he offered gently. "You are a stellar swordsman."

"Thank you, sir."

"But you have the capacity within you to be legendary," Razael's voice took on an unexpected passion. "I want to help you reach your potential. So, if you are willing, I would cherish the opportunity to--"

"I'll do it," Elbaf nodded. "I'll do it sir, just tell me what to do."

Razael smiled so genuinely that the whole balcony was warmed by it.

"Very well." He gave another short bow. "Then I will see you tomorrow, two hours before sunrise."

"Yessir," Elbaf saluted and moved back towards the door.

"Master Elbainsen," Razael called after him. "Bring your father's sword."

Arcus was frustrated, but he tried not to let it show. For the last month and a half he'd been attending courses with Darko and Sami, and for the past month he'd felt outshone in every class. The three of them were identified as the only magical folk in the group and were therefore clumped together for a block of instruction on the subjects of effect spells, battlefield manipulation, and other ways to use magic as a tool to create advantages for their forces.

Darko was the star pupil - that much was certain - but that was no surprise to Arcus. The wizard had the right answer for nearly every question posed by Archmagus Lorehammer, and he had the ability to follow through with whatever course of action he suggested.

Arcus, on the other hand, was limited to shaping ground and stone, manipulating wildlife, vegetation, and the weather - none of which seemed to dazzle their instructor in the slightest.

Sami, for her part, was similarly limited. She seemed to possess a number of powerful abilities that reminded Arcus of a more martial version of what Sister Talia might be in a few years. Sami could cause whole groups of soldiers to fight with renewed vigor and enhanced strength. She knew rituals that could bless, or heal, or protect whole platoons of men at a time, and her ability to heal an individual was nothing short of miraculous. In fact, it was thanks to her that Corporal Felder regained his missing leg. She'd learned of his injury from speaking with the druid, and had visited him in the infirmary that very night.

Other than that one conversation, however, they'd only spoken a few times in passing. She tended to keep to herself around Arcus, Darko, and Elbaf in particular, and the druid was beginning to wonder if she was just shy. He'd decided a week ago that he'd try to break the ice, but hadn't yet had the opportunity.

Today though, their class had ended early and just he and Sami were left in the library for the moment. Scooping up his notes and folding them gently, he approached the young woman.

"Pardon me, Sister--"

"I'm not a *Sister*," she snapped at him, eyes flashing as she glanced at his chest with obvious disapproval. "I am a *Sedhir*, a war-priestess of Lyost, the divine arbiter of justice and vengeance."

She closed the book she was reading with a sharp snap and began to collect her things.

"Ah, erm, right," Arcus stammered, kicking himself. "I meant no offense. I'm--"

"Lieutenant and Black Hand Arcus D'Ari," she finished for him. "We were introduced at the beginning of the course, nearly three months ago, if you recall."

"Did I do something *wrong*?" Arcus raised his hands in exasperation.

"Yes," she frowned disapprovingly. "You and I have nothing to discuss. I am Tirjani, and you are a Hand, a zealot of Imperial will. I don't trust you. I think you're a threat to my godfather, to this school, and, most especially, to me. Are we finished here?" She looked at him with all the grace of an irritated teacher admonishing a youngster.

"I-- No, we're not," Arcus tried to formulate a response to the blistering coldness of the woman. "I'm not a Hand by *choice*!"

She paused, eyes narrow and suspicious.

"How is that possible?" She raised her chin defiantly. "All Hands swear an oath of service on pain of death. Your dedication to the laws of the Empire is legendary, as is your uncompromising treatment of lawbreakers."

"Once upon a time, perhaps," Arcus shook his head ruefully. "But, to my knowledge, that is a fairy tale. The men and women I was trained with were mostly like me, bound to servitude against our wills."

"Why should I believe you?"

"I . . . don't know," Arcus replied. "I guess you have to decide that for yourself. I'm sorry to have bothered you." He turned on his heel and promptly headed for the exit, wishing he hadn't decided to speak with her at all.

"Wait," she called out, hurrying to catch up to him. "I . . . uh, I fear I have prejudged you."

He shrugged, but paused on his path to the door and allowed her to catch up.

"You're the first Hand I have personally interacted with," she admitted. "But news of your order's exploits reach far beyond the borders of the Empire."

"And what do you hear beyond the Empire, priestess?"

"That you are judge, jury, and executioner," she said grimly. "That you extend the Emperor's rule through a combination of fear, magic, and unparalleled dedication. That you do not suffer lawbreakers to live."

"Then you know more truth than many who are young Hands themselves." Arcus smiled darkly. "We are told that ours is a sacred duty. That we preserve the peace, mind the laws of the Empire, and defend her as the most capable of warriors and leaders."

They walked the hall together, passing between shadow and light as they crossed a dozen stained glass windows overlooking the city.

"Maybe that's true for some of my classmates," Arcus sighed. "I hope it is. But since the day I was condemned to servitude, I have found myself straying further and further from what my heart tells me is right. Further from the ideals I once held dear."

They talked for an hour or more, wandering the halls and chatting idly as night began to fall. Arcus told Sami of their adventures so far. She asked questions constantly, but far from finding her irritating, Arcus was genuinely pleased to see her interest. They spoke at length about the minotaur, Vedhellar, and his family. She was as stunned and outraged by the betrayal of Lord Goldrun as he had been. She was similarly shocked by Elbaf's treatment after the assault on the goblin village, and, as Arcus spun the yarn of how they'd come to be at the schoolhouse, she seemed to warm to him considerably.

Eventually they found their way back to the dormitories where they all slept. As Arcus prepared to wish the woman goodnight, a funny look crossed her face.

"The half-orc," she said, her cheeks ever-so-slightly tinged with red. "He is . . . like you?"

"How do you--"

"He didn't choose to be a Hand, either?" she clarified.

"No, and I think sometimes it weighs on him most heavily."

"He seems very brave," she murmured. "And so very far from the world he knew before."

"He is indeed very brave," Arcus agreed warmly. "A man of deep principles and possessing an uncharacteristic heart."

Sami seemed to forget for a moment that he was there, staring off into the distance by the light of a soft lantern hanging from the wall.

"Goodnight, *Sedhir* Sami." Arcus gave a half-bow, rousing her with a small jump from her musings.

"Goodnight, Lieutenant." She smiled back. "I'm glad we finally met. Properly, that is."

Elbaf wasn't drunk, but he'd had enough mead to crack a rare smile as he looked up and down the length of the long wooden table at which he sat. The broad, timeworn slab of wood was chipped, dented, scratched, and even sported a few burn marks up and down its length, but tonight the only thing that mattered were the relaxed, laughing faces of his soldiers. They shared their drink under the roof of the House of Faded Wings, a bar that had, according to the locals, stood in this very spot since before the Empire was ever founded.

Tonight they had the full crew, and the table was crowded, but the men who sat there felt the gaps left by the companions they'd lost along the way. They were, by now, quite deep in their cups, and many a toast had been made to the poor souls of their unforgotten friends.

For nearly five months now, Elbaf, Arcus, and Darko had been attending Redding's school, and in all that time their men had been able to rest, to train, and to recover from the physical and mental exhaustion of their journey across the Empire. Spring had finally come to the Pass after a long and brutal winter, and the cool breezes and heady wildflowers of the high mountains brought a sort of frenzied, pent-up energy to the entire fort.

That energy had driven Elbaf to seek out his men, as he had often done during the long dark of the winter. He spent time with the rest of the officers during the day, but it was these stolen moments with the simple soldiers that offered him the best chance to relax. Darko and Arcus, with their unnatural, sorcerous powers, were these days often embroiled in some discussion of moving mountains, raining fire from the skies, or some other finer point of a magical nature that Elbaf found impossible to relate to. Elbaf found problems with many of the other candidates, as well. The trio from Soelves kept largely to themselves, and he rarely saw them outside of classes. Corvis Caine, the perpetually black-clad mystery figure, remained a complete unknown to him. Sedhir Herzsteller . . . well, to be honest, she was even more confusing than the rogue.

Sami had a way of confounding Elbaf's mind and tying his tongue to knots. He'd tried to speak with her in passing, but he never managed more than a fumbled greeting before shuffling away in embarrassment. Worse, he found himself increasingly irritated with how easily she and Arcus seemed to get along, and, in light of that, he had resolved weeks ago to keep away when the two of them were together.

He felt his cheeks burn from more than drink, and he hid his embarrassment behind the lip of his mug, lest his men take notice.

It was well past midnight now, but Razael had given him the next morning to himself to focus on the quieter, more meditative aspects of becoming Bahram, and Elbaf intended to sleep in as much as he was able. One unexpected benefit of his unfamiliar new training was that he was less plagued by the nightmares, less haunted by his memories, and would daresay that some days he even felt at peace, after a fashion.

The warrior rested his elbows on the table, content to listen to the idle boasting and carefree banter of his men, and scanned the room more out of habit than concern. Nothing looked out of place, all of the locals were, by now, fairly recognizable to him, and he'd just managed to flag down the bartender, Krissa, to order another round when the door flew open with a bang.

The soldiers at the table responded instantly, standing and drawing the shortswords or daggers that they were never without. Elbaf, too, was on his feet in less than a heartbeat, his hand on the hilt of his greatsword.

Elbaf looked to the door and shook his head, certain he was mistaken. But no, the person responsible for the jarring interruption was Sami. She was red in the face and breathing hard.

"Lieutenant," she huffed. "We've been called to the amphitheater immediately."

The amphitheater was one of the primary classrooms they used; it was, in fact, the first room they'd all met in on that first day, months ago.

"I don't--"

"I don't know either," she cut him off, and turned her face back towards the keep. "But it must be serious. Come on, I'm not to head back without you."

Elbaf narrowed his eyes, his heart racing, and felt the hairs on the back of his neck rise as a sense of *wrongness* took hold of his spine.

"Sergeant," he looked to Cormorant, his voice low but urgent. "The second I walk out that door, I want you to take these men back to the barracks."

The man sobered instantly, his body going rigid and his eyes hardening. The rest of the table followed suit, and a split second later they may as well have been statues waiting attentively for orders.

"Pack your things," Elbaf ordered. "I want every one of you ready to go in the next half hour. If you haven't heard from us by then, you're to assemble in the east courtyard, right outside the school."

"Aye, sir, but--"

"Don't take orders from anyone that isn't me, Arcus, or the wizard." Elbaf grabbed the man's shoulder. "Be quick, be quiet, and be careful."

He turned the man loose and stepped to the door where Sami was not-so-patiently waiting.

"You feel it too," she accused, her eyes narrow and her jaw set with concern.

"Feel what?" he deflected.

"Something's off . . ." She chewed her bottom lip as they rushed down the dim, torchlit cobblestones. "I don't know what, but *something* is wrong."

Chapter Twenty-Five

Elbaf's blood ran cold as they entered the room.

The rest of the officer candidates were already at attention in a neat row in the center of the room, all facing a woman who Elbaf recognized immediately.

Annabelle's face was a porcelain painting, a perfect picture of serenity. Everything but her eyes - they were bloodshot and streaked through with menacing black lines. As Elbaf crossed the threshold, she tilted her head to the side ever so slightly, like a cat with a new toy, and gestured to the line.

"Lieutenant Elbainsen," she said, every syllable razor sharp beneath her even tone. "So good of you to join us."

Elbaf froze for a second, at a crossroads, but then proceeded into the room before taking his place at the end of the line. Sami followed suit, coming to attention next to him at the end of the line.

"And look," she practically hissed. "You've brought a blasphemous *witch* from our dear neighbor to the north. How very . . . curious."

Sami stiffened visibly, but did not respond.

Elbaf took in the rest of the room. Their instructors were arranged behind Annabelle, and their expressions could not have been more different. Razael stood with his arms crossed over his chest, obvious distaste written across his face. Lorehammer was utterly and completely expressionless, but Elbaf noted the white in his knuckles where his hand gripped his staff. Colonel Redding was fuming. His foot tapped belligerently, and he was red in the face as he read from a piece of parchment bearing a number of broken, black wax seals.

"Good," Annabelle prompted, stepping to the center of the line. "Now that we're all here, we can get down to--"

"I don't give a damn what this scroll says!" Redding finally exploded, throwing the document to the ground and raising a finger menacingly to Annabelle. "You've lost your damn mind, Major Montagne. If you think you will come here, wake my students in the dead of night, and call together some kind of . . . what, *intervention* to root out heresy?"

Annabelle froze and turned slowly on her heel to face the Colonel.

"I'm not finished, Colonel Redding," she growled as a spiderweb of black lines began to trace itself across her face, emanating from eyes which had now turned to the deepest black. "Now be *silent*."

"Ma'am," Kristoff stepped forward, one hand on the hilt of his saber and the other out in front of himself. "Perhaps it would be best if you calmed down."

Annabelle twitched back towards the students, and Elbaf nearly took a step back in alarm. She turned the midnight pools of emptiness that her eyes had become to the young man in front of her, sizing him up.

"You dare," she hissed, black smoke congealing around her clenched fists. "You *dare?*" Annabelle raised her hand, pointing her palm at Kristoff and then suddenly clenching her fist, and the soldier froze midstep.

Kristoff stiffened, his body wracked by obvious pain, then fell to his knees.

Annabelle twisted her fist and Kristoff writhed on the ground, ripping open his own shirt and holding his chest, which was crisscrossed with wide, quickly spreading blotches of purple and gray. He gurgled and spit up blood on the stone floor and then collapsed again, falling deathly still at last as crimson flowed from his half-opened mouth.

"I have had enough!" she shouted, pacing the room in front of the remaining soldiers and instructors. "Your *miserable* group has caused me endless frustration. You have upset plans laid for *centuries*, you have ruined schemes beyond your comprehension, and your bumbling stupidity has cost me dearly already." She railed against them, confident that fear would keep them rooted firmly in place. "Boric may have misled me, five months ago," she snarled, "but you will not escape me again. I will be finished at long last with this unfortunate *detour*."

Darko watched the woman pacing in front of him and wracked his mind for a course of action that wouldn't leave him just as dead as poor Kristoff a few yards away. He searched the woman's features, her ebony armor, and the room around them for something, *anything* to use against her.

He locked eyes for a moment with Lorehammer. The archmage's eyes were half closed, and his lips were moving swiftly and silently, even to Darko's elven ears.

All hope was *not* lost then, Darko reassured himself. At least, not yet.

Master!

Reia redirected his attention to Annabelle just in time to see her remove a pair of objects from a belt pouch at her waist. In a flash he recognized two of the same black, chalk-like sticks he'd seen her utilize all those months ago at the Altimeer estate.

"No," he gasped, unable to contain himself as she broke the sticks together with a crisp *snap*.

An instant after she broke the chalk, the stone underneath her feet blackened and scorched in a circle almost ten feet wide. There was a flash of black fire that momentarily engulfed her, blinding everyone in the room. A second later, the light faded and a figure stood behind her. If it was a man, it was the largest Darko had ever seen.

The monster held a massive, double-headed ax in one hand and wore heavy slabs of platemail from head to toe. Across its chest was the symbol of Dramugar, inlaid with gold and enamel. His every footstep was a floor-rumbling thud, and smoke curled from under the visor of his broad, horned helmet.

"Traitor!" Redding roared, drawing his blade and striking at the beast's back with a single, fluid movement.

The monster turned with unnatural swiftness, deflecting the Colonel's blade with a bracer and burying his ax in the man's chest. Redding slumped to the ground wordlessly as the beast yanked his gore-soaked weapon free, and all hell broke loose.

The entire line of students drew their weapons as one, and Darko's hands exploded into bright, crackling, teal energy as they made ready to make their last stand.

Before anyone had time to act, however, the room erupted in a soft golden light that stung the eyes of everyone present.

Darko blinked to clear his gaze and tried to make sense of the sudden change before him. Annabelle and the massive fighter were both enclosed in a wide, swirling golden bubble - seemingly frozen in time - and Archmagus Lorehammer was slumped on the ground where he had stood.

Darko recognized the spell, though he had never seen it practiced, even on a smaller scale. To stop time was a feat only the greatest wizards had ever accomplished, and to see it done before him would, in any other circumstances, have been a greatly humbling experience.

"Wait!" Darko shouted, raising his hands as the group surged forward to attack. "Wait!"

They stumbled to a halt, their guards up and confusion in their faces.

"If you touch it, you too will be frozen," Darko explained hurriedly, moving to stand between the soldiers and their prey. "We *must* leave, the spell cannot last long at such a size. The effort to keep it going must be draining Archamgus Lorehammer's very life as we speak."

"Can we not simply kill them now?" Arcus shot back, leveling his blade at the two figures frozen in front of him. "There must be something we can--"

"No," Darko was already kneeling at Lorehammer's side. "We *must* away."

"Who is this?" Elbaf caught Darko's attention with his tone. "Why does he--" The half-orc stood just outside the bubble, studying the massive warrior behind Annabelle.

"Your friend is right," Razael interrupted Elbaf's musing, grabbing him by the arm and turning him away. "We must go."

"Where?" Corvis asked with exasperation. "Where do you propose we--"

"Tirja," Sami interjected. "My brother serves on the Council of Larrin Hold, just across the Pass. He will grant us sanctuary, if I ask him."

"I will not go," Elliot, another of the soldiers from Soelves, raised his chin and looked to Captain Turner and their fallen companion, Kristoff. "We will not abandon our nation."

"Then good luck to you," Corvis frowned, already heading for the door and leaving Elliot and Turner to grieve.

"Elbaf?" Darko asked. "I need your help. I cannot lift the archmagus and, if he is to survive, we must bring him with us."

The half-orc nodded and scooped the frail old man up, throwing him over his shoulder and taking the lead as they headed out of the room.

When they arrived at the courtyard, Arcus thanked the gods. He didn't know how their men had known to assemble, but their entire group was armed, armored, and ready to depart.

"Orders, sir?"

"We're taking the Pass!" Elbaf yelled out. "We may never see our homeland again; if that sits poorly with you, then you may stay with no hard feelings."

Not a single man backed down, and a moment later the entire crew was jogging through the city streets. The winding, serpentine pattern of the city's layout meant that it took the better part of twenty minutes to make the gate, and the men were breathing hard by the time they got there.

Arcus took stock. Their group was augmented by Razael, Sami, and the still unconscious Lorehammer. Corvis was nowhere to be seen, and the rest of their classmates had joined the two remaining men from Soelves in staying behind.

"The gate is closed," Arcus pointed out as they jogged down the homestretch of the city, closing the distance to the outermost wall.

"No, it isn't," Darko mumbled, his hands already beginning to glow a deep, radiant purple.

The closer they got, and the longer that Darko chanted, the brighter the blaze of energy grew until, when they were some fifteen feet away, the mage stopped and planted his feet.

He spoke eldritch words that gave Arcus a headache and seemed to attack his ears from the inside. Then, he stretched his hands out towards the gate. Before their eyes, a rectangle of purple energy traced itself upon the stone of the gate, a little larger than the size of a normal door, and when the rectangle was complete the entire inside flashed pink and then faded.

They were left with what looked like a doorway, and through it they could see the rocky, mountainous terrain of Kyber Pass.

"Hurry," Darko grunted, his shoulders drooping and his brow soaked with sweat. "The doorway will not last long."

Arcus was the first through. He didn't stop to think or to doubt; he simply ran into the doorway without slowing down. As he passed the threshold his stomach dropped through the floor, and for a moment he lost all sense of balance and direction. Then, a moment later, his feet hit the dirt of the road ahead as if he hadn't just traversed through a dozen feet of stone.

Elbaf made sure that he was the last across the threshold of the magical door, unwilling to leave a single man behind. He was taking one last look at the city, hoping against hope to see Elliot or Turner or even the roguish Corvis Cain rounding the corner to join them. Instead, what he saw was a sudden, fiery explosion at the top of the keep. The top of the central tower, not far from where they'd assembled before Annabelle, crumbled and fell into the city with a rumbling boom.

Alarm bells rang out across the city, and he could see the guard mobilizing across the walls. Elbaf was, for a moment, sorely tempted to join them. They knew not the threat they moved to face, and he knew they would stand no chance against her if she'd brought her dragon. As if to confirm his fears, he saw bright bursts of flame across the battlements and the distant cries of battle.

"Elbaf!" Sami called to him from just beyond the gate. "We have to go!"

He sprinted through at last, catching up to Sami and Darko who brought up the rear.

"Darko, what's going on back there?" Elbaf huffed as they ran, still carrying the unconscious archmage across his shoulders. "Can your companion see anything?"

"Yes," Darko said, grimacing from the effort and the pain in his leg. "Orcs flood the city from within, summoned by Annabelle and her mysterious ally."

Elbaf skidded to a halt.

"Splitrock orcs?" he asked.

"Yes." Darko stumbled and stopped as well. "But, Elbaf, there are too many, *far* too many."

"What else can you see?" Elbaf pressed as trumpet calls blared in the far distance. "Those are no orc horns."

"Elbaf, we don't have time," Sami urged him, her eyes similarly glued to the city behind them.

"Darko?"

"Duke Boric and the 7th are outside the walls," Darko admitted. "I think they must have followed Annabelle here or that Duke Boric must have suspected her of such treachery. Even now his men are pushing into the city and supplementing the garrison."

Elbaf swore, torn apart by the options presented to him. He looked back and forth between Sami, the sorcerer, and their men heading up into the pass, then back to the city behind them.

"We should help Boric." The half-orc frowned. "He would help us, were our roles reversed. Perhaps--"

"Elbaf, the Empire is splintering before our very eyes," the mage urged him. "These events are far beyond us. Annabelle could kill us with a single spoken word, should she lay eyes on us."

"But--"

"Elbaf," Darko pressed him. "Your death does your men a great disservice, and you would do well to forestall it as long as you can."

"Darko," Elbaf shook his head. "You don't understand. There is more at stake here for me than I--"

"Is *that* what you care about, Elbaf?" Darko countered. "Your own stakes? If so, then I have dreadfully misread you."

"I--"

"You have peoples' lives *here* that depend on you," Darko pushed him. "The Elbaf I have grown to know and respect would not put his own concerns above them."

"You're right," Elbaf nodded, his cheeks flushed with embarrassment. "We'll--"

"We'll fight another day," Sami reassured him grimly. "This isn't over."

The pass was eight miles of winding, broken ground. High cliffs marked by great piles of craggy granite and limestone curved like a serpent through the high mountains between Tirja and the Empire, the only link between the ancient, bitter foes. With both of the moons new, it was pitch black, save for the feeble light of the stars. Elbaf insisted that they move without torches or lights, so he took the responsibility of leading the column upon himself. Arcus accompanied him, as the most experienced trailblazer, but it was Elbaf's keen darkvision that the group relied upon to move through the rocky area.

They'd been moving for over an hour when they finally heard it - the horrible piercing roar of the dragon. It echoed off the rocks around them and drove the entire group to the ground, huddling under rocks and brush.

"It's still back at Kyber, I think," Darko whispered. "I would wager the city has not yet fallen."

"You'd wager our lives on it?"

"I would, Elbaf," he nodded in the darkness. "If I am right, we would do well to move. We have another few miles to go."

"And if you're wrong it won't matter much either way," Arcus sighed. "We have nowhere to hide in this funnel."

The group was silent as they rushed through the darkness, cursing sharp stones and brambles as they stumbled along. Arcus was the only one of them who had an easy go of it, and Elbaf noticed that the druid seemed to instinctively avoid loose rocks, potholes, and even the brambles of passing thorny bushes. After a while Elbaf stopped warning the druid of upcoming hazards, sparing his breath for warnings passed down the column instead of wasting it telling the druid things he already seemed to know.

The pace they kept was unsustainable. They were half-jogging, and even with their packs lighter than they'd been in months, the men were wearing down as the grueling miles passed. Sometime in the second hour they dropped to a steady march, and even then the soldiers were panting and sweating like racehorses after a sprint.

Elbaf paused for a moment at the head of the group and cast his gaze back along the column. His men were stumbling blind through the rocks. Already most of them had scratches, bruises, or turned ankles from pushing themselves through the treacherous terrain.

"We need to let them rest," Sami said from beside him, her voice even but firm.

Elbaf looked her over, impressed that she, of all of them, seemed to be holding up best under the breakneck pace. A few strands of her hair were out of their usual place, and her breathing was harder than he'd heard it before, but only the faintest hint of perspiration dotted her brow and her eyes were alert and clear.

"I know," Elbaf sighed, wiping his forehead. "But will it be our deaths, I wonder?"

"Who can know?"

"Set a camp," Elbaf called out. "An hour, no more. Get some water, eat something, and try to stay as quiet as possible, men. The long night is nearly over."

Darko sighed with relief. His leg was screaming at him, and pain shot through from his calf to his hip and up into his lower back, and it was only with great difficulty that he managed to sit down under his own power, and not simply fall over.

"*Aesta quellan, Soloran?*" Sami asked from behind him, causing the mage to jump at her soft but unexpected voice.

"Yes," he smiled kindly at the much younger woman. "I am well, or I will be, anyway."

She gave a nod of deference and came to sit beside him.

"You don't speak the mother tongue, *Soloran?*"

"It has been . . . many years since I had need of our ancient language," Darko admitted, feeling an unexpected flush of embarrassment at her use of elven honorifics. "My grandfather spoke it, and my mother as well, but I haven't spoken to them in nearly sixty years, and in all that time I have found no cause to speak it elsewhere."

Sami nodded, tucking her loose hair behind her half-pointed ears and staring up at the skies.

"I learned it in my youth," she confided in him as she fished around in a belt pouch. "From my mother, who lived most of her life in Sionasara's Court in the homeland of our people."

"You *are* half-elven, then?" Darko probed gently. "I didn't want to assume."

"I am," she nodded. "My mother fell in love with a warrior dedicated to the service of Lyost and chose to stay with him in Larrin Hold, where my brother and I still live."

"I . . . I find myself shamed, at times," Darko announced sadly. "Ashamed that I am so far removed from the lore of our people."

"You are perhaps familiar with an old saying of our people." She laid a hand gently on his shoulder. "Let not yesterday's regrets cloud tomorrow's skies."

Darko smiled against his will, surprisingly relieved by a platitude he would normally call trite.

"You are in pain, *Soloran,*" she pointed out. "May I tend to your injury?"

"It is no injury," Darko shook his head regretfully. "An accident of birth ails me."

"Even so," she smiled. "I would do what I can, if you'll permit me?"

He watched with some doubt as she placed her palms on his hip and thigh, fingers splayed out and eyes closed in concentration. Cool blue light bathed his leg from hip to knee, and he found his pain instantly relieved. Sore muscles relaxed in seconds, and the throbbing ache of his poorly formed bones was eased considerably.

"Is that better?" she asked, searching his eyes for lingering pain.

"Better than I would have thought possible," Darko answered, more impressed than he'd expected to be. "In truth, I--"

"Darko," Elbaf interrupted him, approaching from across their small campsite. "Can you give me another update from Kyber?"

"Yes," Darko nodded, recognizing the agitation in Elbaf's voice and guessing at its true cause. "Give me a moment, and I will see what I can see."

Reia?

It is . . . worse than before, Master.

How bad?

Boric's forces are fighting throughout the city, but Dramugar has returned in strength, and he fights for Annabelle. The 7th is faltering, the garrison is overrun, and the orcs seem to have free reign of the city.

Show me.

Darko's vision flickered in and out as he shared vision with his companion. She was circling the city behind them in the form of a hawk, and the peculiar tunnel vision she imparted was disorienting for a moment.

Large portions of the city in the second ring were on fire, but the fighting was the heaviest in the castle itself. The 7th, being primarily a cavalry force, was at a disadvantage in the narrow streets and had almost entirely dismounted upon entering the city.

The outer ring was secure, for now, but the inner two were both hotbeds.

Darko watched as great gouts of flame cropped up, seemingly at random, all over the walls and parapets. Every time, when the flames dissipated, a squad of armor-clad orcs was there on the scorched rocks, ready to wreak havoc.

It had been theorized in the halls of the Academy, years ago, that Dramugar utilized magic to attack his targets and to whisk away his soldiers when the raid was complete. Darko hadn't put much stock in the theory at the time, but he could see now the devastating truth of it.

In the areas where the 7th and the city garrison had managed to link up, they were holding their own. The rest of the city though, where the orcs had free run of the streets, was an absolute madhouse. They were going door to door butchering the residents and torching the buildings.

The writing was on the walls, and to Darko's eye, the outcome of this battle was certain.

Annabelle's dragon was overkill. The creature circled the city, its rider surveying the slaughter below, and intervened only when it seemed Boric and Redding's forces were beginning to turn the tide in one spot or another. It would descend, lay waste to the Imperial soldiers with its horrifying breath, and then climb again and search for new targets.

Darko returned to himself with a shudder to find Elbaf staring at him intently.

"How fares the--"

"No better than Kent," Darko shook his head sadly, his stomach churning. "I will say nothing more."

Elbaf's head hung low with shame, and he left Sami and Darko without another word.

The warrior made his way back across the small camp, his shoulders tense and his thoughts racing. The men all huddled together in clumps of two and three, noting his passage with respectful nods, but no words. He counted them again, compulsively, to ensure no one was lost, no one left behind.

They were all accounted for save Derrin, and Elbaf's heart skipped a beat. He was sure the boy had been there, certain of it.

Elbaf raised his gaze, scanning the horizon at the edge of his vision. He was loath to raise his voice, but he went from clump to clump, asking if anyone had seen Derrin. None of them had, not since the stop at least, but he'd been last spotted by Julias, near the back.

The half-orc hurried back down the path, his eyes peeled for - there he was.

Derrin was standing on a large rock, his face turned toward Kyber, where a faint orange glow tinged the sky.

"Derrin!" Elbaf called, and he watched the young man flinch and turn, his blade half-drawn and his face hardened and battle-ready.

"It's just me," Elbaf called, waving to the young man.

"Sorry," Derrin waved back half-heartedly before turning to face the city again.

"You wish you were there," Elbaf climbed up beside him. "In the city."

"I do," Derrin nodded, speaking through gritted teeth. "I *should* be there."

Elbaf was surprised at the boy's anger, simmering just beneath the surface since the night he'd been separated, when they'd first fought Dramugar's orcs. He tried to think of how to tell the boy that he *understood*. That he felt angry, too. Everything he thought of saying sounded stupid though, so he stood beside his soldier in silence instead.

"We should get back," Derrin announced at last, his cold tone furrowing Elbaf's brow as he turned on his heel, slid down the boulder, and walked towards the camp.

They rested their hour, but by the end of it all eyes had turned silently southward, scanning the pitch blackness for the enemies they imagined would descend on them any second. Even the normally relaxed Razael seemed tense and jumpy. Only Lorehammer, who still had not regained consciousness, was immune to the tension in the air. Finally, Arcus could stand it no longer. He sought out Elbaf and tapped him on the shoulder.

"We should go," he whispered. "If Annabelle hasn't finished with the city by now, she surely will soon. And we're as likely a next target as anywhere else, from what I can tell."

"Right," the half-orc nodded curtly, before calling out to the group. "Break camp, I want to be on the road again in the next five minutes."

Word passed like wildfire through soldiers who were already anxious to move, and they were ready in three. Arcus and Elbaf counted their men twice to be sure, and then set out together at the head of the column.

The ranger judged it was perhaps an hour or two until sunrise and that they were no more than a few miles from the end of the pass, when he at last heard the dreadful approach of the dragon. He cast about in the pre-dawn light, an arrow already nocked against the string of his yew bow as he scanned the skies. Darko's actions confirmed his fears, and the wizard, too, was scanning the horizon behind them.

"What is--"

"Dragon," he interrupted the half-orc at his side as the column passed them by. "She's here."

"No, but she soon will be," Darko corrected them. "She's low over the pass. She's riding the centerline slowly and being very . . . *thorough* in her search for us."

"What can we do?"

"I am afraid I have no brilliant plan for this, Elbaf."

"Arcus, pass the word." The warrior dropped his shoulders. "Double time, and split between the eastern and western walls of the pass, with as much space between as we can manage."

The ranger sprinted back up the column, dividing the men and praying that if it was indeed their time to die, that they would die quickly and without suffering.

Annabelle was either toying with them or afraid she might lose them in the dim lighting of the morning, because she covered and re-covered each strip of pass several times. Between clumps of scrubby brush, and a fair number of overhanging ledges and stands of gnarled mountain aspen, the high-walled canyon had plenty of hiding places for desperate prey. As she drew nearer, however, it became clear that she would reach them long before they would reach the end of the canyon.

Minutes ticked by, and the weight of the dragon drove them into silence.

Arcus nimbly avoided a pile of loose stones at a bend in the path and took a place atop a small boulder instead. He looked down the pass and, though he was quite certain he could see the end of it, his heart fell. He could not see much in the way of cover, only the same scrubby bushes and tumbled rocks that had lined the canyon for the past few miles.

Their soldiers were ragged and worn, bruised and badly mistreated by the terrain, moving much more slowly as the night had progressed. They would be hard pressed to jog at this point, let alone sprint for cover if the need should arise.

"Can one of you . . . I don't know," Elbaf panted, "*make* a cave or something? Grow some shrubs to give us cover?"

"I could--"

"No," Darko warned. "She likely has the ability to sense magic, any spell we work will blaze like a beacon." The wizard's voice trailed off in thought, and he stopped in his tracks.

"What is it?"

"We *can* make it so it doesn't matter," Darko said brightly. "Arcus, you can create fog, yes?"

"I certainly can, but--"

"Do it," Darko nodded. "Lots of it. *All* of it."

Arcus knelt to the ground, his heart reaching out into the rocky soil around him and finding an abundance of moisture. The dew had freshly formed, and even the driest patches of dirt around him were sopping wet. He took a deep breath, pulling the cold mountain air into his lungs, breathing it back out warmer, heavier. All around him wisps of thick silvery fog rose like wraiths from the ground, and within a few moments, visibility had dropped to almost zero.

"Can you raise it?" Elbaf asked from beside him. "Gives us some visibility down here? Otherwise we'll never make any progress at all."

Arcus nodded, looking upward and raising the fog as one thick, solid blanket.

Darko supplemented his magic, and Arcus could feel the rough, jagged edges of the wizard's magic as it manipulated the air around them. Curiously, Arcus could feel a great tingling of energy shooting throughout the fog, almost as if the wizard was charging it intentionally.

"Darko," he said slowly, trying not to break his own concentration. "If you're worried about a beacon then I don't--"

"She'll either see it or she won't," he countered, his voice strained as well. "But if she does, it has to be big enough and bright enough to be useless to her. It's the only way."

They finished their incantations a couple of minutes later and turned back to Elbaf.

"How big is the cloud?"

"A few hundred yards across and spreading," Arcus answered, his breathing heavy. "It'll grow while we travel, but Darko and I will tire out fairly quickly as it does. Our magic will deplete us."

Elbaf nodded and adjusted the straps on his backpack.

"See what you can do about pushing it forward with us." The half-orc frowned. "We'll need all the cover we can get."

Arcus said nothing, but gave a firm nod as a very soft northerly breeze picked up behind them, pushing the fog along at about the pace they could hike.

It didn't take long for Annabelle to find the cloud, and she announced it loudly when she did so. It was less than fifteen minutes later that a mighty, piercing roar filled the air behind them, echoing loudly off the canyon walls until it was deafening.

"Damnit!" Elbaf swore loudly, instinctively dropping to the canyon wall beside him.

"We're still more than two miles out." Arcus shook his head. "That's no easy sprint."

"Darko, what's the situation above?"

"Not good, my friend," Darko shook his head. "She's making up for her lack of sight by filling the canyon with fire. It's slowing her down, but we haven't much time."

"Not enough to get out of the pass, so it doesn't matter."

"What would we do if we *did*, I wonder," Arcus mused, his frustration growing. "The end of the pass may well be open ground - we'd be no better off than we are now."

"Over here," a familiar voice called out softly from just ahead of them.

A black, shadowy figure separated itself seamlessly from the rocks along the cavern, appearing as if by magic in the darkness.

"*Corvis?*"

"In the flesh," the man responded in his trademark buttery smooth voice. "It seems we find ourselves similarly situated."

"How in the hell did you--"

"We'll handle it later," Elbaf waved away Arcus' surprise. "You said you could help?"

"There's a cave over here." The rogue hiked a thumb over his shoulder. "It's hidden well enough to suit our purposes. More importantly, it has a sharp curve just inside that, if we are lucky, will keep out the dragon's breath."

"Good enough." Elbaf whistled sharply, and the men assembled a moment later. "Lead the way."

Corvis turned crisply and headed off down the path, followed promptly by the beleaguered troops.

"Elbaf," Arcus held a hand out to stop him before he followed the rogue, and Elbaf treated him with a curious look.

"What is it?" he asked the ranger with a quick glance behind himself.

"I . . . I don't think I trust the rogue," Arcus admitted. "He kept to himself well enough these past five months, why the change?"

"Mutually assured destruction?" Elbaf answered with a shrug.

"I don't buy it," Arcus insisted. "He could have kept this cave for himself, let us pass by without a word."

"Arcus," Elbaf gripped his shoulder. "What choice do we have?"

The trip to the cave took less than a minute. The mouth of it, barely wider than a man's chest, lay in the shadows and behind a rugged sagebrush. Elbaf had no doubt they would have passed it by unwittingly had they been on their own. Corvis was right about its layout as well. It took a sharp hook about ten yards past the opening, then pushed a further twenty yards or so before terminating in an ancient cave-in.

"How did you know about--"

Elbaf's question was interrupted by another echoing roar, which was close enough to shake the ground beneath their feet. A great rushing wind whistled in the opening of the cave, the eerie sound reflecting strangely across the walls around them.

They were huddled closely together, packed as well as they could be at the back, but judging from the alarmed look on Darko's face there was cause still for worry.

"Something troubles you," Elbaf whispered, trying not to alarm the soldiers. "What is it?"

"I am remembering, with sudden urgency," the mage whispered back, "the *poisonous gas* that makes up part of the dragon's breath."

"Poison gas?" Elbaf growled and rubbed his temples. "*Why* didn't you mention this before?"

"It hadn't come up."

"Can you fix it? Seal the opening or anything?"

"Not without cutting off *our* air supply."

"Wait," Arcus interjected. "I have an idea."

They watched in trepidation as the ranger knelt to the ground and placed his hands upon the bare, dusty stone. The ground shook again, this time much harder.

"Hurry, brother."

Arcus didn't respond, but a crack appeared above them and water started to pour out of it into a second crack that opened in the floor below it. What was at first a trickle grew to a steady stream, and within a few moments there was a solid curtain of fast flowing water that separated the backmost portion of the cave from the tunnel and the entrance.

"This should clean our air." The ranger sat back and dusted off his palms. "In theory."

"And it won't show up as an ongoing enchantment," Darko mumbled his approval. "Brilliant."

They didn't have time to dwell upon Arcus' bright idea though, as Annabelle's wrath roared through the canyon outside. An ugly greenish-red light bathed the entrance, bright enough to reflect all the way along the length of the tunnel to cast an unearthly light upon the water and the men huddled behind it. The ground rumbled, and the rocks overhead radiated heat until the hidden soldiers were sweating in their armor.

Sure enough, greenish gasses leaked into the tunnel and wafted outside the protective curtain of water, but did not pass through it. The fast, cool water seemed to trap the gasses where it touched, and drag them downward into the earth.

The rage of the dragon seemed to thunder overhead forever, and the troops huddled silently within, praying to whatever gods they believed in that the bulwark of the earth would hold.

Even when the ground stopped shaking and the world outside grew silent, no one spoke, least of all with ideas of leaving the cave. The only sounds to be heard were pounding hearts and Kodja's quiet panting. It was impossible to tell how much time had passed.

The silence was at last interrupted by the least likely member of their group.

Corvis Cain stood unexpectedly and cocked his head to the side, earning many looks of confusion in the silent darkness of the cave.

"We're safe." He breathed a sigh of relief. "But I would leave the cave slowly and without weapons drawn."

Chapter Twenty-Six

Arcus waved his hands again and the cracks in the earth sealed, clearing the path of the waterfall, and he stepped out into the cave. It was even hotter outside of their protective nook, and by the time he reached the entrance his cheeks were flushed pink.

He squeezed through the entrance, flinching a little at the heat pouring off the stones, and gaped at what he saw. The canyon walls resembled melted wax, and the entire area was barren. No shrub or even blade of grass had been spared.

Arcus called out to the others, letting them know that the coast was clear as he squinted against the morning light shining off the mirror-bright polished stone all around them. Kodja pushed past him, still panting heavily, but overjoyed to be free of the hot, stifling cave. The rest of the troops squeezed out of the opening and assembled in a loose cluster, each similarly awed by the destruction around them.

"We'll have company in a moment," Corvis Cain alerted them, pointing northward down the pass.

Sure enough, a half-dozen figures approached slowly from the north, longbows at the ready in their hands.

"Form up!" Elbad called, pulling his sword from its scabbard across his back and preparing himself for yet another fight.

But Darko was not convinced.

The mage squinted against the dawning light and studied the warriors approaching them. They looked much like Arcus, with leather armor, longbows, and short swords or sabers at their sides. They traveled with the same practiced gait as he did, and dressed in muted browns and greens that, under normal circumstances, blended in well with the environment of the canyon.

"I don't think these people are with Annabelle," he observed, raising a hand to shade his eyes and allow him a better view. "They don't have the look of Imperial troops at all, in fact."

"They're Tirjani Rangers!" Sami shouted excitedly, waving overhead with both hands at the approaching party.

"Sami?" a surprised female voice called out from the group as they got to within thirty feet or so. "Sami, is that you?"

A lithe huntress, surrounded on either side by two pairs of leather-clad rangers, was shaking her head in astonishment and squinting at their group.

"Katelyn!" Sami yelled back, sprinting towards the group.

The two women met in the middle, with Sami picking the other woman up in a massive bear hug and spinning her around.

"By the gods, am I happy to see you."

"How did you *survive*? We feared the worst when we saw the dragonfire."

"Perhaps you'd care to introduce us?" Darko interjected as the two groups coalesced around the hugging women. "And then we should probably not linger in this canyon."

"Sorry." Sami blushed and released the woman. "This is Katelyn D'Aeri--"

"D'*Aeri?*" Arcus perked up, studying the woman. "I . . . you couldn't possibly be from . . ."

The woman's short, fiercely curled red hair bounced as she studied the man addressing her, and her piercing eyes seemed to drive the poor woodsman to an awkward silence.

"I'm from the Deep Wood," she said, her tone bright and questioning. "Mr . . . ?"

"D-, A-Arcus," he stammered, flushing scarlet. "Arcus D'Ari."

Katelyn's bright, almond-shaped eyes widened, then narrowed again as she studied him with renewed interest.

"Katelyn is an emissary of Sionasara," Sami explained. "High Queen of the Elves. She honors us by commanding our company of rangers."

"Not to mention basically raising you and your rambunctious twin." Katelyn nudged Sami in the ribs, and it was her turn to blush.

"As the wizard said, we should keep moving," Elbaf interrupted, his gaze southward. "There's no telling if she'll be back or when. Sami told us that the people of Larrin Hold would shelter us?"

The atmosphere turned serious again, and Katelyn answered with a curt nod before turning back to the north. She set out at a blistering pace, stepping off lightly in soft, doe-skin boots that made no more sound than a whisper.

"Come along then," she called out. "You're a mile and a half from soft beds and hot food."

Larrin Hold was eerily similar to Fort Kyber. Were it not for the little differences, such as the blue and gold pennants and banners where the black and red of the Empire ought to be, Darko might have been too disconcerted to enter the place. They *must* have been designed by the same minds, if not built by the same hands.

"Welcome to the Capital, Larrin Hold," Sami said, gesturing broadly at the massive curve of the outer wall of the fortress, which formed a graceful arch across the mouth of the pass. "My home."

The pass terminated about three hundred yards from this outermost wall, and directly in the center of it a mighty door was set. It was shorter than the one in Kyber, but much broader. Iron bands as wide as a man's chest wrapped together the tree trunks that made up the thirty foot span of the entrance. Above it sat three low, crenelated towers overlooking the fields and the pass below.

The doors were partially open, at least wide enough for a large wagon to roll through unimpeded, and looked as though they had been for a very, very long time.

"You don't close the gate?" Darko remarked.

"Why would we?" Sami and Katelyn said in unison.

"Aren't you *at war* with us?"

"According to whom?" Sami let out a sardonic bark of a laugh. "We haven't been at war for centuries, not since the civil war."

"*Civil war?*" Darko shook his head. "You mean the War of Liberation?"

"Is *that* what your people call it?" Sami rolled her eyes. "Tell me, do you feel *liberated* as a citizen of the Empire?"

They walked in silence the rest of the way to the gate, where they were met by a young man in fine linens who ran to Sami without a word and wrapped her in an embrace. An honor guard was also present, a dozen men in polished steel scale mail with halberds and peculiar conical helmets.

The guards maintained a respectful distance from the ragged band of travelers, and all eyes were on Sami and the mystery man until he broke away from her at last. Now able to see him clearly, it was remarkable to Darko just how similar the two looked.

"We are in your debt for returning my twin sister unharmed," the man said as he bowed low to them. "Please, let me offer you our warmest hospitality."

The man introduced himself as Connor, and explained that he was one of nine councilmen elected to rule the city. Darko was fascinated by the system of governance. It seemed that each year a new councilman was elected to a nine year term, replacing the longest serving councilman and continuing the government uninterrupted.

Connor walked them around Larrin Hold, and everywhere Darko looked he saw *ancient* architecture, heavily worn but obviously looked after with great care. Any one of these buildings pre-dated those of the Sunset Isle back home, likely by several centuries.

Something struck him as particularly strange, however, and it wasn't until they approached the barracks where they would be staying that it struck him what that might be.

"Where is everyone?" he blurted out, surprising the group at large.

"Sorry?" Connor asked. "How do you mean?"

"These streets, these buildings, this *city*," the mage gestured. "It's all so big. This city is laid out as a teeming metropolis, a home to tens of thousands or more, and yet the streets are mostly empty, and these grand halls are quiet."

"Ah," Connor grew introspective. "You must understand, Tirja's wounds have not yet healed from our last war with the Empire."

Darko tried to express his dissatisfaction with as respectful a frown as he could manage, but judging from the chastised look on their host's face, he didn't succeed.

"The Emperor unleashed a terrible weapon when he broke away from Tirja." Connor turned back towards the barracks and resumed his walk. "If our records are to be believed - and I think they are - we were pushed almost to extinction, massacred by a 'black wind' that gutted the entire nation and brought us to our knees."

The group fell silent and remained so until Connor stopped beside a stout wooden door.

"So you see," he managed a weak smile. "What would we have to gain with a fight against the Empire, especially in the face of such a risk?"

The tour descended into a long silence, with no one sure what to say to such a revelation.

Connor led them to an old stone barracks next, which, though well maintained, was empty for lack of residents.

"You can sleep here," the man gestured at rows of wooden bunks. "At least until we figure out something more suitable," He glanced at Kodja and hesitated. "Your . . . *companion* could sleep in the kennels?"

"He can sleep with us or find his own place," Arcus reassured him. "You don't need to worry about him."

Elbaf, Arcus, Darko, and their soldiers needed no further prompting; they began to unload their gear immediately. The rest of their group split, however, with Archmagus Lorehammer being taken by the guardsmen to an infirmary, Sami leaving with her brother after promising to meet them at dinner, Corvis disappearing out the door without a word, and Razael, who carried no gear but lingered in the doorway a moment before leaving.

"Take your boots off, men," Elbaf advised the soldiers. "Connor said the bathhouse is available for our use, and at this point, if Major Montagne is going to come kill us, we might as well be comfortable."

The men instinctively claimed bunks near one another, despite the hall's capacity being easily six times their numbers. They unpacked as well, but only enough to clean and care for their gear and weapons.

"These men are no more likely to let down their guard than you are," Darko said, shaking his head softly. "And who can blame them? For a year and a half now we've jumped at shadows, and we have no reason to believe our circumstances have meaningfully changed."

"I know," Elbaf sighed quietly. "I just . . . wish it were not so."

Darko patted the much larger man on the back and shuffled to his own bunk, no doubt to rest his tired bones.

Elbaf was restless though, too restless to be confined to a bed this early in the day, so he made his way back outside and looked around.

He saw Razael a few yards away, at the edge of a wide, shallow fountain.

"You are troubled," the Swordmaster observed without turning his gaze from the water. "The warrior from last night, he weighs heavily on your mind."

"How did you know?"

"Your energy is chaotic, unmoored."

"I am finding it . . . difficult," Elbaf admitted as he approached to stand beside the man. "To center myself, as you have instructed."

Razael turned to the half-orc, his eyes kind but his facial expression hardened.

"Because you have yet to accept *who* you are." He tapped Elbaf's chest. "You have yet to accept the source of your--"

"I know who I am," Elbaf countered, taking a step back and turning away.

"Then you know who that was," Razael pressed, pointing southward.

"I don't."

"You *do*," Razael hammered him. "His blood flows in you, and it is from that blood that you draw your power. You *know* that was Dramugar, the same way you know he's-- "

"He's not my father!" Elbaf roared, turning back to his instructor. "I don't care if I share his blood!"

"You will accept the truth of your heritage," Razael frowned. "Or you will never truly center yourself."

But Elbaf would listen no longer, and he stomped off back towards the door.

"You alright?" Arcus asked, watching Elbaf storm angrily into the barracks, throw his gear to the ground, and head off towards the bathhouse.

"I'm fine," the half-orc grumbled, not missing a beat as he headed back out.

"Not terribly convincing," Darko quipped as the man departed. "Do you suppose we ought to pry?"

"No, I don't think so," Arcus sighed as he finished collecting his own sundries.

Within an hour, all the men were fed and bathed and back in their racks.

Soft snores filled the air and conspired to keep Arcus awake. He tossed and turned, trying to clear his mind and regain some of the sleep he'd lost the night before, but he found that every time he closed his eyes his mind was filled with fiery curls and piercing eyes against soft, tan skin.

He must have slept eventually, however, because the next thing he knew someone was tapping his foot from the end of his bed.

"Dinner time, brother," Merryl announced, turning back to his own bunk.

"By the gods . . ." Arcus said, rubbing his temple as he sat up. "Did I truly sleep all day?"

"Who can blame us?" Darko groaned from the next bunk over. "If your magic is as tiring as mine, I would say we earned it."

The ranger smiled and rubbed the sleep from his eyes before rolling to the side of his bed and sliding his boots back over his tired, aching feet.

"Let us hope this dinner party goes better than our last." Darko yawned. "My heart is tired of betrayal and danger."

A young boy in a formal outfit of neutral gray cotton waited patiently as the world-weary travelers gathered themselves. He couldn't have been more than eleven, so Arcus judged him to be a servant or a page. Nonetheless, his manners were impeccable, especially for one so young.

Once the group was assembled, the boy led them through the quiet streets of the city to a large circular building. The structure was three stories tall and ringed with enormous stained glass windows. The creamy granite blocks that comprised it were fit with such masterful precision that no seams were visible unless the observer was very close to the walls and, even then, only if one looked carefully.

"What is this place?" Arcus wondered aloud.

"This is the Senate," the boy responded in a polite, informative tone. "The seat of government of the Republic of Tirja since the time of the Civil War."

Inside, the building was just as grand. The outer wall formed a ring, within which was a broad plaza of checkered granite that featured dozens of seats, all arranged in circles around a central point which was occupied with a large dias. The dias held a pair of banquet tables set with fine cutlery and piled high with foods both foreign and familiar. A small cluster of people waited beside the tables, deep in discussion.

The group turned to face them as they approached, and Arcus felt his heart do a backflip as Lilliana was revealed. She was furthest from him, but she was dazzling in a simple, flowing dress of emerald green. Beside her, perhaps even more beautiful, was Katelyn, with her blazing hair complimenting the rich amber of her own evening gown. Sami was similarly bedecked in formal attire, as were her brother and the rest of the councilmen and women who had joined them for supper.

Introductions went round at length, and at last they were seated. Platters filled with smoked meats, colorful fruit, and earthy vegetables tantalized the guests, but Arcus was too consumed by the conversation to appreciate the food as much as it deserved.

"This hall is grand," Darko noted, gesturing at the rows of empty seats around them. "But I count only nine council members. I'm not sure I understand?"

"You see before you yet another scar of our war with the Empire," Connor answered. "At the birth of the republic, representatives from all of our districts filled this hall. But the desolation wrought by the Black Wind was too great, so most of our citizens moved south, consolidating in the few cities that remained. Those districts have no people now, and so their seats sit empty."

"What exactly *was* the Black Wind?" Darko asked after a few glasses of wine, garnering disapproving looks from their hosts.

"No one knows," Sami answered him, her silver chain earrings glinting in the dim firelight of the oil lamps scattered across the tables. "But our oldest histories speak of a sweeping evil that devoured the very heart of the Kingdom, driving all before it."

"How did Tirja *survive*?" Elbaf wondered aloud, his belly full and his mind afire with tales of wars and histories long past. "If the Emperor had such a weapon?"

"The Dawn Martyr," Lilliana answered, her gaze distant and her voice low and sorrowful. "She . . . stayed the Emperor's Hand, though it ultimately cost her life."

"*The* Dawn Martyr?" Darko shook his head in disbelief. "Impossible. She is a *hero* of the Empire."

"A single individual can be a hero to many nations," Lilliana noted dryly. "And I assure you, the Dawn Martyr would be revered by all mankind if people knew the sacrifices she made nine centuries ago."

They spoke late into the night, and the conversation ranged from mundane topics to more serious matters as the evening lengthened. Eventually though, yawns began to punctuate the conversation more and more frequently. At long last Connor stood, tapping on a crystal glass with the back of a spoon to catch the attention of the group.

"I wish to express again my gratitude for the safe return of my dear sister." He bowed respectfully. "You have done our nation a great service by returning her, and by bringing word of the dangers that lie beyond our borders."

A general wave of agreement washed over the dinner party, and many of the councilmen tapped their knuckles on the tables in what Darko suspected was a similar gesture as applause.

"But the hour is late," Connor continued. "And we would be remiss if we kept you from your well-deserved rest. I would invite you to attend a special senate session in the morning, where we can further discuss how to proceed, what manner of protections and services we can offer you, and what role Tirja may yet have to play."

Darko and the others headed back to their barracks, but unlike most of his companions, the wizard was no more relaxed than when the evening had begun. In fact, the wheels in his mind were turning faster than ever. It seemed that the histories of Tirja and the Empire were more closely linked than he had previously known, and his own education had been compromised. He no longer trusted the validity of the things he thought he knew, and in questioning the Imperial Academy, he had already begun to suspect that this misrepresentation of history was no idle mistake. Further, he was coming to the conclusion that Annabelle was not simply a *symptom* of corruption, but a significant actor in the underlying rot beneath the surface of the Empire.

He intended to make sure.

The rest of the men headed swiftly to bed, leaving Darko alone with his thoughts as he waited for them to fall asleep.

Are you sure about this, Master?
I am. I need more information.
The path you are choosing is a dangerous one.
Potentially, yes.
As you wish, Master.

Good food, strong wine, and warm beds had the room filled once more with snores and deep breathing within a half-hour, and Darko was ready when he heard the last of their men slip finally to sleep.

He sat up soundlessly and set about gathering his spell components as quietly as possible. Despite his physical limitations, he could move swiftly and silently with great skill, and in short order he had assembled a satchel filled with materials and was headed for the door.

Were you able to find a suitable location, Reia?

I was, Master. There is an outbuilding to the south. I don't know its original purpose, but it is empty and unused at the moment.

The building in question was a low stone structure with a vaulted, tiled roof. It had a few high windows, but they looked too small to make an effective entrance. It had only one door, a stout oak affair with a heavy iron handle and a large keyhole.

Darko tried the handle, and found it predictably locked. He pulled a cantrip from his memory, a relatively simple spell that he seldom found use for. He channeled energy into his mouth and lungs, and his lips went cold. His breath turned misty, then thickened to an icy fog as he breathed in deeply the chill air and used it to augment his magic.

The wizard leaned in close to the lock and breathed slowly out. He directed the thick frosty clouds of his breath into the mechanism, and then waited patiently as the mist slowly condensed into a key made entirely of ice. He turned the key and smirked with satisfaction as the lock clicked open and the door swung silently inward.

Darko stepped into the darkened room, shutting the door behind him and summoning a small, softly glowing blob of energy with a flick of his wrist. The fist-sized sphere moved to hover about a foot above his head, and provided steady illumination by which he could examine his new workspace.

Smooth, timeworn wooden floors and clean cut stone walls greeted his gaze, and he was pleasantly surprised to find that, aside from a few wooden boxes stacked in one corner, the entire twenty-by-twenty shed was empty.

Reia joined him, landing lightly on the floor in her true form and looking around.

It is a suitable location, Master, but--

Are you truly so concerned?

I am, Master. We don't know what she's capable of.

We'll be careful, use every precaution and protection, I promise.

Darko pulled ashes, blue candles, and the rest from his pouch and began to arrange it in the prescribed manner. He made good on his promise to Reia, and at every stage he layered wards and protective enchantments. Hours passed before he was ready to begin the ritual, and already the room was humming with arcane power. Layer upon layer of tightly woven magic filled the space with a palpable buzz, but at last he was ready.

He took his place at one edge of the rune-covered circle and waited as Reia took hers opposite him. As she approached the edge of the circle and came to a halt, the entire ring erupted in a scintillating blaze of energy, swirling through an impossible rainbow of colors.

Master?

Yes, Reia?

Promise me if anything goes wrong you'll pull back, with or without me.

Reia, I couldn't leave--

Promise me, or I'll have no part of this.

Silence met her demand. Darko had never known her to give him an ultimatum; it violated the unspoken dynamic between them in a jarring and uncomfortable way and, quite frankly, it wasn't something he'd thought possible.

Reia, my dearest friend, we'll be quick and we'll be careful. We'll be in and out--

Promise me.

I . . . promise.

The tiny demon nodded her agreement and Darko felt a strange flutter across his heart and mind, as though deep magics were being emplaced as he made his bargain. He turned his attention inward in alarm and found thin, silvery cords of energy laced around his mind that he had no hand in making.

Reia . . .

Just a little insurance, Master.

Darko studied the small creature before him. He noted the well-concealed look of concern in her eyes and the nervousness of her carriage, and wrestled with himself over how to react. In the end, he concluded that she was trying to protect him, and that after a century of friendship, he should trust her good intentions over his own suspicions.

Ready, Reia?

I am.

They stepped into the circle together and slowly made their way inward until they were once again seated before the onyx and mirror on the ground between them. Darko found it easier for him to complete the spell this time, though no less taxing. By the time he and Reia were floating together in the endless starry void, he was drenched in sweat and breathing hard.

Master, you are still tired from your previous exertions. Perhaps it is unwise to perform the bonding ritual?

I have no intention of performing a bond, Reia, don't worry.

No? Then what is your aim, Master?

The safest way to observe Annabelle is in my astral form. She'll have no idea I'm even there.

And I will be your anchor?

Exactly. You will keep me grounded, and through our link, I will remain tethered to this place - to safety.

Darko studied his oldest and dearest friend, somehow finding comfort and care in the hollow voids of bright violet that were her eyes. Her body, now again as large as his own, was a thing of beauty. She radiated power and confidence, surety and grace. He felt secure in the knowledge that she would be his way back and felt no fear at leaving.

Ready?

Ready.

Darko, sealed safely within the spinning rings of runes and circles of power, directed his energies to a new undertaking - separating his physical form from the essence of his consciousness and spirit. He understood the magic in theory, but it was a complex effect to accomplish. He used his power to isolate all of the various parts of himself in his mind, to compartmentalize all that he consisted of in preparation for the split. Here he placed his ego, there his body, and over there his mind. He closed his eyes and imagined his body with criss-crossing lines separating all of the pieces of himself from one another, toying with the idea of which pieces he should bring and what he should leave behind.

As he began to separate these various constituent pieces, he could feel the energy flowing in and around him begin to make those divisions more and more *real*. Pain shot through his body, and his mind ached as he flinched with surprise at the sensation.

He wasn't ready. The categories into which he was sorting himself were only temporary and preparatory in nature, and he hadn't intended to begin the actual separation yet - the magic seemed to have begun it for him as soon as he thought up the divisions. He paused his work in frustration and sought a different way to approach the problem.

Master, you cannot execute this spell in bits and pieces. You cannot gently and comfortably split your existence.

I'm trying to take it slowly so I don't make any mistakes.

Yes, Master, and in doing so you are committing a grave error. To travel astrally is not to gently cross stepping stones in a stream, it is a wild and dangerous leap into the unknown.

Darko mulled over her words. They made a certain amount of sense, of course, but the idea was intimidating. The 'wild and dangerous leap' in question was not theoretical. It could have grave consequences for him.

Nonetheless, the need was great and he was committed.

Darko steadied himself again, centering his energy within his body and concentrating on his *self*. Not one specific part, but the entirety of what it was to *be*. He felt a bizarre tingling sensation flooding his body that seemed both to dull his senses and to heighten his awareness. The buzzing grew stronger and stronger until, with an almost audible snap, it stopped completely.

He was, for a moment, too nervous to open his eyes.

He could feel Reia's gaze upon him though and quickly grew self-conscious. Upon opening his eyes he was flooded with a sense of relief and awe - his body was floating in front of him, suspended as though in water. His body was still, unmoving, and he felt very odd seeing himself from the perspective of an outsider.

Well done, Master.

He inspected himself, finding that he was a misty, silver-gray copy of the body he'd inhabited all his life. He was translucent as well, and he could see *through* his body with relative ease.

He tried to move, mimicking swimming for lack of a better idea, and was surprised by Reia's soft, melodic laughter.

Move with your mind, Master. Will yourself to travel through space.

He made a face at her, mentally reminding himself to address her apparent familiarity with astral travel at a later date, and tried to put her words into practice. He directed his will towards circling his body, and found himself moving with sudden speed. Once he learned the methodology, the execution was simple enough.

He floated to the front of himself, between his body and Reia, and was interested to find that there was a bright, faintly pulsing silvery dot on his body's forehead.

Your anchor, Master.

Darko studied the mark. It was faint but clear and much weaker than he'd hoped.

It seems so small. This is meant to guide me back?

That's where I come in, Master.

She smiled in his mind, and he turned back to her. She had her arms open as if to embrace him, and she began to shimmer with swirls of bright violet energy before his very eyes.

Pass through me, Master, and our spirits will link. I will become your beacon.

Darko took the spiritual equivalent of a deep breath and willed himself to fly through Reia, aiming for her heart. He closed his eyes at the last moment, bracing for the impact he knew would occur.

He *expected* resistance, but found none. Instead, he felt his new form energized as though struck by lightning. As he opened his eyes and turned around, he was nearly blinded by the overwhelming radiance of his companion.

Reia's form had been utterly consumed, and replaced by a body of brilliant silver light flecked with bright purple motes of swirling energy.

Reia?

I am here, Master.

Reia's voice was magnified, and he felt it within his chest as much as in his mind.

I will be your anchor, Master, and your protector.

Darko was overwhelmed with gratitude and felt much more secure in his decision in the face of her brilliance.

Go Master, this spell will continue to drain energy from your physical form. You won't feel it while you are apart from your physical body, but it will occur nonetheless.

Thank you, Reia.

Don't lose sight of me, Master. Whatever you do, don't let our link be broken.

Darko nodded and turned his attention southward, picturing the soaring towers and mighty walls of Kyber. His thoughts carried him, slowly at first and then with startling speed, through the starry expanse of the void. He tried to reconcile the bizarre feeling of being still and unmoving, as well as the scenery hurtling past him on either side.

Great spinning planets, blazing stars, and sparkling clouds of dream-stuff raced past him as blurs, but he had his gaze firmly locked upon the horizon. Faster and faster he flew, until all around him was a tunnel of swirling light and energy, and the only thing that seemed at all stable was the pinprick of light ahead of him and the steady glow of silver light from over his shoulders.

His arrival was even more jarring. He snapped into existence with an alarming suddenness that filled him with vertigo and dizziness. The lack of transition between hurtling through the cosmos and standing still was so disorienting that for a moment he failed to take in his surroundings.

But that didn't last long.

From his vantage atop the ruined central tower, Darko gaped at the wreckage of Fort Kyber all around him. The city itself had been razed to the foundations, and great corpse-piles dotted the city, still smoldering from the burning of thousands of bodies.

Dozens of large, circular canvas tents dotted the city below as well, and a small army of the heavily armored Ohryics seemed to occupy them and the city at large. Of the 7th, there was no sign, save the towering plumes of black smoke and the wreckage of the city and hills outside the walls. Darko had no doubt that any who had survived the assault on the city were by now long gone - if they had managed to escape the dragon's wrath at all.

Focus, Master, our time is limited.

Darko agreed silently, instinctively turning back to ensure that he could see the shining silver light that was Reia in the far distance. Confident that she was still there, and that his escape route was secure, he turned his energies to finding his prey - Annabelle and her dragon must be close, and now that he knew what he was looking for he should have little trouble finding them.

He turned inward, finding that his connection to his powers felt somehow both clearer and more difficult. Drawing the power was challenging, like he was trying to suck air through a straw, but once he had summoned it, it was more easily manipulated than he'd ever experienced. He made a note to study the effect more fully later, and magically augmented his senses - extending his perception in both the physical and the metaphysical planes - to seek out the ripple of power he suspected the dragon would produce.

There.

Below him in the tower there was an unmistakable aura of magical energy that could only come from something so powerful as the dragon. He kicked himself for not sensing it before, on their journey across the Empire, but just as swiftly dismissed his self-criticism: the creature was intelligent, and likely a very capable spellcaster in its own right. It had more than enough magical strength to conceal itself from him.

Even so, the force emanating from below was daunting - it dwarfed his own power in many ways, and it felt foreign, *alien*, to his own magics.

Careful.

Darko did not begrudge her worry.

The wizard took a moment to locate the focal point of the dragon's energy and to re-orient himself towards it, then began to move ever so slowly forward. He floated through the stone floor of the tower and was overcome by a peculiar sense of surreality as walls, floors, and all the rest of the intervening structure was rendered functionally irrelevant.

He entered a large, opulently dressed room and halted abruptly, freezing in place by instinct.

Annabelle was sitting behind a broad desk - no doubt the late Colonel Redding's - across from a woman Darko didn't recognize. She wore the same armor and cleric's garb as Annabelle, though she stood a few inches shorter. So similar were they in appearance that Darko could have mistaken them for twins, in fact.

" . . . remains the possibility, however remote, that they survived, Herestia," Annabelle frowned to the second woman, rubbing her temples in frustration. "If they bring back word to the Empire before we are ready, all could be lost."

"*Nothing* in that canyon survived my wrath, sister," the shorter woman shook her head with a cruel smirk. "The Brood's work remains undamaged, and with Boric finally out of the picture, we are in a place of greater advantage than we have been in decades, *Annabelle*."

"Don't call me that," Annabelle hissed. "It's bad enough adopting that stupid name around these pathetic humans."

Darko blanched at the woman's words, noting with grave concern the biting, sibilant voice of the newcomer, Herestia, and her use of one word in particular - *sister*.

"Besides, your overconfidence is precisely the reason why *I* was chosen to lead this mission and not you," Annabelle glared.

"And yet it is you, Korreva," Herestia jabbed a finger at Annabelle, "who toys with the Littovar, knowing the effects it has--"

"Do not question my methods, little sister," Annabelle snapped. "If I use the chalk, it is because it is *my right* to do so. It was I who first traced the Blackfalls to their origin, just as it was I who--"

Annebelle froze, and Darko could see a vein pulsing in her forehead as her eyes darted back and forth. His non-existent blood ran cold as the woman began to scan the room, her head weaving to and fro like a cobra.

"Korreva, what are you--"

"Shh," Annabelle hissed, the area around her eyes darkening to a spiderweb of pitch black.

Darko's heart, if it had been a part of him, surely would have stopped as she turned directly to face him. Annabelle's eyes clouded over with pure black and then cleared once again, revealing startlingly green reptilian eyes reminiscent of the dragon they'd seen months before.

Over and over he told himself she couldn't see him - that it was *impossible* to detect him - but as her gaze at last locked with his, he knew the dreadful truth and recognized the enormity of his mistake.

"Well hello, little elf." Annabelle smiled.

Run!

Darko spun in place and shot off like a lightning bolt, using every ounce of his consciousness to gain distance from the two dragonesses he had so foolishly chosen to spy on. Ahead he could see the unwavering light of Reia's beacon and he focused on it, pushing his fear to the back of his mind.

He could *feel* her behind him, pursuing him through the astral realm in a way that shouldn't have been possible. He theorized that she had accessed the 'tunnel' he was creating as he hurtled through the planes, and that his escape route was also the method by which she might well catch him.

You're nearly here, Master. You'll be ok.

Reia urged him from miles away, her voice a steady, familiar warmth just out of reach as the lights and sounds of the material plane were replaced by the roiling void of the cosmos once again.

He dared to look behind himself - only for a moment - and saw Annabelle in her true form, that of a massive, glittering black dragon. Her broad toothy maw seemed to smile, and her powerful wings were pulled back like a falcon diving as she closed the space between them.

He turned forwards once again to see the spinning circles and floating runes of his enchantment, and at the heart of it floated Reia and his own motionless body.

Darko crashed into the circle at a speed beyond reckoning, beating Annabelle there by only the tiniest fraction of a second. Her snout ricocheted off the swirling protective bubble and she reared back in surprise.

She brought her massive claws to bear, grasping the sphere of magic surrounding them and digging the razor sharp points into it. The shields sparked and crackled, a broad spider web of purple cracks shooting across its surface in protest.

Darko turned to Reia, returning to himself in a blinding flash, and knowing full well that there was no way to undo the magical protections and return to the material world safely in the fleeting time they had.

Time seemed to slow as Reia turned to him with a look of unexpected calm, mixed with a deep and obvious sadness.

Forgive me, Master.

She raised her hand, palm out, to face him and spoke in a language he didn't recognize. The effect was as immediate as it was uncomfortable, and he felt himself blown backwards as if by an explosion. He was overwhelmed with a feeling of falling and found himself unable to move as he rocketed away from the protective haven of the magical shell.

He watched helplessly as Annabelle broke through the shields at last, her murderous claws reaching inward toward his trapped friend. Darko tried to cry out, but he was winded by an impact like a hammer blow as he slammed back into his body on the floor of the shed in the heart of Larrin Hold.

Immediately he started to black out, his blurry vision revealing his battered reflection in the mirror in the middle of the now smoking and ruined magical circle. Blood poured from his nose, his mouth, and his eyes as he crawled hand over hand towards the door. He never made it, and the last thing he saw before the darkness finally claimed him were the stars above, revealed by a massive split where the building itself had cracked in half down to the foundation.

Chapter Twenty-Seven

"You're not attending the Senate meeting?"

Lilliana's soft voice caused Arcus to pause his pacing and turn. She was radiant as ever and clothed more recognizably in hunter's garb. She wore the same elegant clothes as the first time he'd seen her, and he caught himself admiring the intricate beadwork and simple lines of her outfit as she approached.

"In light of the events of last night," Arcus smiled thinly, "they decided it best that our party perhaps sit this meeting out."

"I suppose that makes sense from their perspective." Lilliana nodded, walking to stand alongside him. "And how is your companion, the wizard?"

"I don't know," Arcus sighed heavily. "He lost a lot of blood doing . . . whatever it was he was trying to do. Sami says his body is stabilized now. She's . . . less confident that his mind remains intact."

"And Lorehammer?"

"Not much different, I'm afraid." Arcus scuffed his foot in frustration. "Sami says that physically he's fine, but that he is gravely depleted and she isn't sure when he might awaken."

"And so you pace the great walls of Larrin Hold," she nodded at the breathtaking view around them. "To wear pathways in the stones while you worry?"

Arcus found himself reluctantly chuckling.

"I suppose so, my lady." He nodded toward the opening to Kyber Pass, a few hundred yards away in the valley below. "I keep expecting Annabelle and her army to come charging out, I think."

"Annabelle's dragon companion cannot physically enter Tirja," Lilliana replied with unexpected sadness. "Ancient magics, wrought at terrible cost, prevent it."

"Then why don't I feel safe?"

"You are wise to keep your guard up," Lilliana answered. "If Annabelle has aligned herself with The Brood then she may have other powerful allies as well."

"*The Brood?*"

"A coven of sorceresses," Lilliana's eyes glazed over as she spoke. "*Dragonesses*, I should say. A clutch of siblings dedicated to their own mysterious agenda, who have brought destruction to this part of the world for the better part of two millenia, perhaps longer."

"*More* dragons . . ." Arcus scratched his head. "To learn that these monsters exist is--"

"Monsters?" Lilliana's tone took a sharp note. "And what makes them monsters?"

"I . . . Well, I mean, they . . ." Arcus tried to think of a reason that didn't boil down to his own terror. "You should have *seen* Kent, my lady. I--"

"So you've 'met' a dragon," Lilliana frowned. "And now you're an expert. How novel."

The woman's stride lengthened in agitation and Arcus struggled to keep up with her.

"My lady," Arcus huffed along behind her. "Please, I am not sure what I said to offend you, but I am sorry for it."

"You would do well to reserve judgment regarding things you know *nothing* about," she admonished him, coming to an abrupt halt and spinning around to face the druid. "The dragons are an ancient, *noble* race, firstborn among the--"

She stopped and rubbed her temples, taking a deep breath to cool her temper. "You're so . . . *young*, Arcus," she sighed. "And there is so much more gray in the world than you can possibly know."

He felt the need to apologize, and tried to think of something to express how unintended the insult was - or at least something clever or funny - but came up short. Thankfully, she rescued him from the awkward silence with a suggestion of her own.

"Come with me," she said. "Let's take a walk in the grass, my feet have had enough of cold stone and boots."

Surprised, Arcus allowed her to lead the way down to the courtyard and then out past a pair of startled guardsmen.

"If you will indulge me," Lilliana said, sitting on the grass just outside the gates and pulling her leather boots off. "I find that when I am frustrated, or when anxiety begins to get the best of me, that the feel of fresh earth and grass beneath my feet is immensely soothing."

She stood again and, holding her boots in one hand, set off into the knee high grass, still glistening with morning dew. Arcus hurried to follow her, yanking off his own worn leather footwear and jogging to catch up to her practiced stride.

"My lady," he said when he finally caught her again. "Thank you for--"

"Shh," she smiled. "Walk. Feel. Relax. Let the earth calm the storm inside you, then we can talk."

Arcus closed his mouth, wise enough not to argue with the woman, and found that she was right. With every step he could feel the soft mountain grasses tickling his toes and the cool, wet earth yielding beneath his footfalls. His tensions seemed to drain down into the ground, swallowed by the enormous, unchanging patience of the mountains.

They walked together for a candlemark or so, watching the early morning sun burn off wisps of mist and fog over the valley. For a time, Lilliana seemed to hold a sort of *tension*. The more centered and calm Arcus became, the more apparent it was to him that it was Lilliana who needed this walk the most.

He took to observing her, worrying over the wrinkle in her brow and the faint but unmistakable curl of a frown at the edge of her lips. His gaze did not go unnoticed for long though, and she treated him with a half-hearted smile.

"You are growing more perceptive," she chuckled softly. "I cannot say I am surprised. Nizhóni has a way of permanently altering those who visit there, and your visit was more . . . complex than most."

"Is that why I keep . . . I don't know how to explain it," Arcus mulled the changes in his mind. "*Feeling* things?"

"It is, Groveborn," she nodded. "Nizhóní has given you new life, and with it a broader understanding of the Great Web around us all. Your connection will continue to deepen as your bond with Nizhóní grows."

Rather than surprise, Arcus felt a certain reassurance from her words. The Great Web - at least as far as his people knew it - was the vast network of all living things and of all the natural world at large. Arcus had already dedicated most of his life to it, in his own way, and to learn his connection would only grow was a great relief to his tired heart.

"So it is only by being close to the Grove that this . . . connection will continue to grow?"

"No," she laughed. "But it will be much easier - and more fruitful - the longer you remain near Nizhóní's physical form. Rest assured though, Groveborn, your fates are bound together now, threads in the same string, in the fabric of time."

"I don't understand though," Arcus pressed. "I'm not 'near' Nizhóní, am I?"

Lilliana paused and studied him carefully. Her gaze seemed to pierce his very soul and Arcus felt suddenly bashful.

"You see this cloak?" She spun in a slow circle, allowing him to fully appreciate the myriad feathers and leaves all intricately woven together. "*This* is the physical anchorpoint of the Grove. I am her guardian, just as she is my home, and she never leaves my side. She is my dearest and most precious friend, as well as my most solemn responsibility."

"I don't understand." Arcus was awed by the power of the garment. "How can something so small, so fragile, be an artifact of such power?"

"Things are often more than they appear, Groveborn." She placed a hand gently upon his shoulder. "To truly serve the balance, you *must* learn this critical lesson."'

"I will do my best."

"That is all we can do." She returned to her walking. "Isn't it?"

A few more minutes passed in quiet contemplation before Arcus interrupted it.

"My lady," he braced, unsure if reopening the topic was a good idea but committed to pressing on regardless. "Can you tell me more about dragons?"

Lilliana's step faltered, and she turned to Arcus in surprise. The ranger searched her face, but though she seemed conflicted, he saw no trace of anger there.

"What do you want to know?"

"Er, well . . . everything, I guess," he admitted, realizing he had no specific question in mind. "How many are there? Are they all like Annabelle's? I--"

"Slow down." She laughed and rolled her eyes gently. "When Scera was young, there were *thousands* of dragons. They thrived in the youth of the world and were the favored children of the gods. Now . . . now they are much fewer in number, and those that still live here on Scera often cluster together out of sight and out of mind."

"But why should they hide? What could possibly have happened to them?"

"Mortals are relentless in their thirst for blood, even the 'finer' races like the elves and the dwarves," she answered sadly. "Dragons are powerful, but they are not invincible. The mortal races hunted them nearly to extinction. Most of them either died here on Scera or retreated to other, less hostile planes of existence where they live more freely."

"But why wouldn't they *all* simply abandon Scera, then?"

"Dragons were given a . . ." Lilliana frowned faintly. "A *responsibility*, by the gods. They were to rule Scera so long as they cared for it, and help maintain the balance that had been so lovingly created. Like all creatures possessed of intellect, however, many turned to self-serving pursuits and abandoned the balance in favor of what would benefit them most."

Arcus tried to imagine a world filled with dragons, finding it quite impossible to do so.

"Some stayed - remained committed to their purpose - and even fought wars against the worst of their own kind." Lilliana shrugged. "But, perhaps they were not enough. Perhaps the gods grew angry, and that is why the dragons fell from their graces."

"A war between dragons," Arcus shuddered at the thought. "What a horror that must be."

"It was. The land was ravaged for millenia, until--" Lillina's jaw popped open in surprise, and Arcus couldn't help but turn to follow her gaze.

A lone rider, slumped over his saddle, was visible at the edge of the pass. The rider wore the armor of the 7th, and Arcus recognized the purple and silver trim and the heavy build even from this distance.

"Boric," they both gasped in unison.

Lilliana wasted no time.

The druidess crouched to the ground amid an explosion of feathers, and before Arcus could even react, a massive blue-tailed hawk was in her place. She leapt into the sky with a powerful wingbeat and rocketed off towards their mutual friend. Arcus was right behind her. He felt a surge of power within himself and his magic flowed with uncommon ease - a fact he now knew to attribute to Nizhóní - and he began to shift into the familiar form of a massive wolf as he sprinted across the grassy field. His limbs stretched and his joints rearranged in a flowing wave, starting with his toes and ending at his new, fang-filled snout. His saber and his armor morphed into tough, thick fur, and the cold air whistled past his keen new ears as he tore up the ground between himself and his injured comrade.

The Duke's body was slumped over the neck of his horse, and the poor mount was limping badly. He could see that Boric had been cradling his sword arm, and that rivers of dried blood ran from it and down the flank of his horse. His enhanced canine eyes also picked out several arrows sprouting from Boric's unmoving back as he neared.

Arrows and blood, far too much blood.

They were seconds away, with Lilliana just fifteen yards ahead of him, when Boric slipped at last from the saddle with a dull, heavy thud. Lilliana transformed seamlessly back into her natural form and lifted the man from the ground, cradling his head against her shoulder. Arcus slid to a halt as well, his body stretching and twisting as he changed from wolf to man with barely a stutter in his stride.

"Lilliana!" he called out as he ran the last few feet. "Is he--"

A blackened spike of cracked bone erupted from Lilliana's back in front of him, flecking his face and chest with blood and stopping him in his tracks. A heartbeat passed and Arcus stood frozen, his mind unable to comprehend what he was seeing.

Lilliana's body - suddenly limp - slid to the side and fell to the ground, revealing the snarling, inhuman rider's face. Arcus recognized the drawn, lifeless skin of the Duke's face and knew that it *was* Boric, but that he was no longer among the living.

Boric hissed at him through curled, cracked lips and staggered to his feet, where Arcus finally got his first good look at the man. His sword arm had been severed just above the wrist, and the flesh had - from the looks of it - been burned away nearly up to the elbow. What remained were the broken off shafts of the bones in his forearm, now soaked with Lilliana's blood from where he'd impaled her.

"Lilliana!" Arcus called out, drawing his blade and taking a step back. "Lilliana?"

She made no move nor made any sound, but the undead form of the Duke did. He stepped over her crumpled body and with his good hand drew forth his own blade, a stunning longsword of impeccable craftsmanship.

What captured Arcus most, what held him at bay, was the look of cunning intellect behind the grayish eyes of the monster in front of him. These were not filled with the same mindless hunger of the undead at the Altimeer Estate, but were instead possessed of keen awareness.

Without warning, the creature lunged, letting loose a wicked downstroke that Arcus only barely managed to deflect. The power behind the swing was sobering. Even with a glancing blow it was enough to rattle Arcus to his core. Boric followed with an onslaught of blows, sending Arcus scrambling backwards as he desperately tried to avoid the creature's flashing blade. Sweat soaked Arcus' brow and back, and his sword arm was already tiring from the violence of the impacts he deflected; he was forced to recognize the obvious - he was not prepared for this fight.

Boric's body was as heavily armored as it had been in life, and Arcus had no confidence that he could wound the monster regardless. Arcus, on the other hand, wore only his traveling clothes for protection, and had only his scimitar to fight with. When the monster moved, it was with an unearthly quickness. When it struck, it was with a strength that *must* have been a product of the foul energies animating it. And worst of all, it seemed utterly immune to fatigue.

Arcus ducked under another particularly brutal swing and drove his blade into his enemy's waist, hoping against hope that he was wrong. His saber bit deeply, burying itself in the thin joint of the monster's armor and unleashing a gush of thick, half-congealed blood.

Boric staggered back a moment, yanking the blade free from Arcus' hand to remain buried in his gut, and regarded the offending weapon. After a moment, the creature returned its baleful gaze to the druid, and he could see fresh fire in its merciless eyes.

Arcus took another step back, then by instinct dug deep within himself for the sacred energies of the world. He could feel Boric's presence like a disease in front of himself, but the Great Web was a light that could not be dimmed, even in proximity to such an abomination.

The ranger reached down to the ground, his arms swirling with incandescent motes of greenish energy, and the ground rippled in response. The grasses of the plain shot upward around Boric, wrapping him in thousands of interwoven stalks and vines sprouting from the earth. The beast pressed on, pulling against the undergrowth shooting up to hold it in place.

The creature was relentless, and even as Arcus dug deeper and the earth itself began to reach up and grasp at the monster's legs, it pushed forward, making its way inexorably towards the ranger. The monster's vile energy soaked the ground like crude oil, weakening the hold of Arcus' magic, and allowing the unholy creation to continue in its deadly mission.

He was running out of options, and running out of time, but Arcus refused to give in. He cast around for another solution - any solution - that would allow him to either destroy this monster or recover Lilliana and escape.

Suddenly, he was blinded by an overwhelming wave of brilliant golden energy that drove all conscious thought out of his mind. He saw the silhouette of Boric's body, highlighted against the wash of pure light that originated from somewhere behind it. The stark black shape of the walking corpse disintegrated before Arcus' eyes, ripped apart into motes of dust, and then to nothing at all. With its destruction, the light began to fade until it merged seamlessly with the light of the morning sun.

As his vision returned to normal Arcus could see Lilliana, still on the ground, but propping herself up with one hand while the other remained pointed towards Arcus, palm forward. The golden light of the spell lingered long enough for Arcus to watch as the last radiant rays returned to Lilliana's hand. Her skin, no longer bathed in the soft warmth of the spell, was pale. She shuddered, her eyes rolling back in her head, and collapsed once again before Arcus could reach her.

He ran to her side, sliding across the last few feet of grass to reach her faster, and lifted her from the earth as she had lifted Boric minutes before.

"My lady," he whispered.

He blinked back tears as he was finally able to examine her wound more closely.

Boric's bones had left twin holes, just below her heart, that had impaled her through-and-through. Dark red blood flecked with glittering gold flowed freely from the wounds and from the corner of her mouth, foaming a bit with every ragged breath she took.

The woman's wounds were far, far beyond anything Arcus could heal, and hot, bitter tears ran down his cheeks as he confirmed what he already knew - she was dying, and there was nothing he could do about it.

"Groveborn," she gasped, coughing from the effort. "Do not weep for me."

"How can I not weep?" He brushed her hair back. "You have taught me so much already, and you gave me back my life, my freedom. It should have been me--"

"Shh." She smiled at him with great difficulty. "My time is short, Groveborn. First, Nizhóni is yours now, to care for and to protect. In this you cannot fail. You--"

"My lady." Arcus was stunned. "I can't--"

"You *can*, Groveborn." She coughed again. "You *must*."

Arcus' breath caught as the woman took another slow gurgling breath, but at last she again began to speak.

"I have only one gift left to give, I'm afraid." She winced in pain, screwing her eyes shut. "Time, as much of it as I can manage. When I am gone . . . Listen closely to me, Groveborn. When I'm gone you must seek out Queen Sionasara. She is . . . dear to me. It is my hope that she will aid you--"

A coughing fit wracked her body, and Arcus couldn't help but notice blackish threads in the blood pouring from her wounds now and a network of spidery black lines beneath the skin of her neck.

"Damn her," she grimaced. "Annabelle wields the Littovar, an ancient weapon of shadow and death. Sionasara knows better than any soul living the gravity of this threat and how it might be stopped."

"My lady," Arcus hesitated to interrupt her again, but the blackness was spreading, growing in thin tendrils below her pallid flesh. "Are you--"

"You have nothing to fear from my death, Groveborn," she shook her head almost imperceptibly. "My magic runs deeper than hers."

As she spoke, the corners of her mouth turned up into a faint but unmistakable smile, and power began to radiate off of her with all the warmth of a noonday sun. The grass all around them waved in a breeze that wasn't there, and the sun itself seemed to shine brighter upon them.

Arcus' jaw opened in awe as the blackness spreading beneath her skin began to recede. Her blood began to change, too. The faint shimmering flecks now burned brightly, like fresh-forged drops of the purest gold. The ground below them shook, and the clouds above swirled in intricate, criss-crossing patterns unlike he had ever seen.

"Do not mourn, child. There is no time."

As she spoke, her voice took on a powerful, ethereal tone. It surrounded him, rustling like leaves in a distant wind and echoing in the chambers of his heart.

Then, her entire body was bathed in golden light, glowing softly at first and then with gathering intensity. Her physical form grew lighter and lighter until it floated free of Arcus' grasp. The ground shook, and instinctively, he stood up and stepped back.

He watched in wonder as the woman's limp body began to transform, slowly at first and then with growing speed. Her skin turned to shining scales, mighty wings sprouted from her back, and her beautiful face lengthened into the regal countenance of a mighty dragon. Gone was the timeless, inhuman form she had inhabited, and in its place was that of an enormous golden dragon. She was a third again as large as Annabelle's dragon and in every way sleeker and more beautiful. Where Annabelle's monster had been a thing of violence and destruction, here was a masterpiece of gentle grace.

Arcus saw that her wounds grew too - a great ragged hole still pierced her body - but it bled no more, and all traces of the shadows were gone.

A voice called to him, so impossibly vibrant and beautiful that he couldn't help but fall to his knees.

"Groveborn, one last boon I grant you: Shelter in the eye of the storm," Lilliana's voice grew weaker with each word. "But take heed - when the last leaf falls under the same moons, one year from now, so too will your protection."

Lilliana's body settled gently upon the ground, curled up like a giant sleeping house cat in a patch of morning sunlight. Arcus watched as the brilliant shine of her body dulled and faded. He stood silently as flowering vines blossomed up around her, creeping up along her body until she was covered all over in soft, white seven-star lilies.

Then - one final beautiful act of nature - a sapling appeared in the middle of her body, leaving her hill-like form curled around it. It sprouted up with sudden vitality, growing in seconds to a towering willow tree, complete with slowly waving branches and thousands of vibrant green leaves.

A soft breeze swirled past him and he felt a sudden weight upon his shoulders. He was startled to realize that he was suddenly wearing Nizhóní.

Arcus saw the tree mature in moments, and then - with startling clarity - he saw a single leaf fade to yellow, then brown, then drop gracefully from the nearest branch to land upon the ground.

The moment it touched the grass, a powerful gust of wind blew past him, shaking the tree but not pulling a single leaf free from it. The wind rushed outwards past him to the mouth of the pass and then shot skyward in a cloud of dust. He stood in peculiar calm, not feeling any wind at all but witnessing the power of it right in front of himself. It grew before his eyes, swirling into a cyclone of immeasurable size in the space of a few heartbeats. In moments, the wind was so thick with debris at the mouth of the pass that he couldn't see through it at all.

But it wasn't just the pass.

A solid, gray-and-brown wall of hurricane winds stretched across his vision as far as he could see in either direction. The wall of raw, surging, elemental power crackled with lightning and hail for miles and miles, disappearing over the horizon along the very borders of the land of Tirja.

He was staggered by the unbelievable power before him, but a dreadful sound brought him swiftly back to his senses - alarm bells, ringing out from the city behind him.

Elbaf missed a swing, eliciting a disapproving look from his instructor. He shrugged off his frustration, letting his blade droop as he rolled his neck and stretched his shoulders a moment. They were sparring in the East Courtyard, not far from the Senate hall where the Tirjan councilmen debated their futures.

Their men were scattered throughout the city, enjoying the rare freedom to do as they pleased without a pressing deadline or the threat of death hanging over their heads.

Elbaf had been training with Razael for the past two hours, but he was having a great deal of difficulty concentrating. He wasn't performing at his best, and Razael was capitalizing on it - and Elbaf had the bruises to show for it already.

"I cannot help but think your mind is elsewhere," Razael announced, nonplussed, as Elbaf nearly missed another easy parry.

The Swordmaster let his blade drop until the point nearly touched the surface of the stone plaza and leveled an irritated scowl at his apprentice.

His pride injured, Elbaf opened his mouth to argue - but he thought better of it.

"I'm not sure." He ran a hand through his hair and cast a sidelong glance at the Senate building in the near distance. "Something--"

"Is *distracting* you," Razael prompted as he sheathed his sword and treated Elbaf to a wry grin. "I wonder, is it the weight of the council's decision, or does a specific person scatter your thoughts this morning?"

Elbaf huffed and kicked the scuffed road below his boot, suddenly warm in the face.

"Some of both," he admitted. "But more of--"

Alarm bells cut through the air, driving them to silence.

"The pass," Razael narrowed his eyes. "Something's wrong."

The Swordmaster and Elbaf sprinted together down the street, turning a corner onto the main thoroughfare that led from the Southern Gate all the way through the city.

Elbaf could see what looked like every citizen - and every guard - in the city pouring toward the gate and to the main wall like a horde of angry ants. Razael took off in a dead sprint, rapidly growing the distance between himself and Elbaf, who skidded to a sudden halt.

Something was wrong, *all* wrong.

He looked back over his shoulder at the quiet streets behind himself, now completely deserted. He narrowed his eyes, squinting at the Senate hall a few hundred yards away and wishing - for the first time in his life - for Darko's elven vision.

At first he wasn't sure what he was looking for, but then it hit him. Why hadn't the Senate building emptied? Hadn't the council heard the alarms?

He waited another few moments, doubting the uneasy feeling in his belly as Razael and the rest of the town guard got further and further away from him. Elbaf shook his head, taking another few steps in the direction of the gate before growling at himself in frustration, turning on his heel, and sprinting back towards the Senate.

The closer he got to the high stone walls, the more his conviction grew - they *had* to be able to hear the bell.

Elbaf hit the outer door and was surprised to find it didn't open to his push. He looked the door up and down and noticed something that set his heart racing, a small trickle of blood was flowing out from under the door, pooling in an area about the size of a playing card under the otherwise tight seam.

Elbaf stepped back and then threw his shoulder into the door, which let out a satisfying crack as the lock gave way. He shoved it open and found the bodies of two of the Senatorial honor guards had been pushed up against it - no doubt the source of the blood. Both had lethal knife wounds, and from the quick glance they received from Elbaf, he guessed they'd been ambushed individually from behind.

The half-orc sprinted down the hall, drawing his sword and gripping it tightly as he made his way through the building to the large central courtyard. On the way he found another three guards, all cut down with similarly wicked knife-wounds to their backs or with mottled purple strangulation marks around their necks.

With each grisly new discovery, the knot in his stomach grew.

In total, it took him no more than a minute or two to get from the entrance to the central plaza - but as the death toll mounted, it seemed to stretch on forever. He could see the last door and hit it at a sprint. He burst through it, splintering the wood and sending bits of wood and metal showering outward into the room with a bang. The warrior skidded to a halt on the checkered stone floor, taking in the scene before him and struggling to make sense of what he saw.

Private Derrin was standing over Sami's brother and had a garrote around the poor councilman's neck. A vile grin was plastered across his face, and his eyes were wide with excitement as the much smaller, much weaker man grasped at the short chain encircling his throat.

The rest of the council members were littered about, most of them with knives buried in their bodies, and Sami lay about fifteen feet away, a knife in her side, a sizable cut on the left side of her head, and a thin chain wrapped around her throat.

"Derrin!" Elbaf roared, approaching the other warrior cautiously. "Have you lost your mind, man? What--"

"*Derrin,*" the young soldier mocked him with a laugh, giving the garrote in his hands one more savage yank and then kicking Connor's body over at his feet.

"Derrin! What are you doing, Derrin? What's wrong with you, Derrin?" he continued mocking.

Derrin laughed a cold, heartless laugh that sent a shiver down Elbaf's spine as he drew his own blade and pointed it directly at the half-orc.

"You're not supposed to be here, Elbaf." The man shook his head. "You're supposed to be on the wall, with everyone else. You were never supposed to see this, and now you've left me very little in the way of options."

"Derrin--"

"Derrin's been dead a good long while," the man snapped. "And I've been wearing this filthy disguise for nearly six months, ever since you and your damned imperials attacked our camp outside of Kent!"

Elbaf resisted the impulse to charge, barely. Instead, he kept a careful eye on the man while performing a quick scan of the room - none of the people strewn about were moving, and he would be of no help if he met a similar fate.

"Who are you?"

"Questions," the man snorted in disgust. "Your friends lay dead around you - you yourself will be dead in a moment - and you're asking me questions? Pathetic."

"I said, who--"

"You know, he cried in the end." Derrin smiled at him. "That *boy* who wanted to be a soldier - who wanted to be a *hero*. He asked for you, begged for help as I gutted him in the underbrush. And where were you?"

The bottom fell out of Elbaf's stomach as the thought of Derrin's final, terrified moments filled his mind.

"And *you*, you didn't even realize he was gone," his enemy snarled. "Your men call you a leader, but deep down you know you don't deserve it any more than you deserve the honor of the Warchief's bloodline."

"Enough!" Elbaf roared, charging forward and letting loose a wild sideways swing of his greatsword.

"You're *weak*," the man accused him, nimbly rolling to the side to dodge the blow. "You're a *failure*, and the only reason I didn't slit your throat in your sleep is because the Warchief - a *true* leader - ordered it."

Elbaf was beyond words, pursuing the smaller fighter back and forth across the stone floor, his blade flashing in lethal spirals and swirls.

"'*Watch him*,' I was told." He spat on the ground before sidestepping another careless swing. "'*Discover if he is worthy of my bloodline*,' the warchief said. Above all, no harm was to come to you until he'd made his decision."

Elbaf's sword moved with glorious, deadly purpose, but found only air. Derrin moved like a shadow, and Elbaf was beginning to tire before even landing a blow.

"But you *are* unworthy," Derrin snarled at him. "Undeserving of your heritage--"

Something within Elbaf snapped, and his mind went deadly calm. Rage simmered below the surface, but all of his thoughts were crystal clear.

He twisted his body in the middle of his next swing, letting go with one hand from his blade and planting it firmly in Derrin's stomach with a satisfying thump. The blow sent the man sprawling, and he only barely parried Elbaf's next blow before scrambling to his feet with a backwards roll.

"Very well." The man grinned again - a manic, violent expression of anticipation. "But let's see how you do when I shed this flimsy disguise."

Derrin reached up to his collar and pulled out an amulet he was wearing from beneath his tunic. A talisman of sorts - a tangle of wire wrapped around a rodent skull

- hung from the thin, knotted leather string of the amulet, and he yanked it from his neck with a soft snap.

Immediately, his appearance shifted dramatically. Derrin's small, wiry build was replaced by the towering body of a fully-grown Ohryic, complete with a thick layer of brushed steel scale-mail. Even the man's sword grew, now sized appropriately for his much larger frame.

"That's right, *runt*," the towering fighter said, his voice now guttural and low. "I am Gur Lagash, warrior of the Splitrock, and I will have your skull for the Warchief's throne."

Elbaf realized with dismay just how drastically this new development shifted the balance of their fight. Elbaf wore no armor, and any advantages he'd had in reach, in strength, or in stature were now totally reversed. He took a half step back, marginally increasing the distance between them while he lifted his sword into a ready position. The half-orc's stalwart instructor came to mind, and he found himself paying heed to every lesson, great and small, that he had learned these past few months.

"You look ready to surrender already, mongrel." Gur smiled, baring his fangs at Elbaf and chuckling darkly.

Elbaf ignored the comment, focusing instead on reading his opponent's body language.

The massive orc charged without warning, driving Elbaf backwards under a series of powerful overhand cuts that Elbaf expertly parried. Gur pushed, and Elbaf allowed himself to give ground under the onslaught. He kept a steady pace backwards, circling the room and carefully avoiding anything that might cause him to trip or lose his footing, and all the while he watched and he learned.

There.

Elbaf finally found what he was looking for, the subtle tell in his opponent - the key that would enable his victory. Gur led ever-so-slightly with his left foot, and with every strike he telegraphed the direction of his swing. Taking his shoulders into account, Elbaf could predict his every move.

He pictured the chessboard that Razael would often bring to their lessons and began to plan his next move until an idea came to mind. Elbaf conserved energy, exerting precisely the amount he needed to deflect the larger warrior's blows and nothing more.

The half-orc also adjusted his direction of travel, weaving in and out of obstacles with a new purpose in mind until a heavy wooden chair - one of the dozens circling the room - was directly at his back. Then he planted his feet and dug in. Gur took the bait, certain that he had cornered the smaller fighter at last.

Elbaf adjusted his technique, leaving openings that Gur eagerly exploited with a series of predictable overhand strikes. Gur smiled as he rained down blow after blow, and Elbaf could see the confidence in his eyes as he hammered the half-orc's defenses.

Elbaf waited for the perfect moment, when the bloodlust had fully consumed Gur beyond reason, before making his move. He twisted in a flash, leaving only empty space where he'd been a moment before. Gur's blade bit deeply into the heavy wooden chair, lodging itself securely in the backrest and nearly splitting it in half in the process.

The half-orc continued his spin, converting it into a lightning fast strike. He put all of his force behind the swing, driving the keen edge of his blade downward in a fatal strike to the back of his opponent's neck. Blood sprayed out in an arc as Gur's head left his body, staining the debris-strewn plaza until it rolled to a stop a few feet away.

The Ohryic's body slumped down a moment later, landing in a crumpled heap at Elbaf's feet and throwing the entire room into near silence. Elbaf's heavy breathing and pounding heart filled his ears, and he had to force himself to calm down.

He wiped his brow with the back of his hand and stepped around his fallen foe, making a beeline for Connor. He found the man was still drawing soft, raspy breaths and wasted no time in removing the chain from around his neck. He helped Connor sit up, taking note of the deep purplish tinge of his face and neck, and checking him over for any other wounds. He'd nearly finished when the soft scrape of metal on stone pierced the fog in his mind.

He spun to his feet, blade raised, and scanned the room for what was sure to be another threat. Instead, he saw Sami feebly reaching for her throat, grasping weakly at the cord there.

All thoughts of Connor erased, Elbaf rushed to the woman and gently unwrapped the garrote from her slender neck. It was a weapon he'd never seen before, with weights on each end that would enable it to be thrown with lethal efficiency. The cleric coughed, a painful, body-wracking affair that made Elbaf wince as he untangled the chain. Her eyes fluttered open, and she flinched at the sight of Elbaf's face, an expression that hit the warrior like a punch in the gut.

"It's alright," Elbaf reassured her, cradling her gently. "You're safe now. I've got you."

Printed in the USA
CPSIA information can be obtained
at www.ICGtesting.com
JSHW010923270924
70567JS00004B/14

9 781964 893006